For Pam

CHAPTER 1

A LITTLE WEIRD

I'LL TRY TO EXPLAIN, BUT IT WAS A LITTLE WEIRD.
MY NAME IS **DANIEL JACKSON LIM**, BUT EVERYONE CALLS ME **D.J.** AND I WASN'T GOOD AT ANYTHING.
THEN A BOY FELL FROM THE SKY.
BOOM
BUT HE **WASN'T** A BOY.

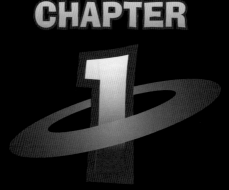

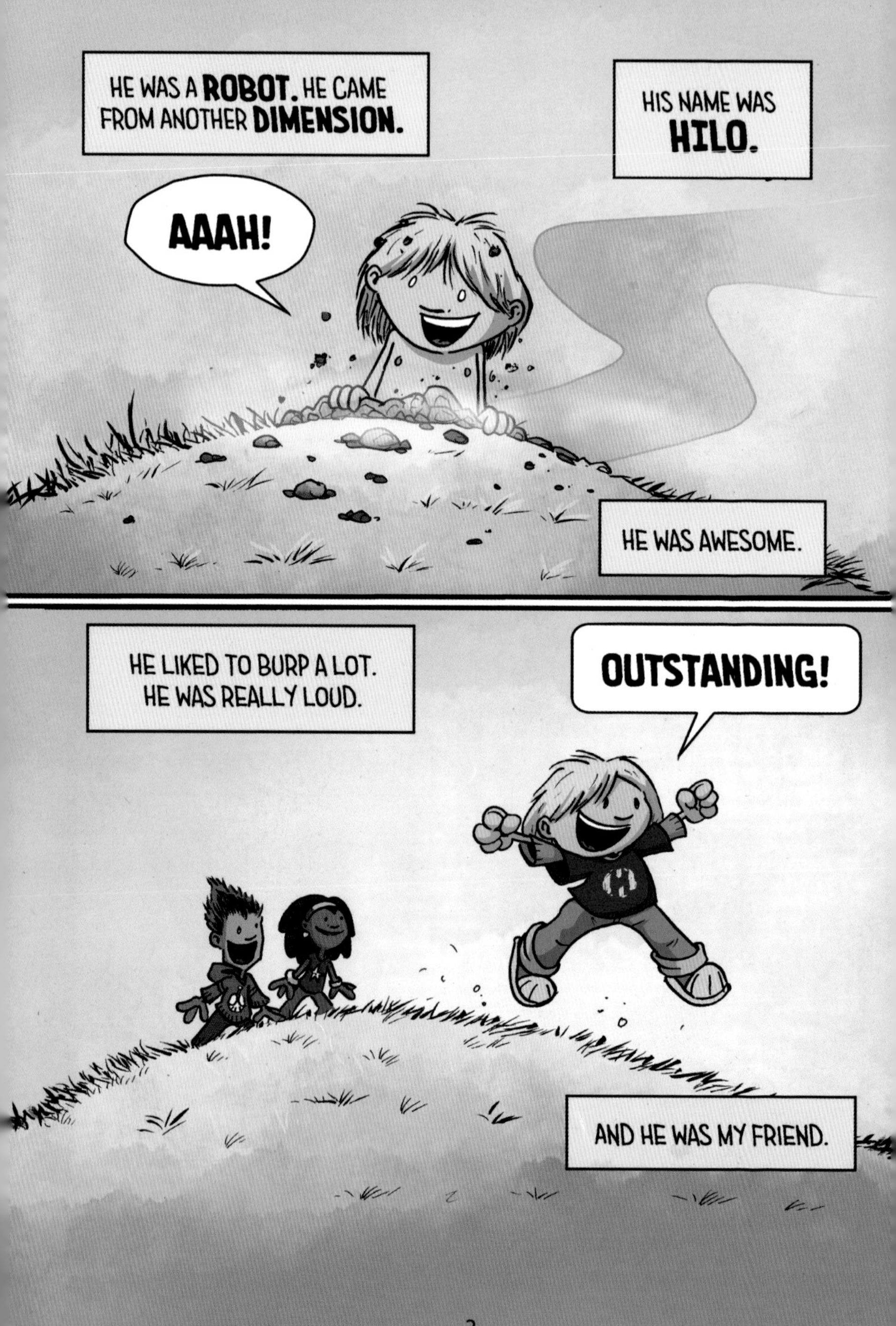
HE WAS A **ROBOT.** HE CAME FROM ANOTHER **DIMENSION.**
HIS NAME WAS **HILO.**
AAAH!
HE WAS AWESOME.
HE LIKED TO BURP A LOT. HE WAS REALLY LOUD.
OUTSTANDING!
AND HE WAS MY FRIEND.

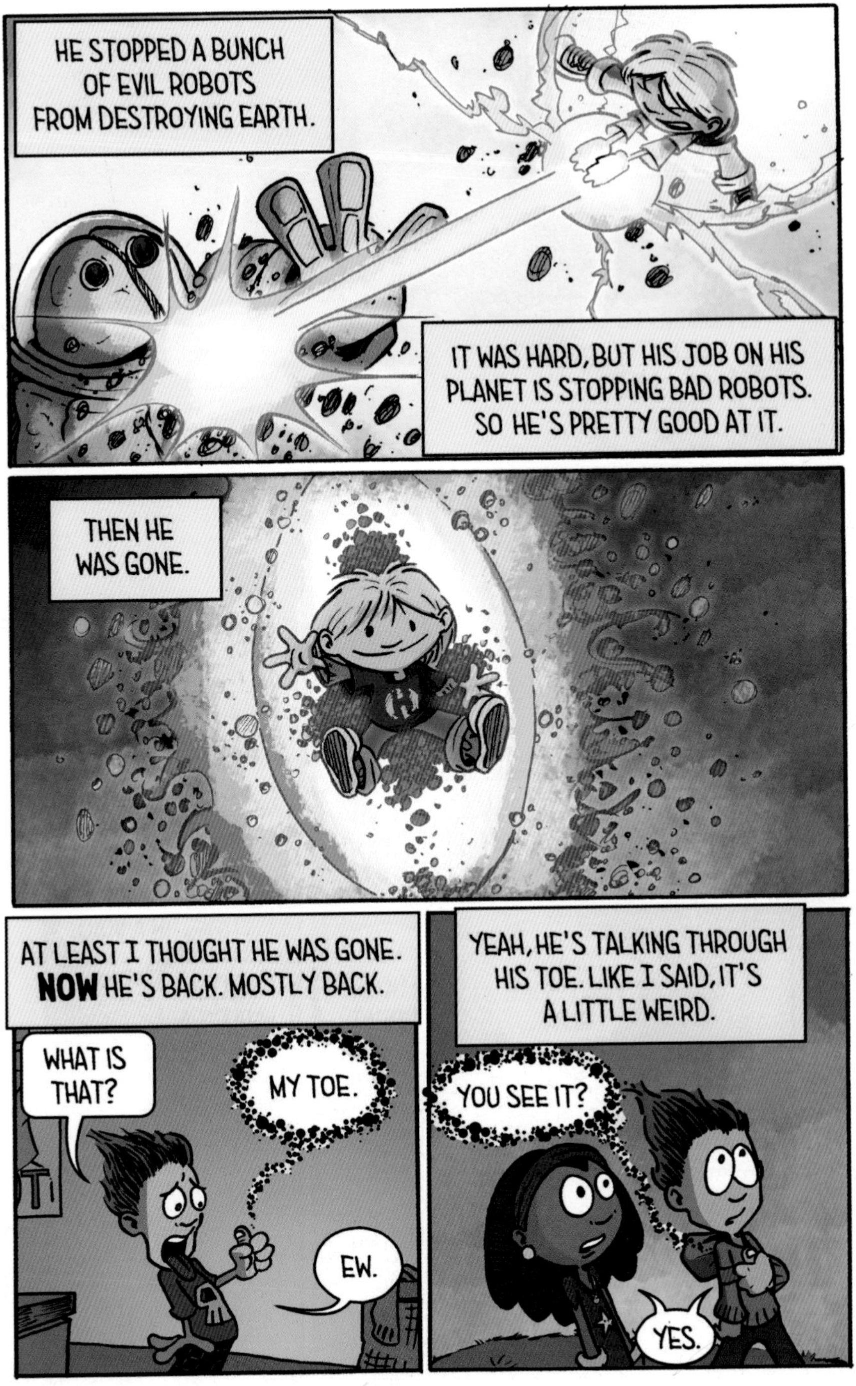
HE STOPPED A BUNCH OF EVIL ROBOTS FROM DESTROYING EARTH.
IT WAS HARD, BUT HIS JOB ON HIS PLANET IS STOPPING BAD ROBOTS. SO HE'S PRETTY GOOD AT IT.
THEN HE WAS GONE.
AT LEAST I THOUGHT HE WAS GONE. NOW HE'S BACK. MOSTLY BACK.
WHAT IS THAT?
MY TOE.
EW.
YEAH, HE'S TALKING THROUGH HIS TOE. LIKE I SAID, IT'S A LITTLE WEIRD.
YOU SEE IT?
YES.

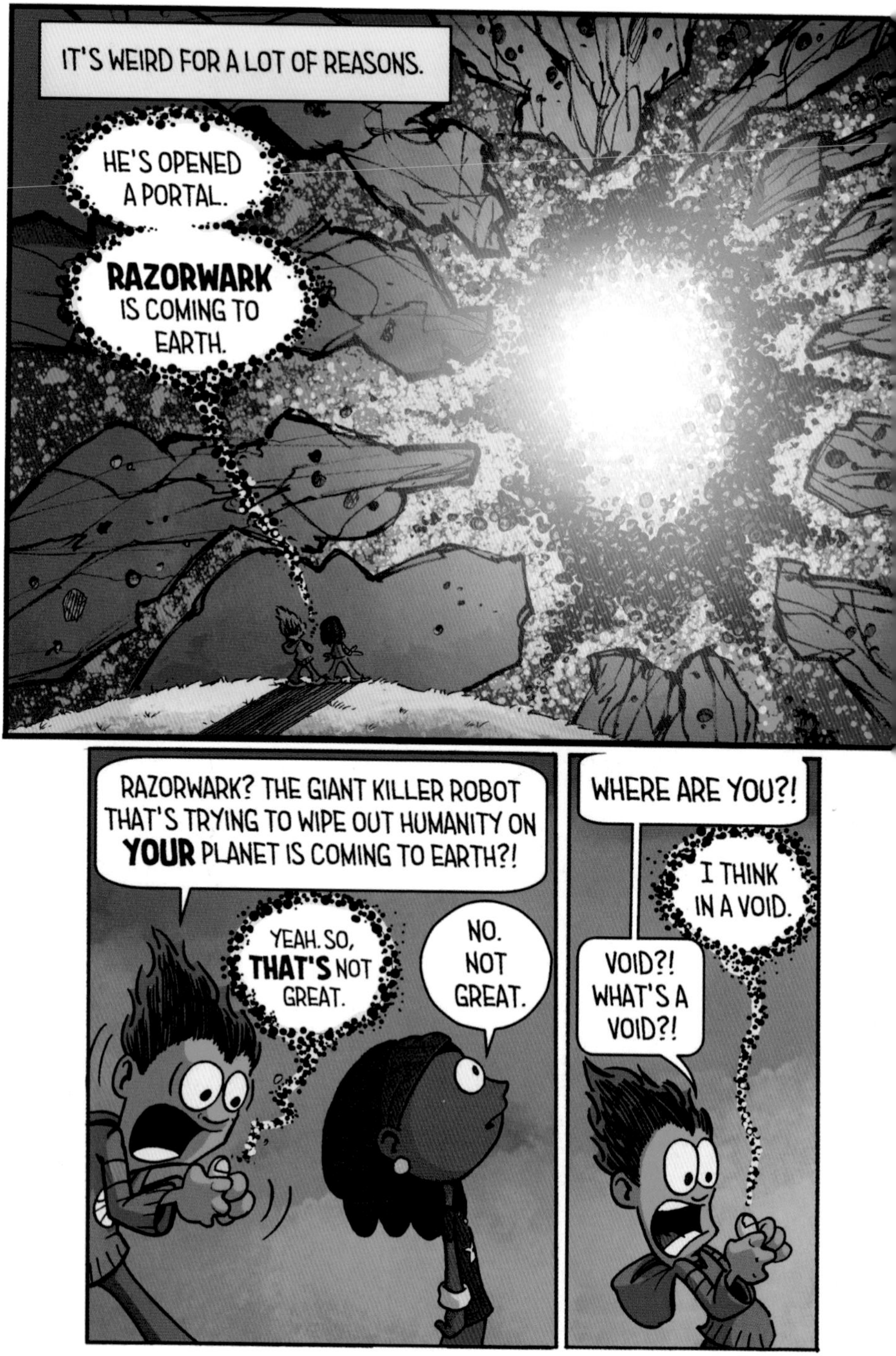
IT'S WEIRD FOR A LOT OF REASONS.
HE'S OPENED A PORTAL.
RAZORWARK IS COMING TO EARTH.
RAZORWARK? THE GIANT KILLER ROBOT THAT'S TRYING TO WIPE OUT HUMANITY ON **YOUR** PLANET IS COMING TO EARTH?!
YEAH. SO, **THAT'S** NOT GREAT.
NO. NOT GREAT.
WHERE ARE YOU?!
I THINK IN A VOID.
VOID?! WHAT'S A VOID?!

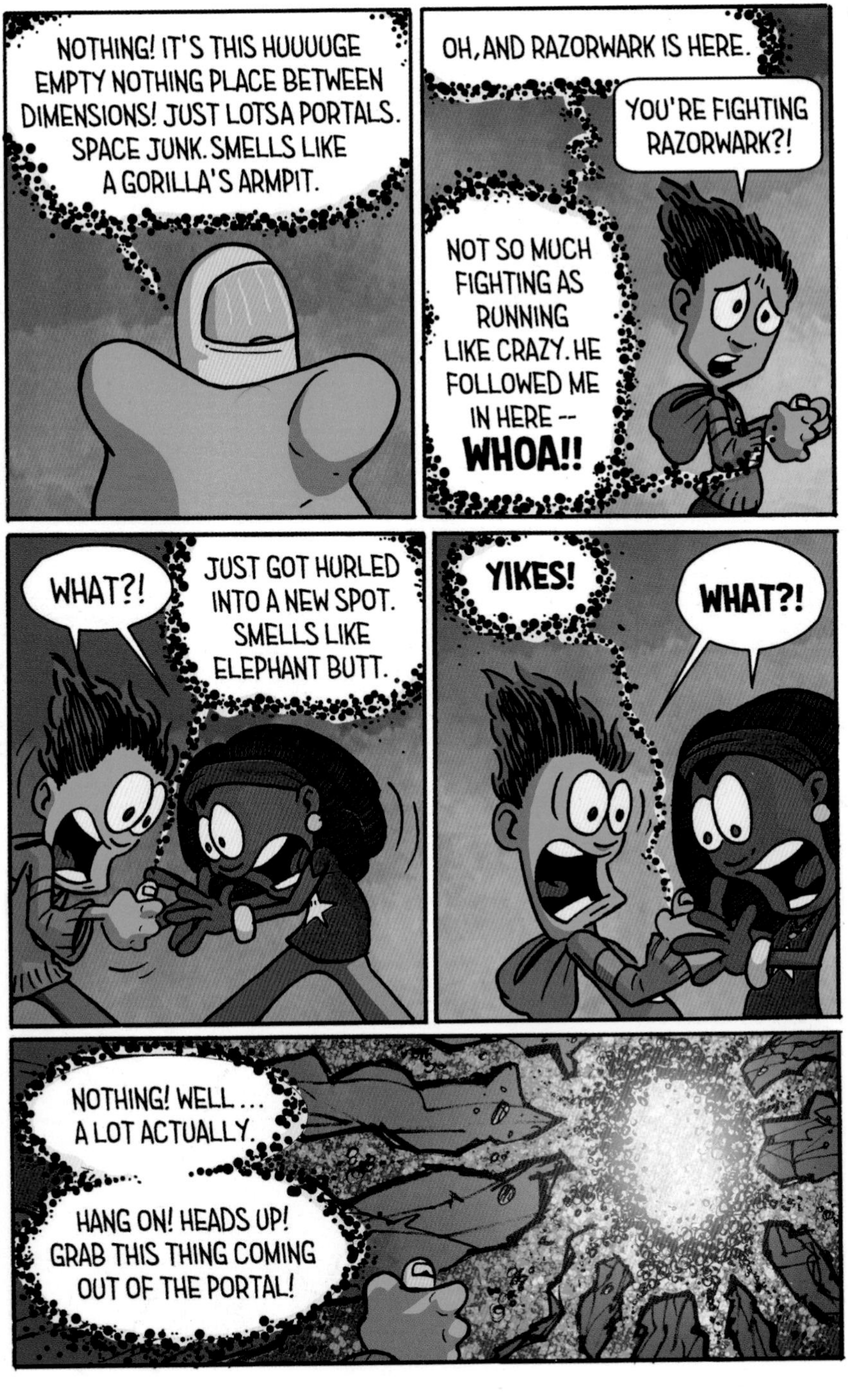
NOTHING! IT'S THIS HUUUUGE EMPTY NOTHING PLACE BETWEEN DIMENSIONS! JUST LOTSA PORTALS. SPACE JUNK. SMELLS LIKE A GORILLA'S ARMPIT.
OH, AND RAZORWARK IS HERE.
YOU'RE FIGHTING RAZORWARK?!
NOT SO MUCH FIGHTING AS RUNNING LIKE CRAZY. HE FOLLOWED ME IN HERE -- WHOA!!
WHAT?!
JUST GOT HURLED INTO A NEW SPOT. SMELLS LIKE ELEPHANT BUTT.
YIKES!
WHAT?!
NOTHING! WELL . . . A LOT ACTUALLY.
HANG ON! HEADS UP! GRAB THIS THING COMING OUT OF THE PORTAL!

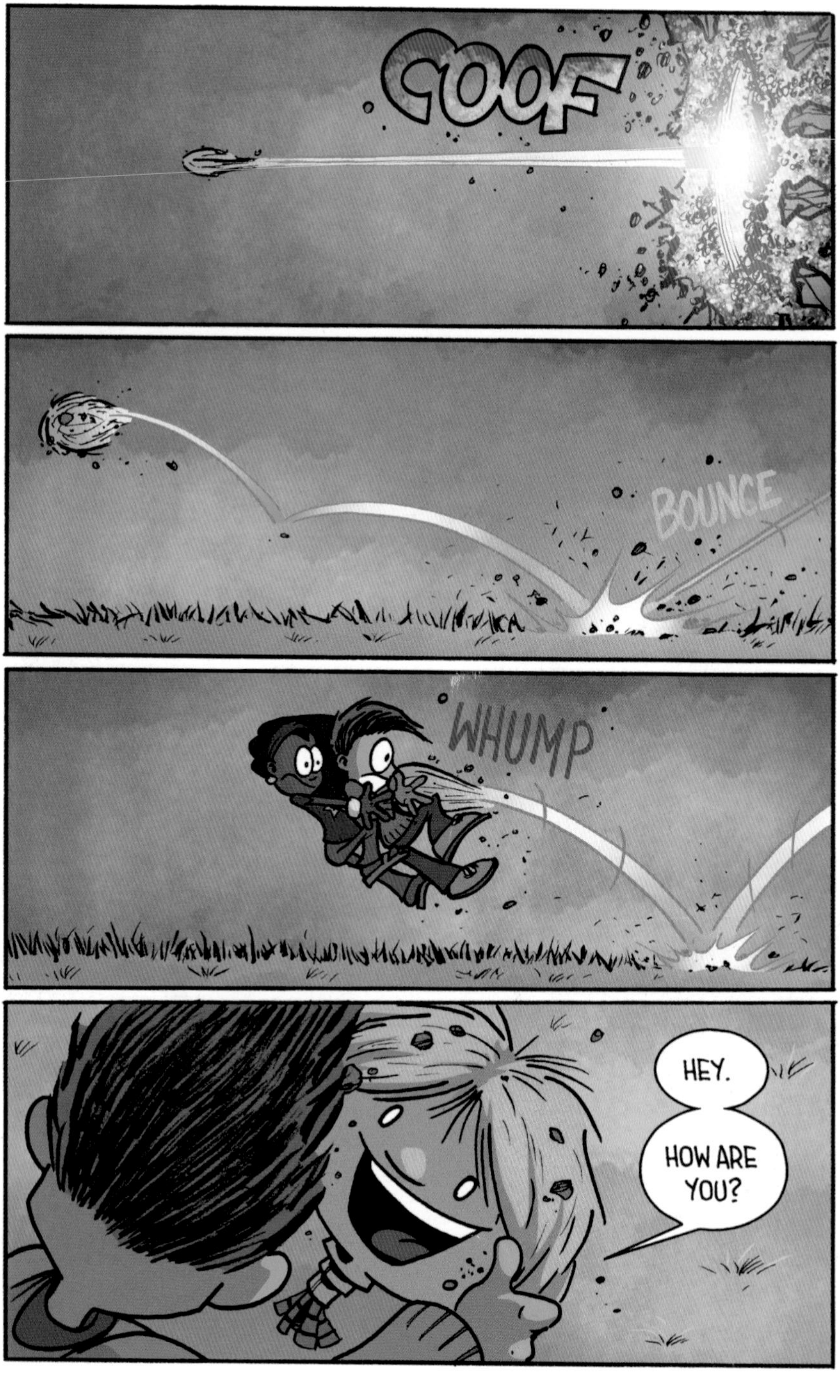
COOF
BOUNCE
WHUMP
HEY.
HOW ARE YOU?

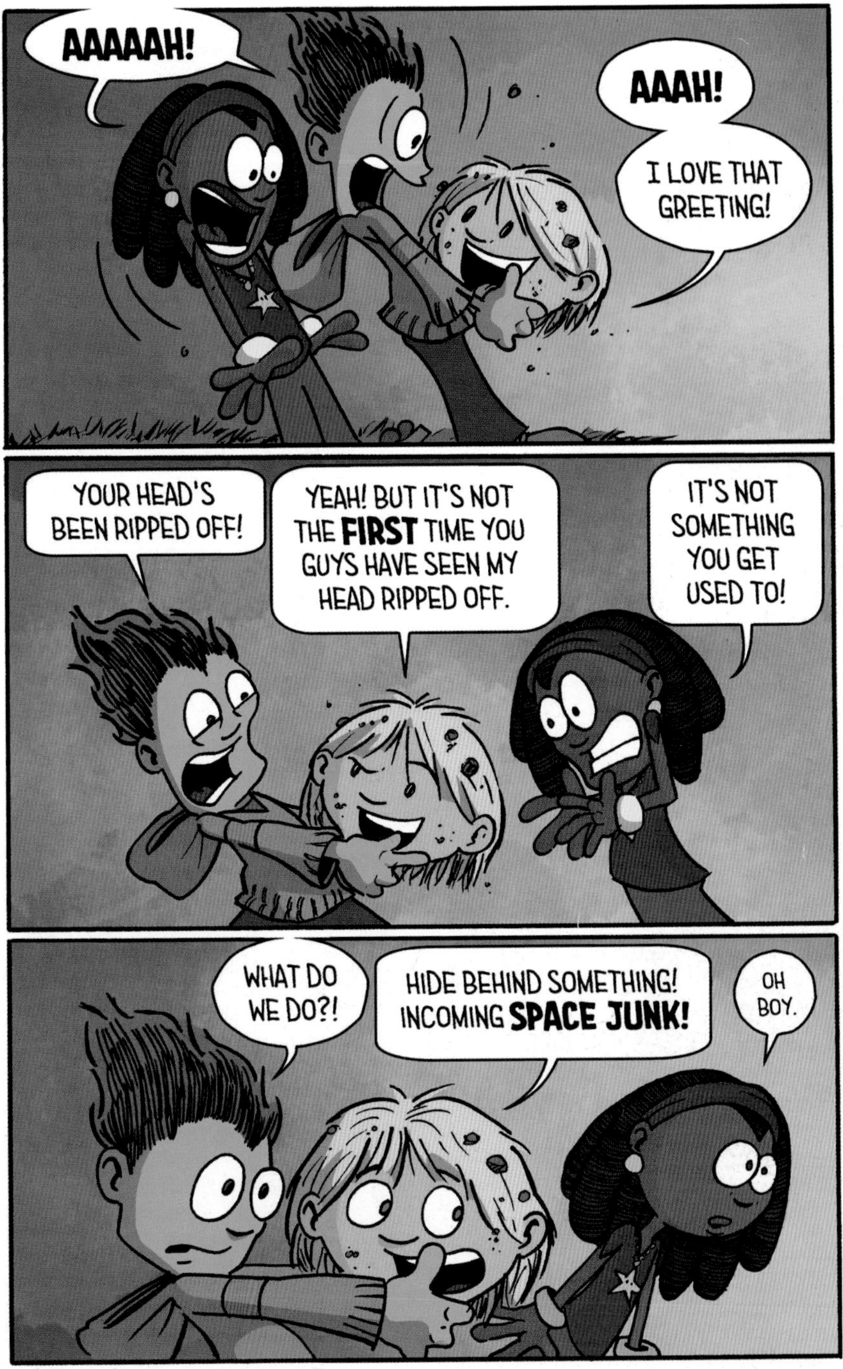
AAAAAH!
AAAH!
I LOVE THAT GREETING!
YOUR HEAD'S BEEN RIPPED OFF!
YEAH! BUT IT'S NOT THE **FIRST** TIME YOU GUYS HAVE SEEN MY HEAD RIPPED OFF.
IT'S NOT SOMETHING YOU GET USED TO!
WHAT DO WE DO?!
HIDE BEHIND SOMETHING! INCOMING **SPACE JUNK!**
OH BOY.

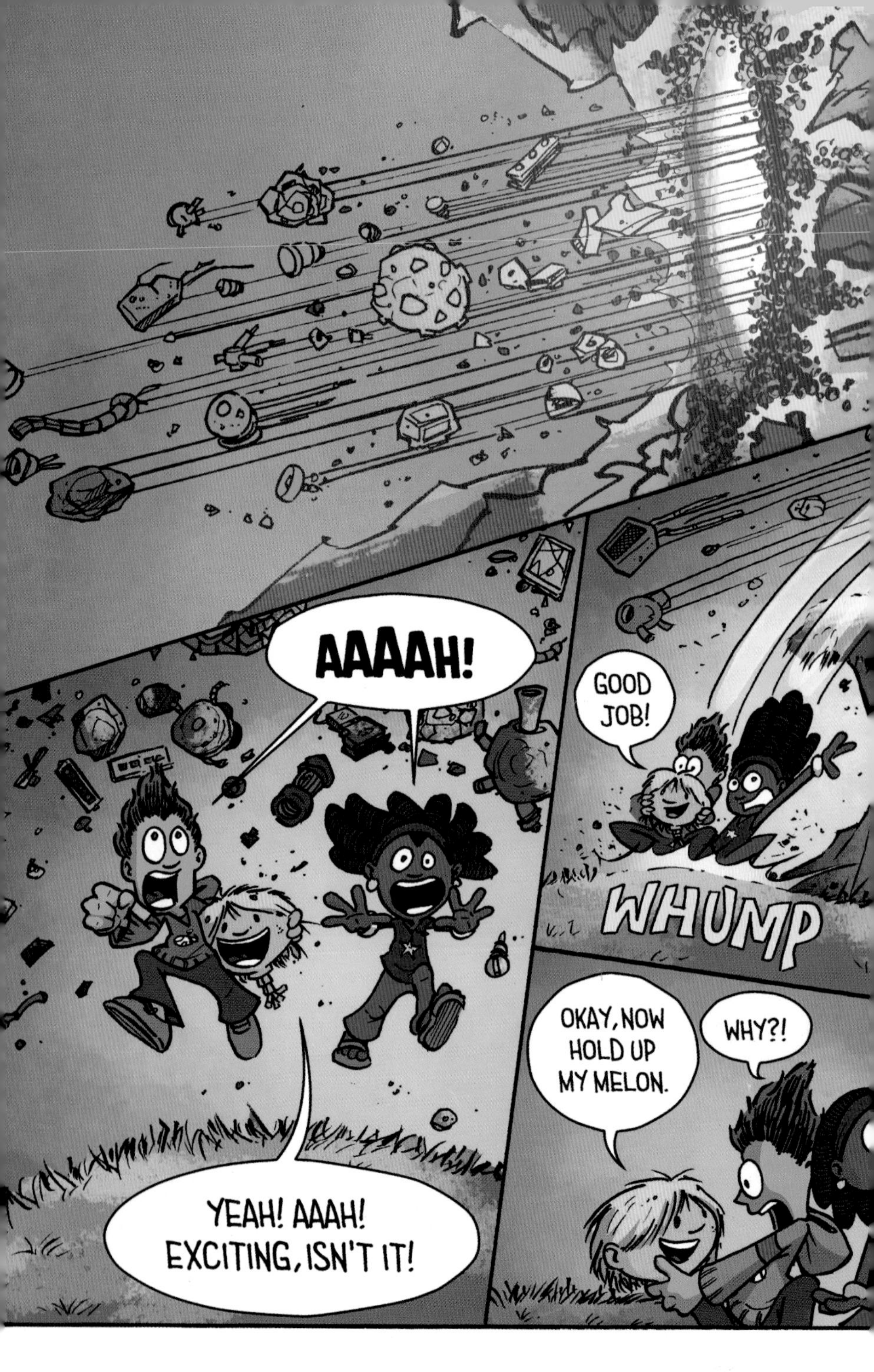
AAAAH!
YEAH! AAAH! EXCITING, ISN'T IT!
GOOD JOB!
WHUMP
OKAY, NOW HOLD UP MY MELON.
WHY?!

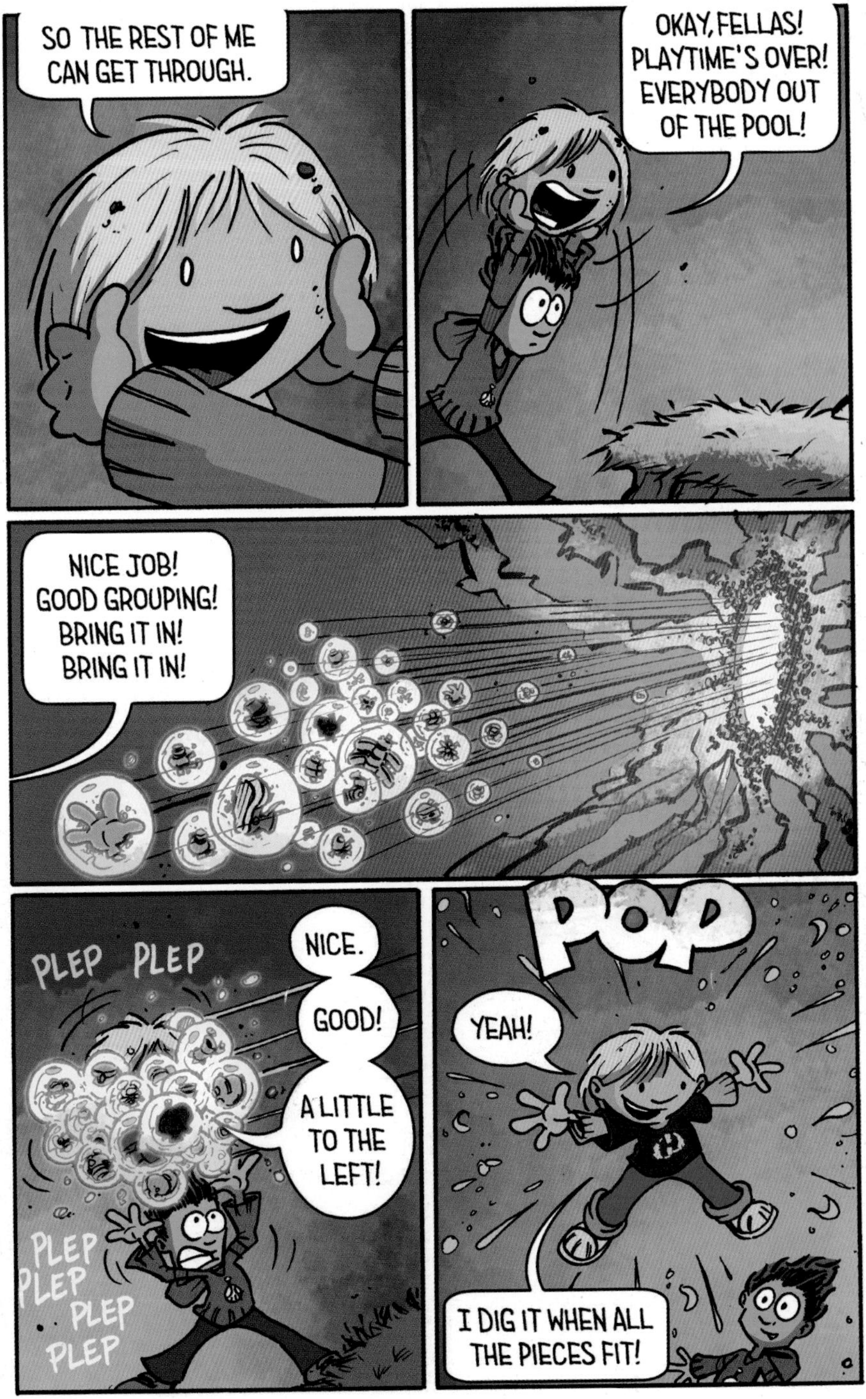
SO THE REST OF ME CAN GET THROUGH.
OKAY, FELLAS! PLAYTIME'S OVER! EVERYBODY OUT OF THE POOL!
NICE JOB! GOOD GROUPING! BRING IT IN! BRING IT IN!
PLEP PLEP
NICE.
GOOD!
A LITTLE TO THE LEFT!
PLEP PLEP PLEP PLEP
POP
YEAH!
I DIG IT WHEN ALL THE PIECES FIT!

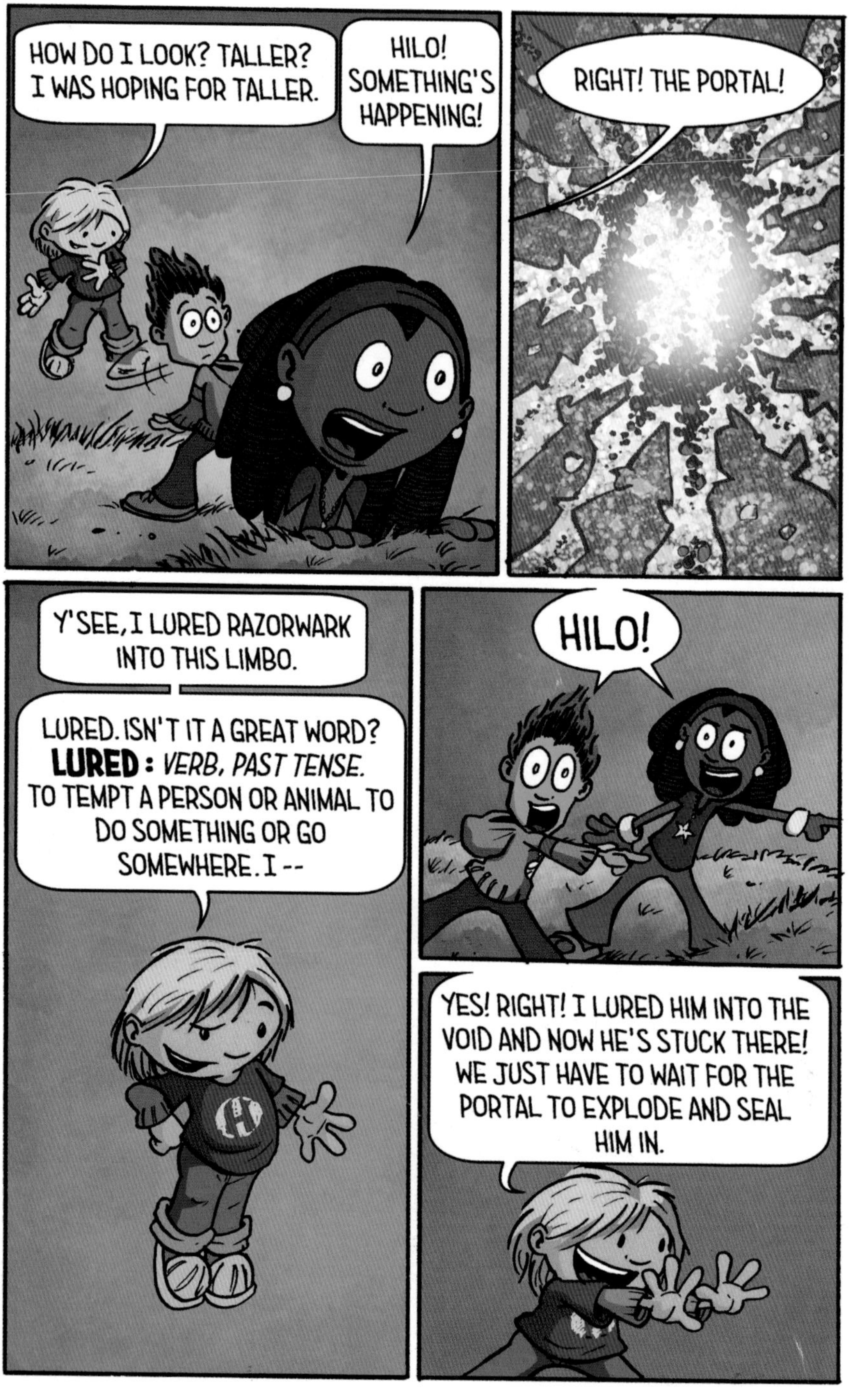
HOW DO I LOOK? TALLER? I WAS HOPING FOR TALLER.
HILO! SOMETHING'S HAPPENING!
RIGHT! THE PORTAL!
Y'SEE, I LURED RAZORWARK INTO THIS LIMBO.
LURED. ISN'T IT A GREAT WORD? **LURED :** *VERB, PAST TENSE.* TO TEMPT A PERSON OR ANIMAL TO DO SOMETHING OR GO SOMEWHERE. I --
HILO!
YES! RIGHT! I LURED HIM INTO THE VOID AND NOW HE'S STUCK THERE! WE JUST HAVE TO WAIT FOR THE PORTAL TO EXPLODE AND SEAL HIM IN.

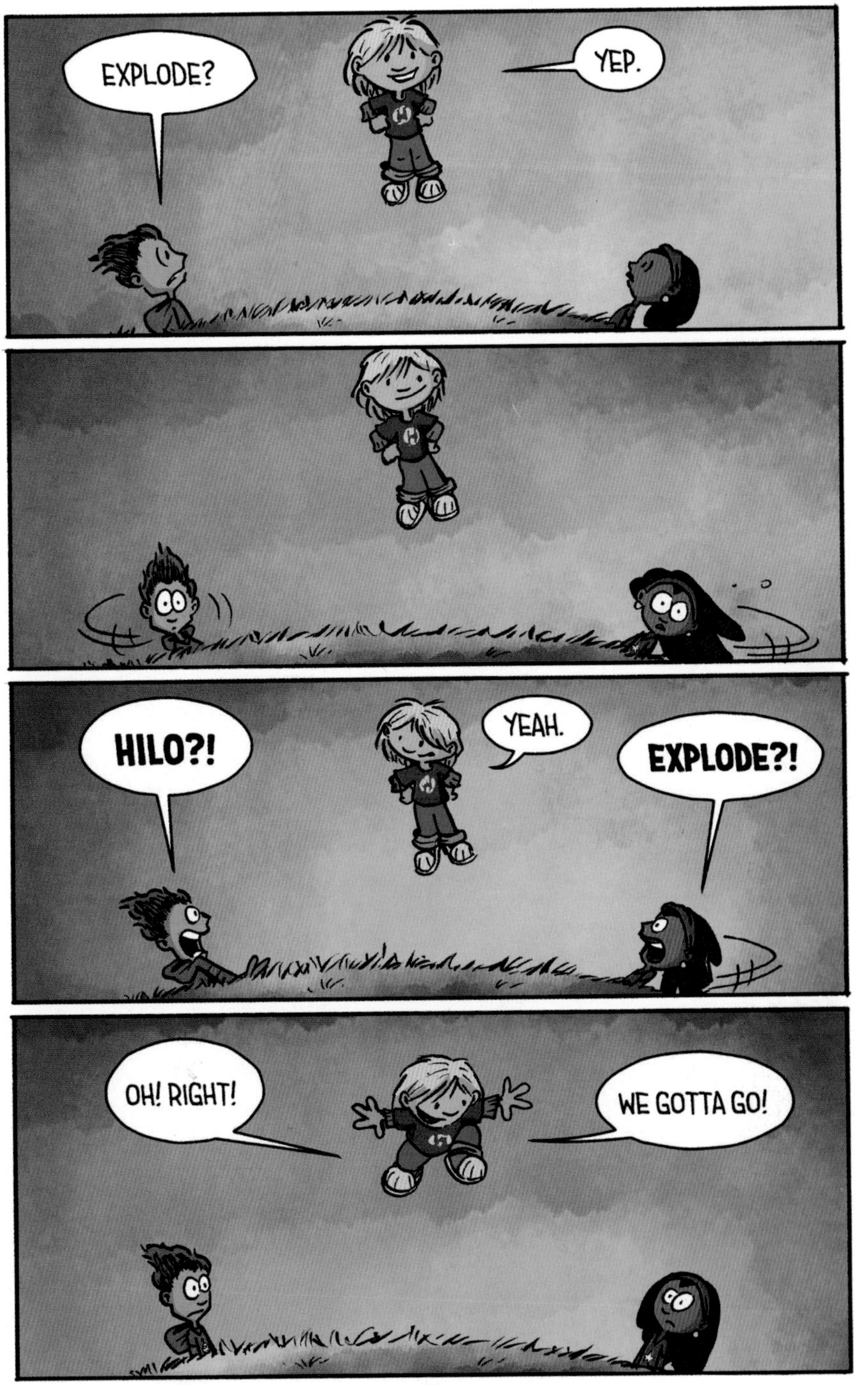
EXPLODE?
YEP.
HILO?!
YEAH.
EXPLODE?!
OH! RIGHT!
WE GOTTA GO!

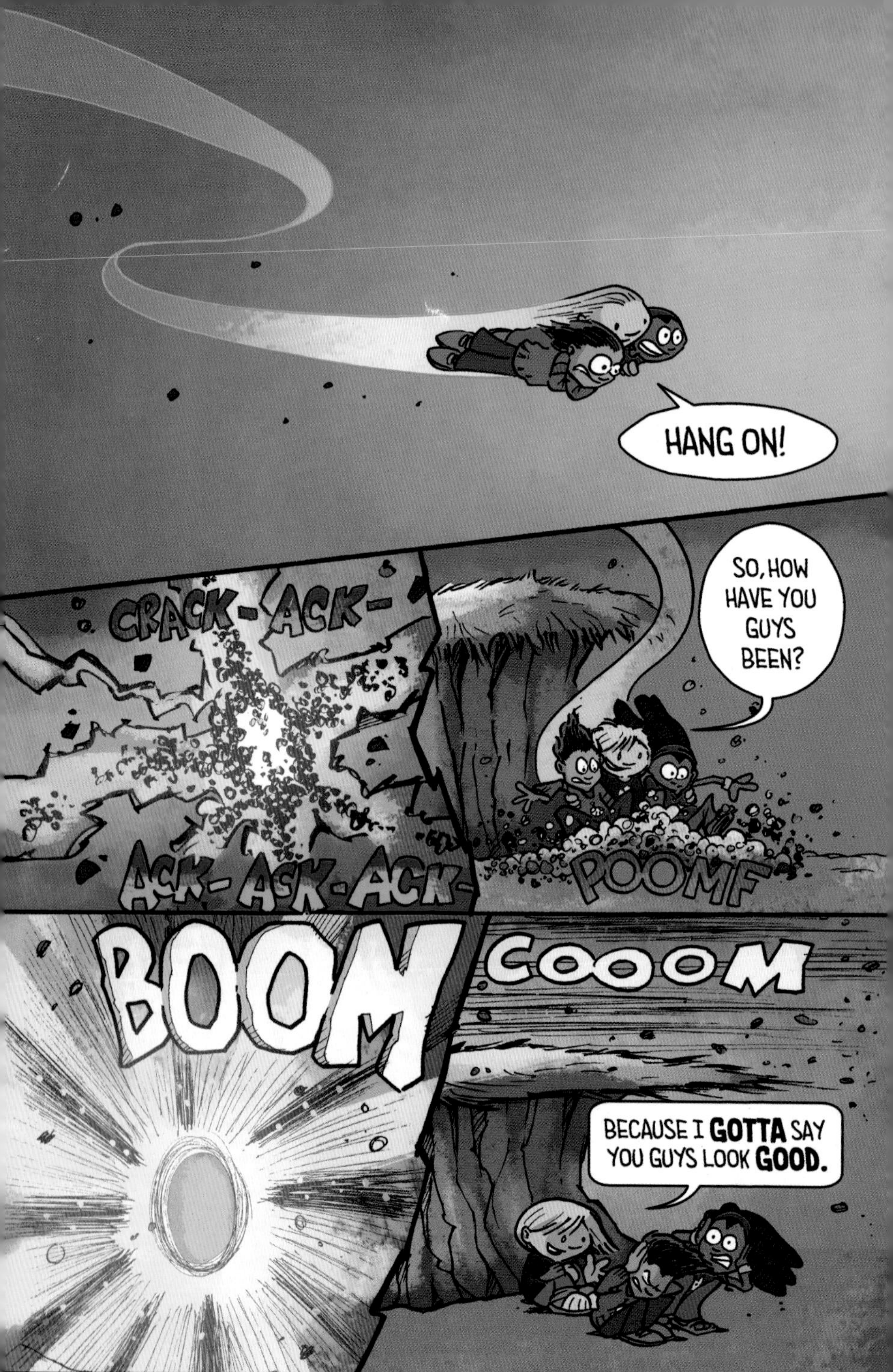
HANG ON!
CRACK-ACK-
ACK-ACK-ACK-
SO, HOW HAVE YOU GUYS BEEN?
POOMF
BOOM
COOOM
BECAUSE I **GOTTA** SAY YOU GUYS LOOK **GOOD.**

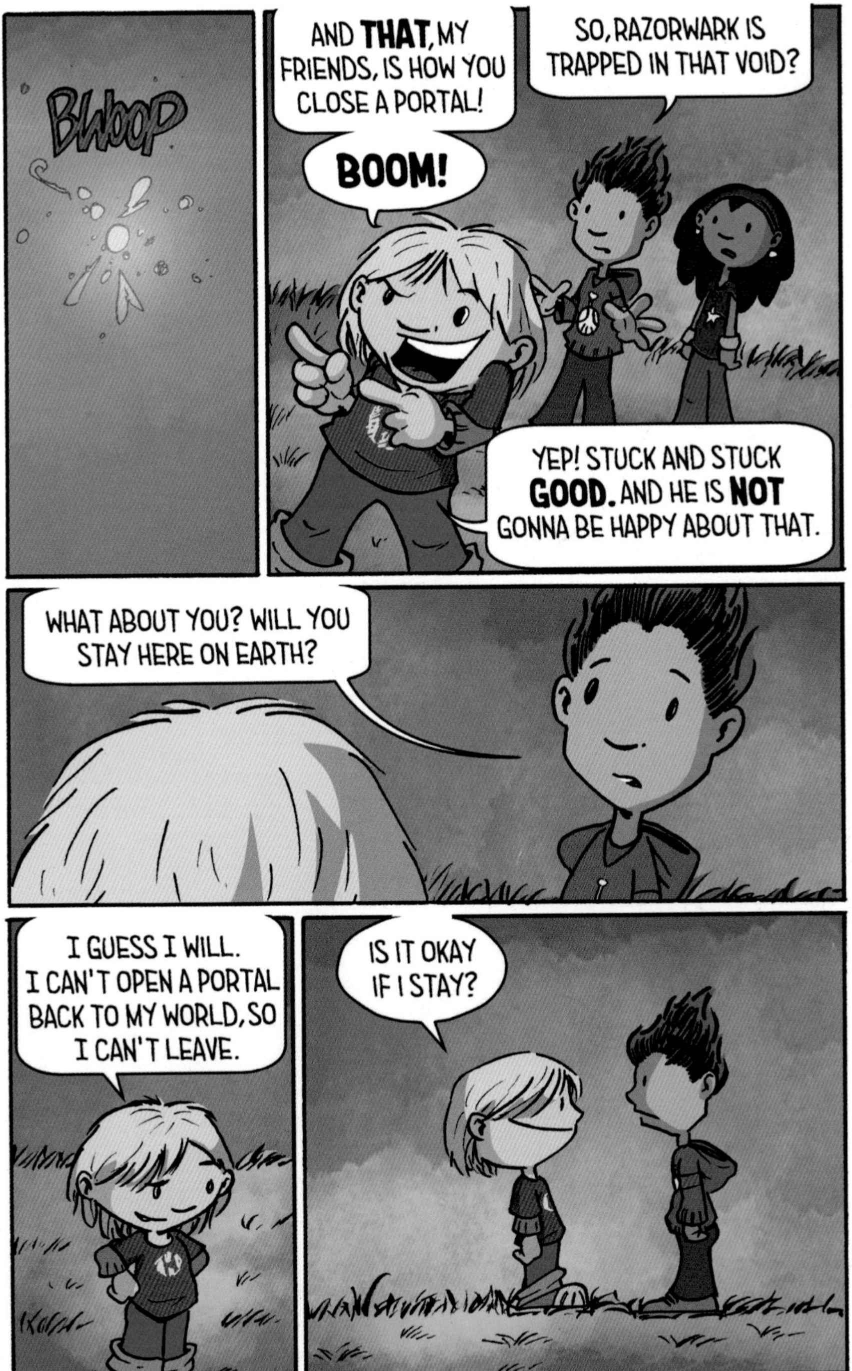
BWOOP
AND THAT, MY FRIENDS, IS HOW YOU CLOSE A PORTAL!
BOOM!
SO, RAZORWARK IS TRAPPED IN THAT VOID?
YEP! STUCK AND STUCK GOOD. AND HE IS NOT GONNA BE HAPPY ABOUT THAT.
WHAT ABOUT YOU? WILL YOU STAY HERE ON EARTH?
I GUESS I WILL. I CAN'T OPEN A PORTAL BACK TO MY WORLD, SO I CAN'T LEAVE.
IS IT OKAY IF I STAY?

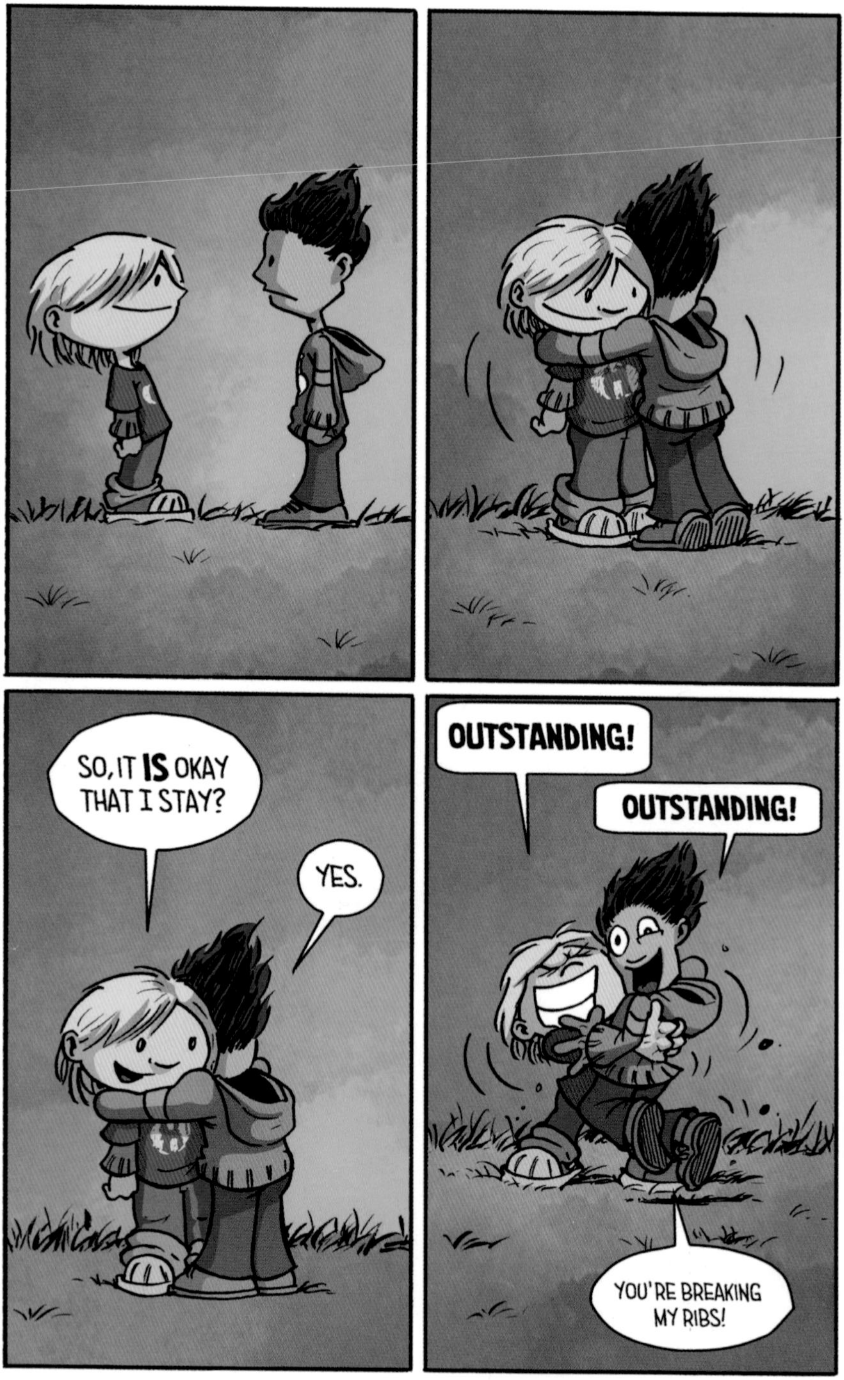
SO, IT **IS** OKAY THAT I STAY?
YES.
OUTSTANDING!
OUTSTANDING!
YOU'RE BREAKING MY RIBS!

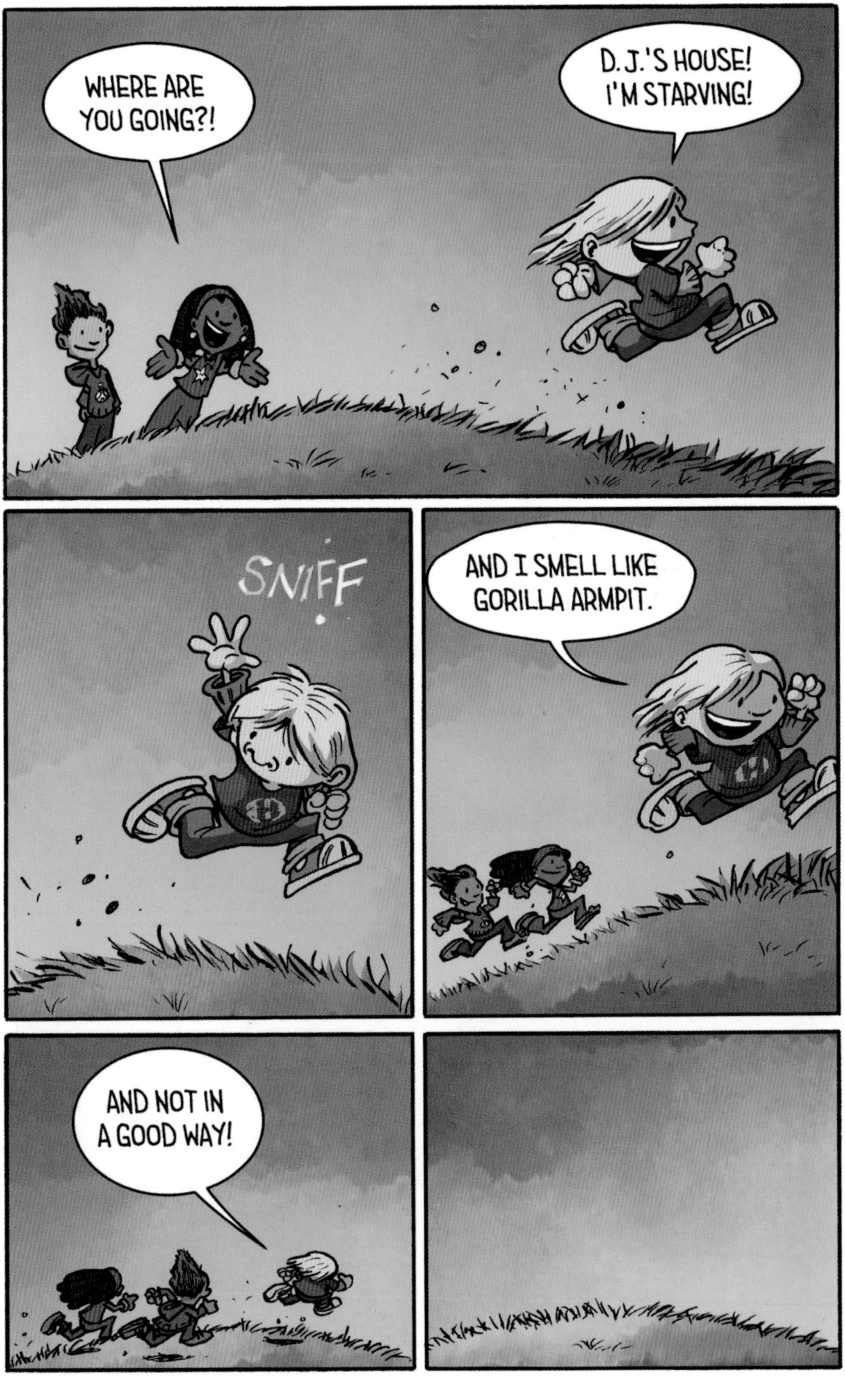

WHERE ARE YOU GOING?!
D.J.'S HOUSE! I'M STARVING!
SNIFF
AND I SMELL LIKE GORILLA ARMPIT.
AND NOT IN A GOOD WAY!

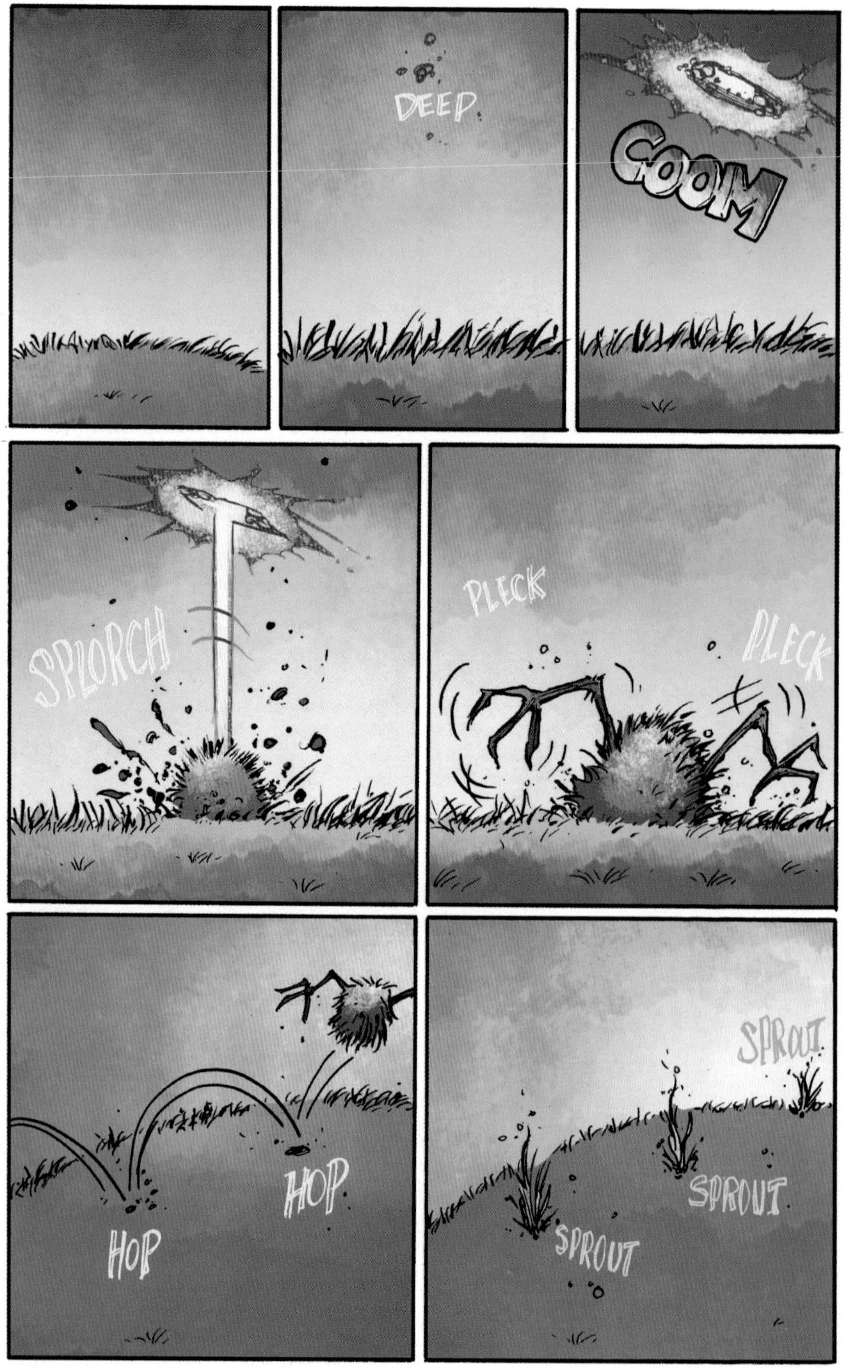
DEEP
GOOM
SPLORCH
PLECK
PLECK
HOP
HOP
SPROUT
SPROUT
SPROUT

CHAPTER 2

KNOCK KNOCK

SO, HILO IS STAYING. IT'S FUN.
MORE RICE AND MILK?
YES!
OUTSTANDING!
MILK
HE'S WORKING ON FITTING IN.
I'M ON THE SCHOOL BUS! TRANSPORTATION!
WHOOO!
PLEASE BE COOL.
BEING COOL!

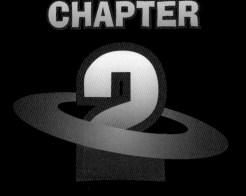

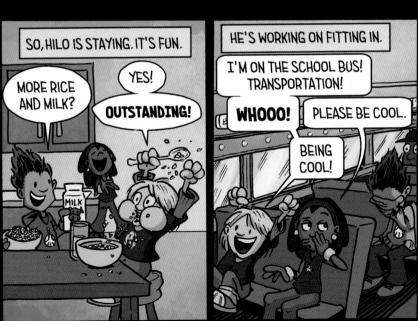

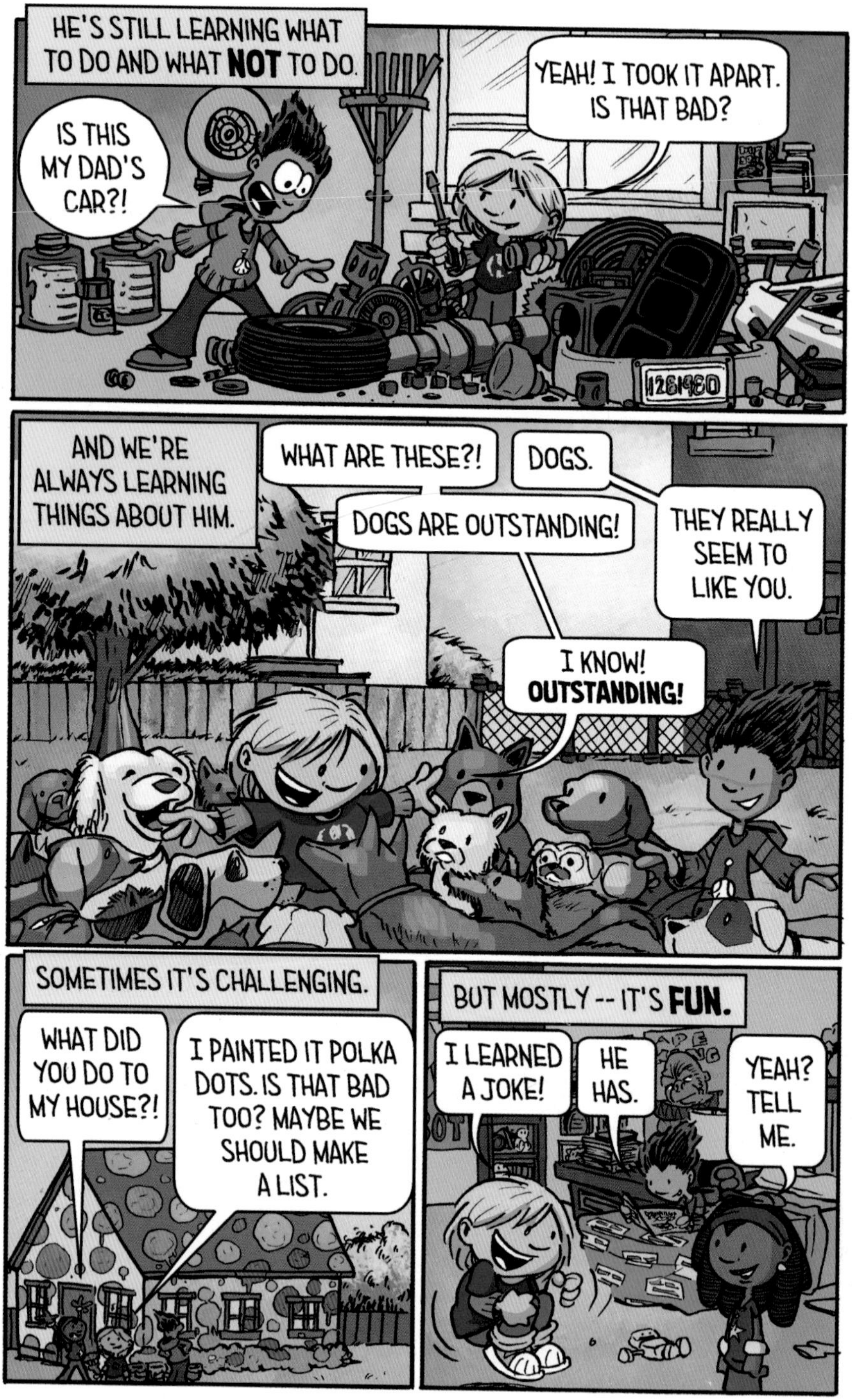
HE'S STILL LEARNING WHAT TO DO AND WHAT **NOT** TO DO.
IS THIS MY DAD'S CAR?!
YEAH! I TOOK IT APART. IS THAT BAD?
1281980
AND WE'RE ALWAYS LEARNING THINGS ABOUT HIM.
WHAT ARE THESE?!
DOGS.
DOGS ARE OUTSTANDING!
THEY REALLY SEEM TO LIKE YOU.
I KNOW! **OUTSTANDING!**
SOMETIMES IT'S CHALLENGING.
WHAT DID YOU DO TO MY HOUSE?!
I PAINTED IT POLKA DOTS. IS THAT BAD TOO? MAYBE WE SHOULD MAKE A LIST.
BUT MOSTLY -- IT'S **FUN.**
I LEARNED A JOKE!
HE HAS.
YEAH? TELL ME.

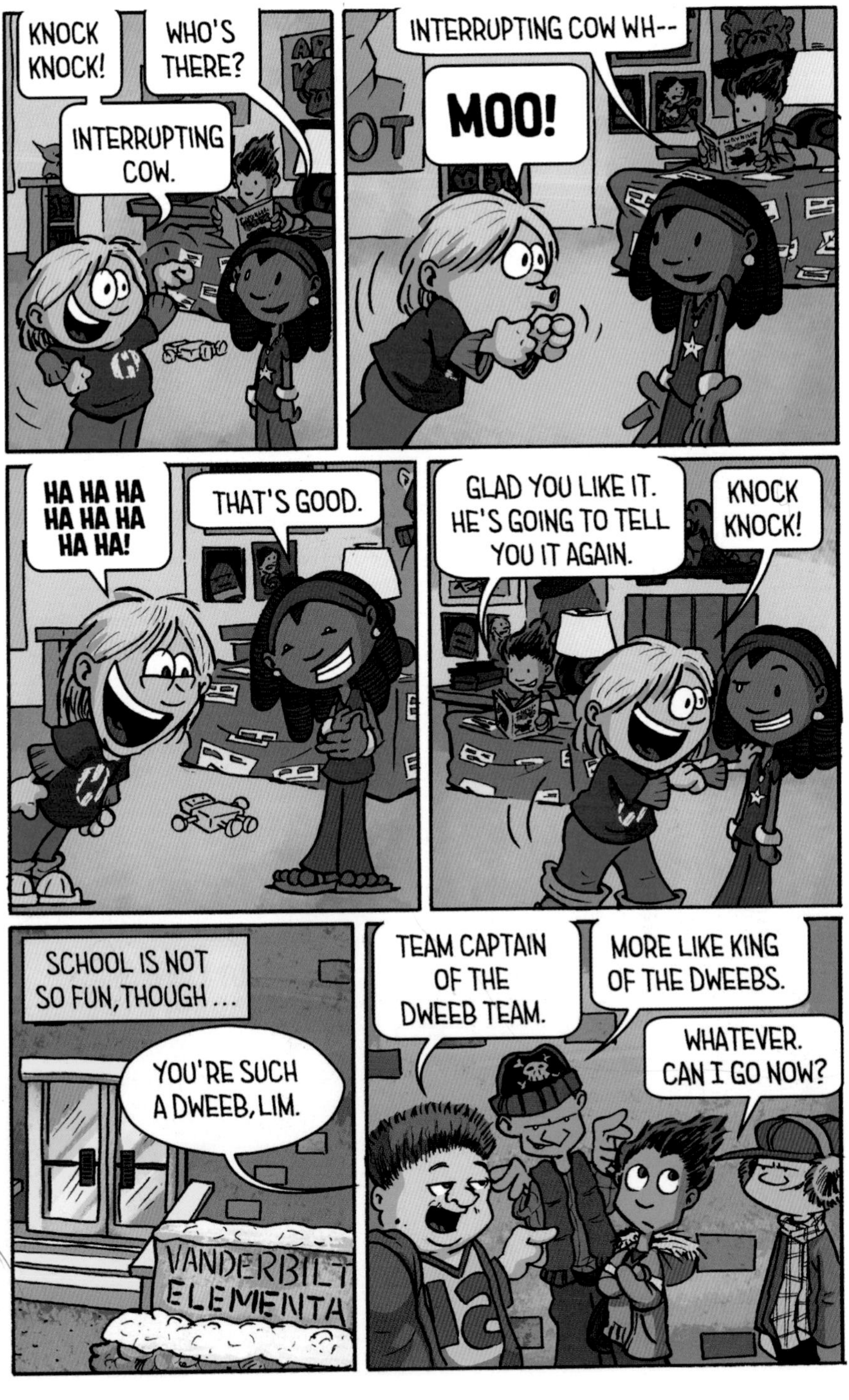
KNOCK KNOCK!
WHO'S THERE?
INTERRUPTING COW.
INTERRUPTING COW WH--
MOO!
HA HA HA HA HA HA HA HA!
THAT'S GOOD.
GLAD YOU LIKE IT. HE'S GOING TO TELL YOU IT AGAIN.
KNOCK KNOCK!
SCHOOL IS NOT SO FUN, THOUGH . . .
YOU'RE SUCH A DWEEB, LIM.
VANDERBILT ELEMENTA
TEAM CAPTAIN OF THE DWEEB TEAM.
MORE LIKE KING OF THE DWEEBS.
WHATEVER. CAN I GO NOW?

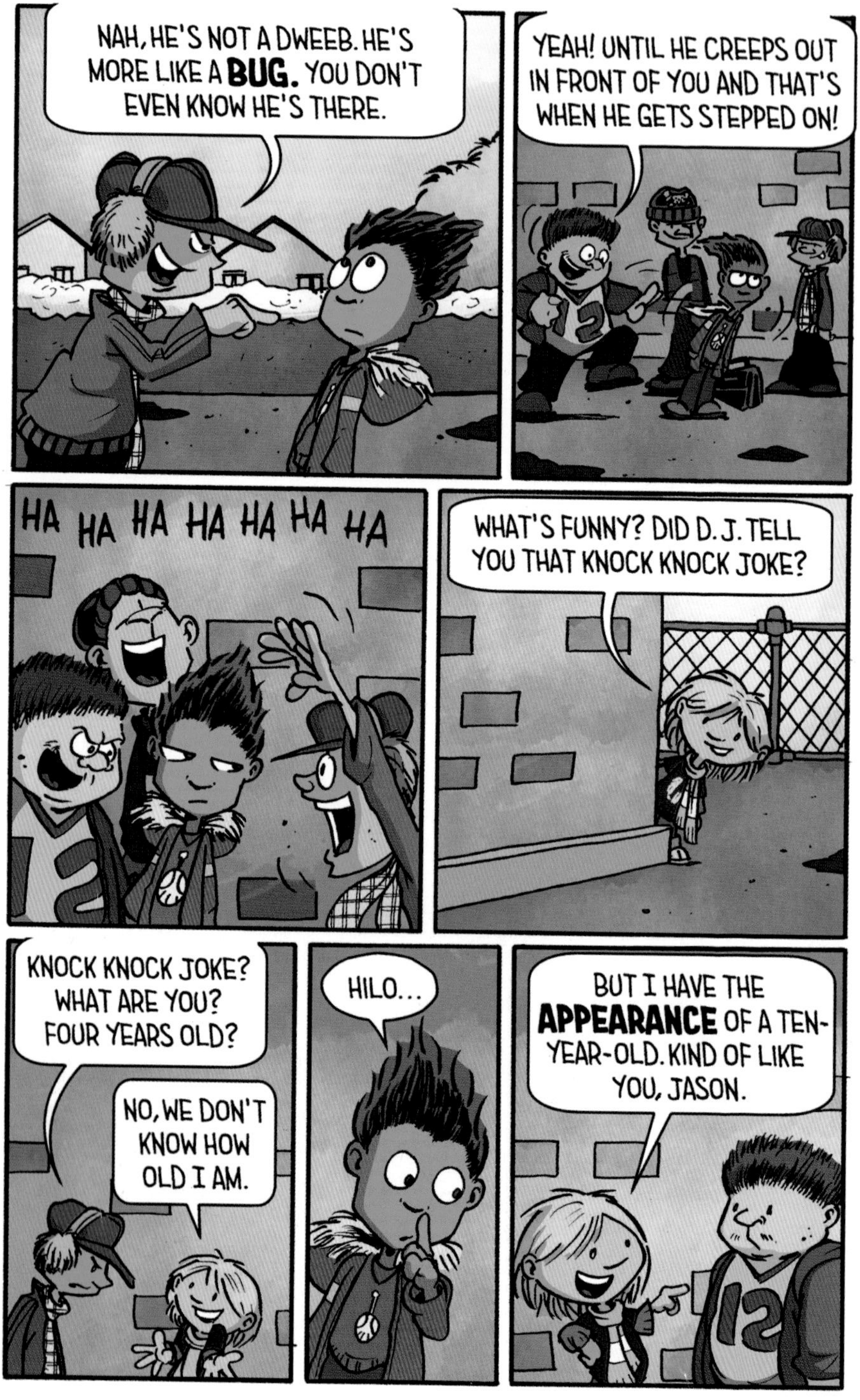
NAH, HE'S NOT A DWEEB. HE'S MORE LIKE A **BUG.** YOU DON'T EVEN KNOW HE'S THERE.
YEAH! UNTIL HE CREEPS OUT IN FRONT OF YOU AND THAT'S WHEN HE GETS STEPPED ON!
HA HA HA HA HA HA HA
WHAT'S FUNNY? DID D. J. TELL YOU THAT KNOCK KNOCK JOKE?
KNOCK KNOCK JOKE? WHAT ARE YOU? FOUR YEARS OLD?
NO, WE DON'T KNOW HOW OLD I AM.
HILO...
BUT I HAVE THE **APPEARANCE** OF A TEN-YEAR-OLD. KIND OF LIKE YOU, JASON.

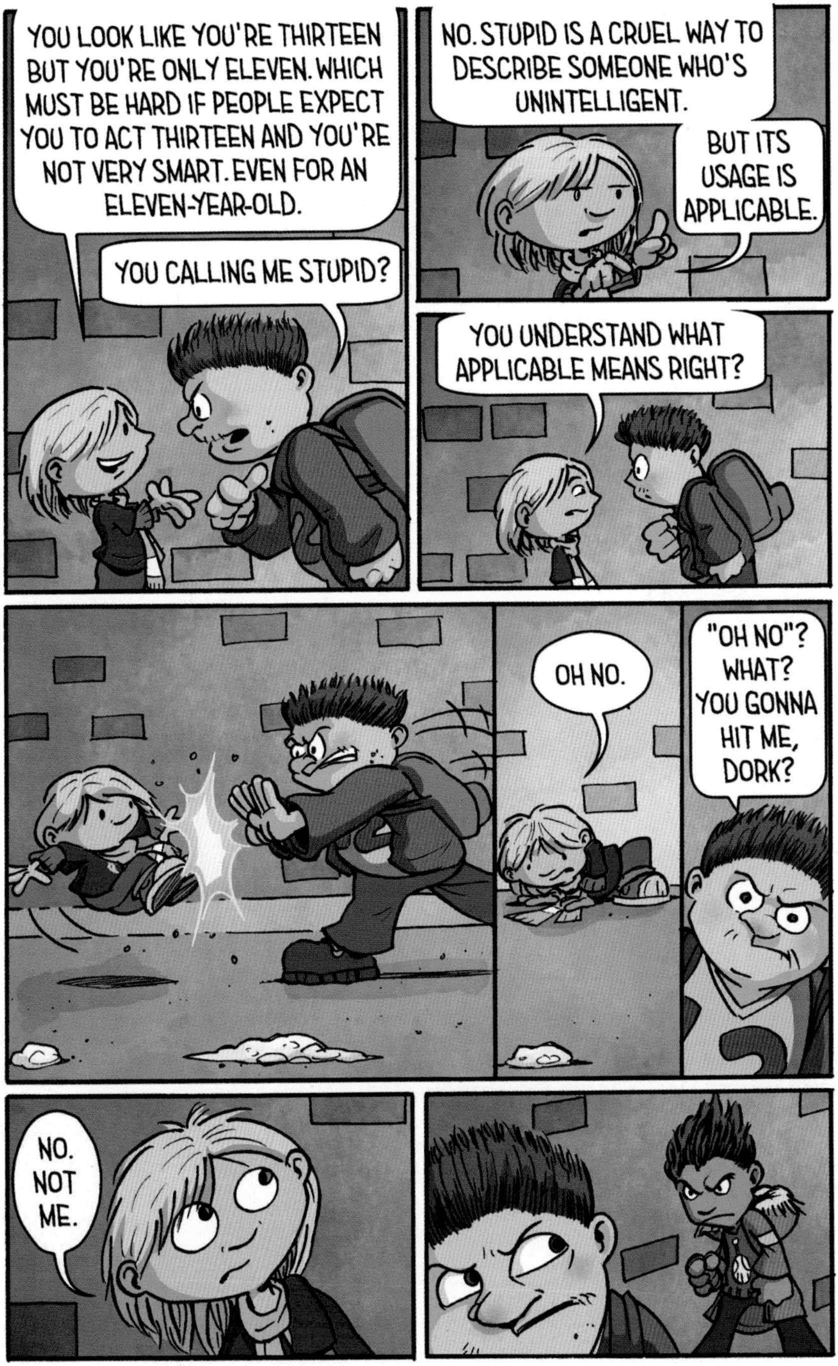
YOU LOOK LIKE YOU'RE THIRTEEN BUT YOU'RE ONLY ELEVEN. WHICH MUST BE HARD IF PEOPLE EXPECT YOU TO ACT THIRTEEN AND YOU'RE NOT VERY SMART. EVEN FOR AN ELEVEN-YEAR-OLD.
YOU CALLING ME STUPID?
NO. STUPID IS A CRUEL WAY TO DESCRIBE SOMEONE WHO'S UNINTELLIGENT.
BUT ITS USAGE IS APPLICABLE.
YOU UNDERSTAND WHAT APPLICABLE MEANS RIGHT?
OH NO.
"OH NO"? WHAT? YOU GONNA HIT ME, DORK?
NO. NOT ME.

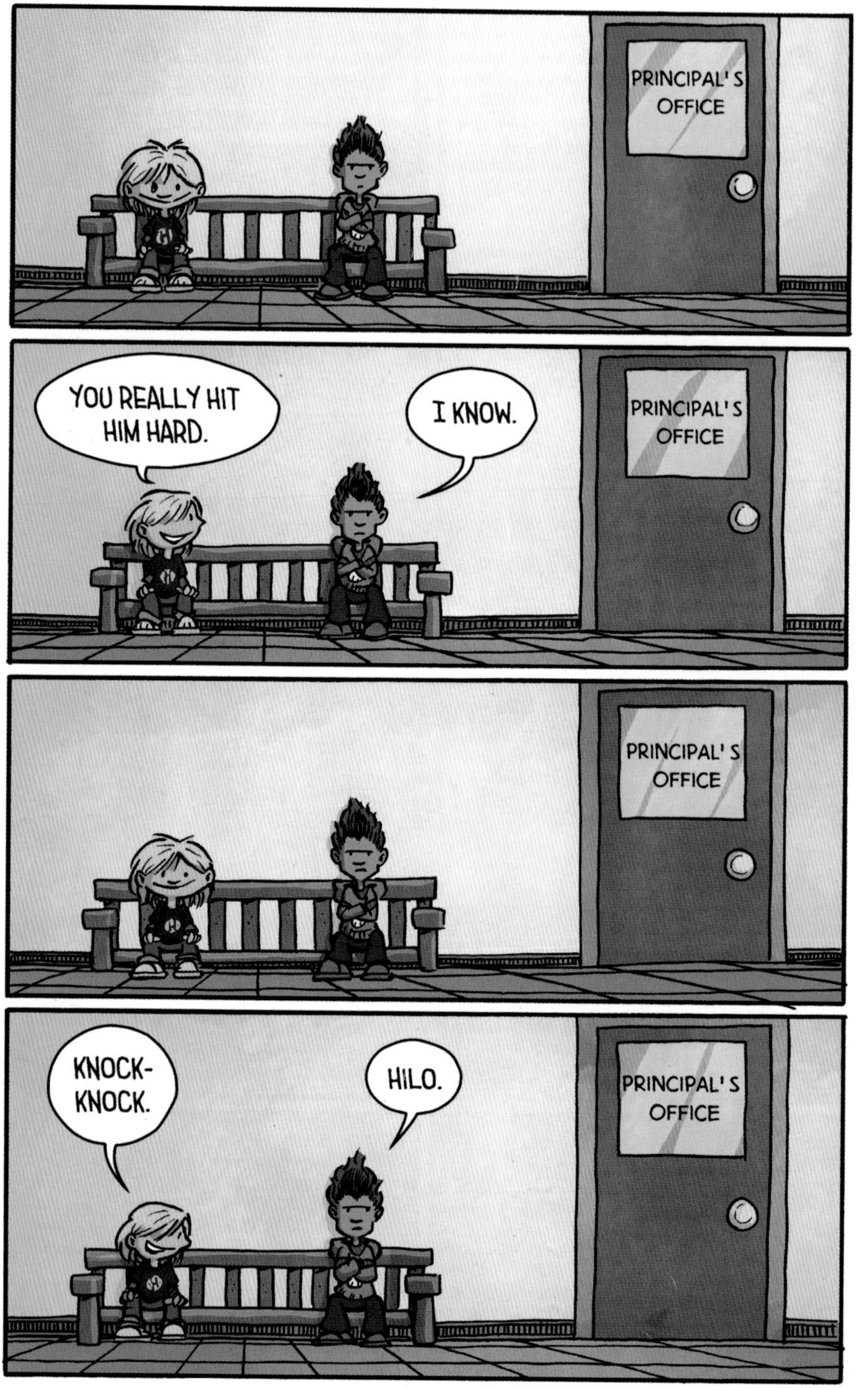
PRINCIPAL'S
OFFICE
YOU REALLY HIT HIM HARD.
I KNOW.
PRINCIPAL'S
OFFICE
PRINCIPAL'S
OFFICE
KNOCK-KNOCK.
HILO.
PRINCIPAL'S
OFFICE

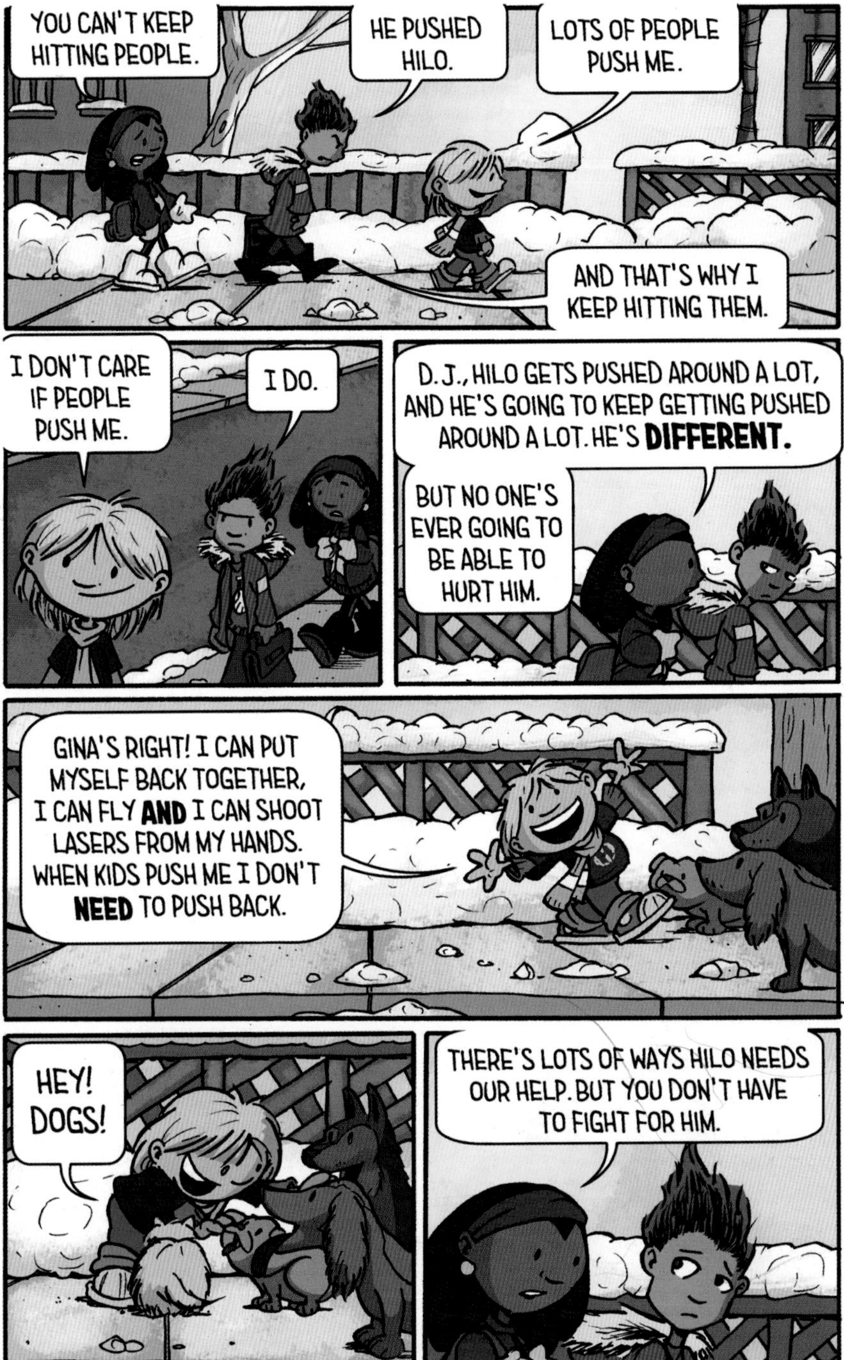

YOU CAN'T KEEP HITTING PEOPLE.
HE PUSHED HILO.
LOTS OF PEOPLE PUSH ME.
AND THAT'S WHY I KEEP HITTING THEM.
I DON'T CARE IF PEOPLE PUSH ME.
I DO.
D. J., HILO GETS PUSHED AROUND A LOT, AND HE'S GOING TO KEEP GETTING PUSHED AROUND A LOT. HE'S DIFFERENT.
BUT NO ONE'S EVER GOING TO BE ABLE TO HURT HIM.
GINA'S RIGHT! I CAN PUT MYSELF BACK TOGETHER, I CAN FLY AND I CAN SHOOT LASERS FROM MY HANDS. WHEN KIDS PUSH ME I DON'T NEED TO PUSH BACK.
HEY! DOGS!
THERE'S LOTS OF WAYS HILO NEEDS OUR HELP. BUT YOU DON'T HAVE TO FIGHT FOR HIM.

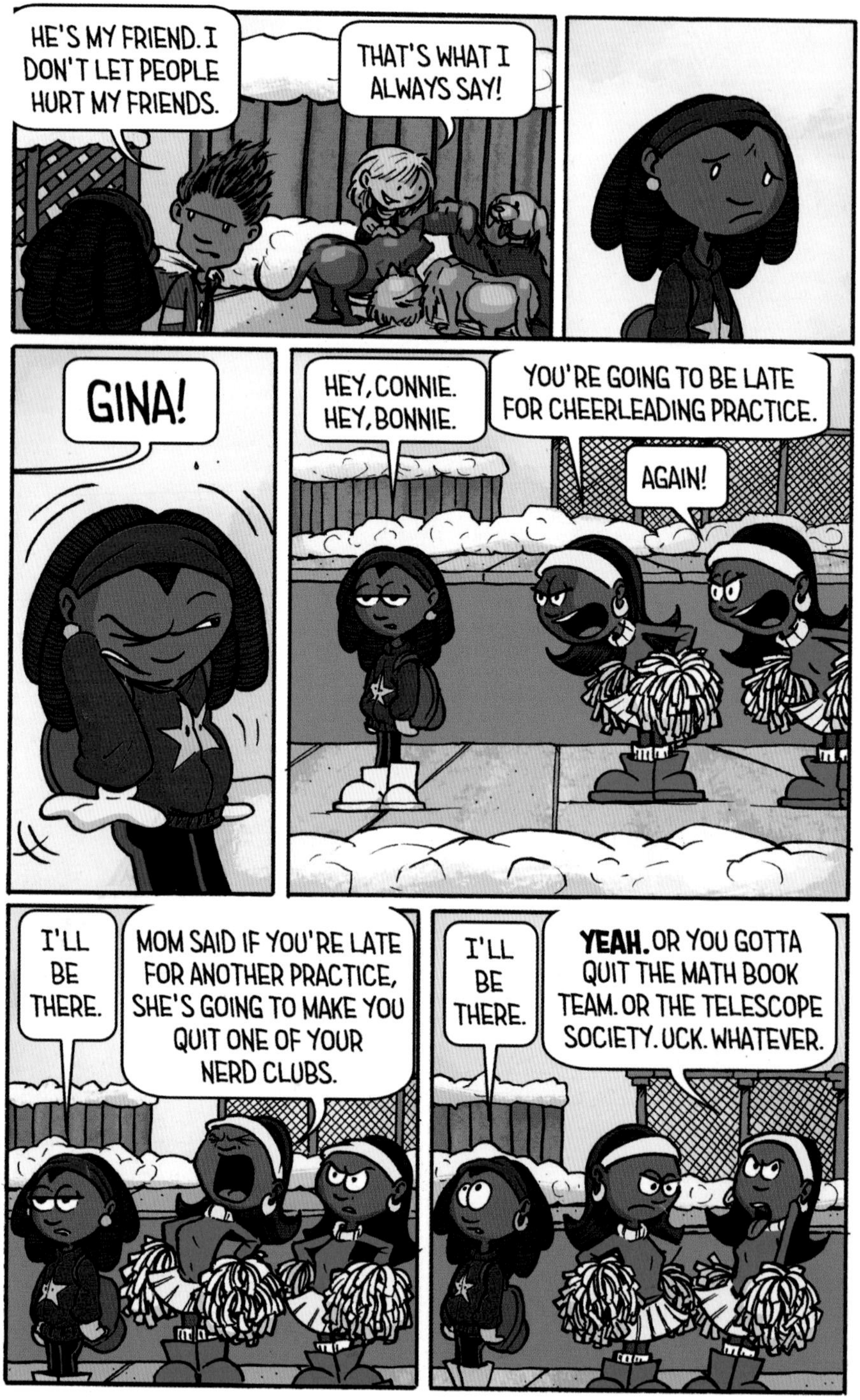
HE'S MY FRIEND. I DON'T LET PEOPLE HURT MY FRIENDS.
THAT'S WHAT I ALWAYS SAY!
GINA!
HEY, CONNIE. HEY, BONNIE.
YOU'RE GOING TO BE LATE FOR CHEERLEADING PRACTICE.
AGAIN!
I'LL BE THERE.
MOM SAID IF YOU'RE LATE FOR ANOTHER PRACTICE, SHE'S GOING TO MAKE YOU QUIT ONE OF YOUR NERD CLUBS.
I'LL BE THERE.
YEAH. OR YOU GOTTA QUIT THE MATH BOOK TEAM. OR THE TELESCOPE SOCIETY. UCK. WHATEVER.

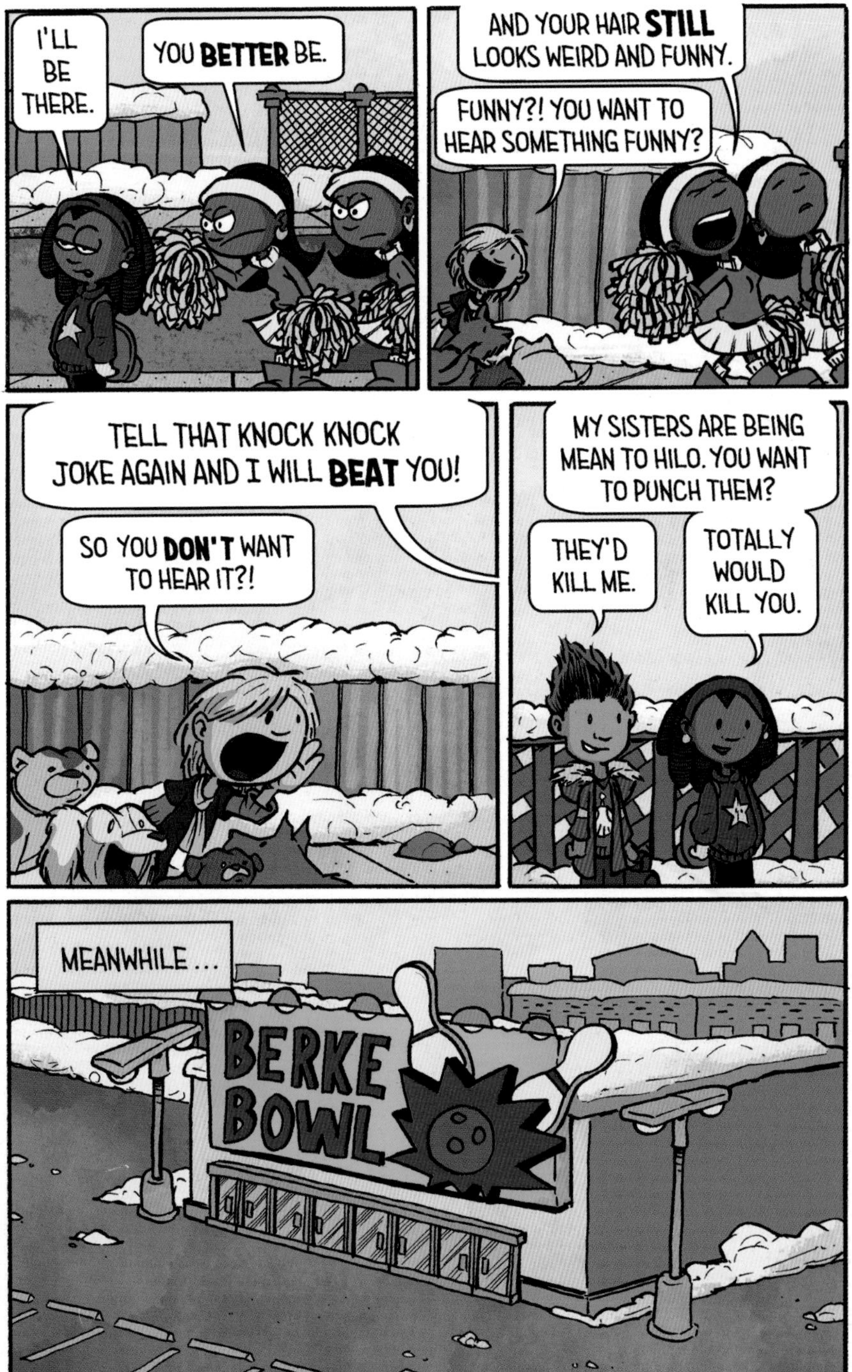
I'LL BE THERE.
YOU BETTER BE.
AND YOUR HAIR STILL LOOKS WEIRD AND FUNNY.
FUNNY?! YOU WANT TO HEAR SOMETHING FUNNY?
TELL THAT KNOCK KNOCK JOKE AGAIN AND I WILL BEAT YOU!
SO YOU DON'T WANT TO HEAR IT?!
MY SISTERS ARE BEING MEAN TO HILO. YOU WANT TO PUNCH THEM?
THEY'D KILL ME.
TOTALLY WOULD KILL YOU.
MEANWHILE...
BERKE BOWL

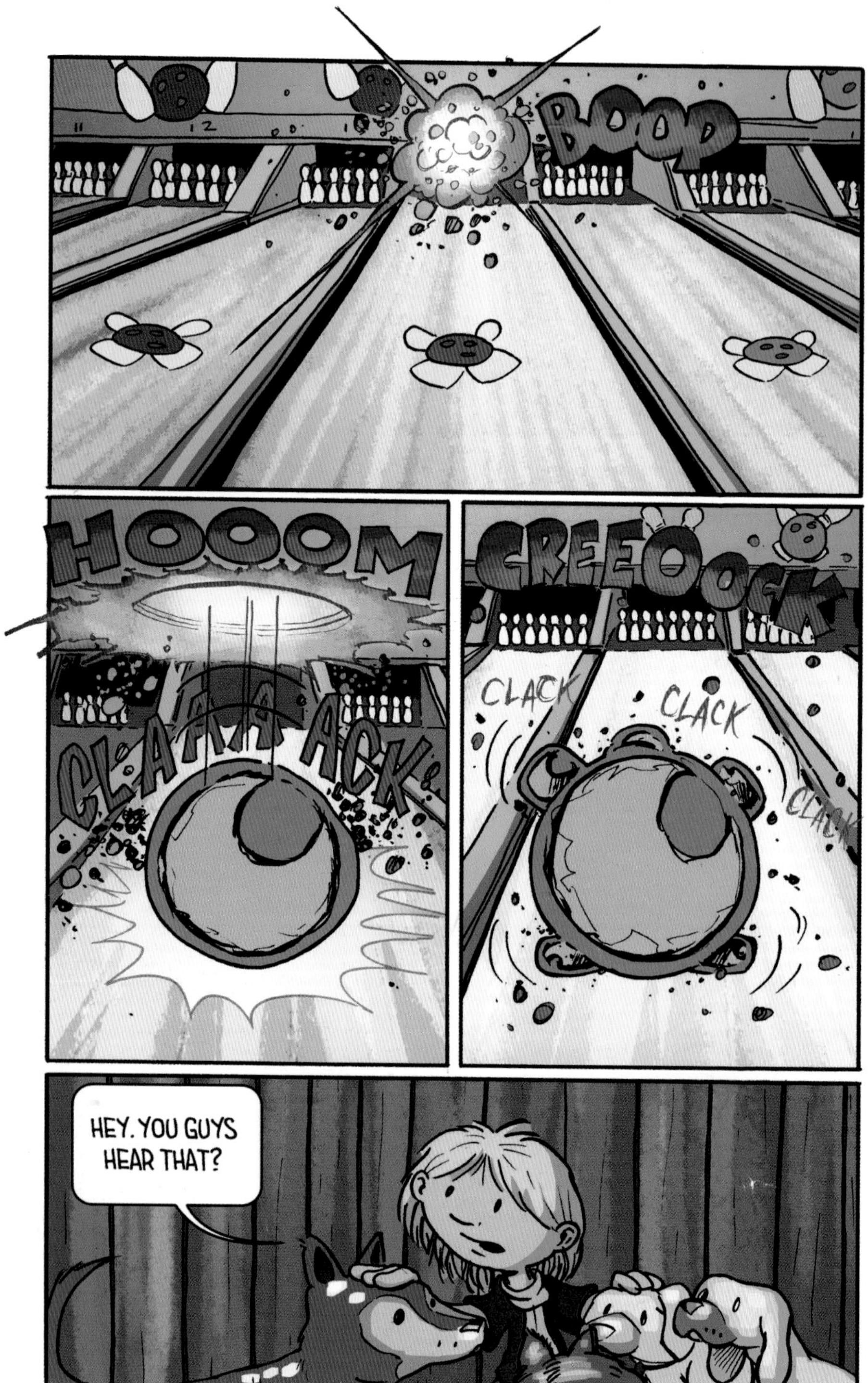
BOOP
HOOOM
CLAAAACK
GREEOOCK
CLACK
CLACK
CLACK
HEY. YOU GUYS HEAR THAT?

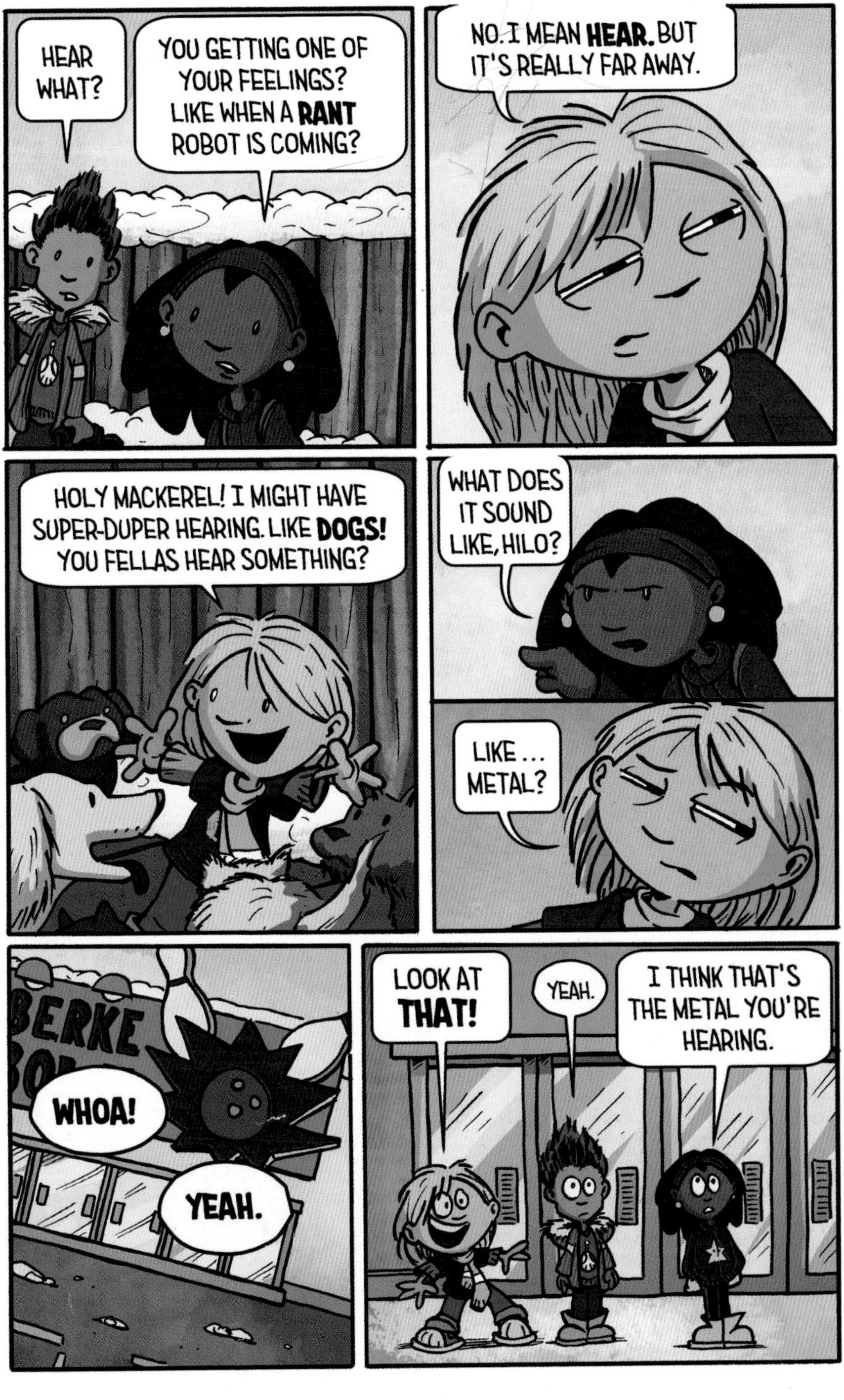
HEAR WHAT?
YOU GETTING ONE OF YOUR FEELINGS? LIKE WHEN A **RANT** ROBOT IS COMING?
NO. I MEAN **HEAR.** BUT IT'S REALLY FAR AWAY.
HOLY MACKEREL! I MIGHT HAVE SUPER-DUPER HEARING. LIKE **DOGS!** YOU FELLAS HEAR SOMETHING?
WHAT DOES IT SOUND LIKE, HILO?
LIKE . . . METAL?
BERKE
WHOA!
YEAH.
LOOK AT **THAT!**
YEAH.
I THINK THAT'S THE METAL YOU'RE HEARING.

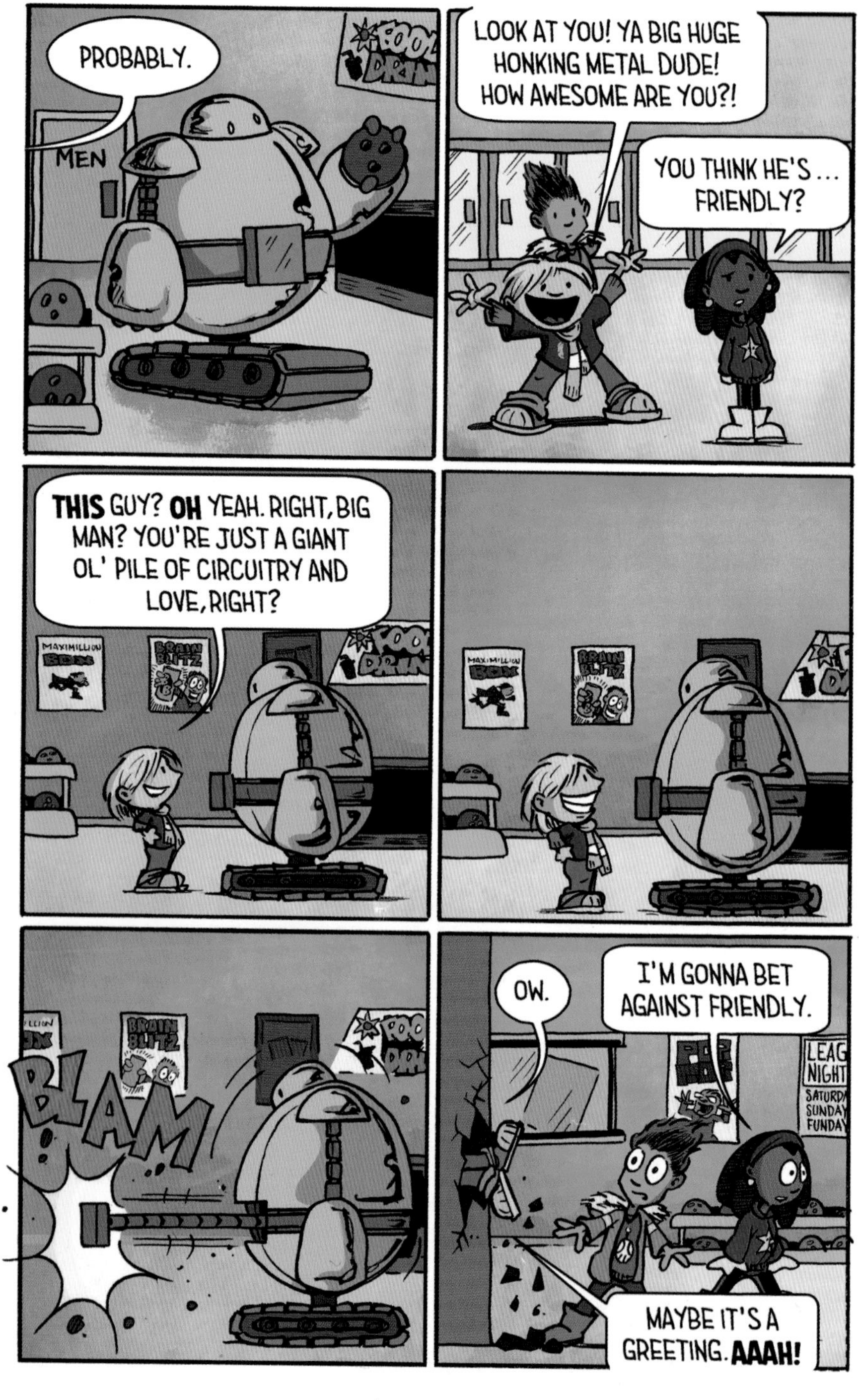

PROBABLY.
MEN
LOOK AT YOU! YA BIG HUGE HONKING METAL DUDE! HOW AWESOME ARE YOU?!
YOU THINK HE'S ... FRIENDLY?
THIS GUY? **OH** YEAH. RIGHT, BIG MAN? YOU'RE JUST A GIANT OL' PILE OF CIRCUITRY AND LOVE, RIGHT?
BRAIN BLITZ
BLAM
OW.
I'M GONNA BET AGAINST FRIENDLY.
MAYBE IT'S A GREETING. **AAAH!**

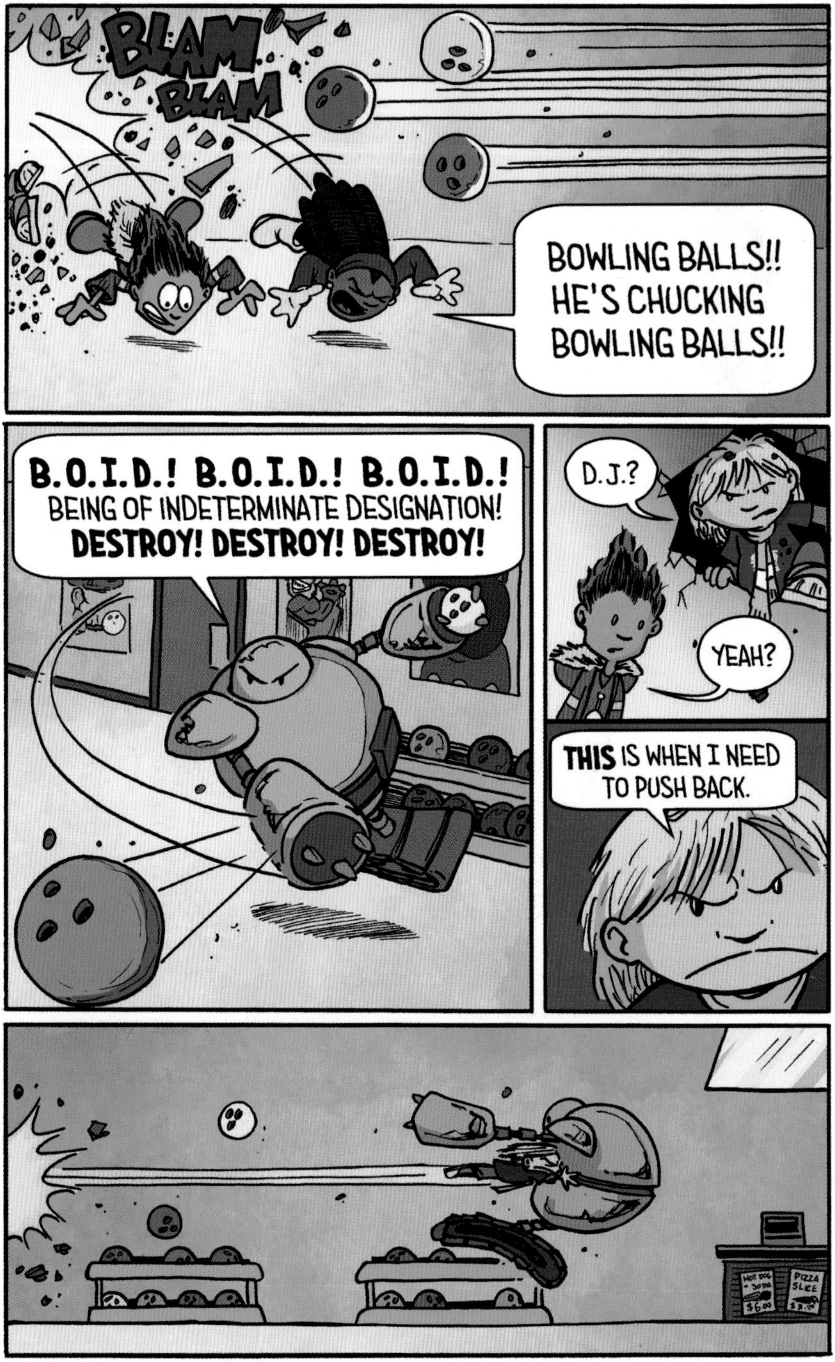
BLAM
BLAM
BOWLING BALLS!! HE'S CHUCKING BOWLING BALLS!!
B.O.I.D.! B.O.I.D.! B.O.I.D.! BEING OF INDETERMINATE DESIGNATION! DESTROY! DESTROY! DESTROY!
D.J.?
YEAH?
THIS IS WHEN I NEED TO PUSH BACK.

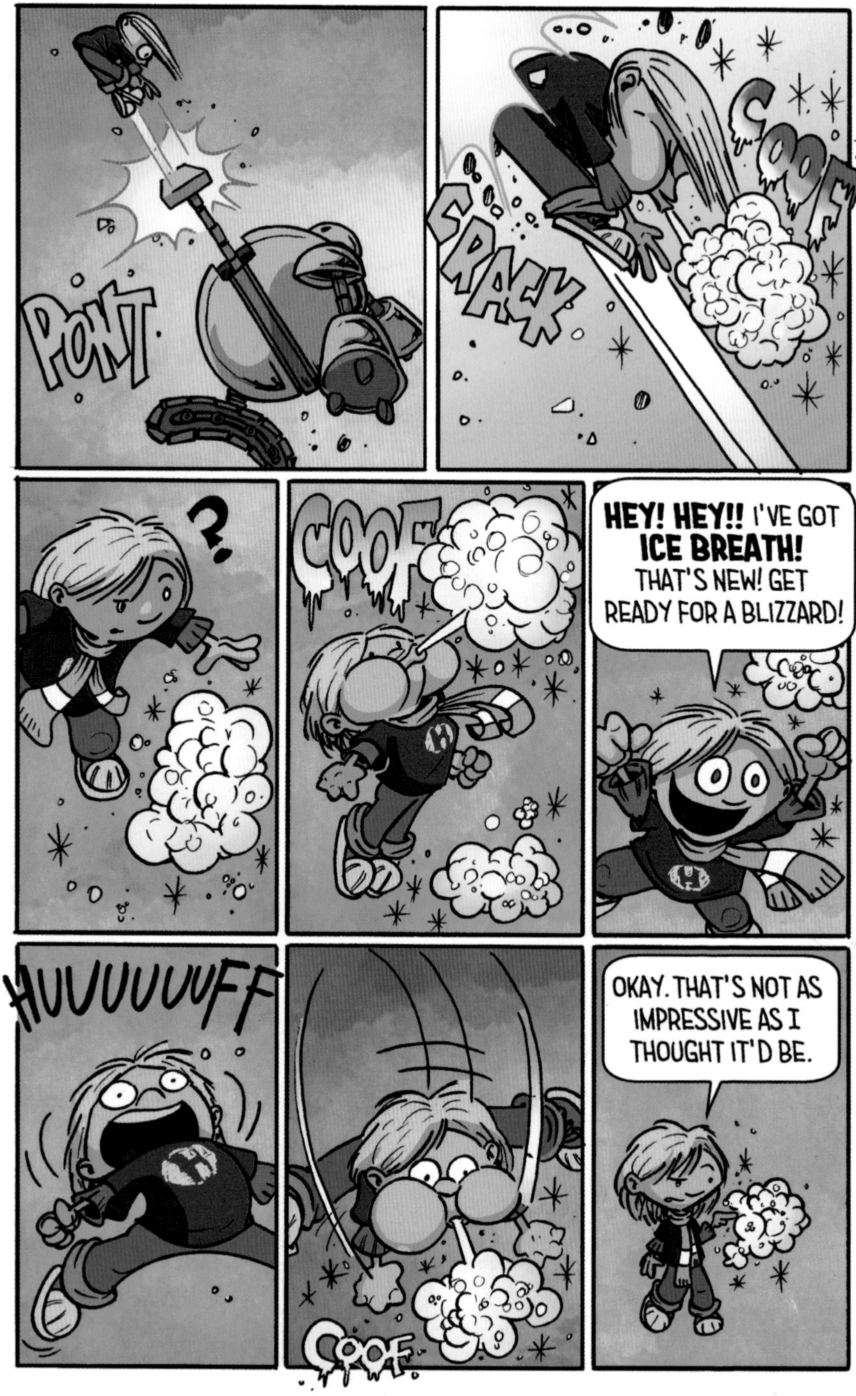
PONT
CRACK
COOF
COOF
HEY! HEY!! I'VE GOT ICE BREATH! THAT'S NEW! GET READY FOR A BLIZZARD!
HUUUUUUFF
COOF
OKAY. THAT'S NOT AS IMPRESSIVE AS I THOUGHT IT'D BE.

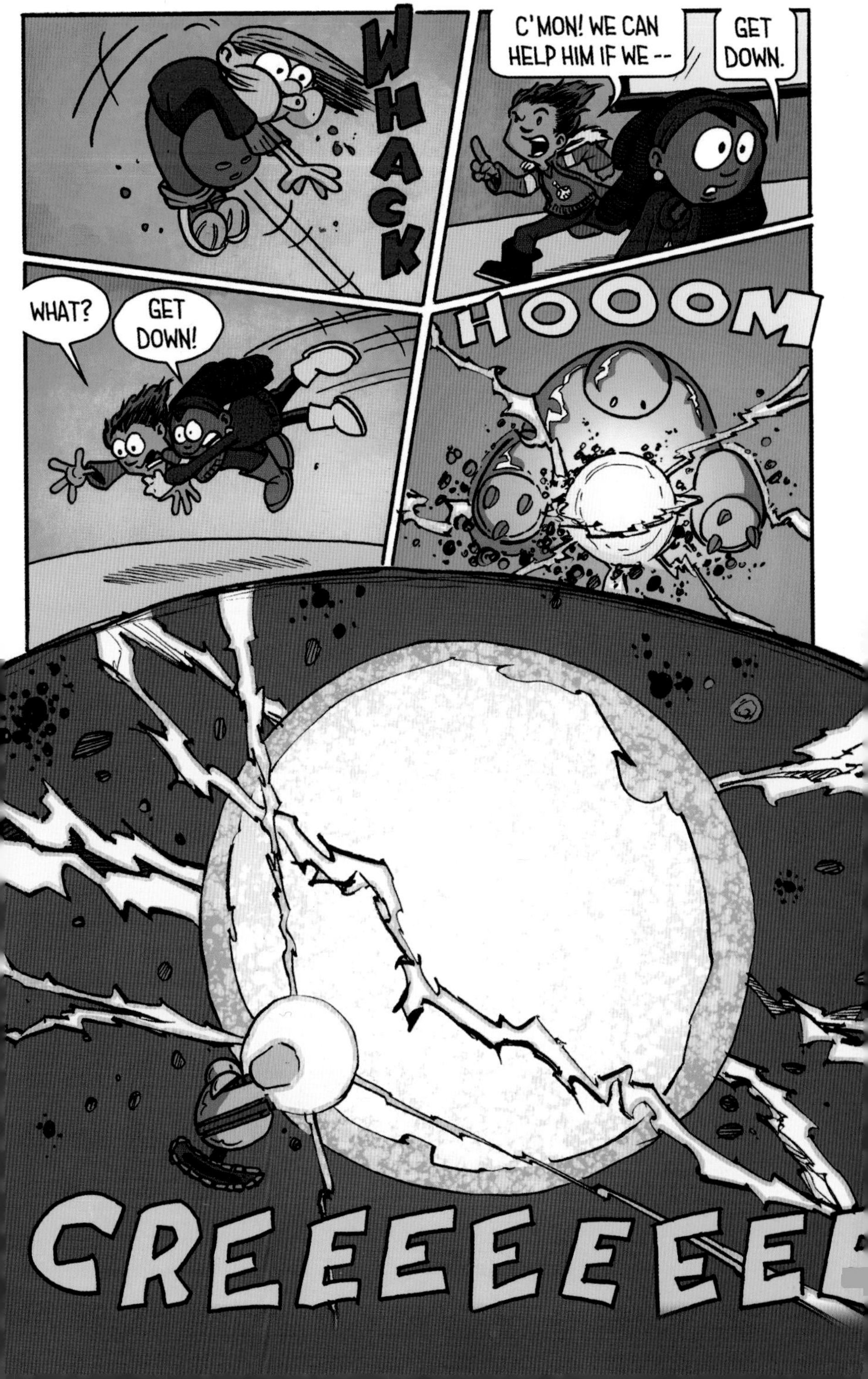
WHACK
C'MON! WE CAN HELP HIM IF WE --
GET DOWN.
WHAT?
GET DOWN!
HOOOM
CREEEEEEE

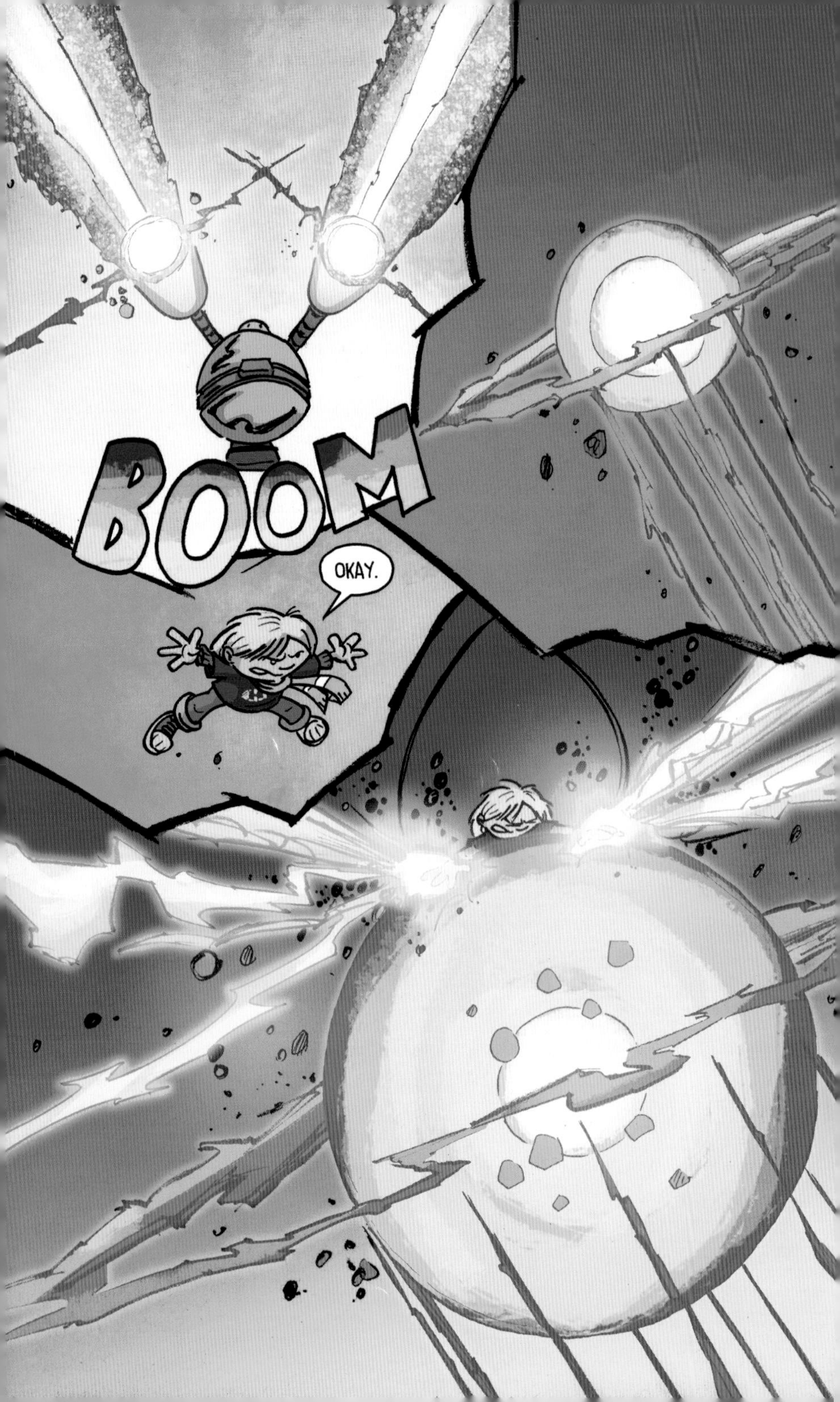
BOOM
OKAY.

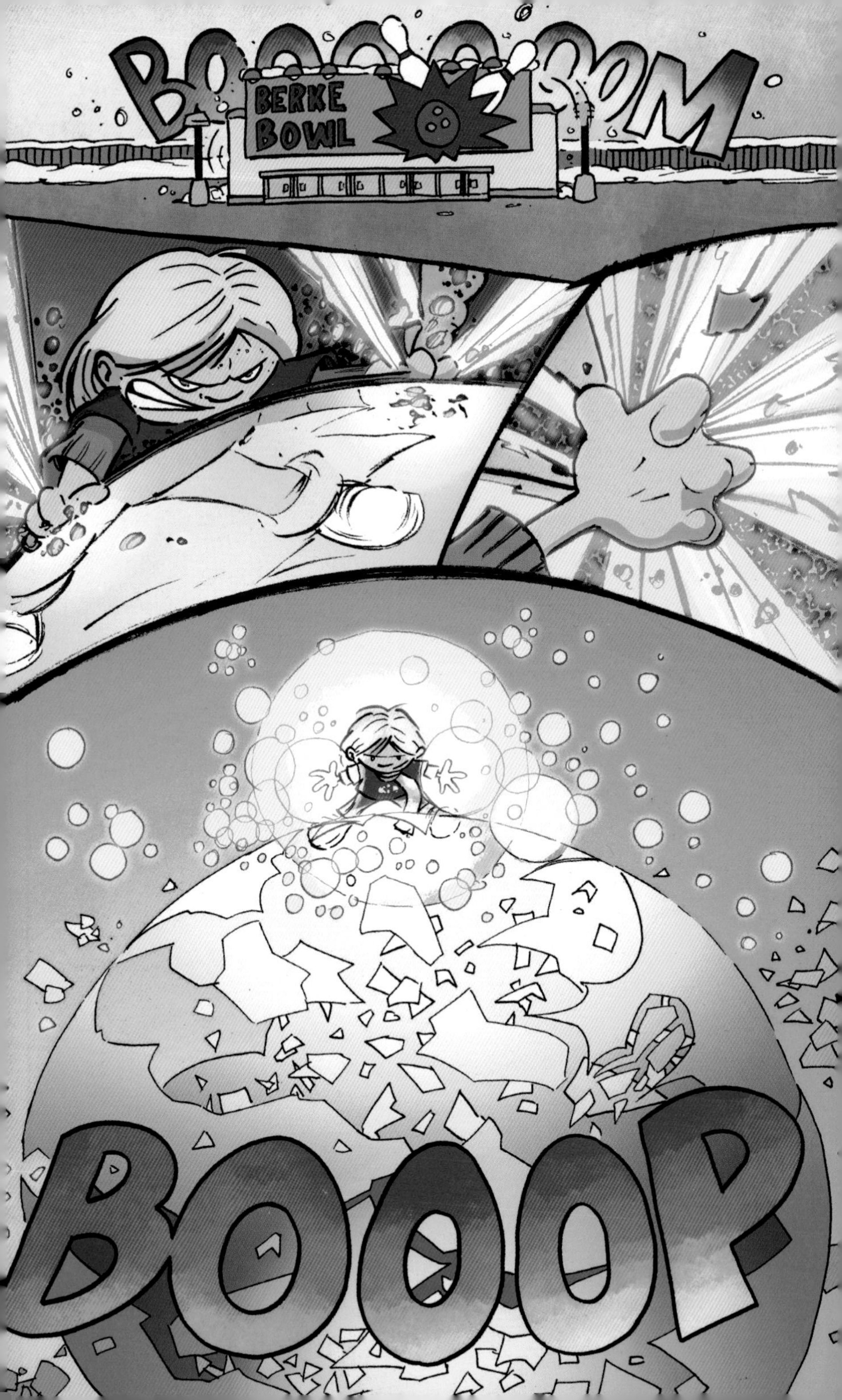
BOOOOOOOM
BERKE BOWL
BOOOP

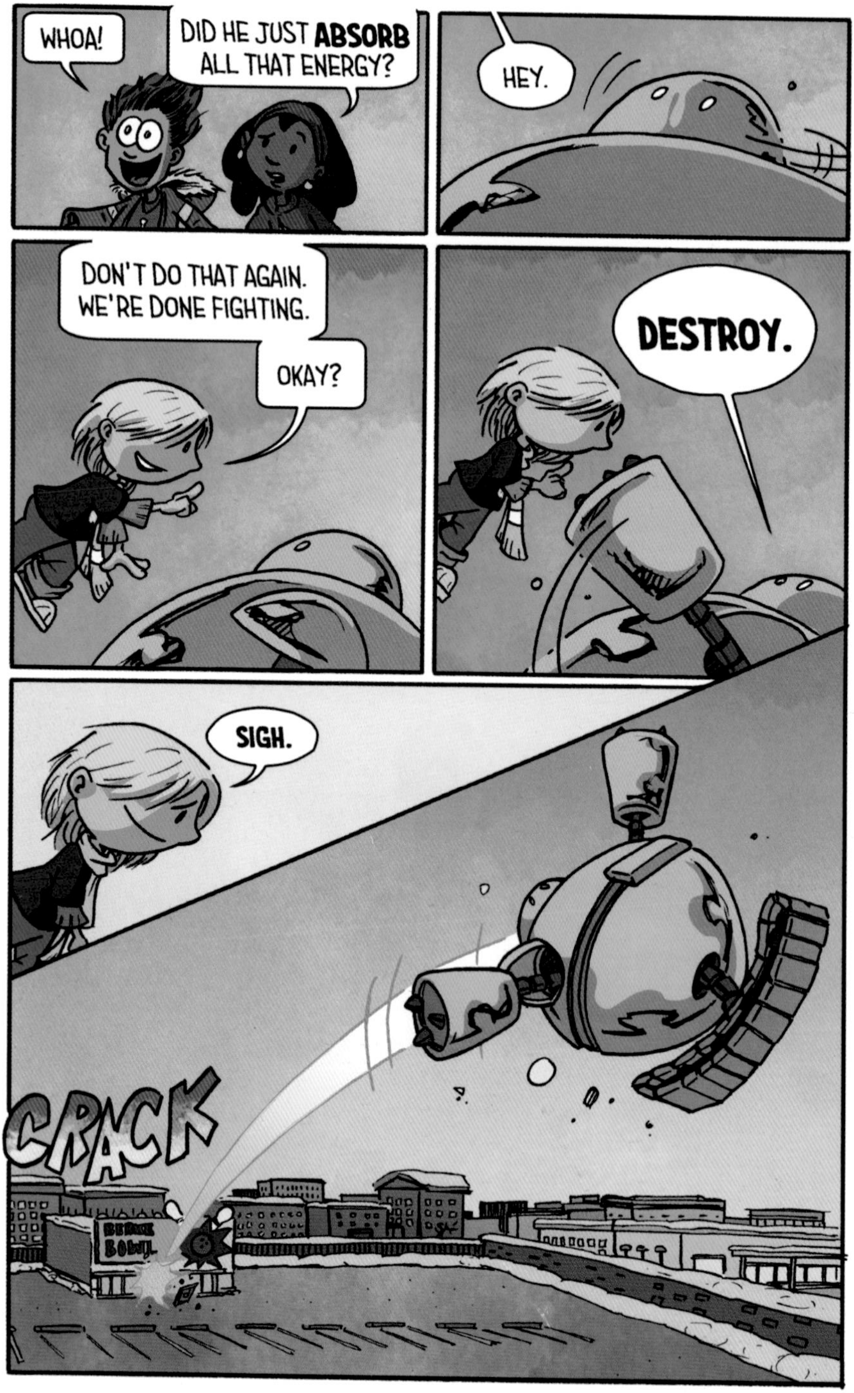
WHOA!
DID HE JUST ABSORB ALL THAT ENERGY?
HEY.
DON'T DO THAT AGAIN. WE'RE DONE FIGHTING.
OKAY?
DESTROY.
SIGH.
CRACK

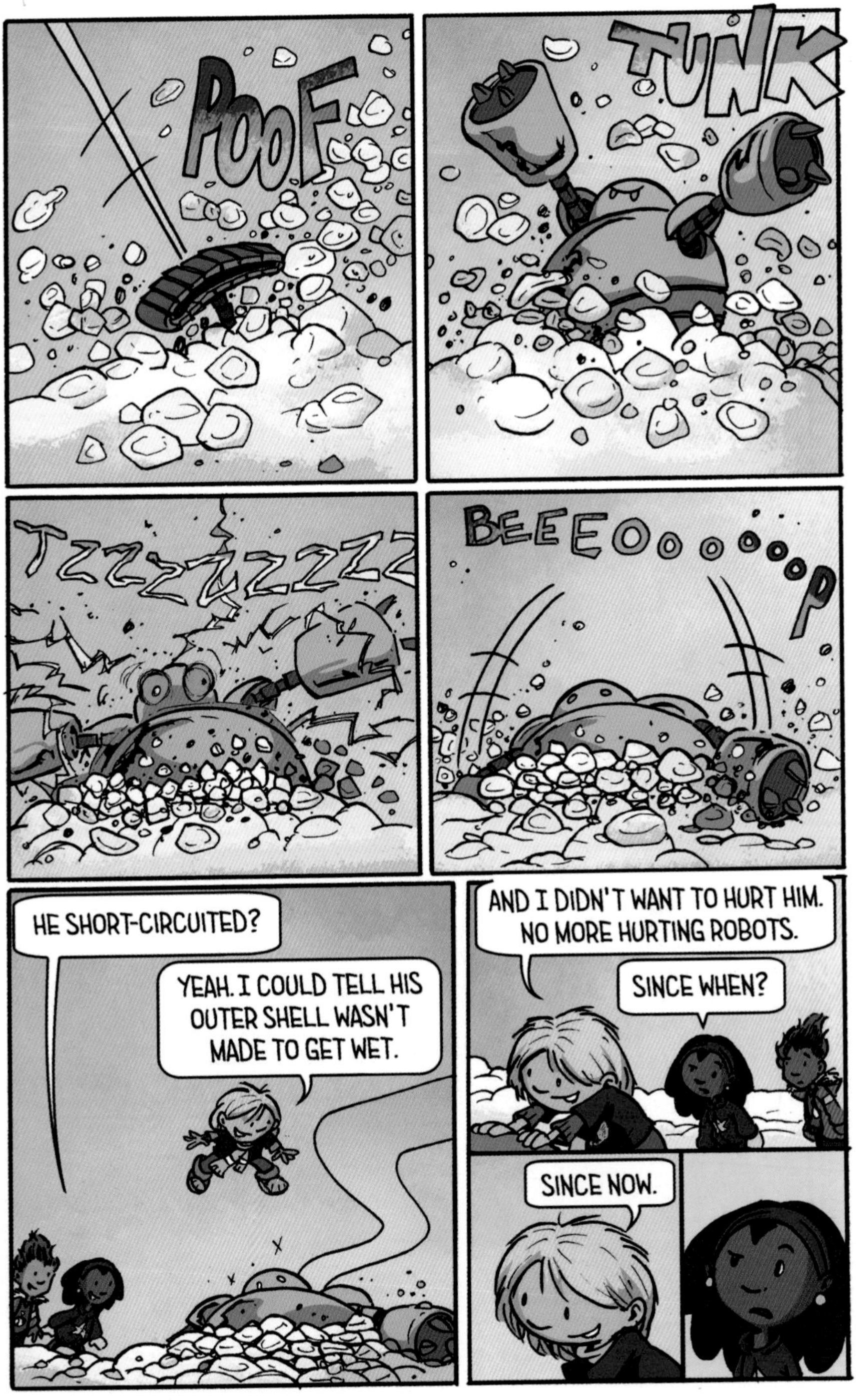
POOF
TUNK
TZZZZZZZZZZ
BEEEOooooooP
HE SHORT-CIRCUITED?
YEAH. I COULD TELL HIS OUTER SHELL WASN'T MADE TO GET WET.
AND I DIDN'T WANT TO HURT HIM. NO MORE HURTING ROBOTS.
SINCE WHEN?
SINCE NOW.

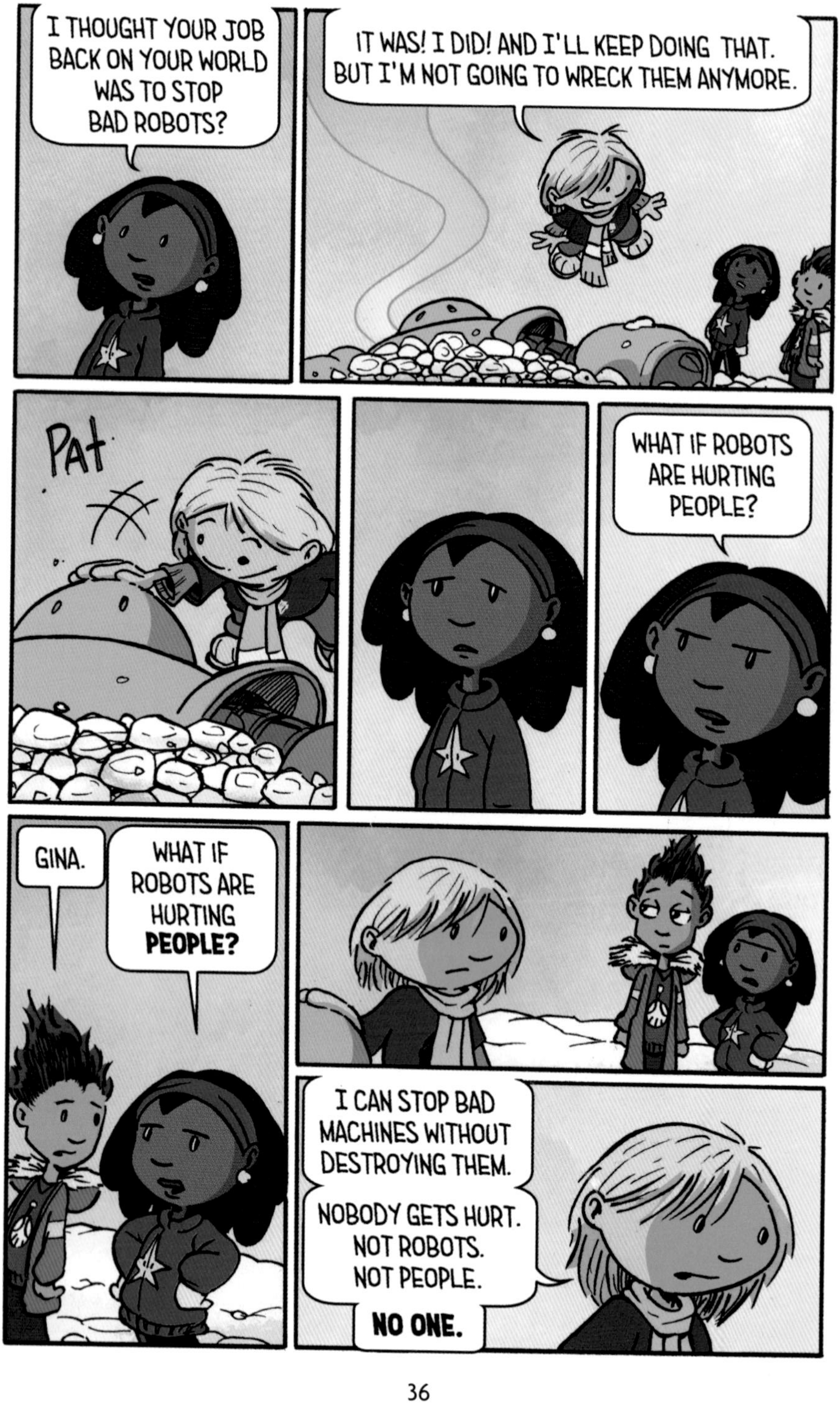

I THOUGHT YOUR JOB BACK ON YOUR WORLD WAS TO STOP BAD ROBOTS?
IT WAS! I DID! AND I'LL KEEP DOING THAT. BUT I'M NOT GOING TO WRECK THEM ANYMORE.
PAT
WHAT IF ROBOTS ARE HURTING PEOPLE?
GINA.
WHAT IF ROBOTS ARE HURTING **PEOPLE?**
I CAN STOP BAD MACHINES WITHOUT DESTROYING THEM.
NOBODY GETS HURT. NOT ROBOTS. NOT PEOPLE.
NO ONE.

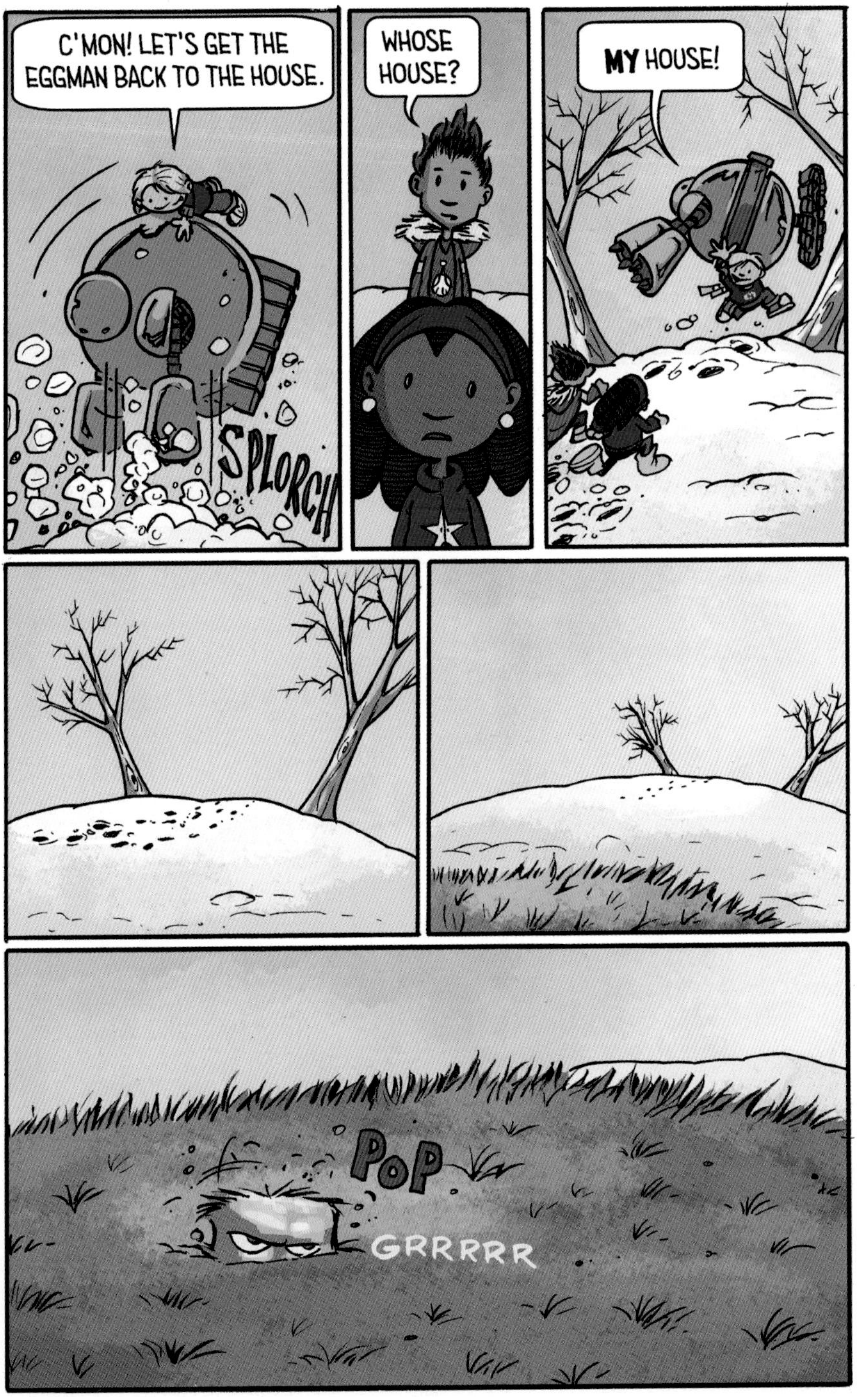
C'MON! LET'S GET THE EGGMAN BACK TO THE HOUSE.
SPLORCH
WHOSE HOUSE?
MY HOUSE!
POP
GRRRRR

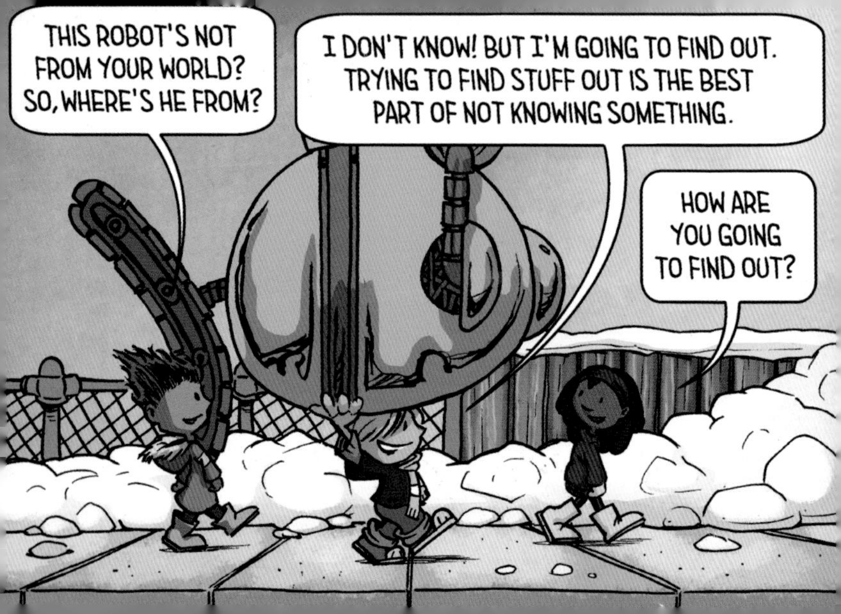
THIS ROBOT'S NOT FROM YOUR WORLD? SO, WHERE'S HE FROM?
I DON'T KNOW! BUT I'M GOING TO FIND OUT. TRYING TO FIND STUFF OUT IS THE BEST PART OF NOT KNOWING SOMETHING.
HOW ARE YOU GOING TO FIND OUT?

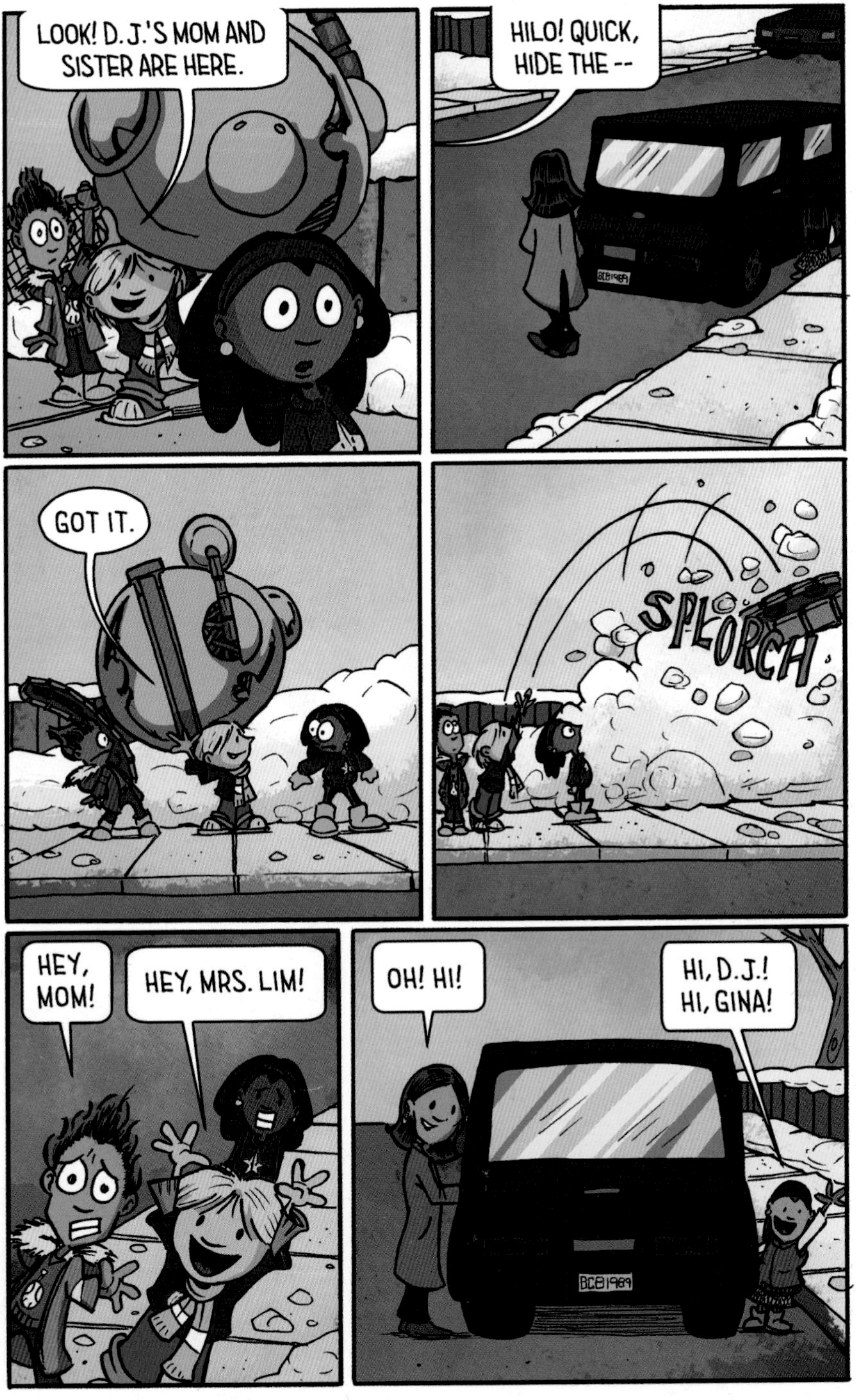

LOOK! D.J.'S MOM AND SISTER ARE HERE.
HILO! QUICK, HIDE THE --
GOT IT.
SPLORCH
HEY, MOM!
HEY, MRS. LIM!
OH! HI!
HI, D.J.! HI, GINA!

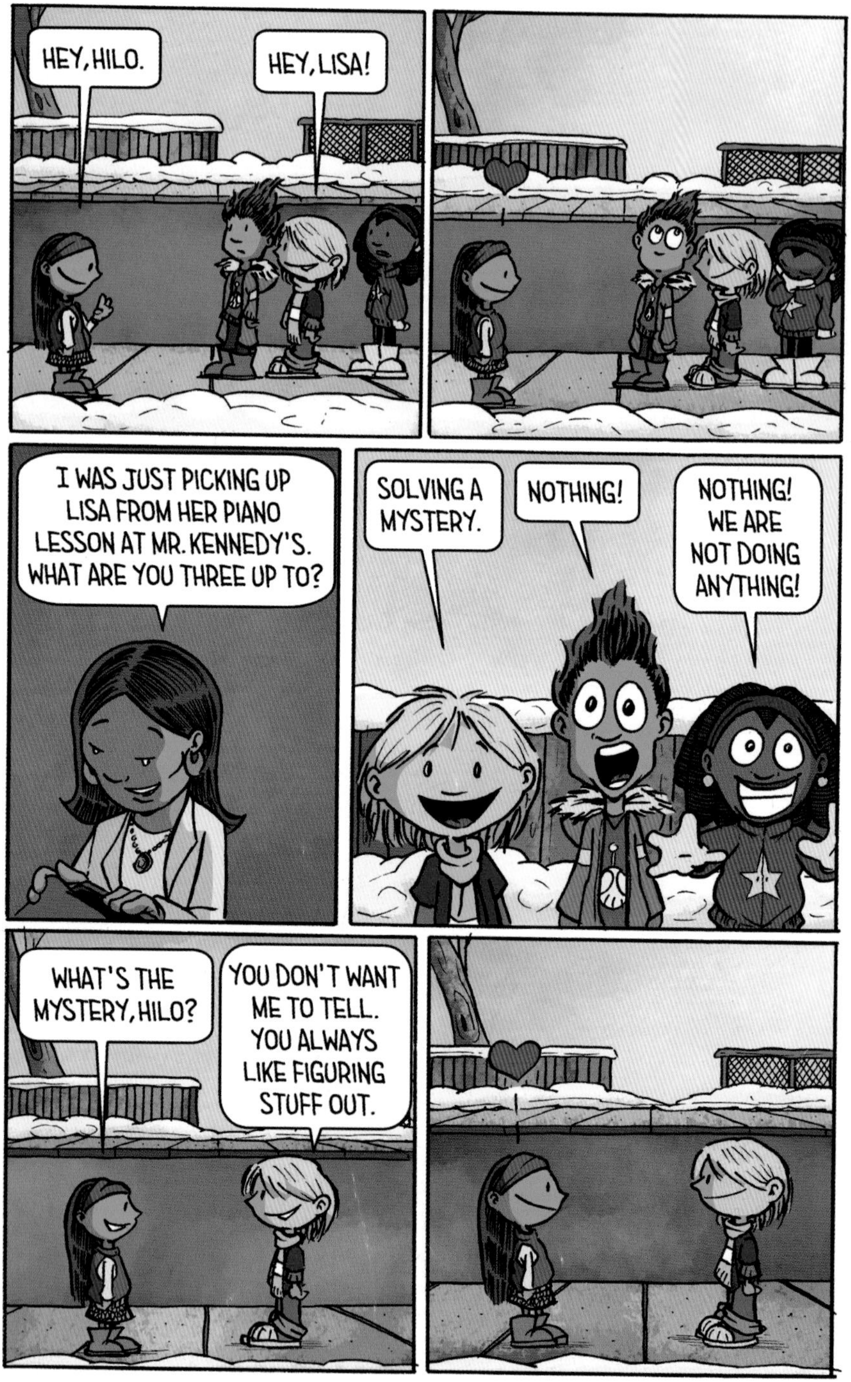
HEY, HILO.
HEY, LISA!
I WAS JUST PICKING UP LISA FROM HER PIANO LESSON AT MR. KENNEDY'S. WHAT ARE YOU THREE UP TO?
SOLVING A MYSTERY.
NOTHING!
NOTHING! WE ARE NOT DOING ANYTHING!
WHAT'S THE MYSTERY, HILO?
YOU DON'T WANT ME TO TELL. YOU ALWAYS LIKE FIGURING STUFF OUT.

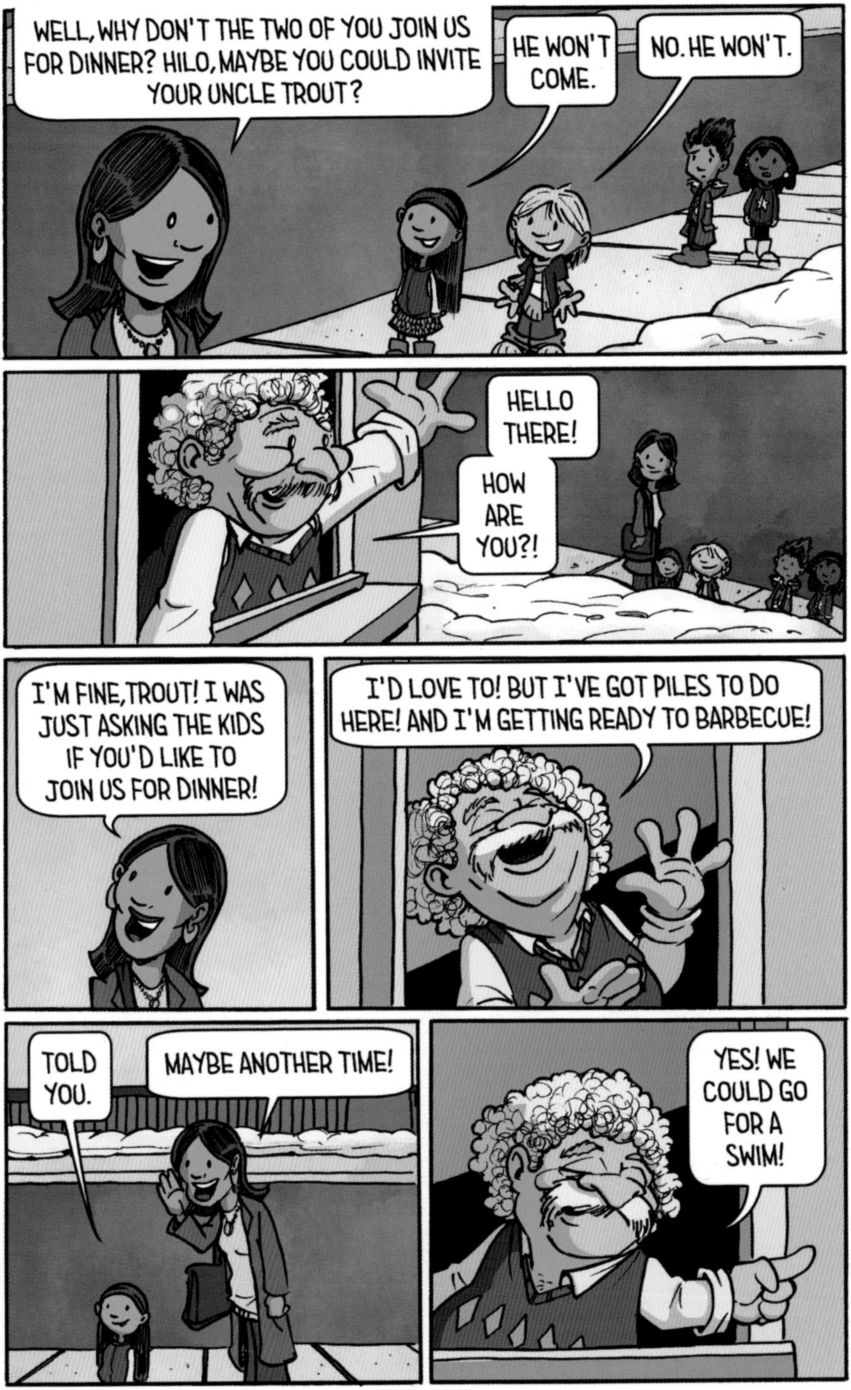
WELL, WHY DON'T THE TWO OF YOU JOIN US FOR DINNER? HILO, MAYBE YOU COULD INVITE YOUR UNCLE TROUT?
HE WON'T COME.
NO. HE WON'T.
HELLO THERE!
HOW ARE YOU?!
I'M FINE, TROUT! I WAS JUST ASKING THE KIDS IF YOU'D LIKE TO JOIN US FOR DINNER!
I'D LOVE TO! BUT I'VE GOT PILES TO DO HERE! AND I'M GETTING READY TO BARBECUE!
TOLD YOU.
MAYBE ANOTHER TIME!
YES! WE COULD GO FOR A SWIM!

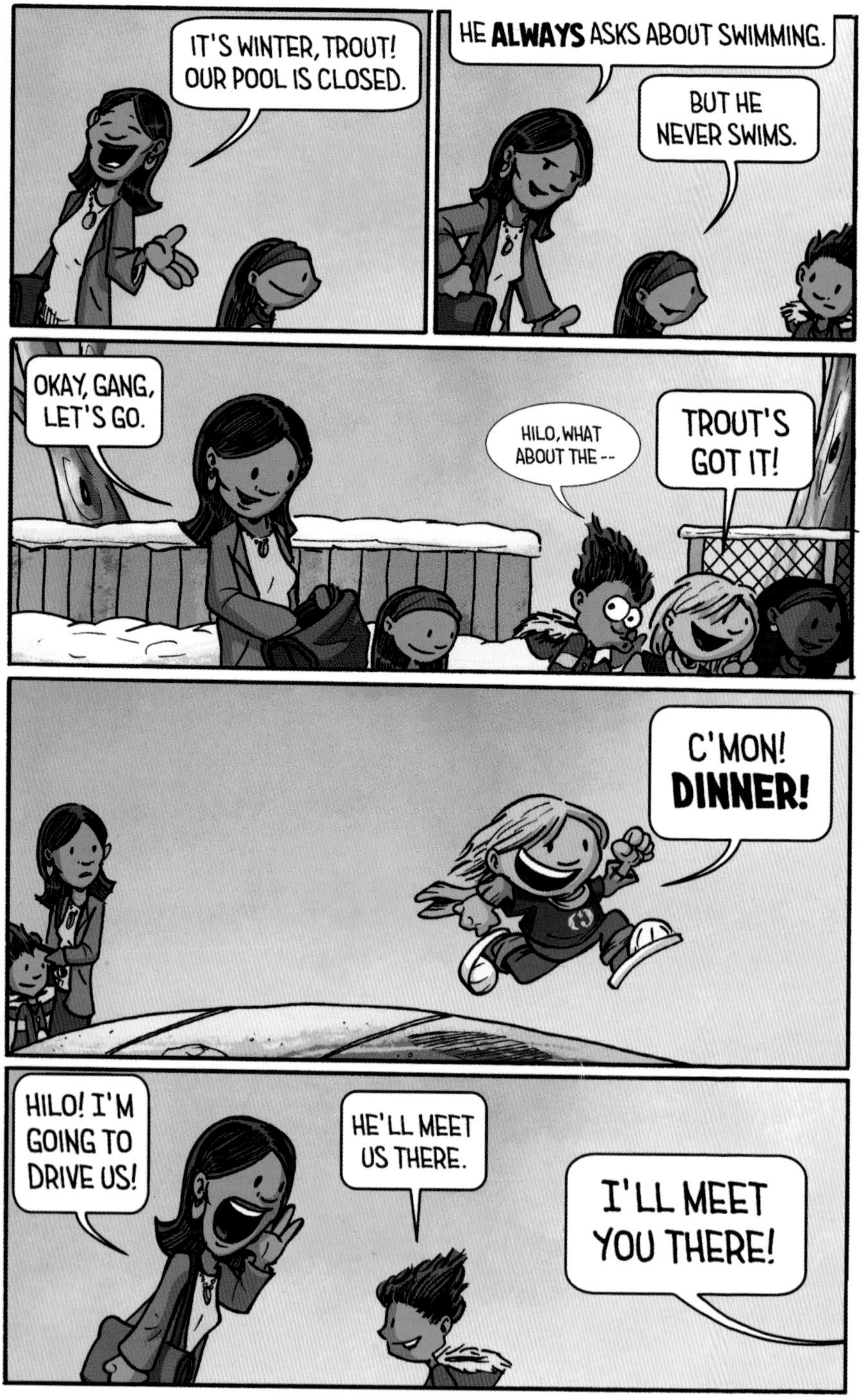
IT'S WINTER, TROUT! OUR POOL IS CLOSED.
HE **ALWAYS** ASKS ABOUT SWIMMING.
BUT HE NEVER SWIMS.
OKAY, GANG, LET'S GO.
HILO, WHAT ABOUT THE --
TROUT'S GOT IT!
C'MON! **DINNER!**
HILO! I'M GOING TO DRIVE US!
HE'LL MEET US THERE.
I'LL MEET YOU THERE!

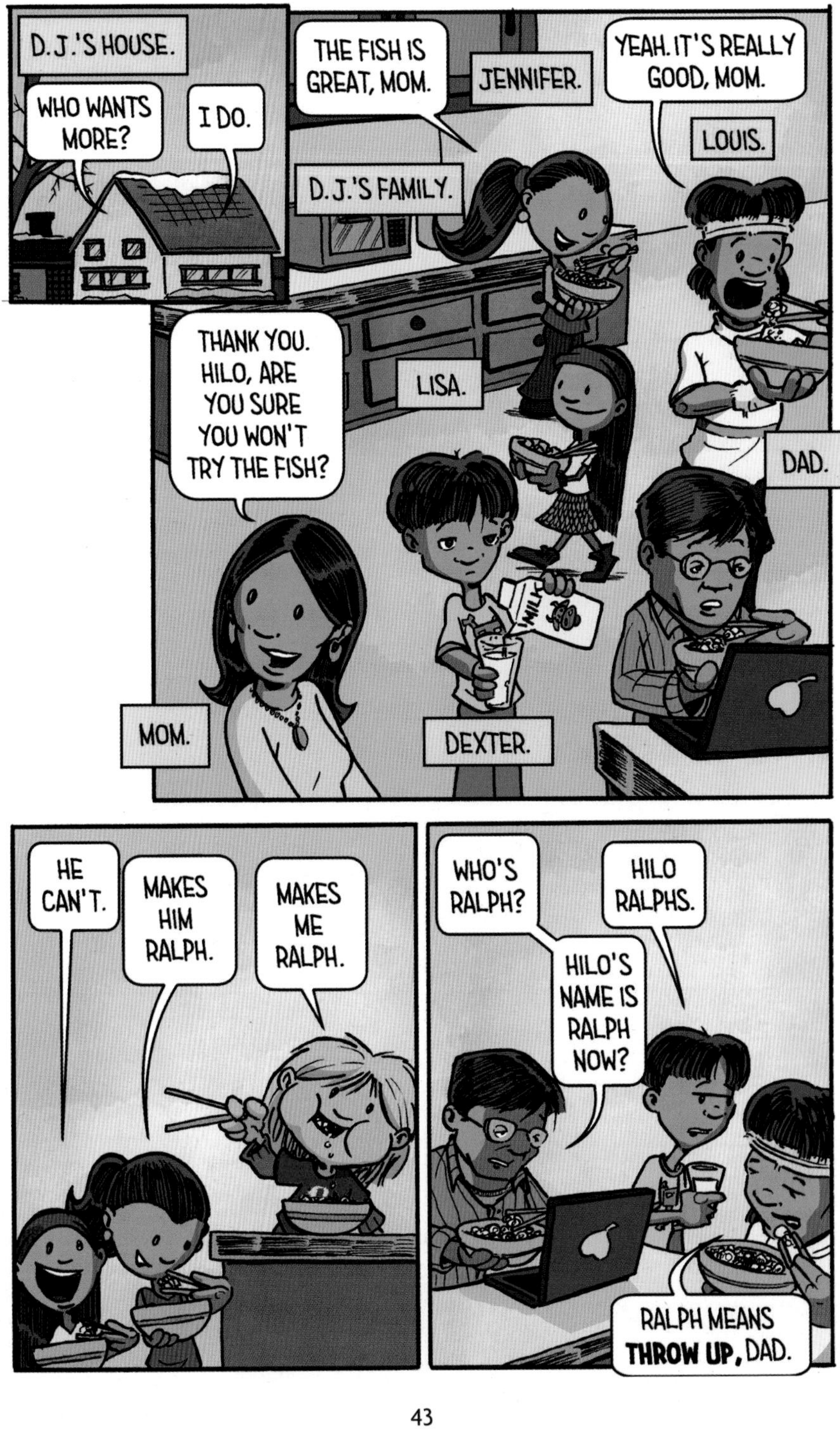

D.J.'S HOUSE.
WHO WANTS MORE?
I DO.
THE FISH IS GREAT, MOM.
JENNIFER.
YEAH. IT'S REALLY GOOD, MOM.
LOUIS.
D.J.'S FAMILY.
THANK YOU. HILO, ARE YOU SURE YOU WON'T TRY THE FISH?
LISA.
DAD.
MILK
MOM.
DEXTER.
HE CAN'T.
MAKES HIM RALPH.
MAKES ME RALPH.
WHO'S RALPH?
HILO RALPHS.
HILO'S NAME IS RALPH NOW?
RALPH MEANS **THROW UP,** DAD.

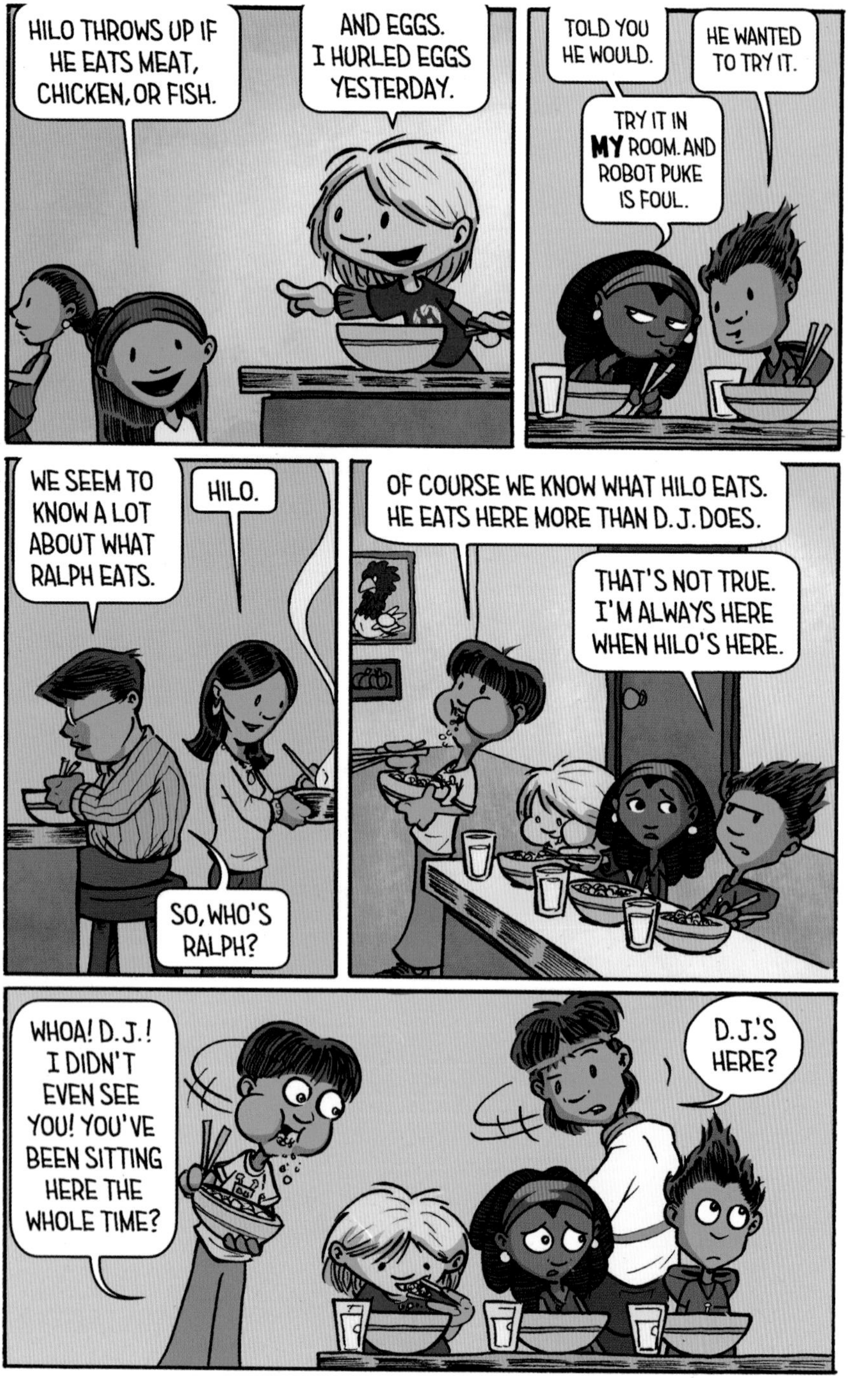
HILO THROWS UP IF HE EATS MEAT, CHICKEN, OR FISH.
AND EGGS. I HURLED EGGS YESTERDAY.
TOLD YOU HE WOULD.
HE WANTED TO TRY IT.
TRY IT IN **MY** ROOM. AND ROBOT PUKE IS FOUL.
WE SEEM TO KNOW A LOT ABOUT WHAT RALPH EATS.
HILO.
SO, WHO'S RALPH?
OF COURSE WE KNOW WHAT HILO EATS. HE EATS HERE MORE THAN D. J. DOES.
THAT'S NOT TRUE. I'M ALWAYS HERE WHEN HILO'S HERE.
WHOA! D. J.! I DIDN'T EVEN SEE YOU! YOU'VE BEEN SITTING HERE THE WHOLE TIME?
D. J.'S HERE?

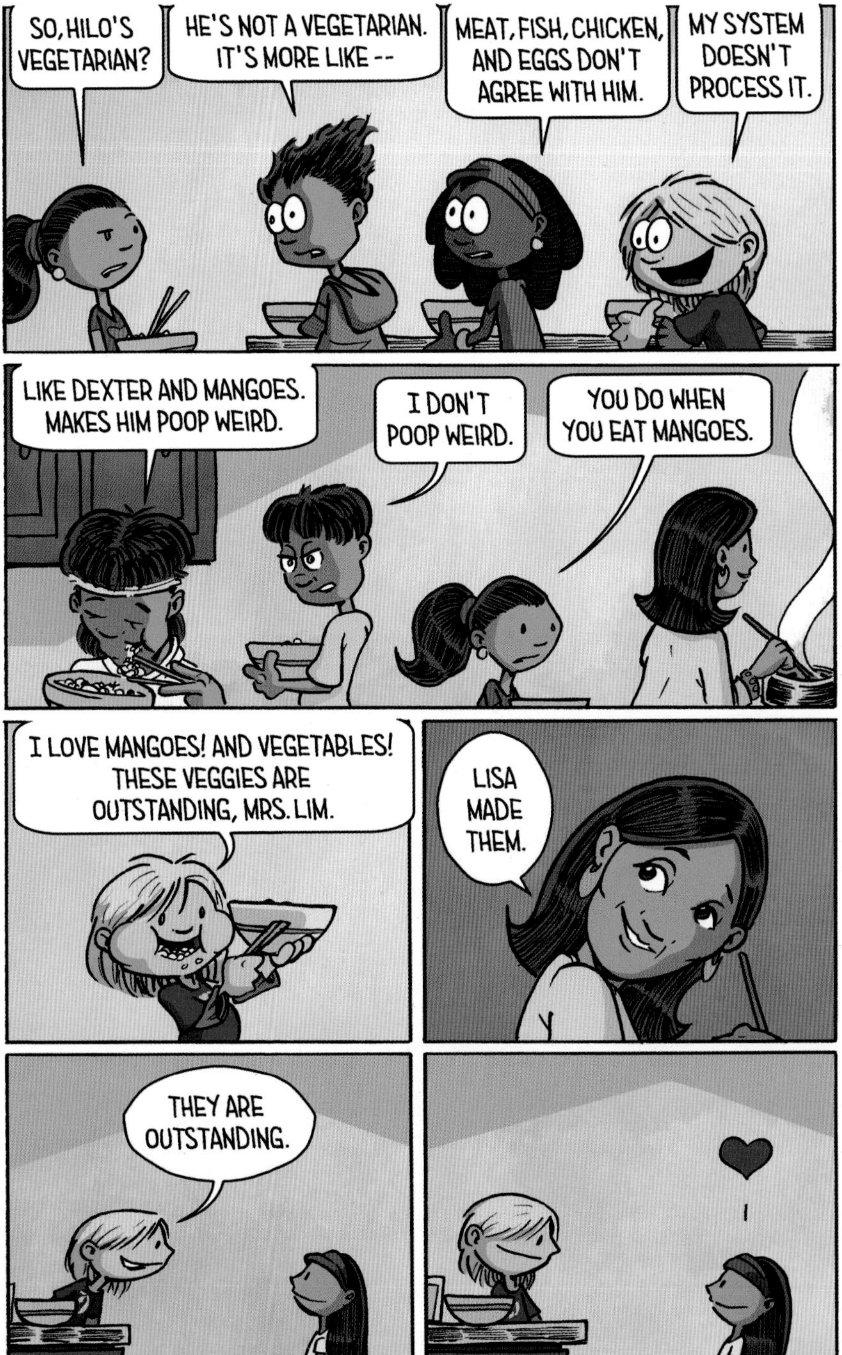

SO, HILO'S VEGETARIAN?
HE'S NOT A VEGETARIAN. IT'S MORE LIKE --
MEAT, FISH, CHICKEN, AND EGGS DON'T AGREE WITH HIM.
MY SYSTEM DOESN'T PROCESS IT.
LIKE DEXTER AND MANGOES. MAKES HIM POOP WEIRD.
I DON'T POOP WEIRD.
YOU DO WHEN YOU EAT MANGOES.
I LOVE MANGOES! AND VEGETABLES! THESE VEGGIES ARE OUTSTANDING, MRS. LIM.
LISA MADE THEM.
THEY ARE OUTSTANDING.

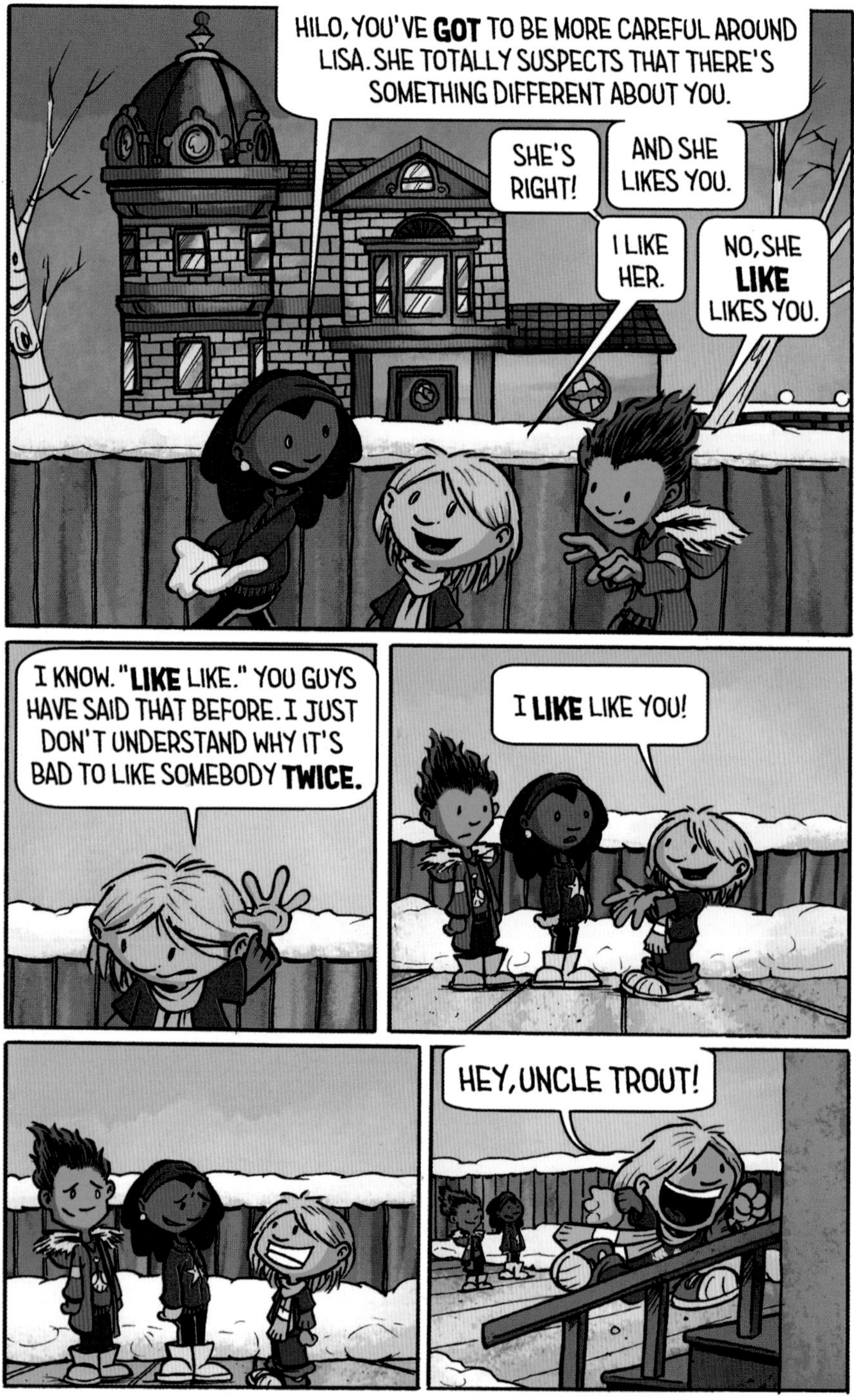
HILO, YOU'VE **GOT** TO BE MORE CAREFUL AROUND LISA. SHE TOTALLY SUSPECTS THAT THERE'S SOMETHING DIFFERENT ABOUT YOU.
SHE'S RIGHT!
AND SHE LIKES YOU.
I LIKE HER.
NO, SHE **LIKE** LIKES YOU.
I KNOW. "**LIKE** LIKE." YOU GUYS HAVE SAID THAT BEFORE. I JUST DON'T UNDERSTAND WHY IT'S BAD TO LIKE SOMEBODY **TWICE.**
I **LIKE** LIKE YOU!
HEY, UNCLE TROUT!

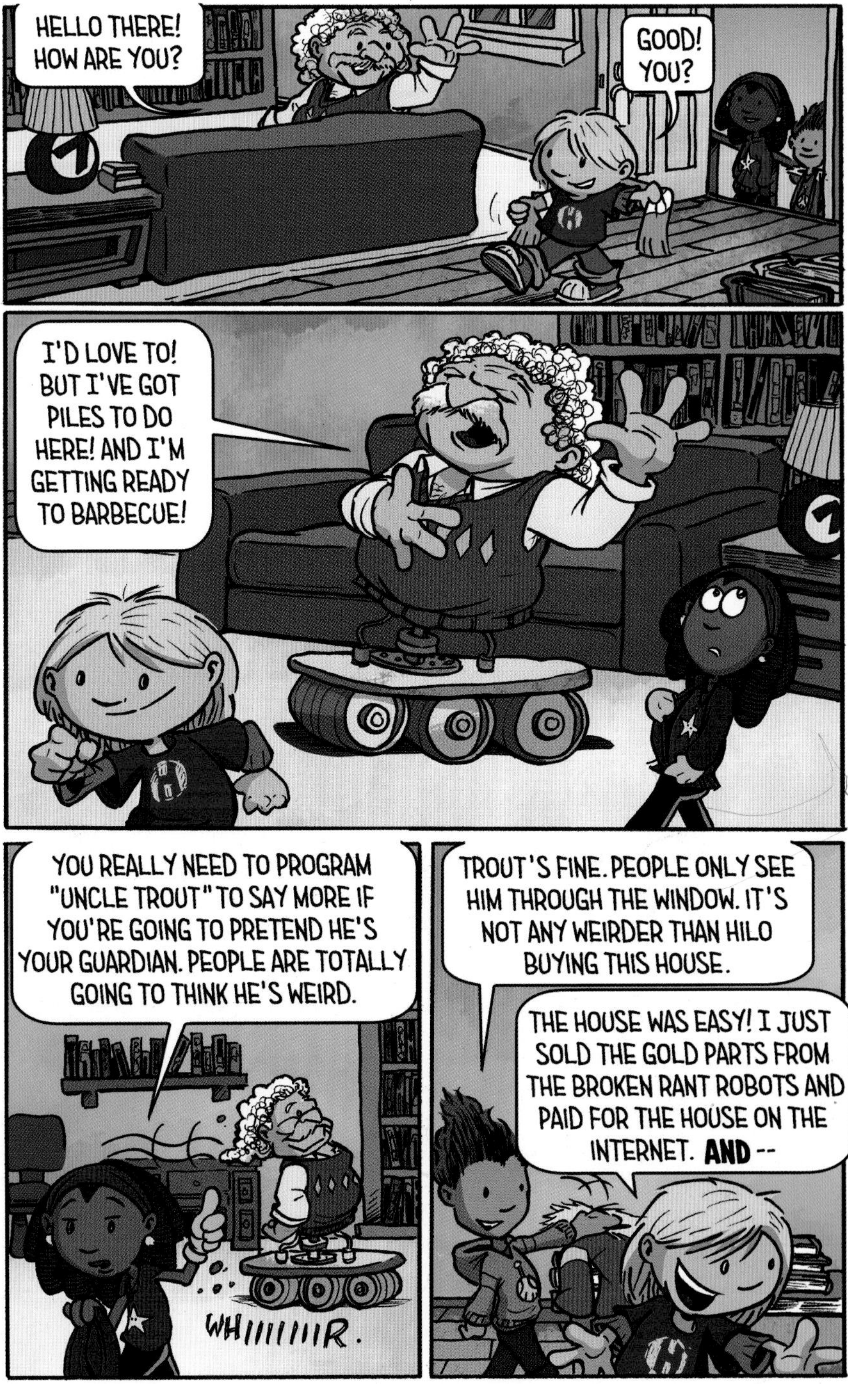
HELLO THERE! HOW ARE YOU?
GOOD! YOU?
I'D LOVE TO! BUT I'VE GOT PILES TO DO HERE! AND I'M GETTING READY TO BARBECUE!
YOU REALLY NEED TO PROGRAM "UNCLE TROUT" TO SAY MORE IF YOU'RE GOING TO PRETEND HE'S YOUR GUARDIAN. PEOPLE ARE TOTALLY GOING TO THINK HE'S WEIRD.
WHIIIIIIR.
TROUT'S FINE. PEOPLE ONLY SEE HIM THROUGH THE WINDOW. IT'S NOT ANY WEIRDER THAN HILO BUYING THIS HOUSE.
THE HOUSE WAS EASY! I JUST SOLD THE GOLD PARTS FROM THE BROKEN RANT ROBOTS AND PAID FOR THE HOUSE ON THE INTERNET. AND --

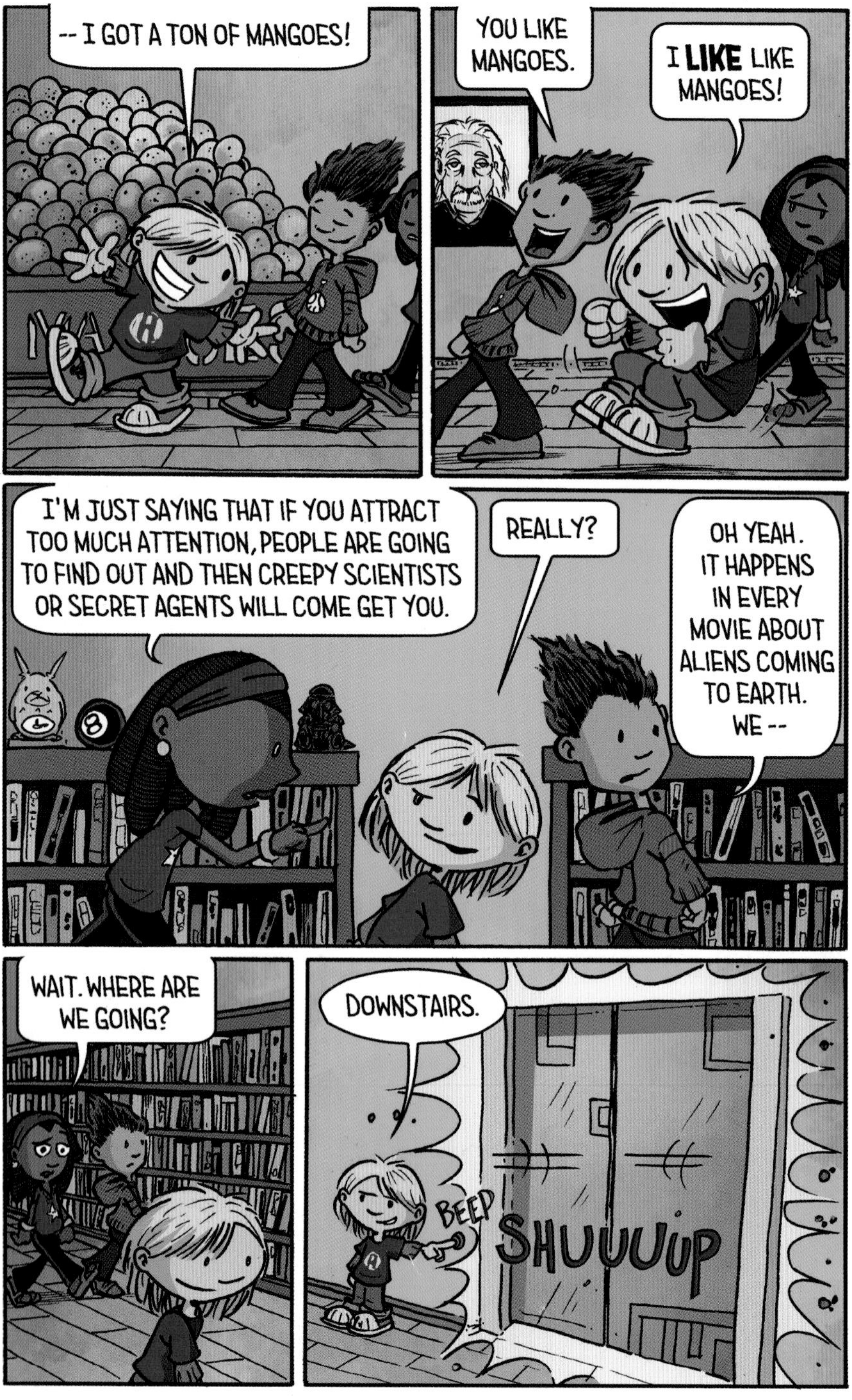

-- I GOT A TON OF MANGOES!
YOU LIKE MANGOES.
I LIKE LIKE MANGOES!
I'M JUST SAYING THAT IF YOU ATTRACT TOO MUCH ATTENTION, PEOPLE ARE GOING TO FIND OUT AND THEN CREEPY SCIENTISTS OR SECRET AGENTS WILL COME GET YOU.
REALLY?
OH YEAH. IT HAPPENS IN EVERY MOVIE ABOUT ALIENS COMING TO EARTH. WE --
WAIT. WHERE ARE WE GOING?
DOWNSTAIRS.
BEEP
SHUUUUP

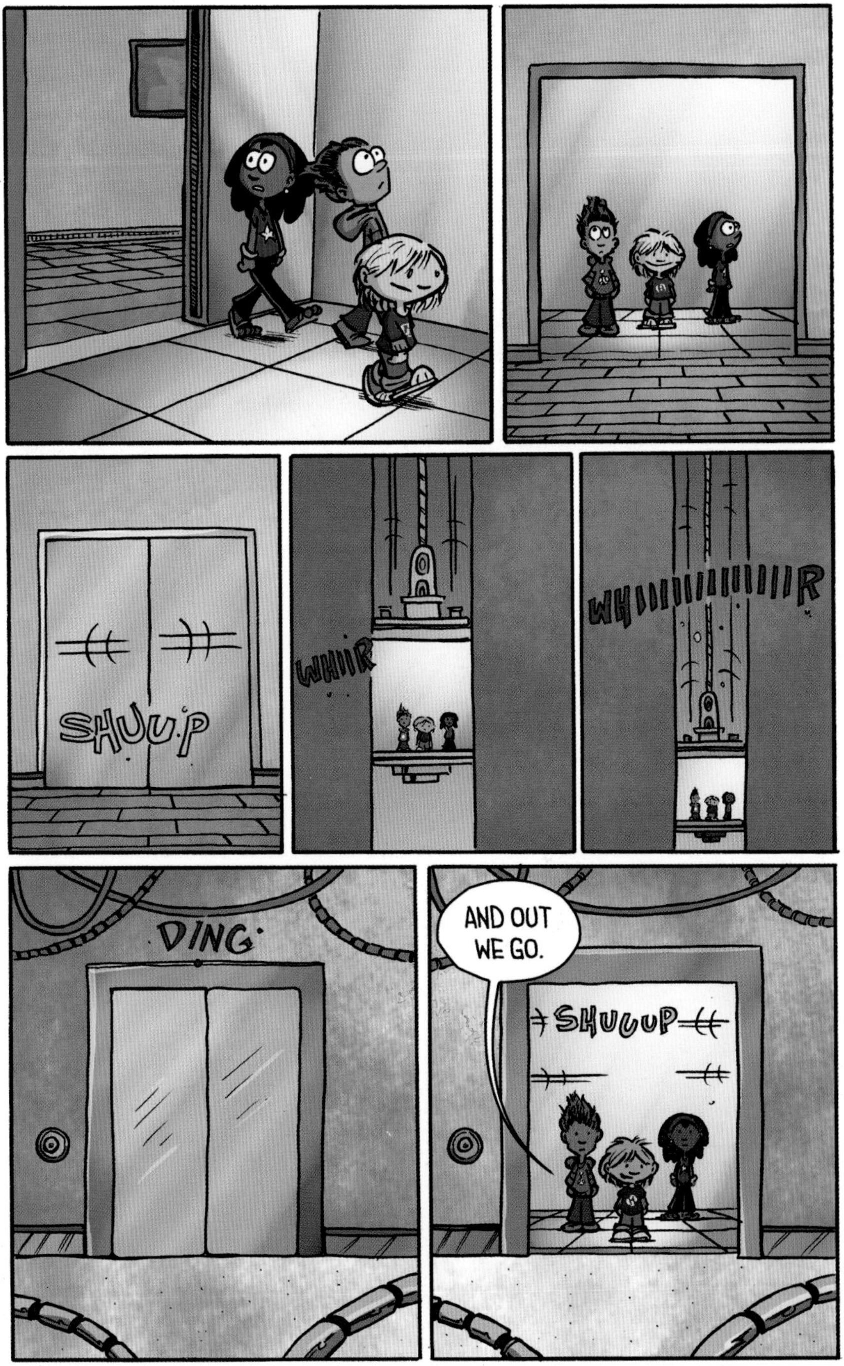
SHUUP
WHIIR
WHIIIIIIIIIIIIIR
DING
AND OUT WE GO.
SHUUUP

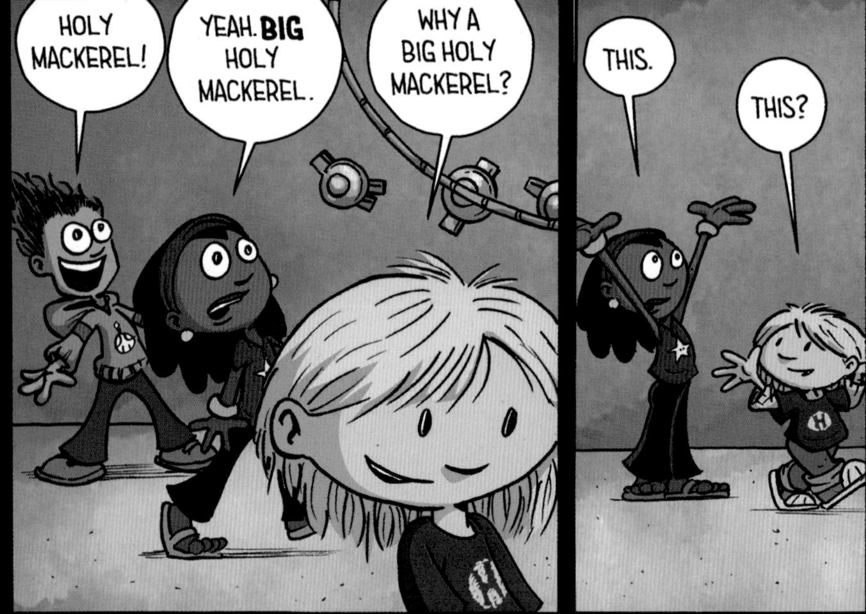
HOLY MACKEREL!
YEAH. BIG HOLY MACKEREL.
WHY A BIG HOLY MACKEREL?
THIS.
THIS?

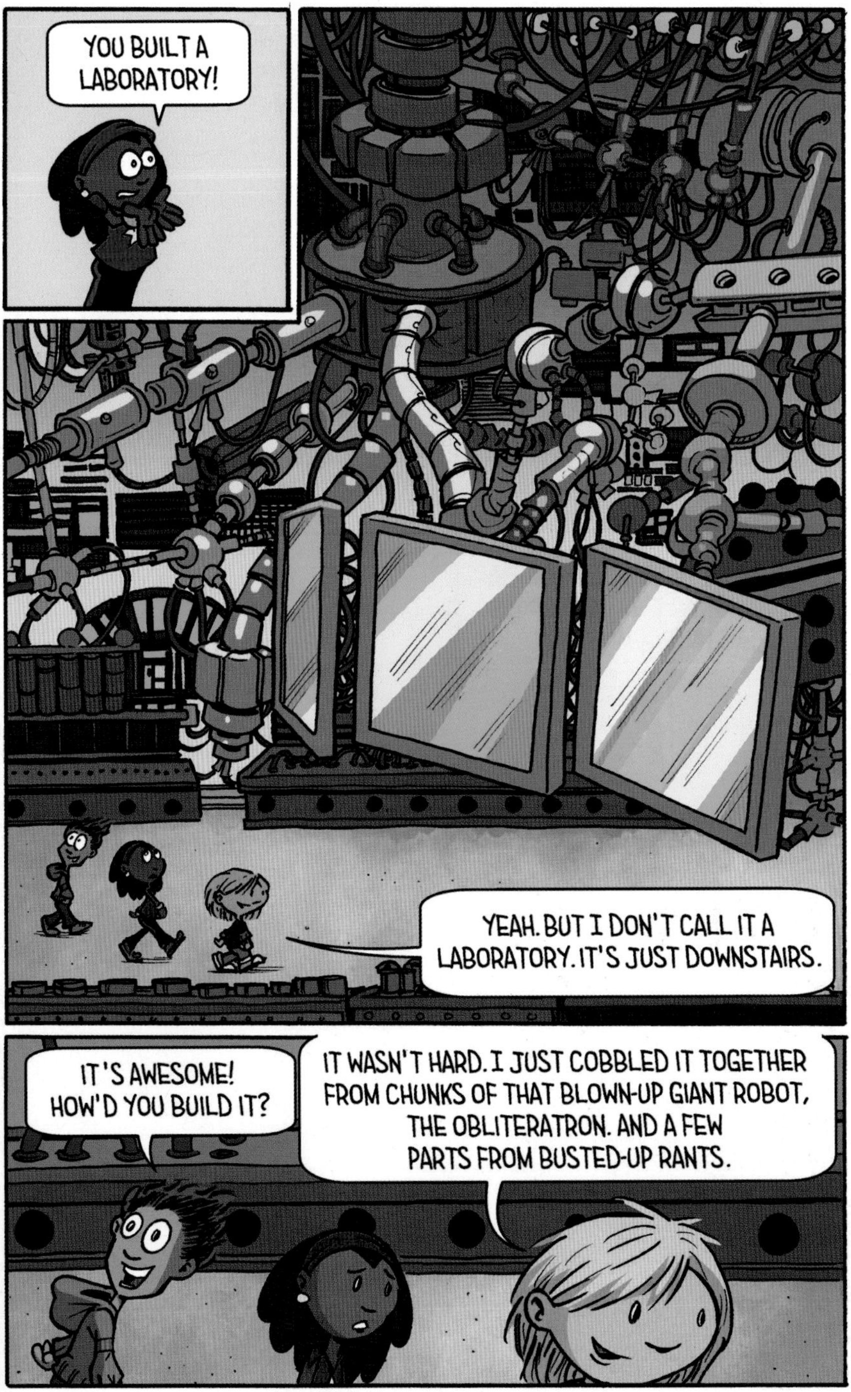
YOU BUILT A LABORATORY!
YEAH. BUT I DON'T CALL IT A LABORATORY. IT'S JUST DOWNSTAIRS.
IT'S AWESOME! HOW'D YOU BUILD IT?
IT WASN'T HARD. I JUST COBBLED IT TOGETHER FROM CHUNKS OF THAT BLOWN-UP GIANT ROBOT, THE OBLITERATRON. AND A FEW PARTS FROM BUSTED-UP RANTS.

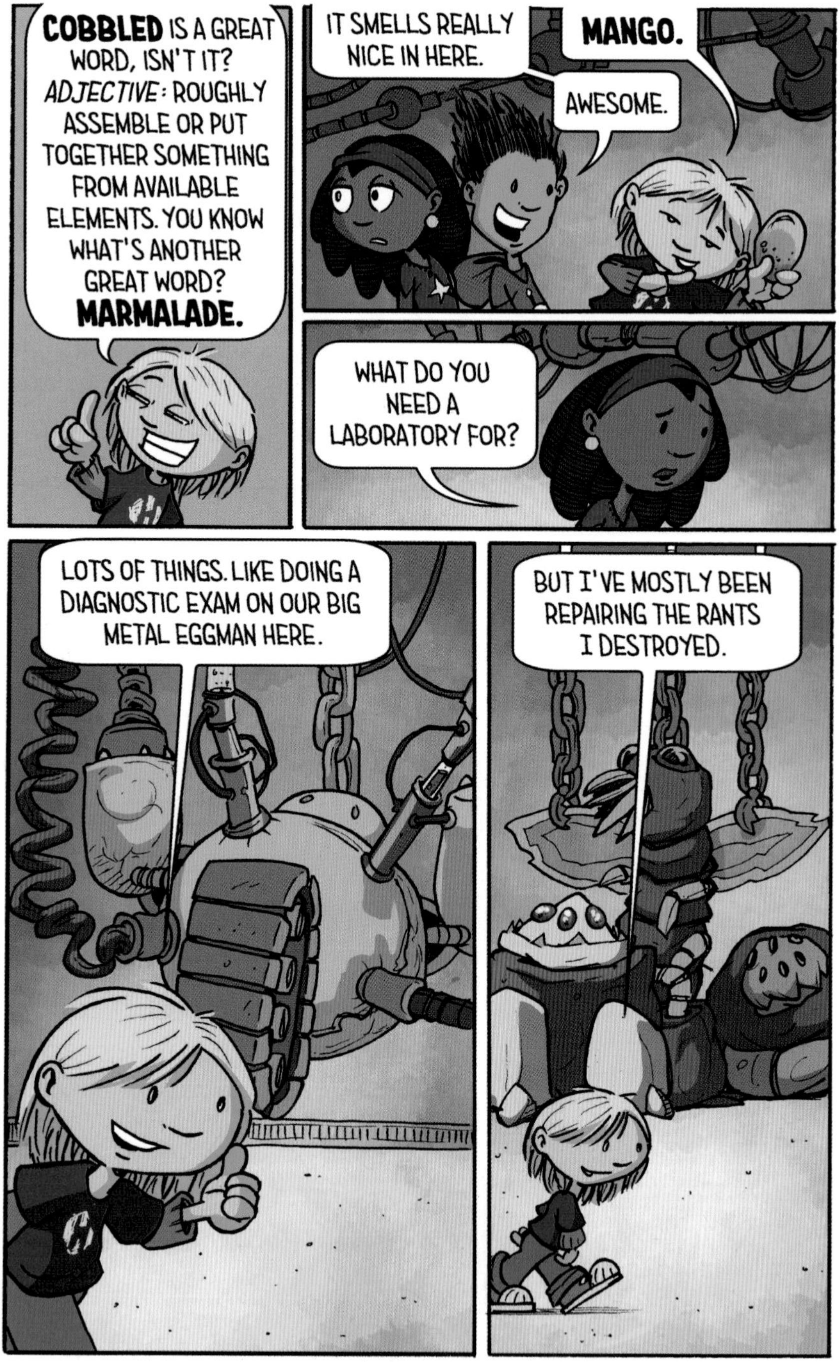
COBBLED IS A GREAT WORD, ISN'T IT? *ADJECTIVE*: ROUGHLY ASSEMBLE OR PUT TOGETHER SOMETHING FROM AVAILABLE ELEMENTS. YOU KNOW WHAT'S ANOTHER GREAT WORD? **MARMALADE.**
IT SMELLS REALLY NICE IN HERE.
MANGO.
AWESOME.
WHAT DO YOU NEED A LABORATORY FOR?
LOTS OF THINGS. LIKE DOING A DIAGNOSTIC EXAM ON OUR BIG METAL EGGMAN HERE.
BUT I'VE MOSTLY BEEN REPAIRING THE RANTS I DESTROYED.

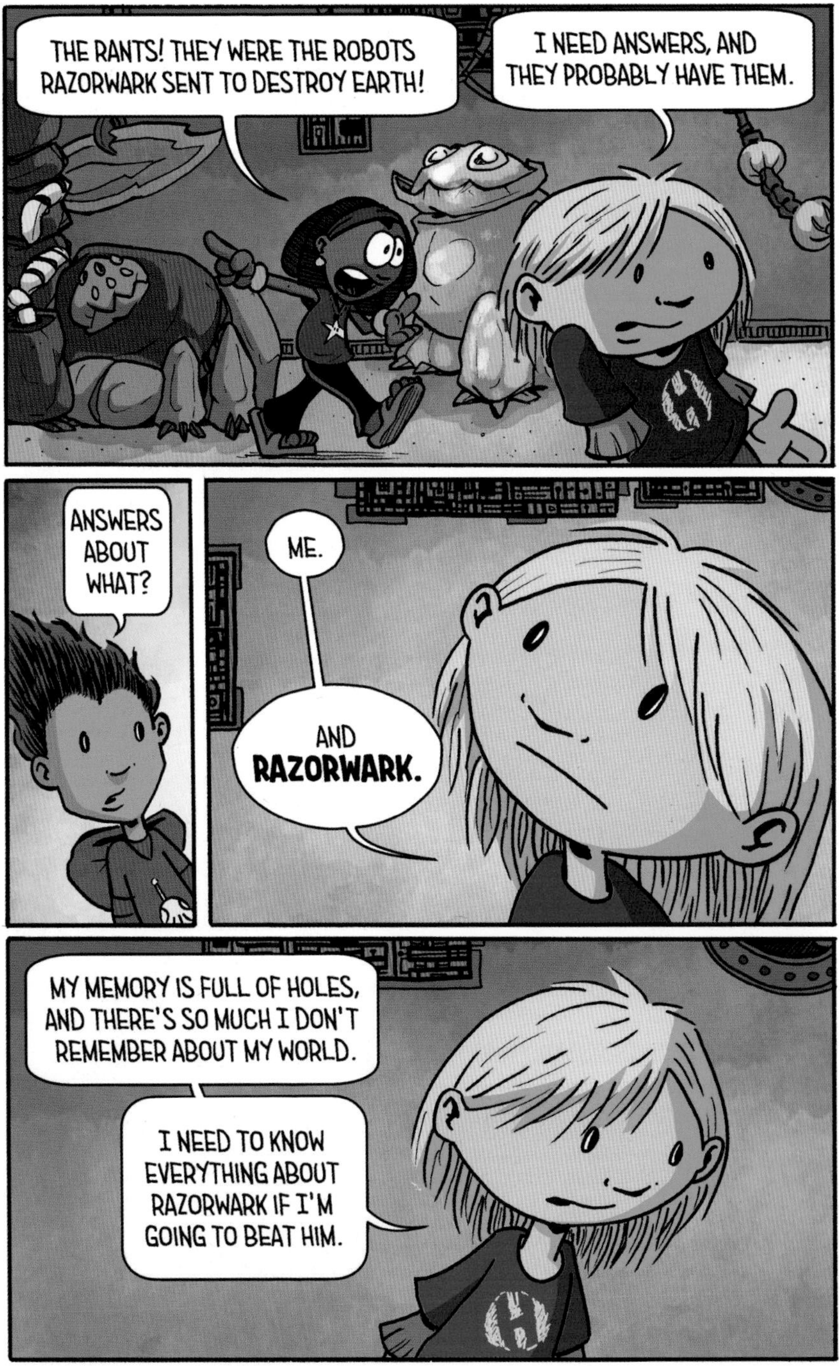
THE RANTS! THEY WERE THE ROBOTS RAZORWARK SENT TO DESTROY EARTH!
I NEED ANSWERS, AND THEY PROBABLY HAVE THEM.
ANSWERS ABOUT WHAT?
ME.
AND **RAZORWARK.**
MY MEMORY IS FULL OF HOLES, AND THERE'S SO MUCH I DON'T REMEMBER ABOUT MY WORLD.
I NEED TO KNOW EVERYTHING ABOUT RAZORWARK IF I'M GOING TO BEAT HIM.

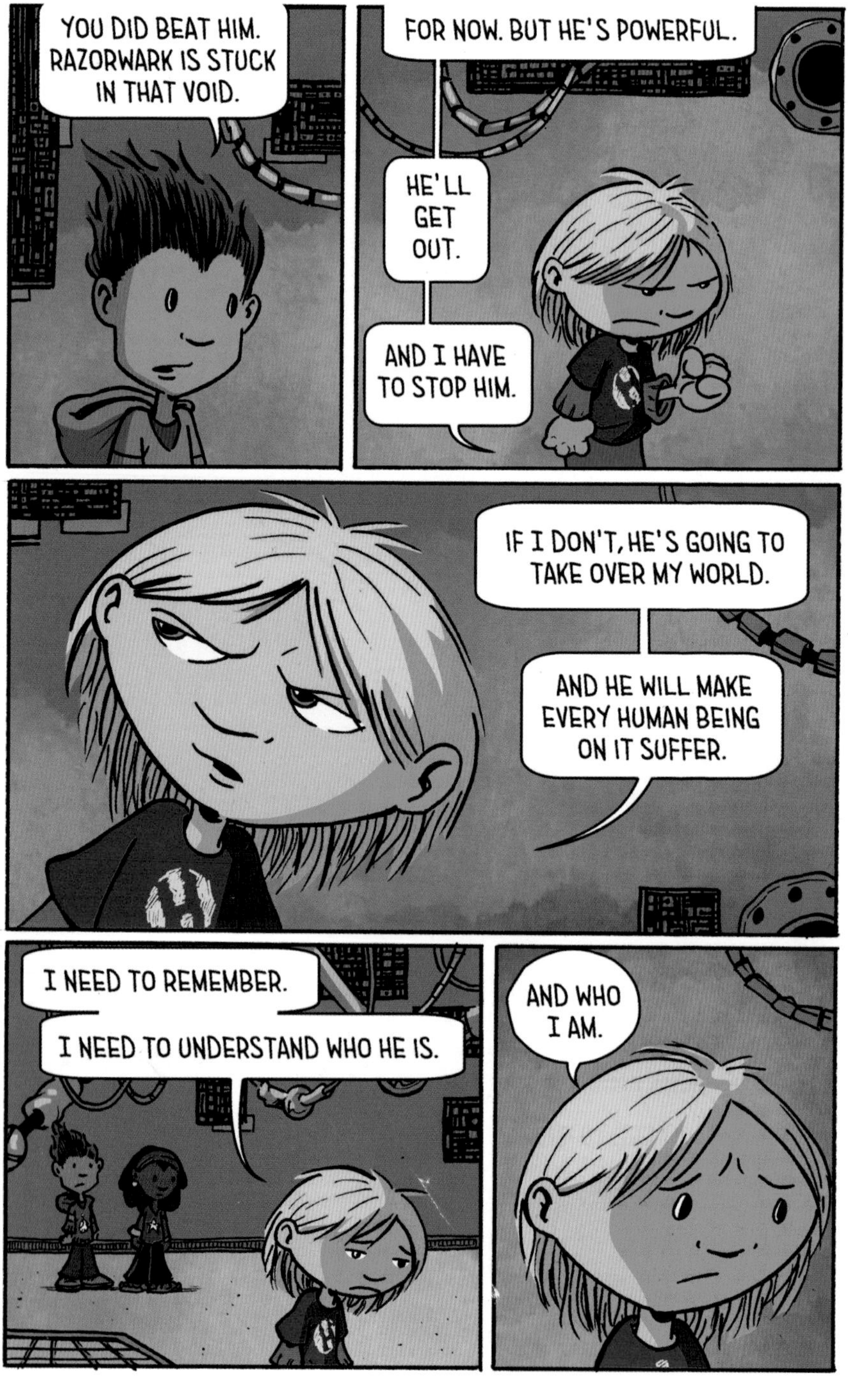
YOU DID BEAT HIM. RAZORWARK IS STUCK IN THAT VOID.
FOR NOW. BUT HE'S POWERFUL.
HE'LL GET OUT.
AND I HAVE TO STOP HIM.
IF I DON'T, HE'S GOING TO TAKE OVER MY WORLD.
AND HE WILL MAKE EVERY HUMAN BEING ON IT SUFFER.
I NEED TO REMEMBER.
I NEED TO UNDERSTAND WHO HE IS.
AND WHO I AM.

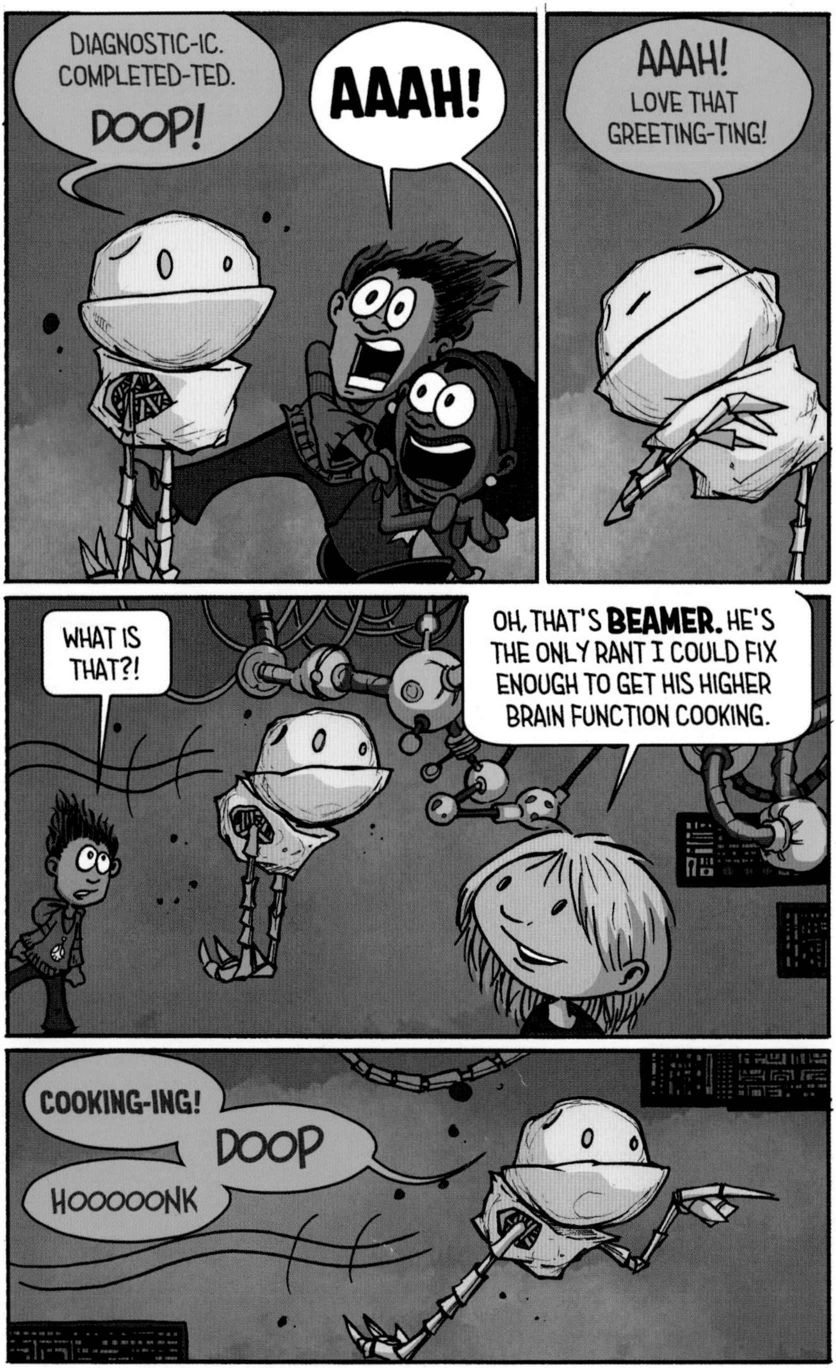
DIAGNOSTIC-IC. COMPLETED-TED. DOOP!
AAAH!
AAAH! LOVE THAT GREETING-TING!
WHAT IS THAT?!
OH, THAT'S BEAMER. HE'S THE ONLY RANT I COULD FIX ENOUGH TO GET HIS HIGHER BRAIN FUNCTION COOKING.
COOKING-ING!
DOOP
HOOOOONK

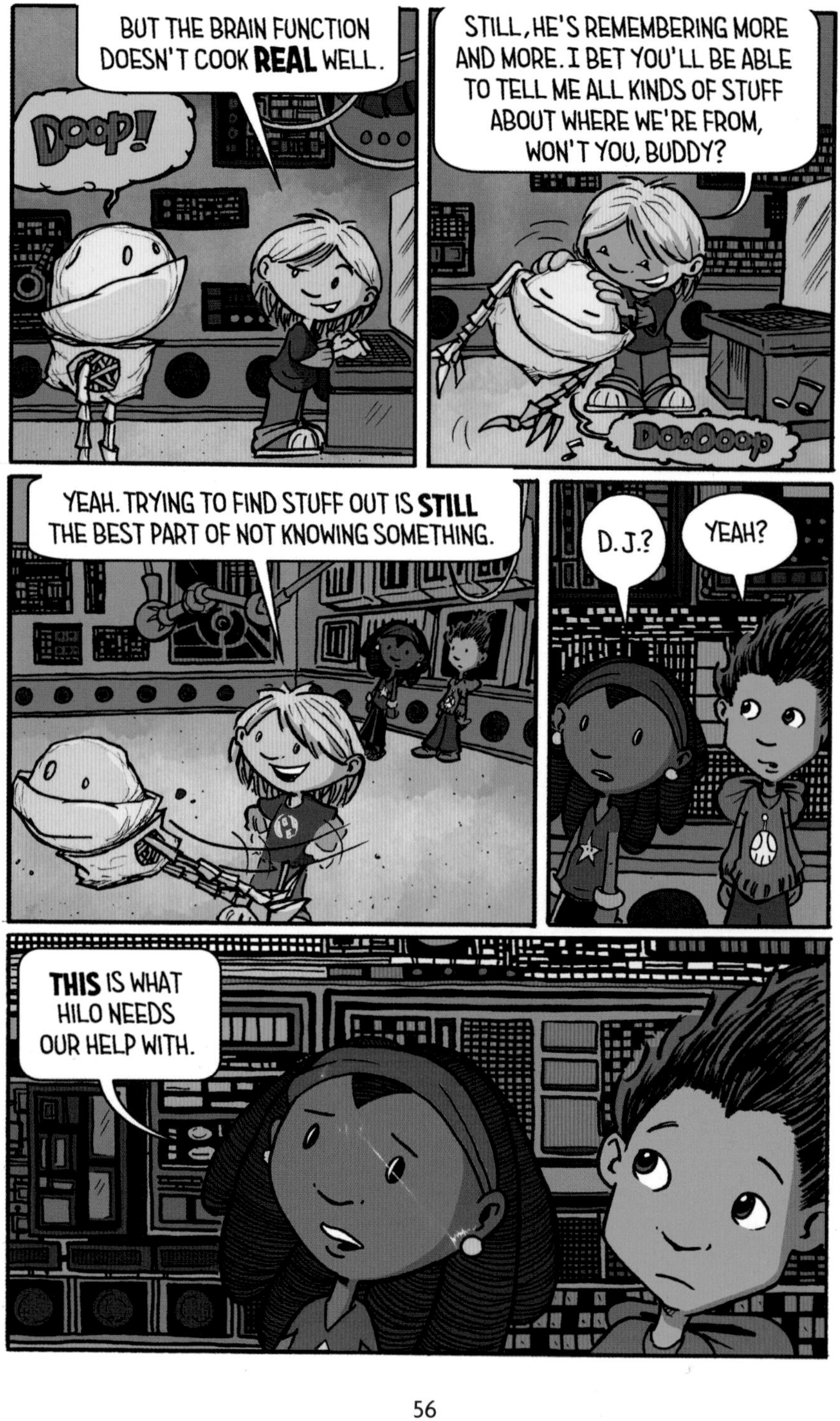
BUT THE BRAIN FUNCTION DOESN'T COOK **REAL** WELL.
DOOP!
STILL, HE'S REMEMBERING MORE AND MORE. I BET YOU'LL BE ABLE TO TELL ME ALL KINDS OF STUFF ABOUT WHERE WE'RE FROM, WON'T YOU, BUDDY?
DOOOOOP
YEAH. TRYING TO FIND STUFF OUT IS **STILL** THE BEST PART OF NOT KNOWING SOMETHING.
D.J.?
YEAH?
THIS IS WHAT HILO NEEDS OUR HELP WITH.

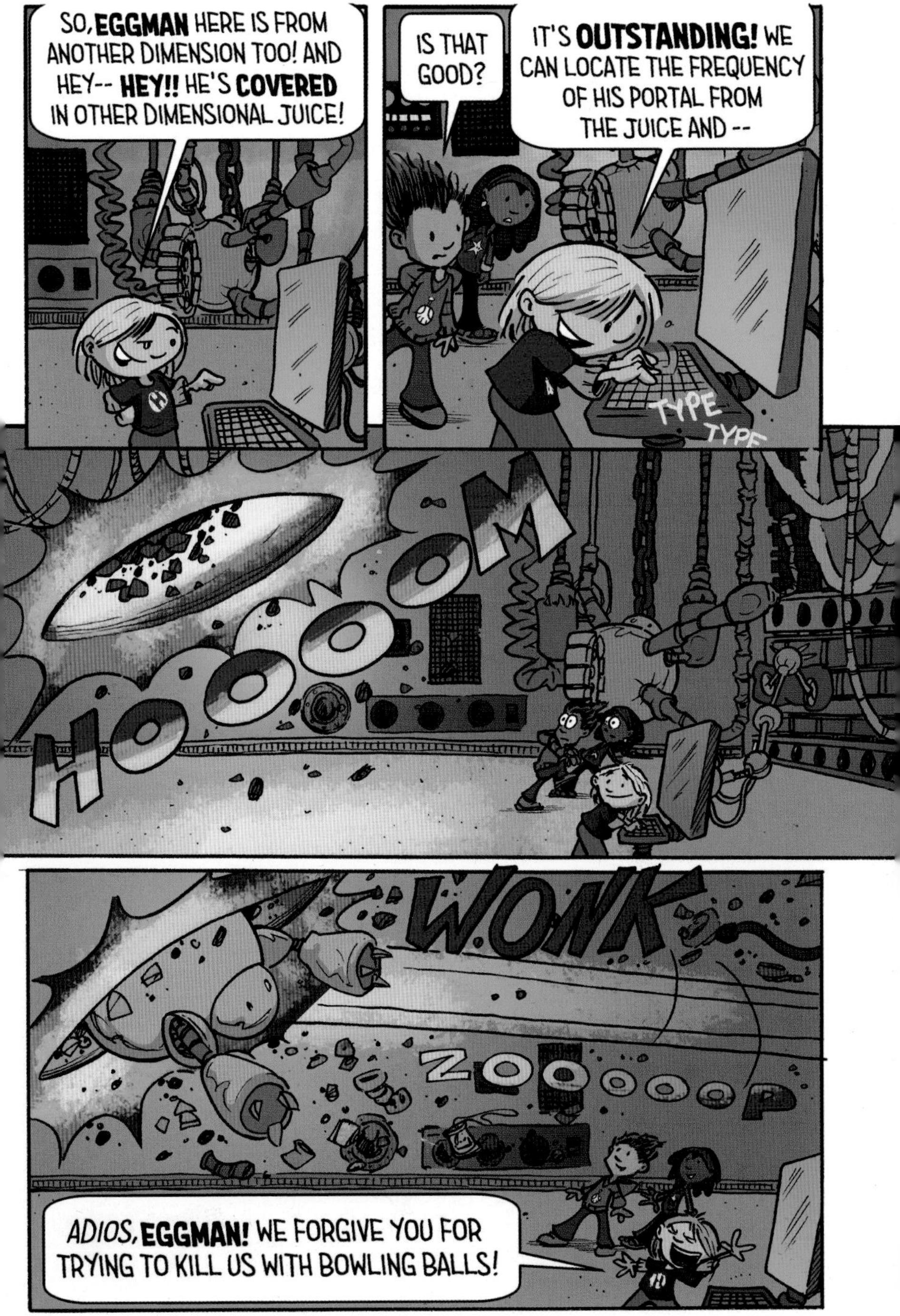
SO, **EGGMAN** HERE IS FROM ANOTHER DIMENSION TOO! AND HEY-- **HEY!!** HE'S **COVERED** IN OTHER DIMENSIONAL JUICE!
IS THAT GOOD?
IT'S **OUTSTANDING!** WE CAN LOCATE THE FREQUENCY OF HIS PORTAL FROM THE JUICE AND --
TYPE TYPE
HOOOOOOM
WONK
ZOOOOOOP
ADIOS, **EGGMAN!** WE FORGIVE YOU FOR TRYING TO KILL US WITH BOWLING BALLS!

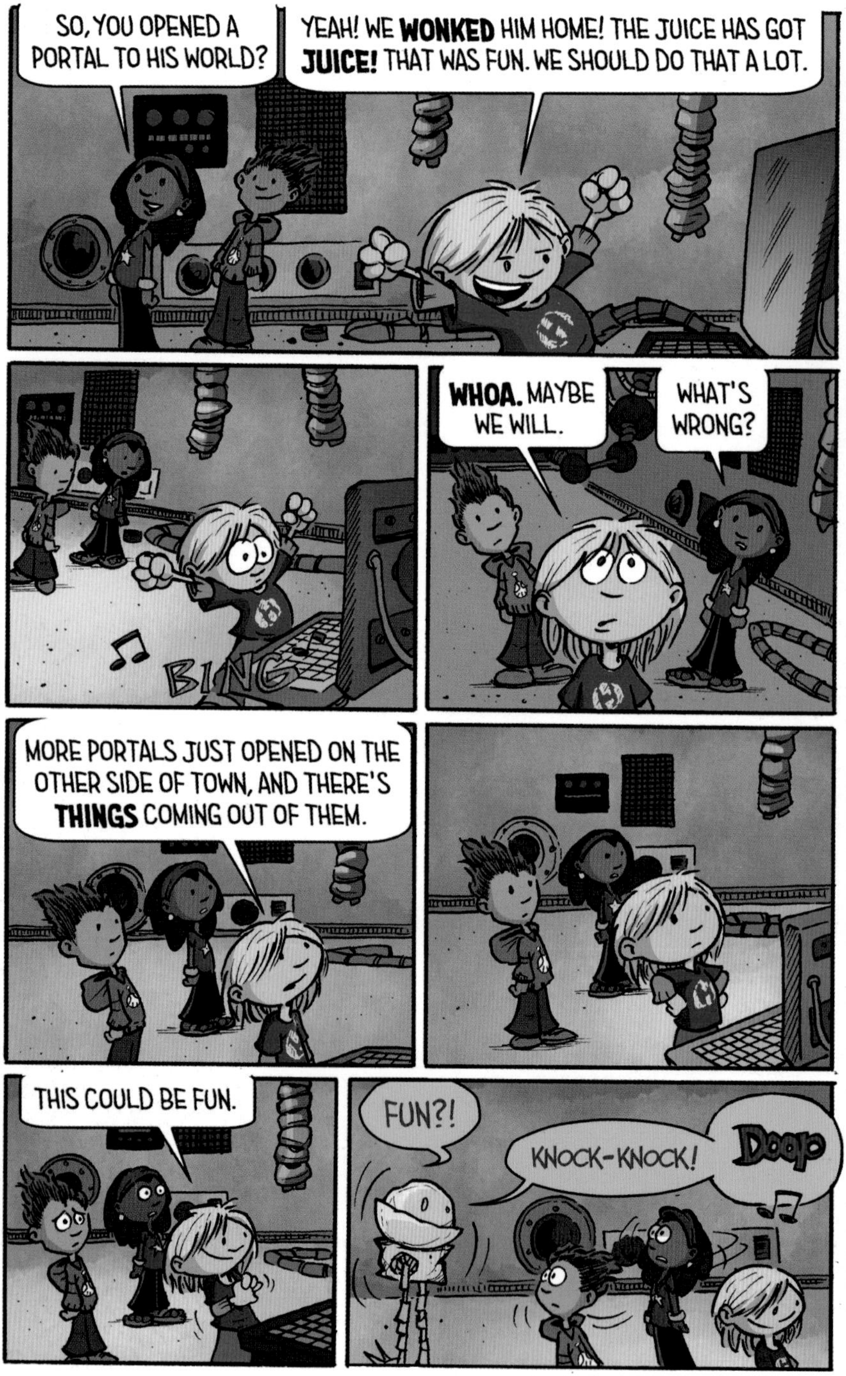
SO, YOU OPENED A PORTAL TO HIS WORLD?
YEAH! WE **WONKED** HIM HOME! THE JUICE HAS GOT **JUICE!** THAT WAS FUN. WE SHOULD DO THAT A LOT.
BING
WHOA. MAYBE WE WILL.
WHAT'S WRONG?
MORE PORTALS JUST OPENED ON THE OTHER SIDE OF TOWN, AND THERE'S **THINGS** COMING OUT OF THEM.
THIS COULD BE FUN.
FUN?!
KNOCK-KNOCK!
DOOP

CHAPTER 5

POLLY

HOOOM
WHUMP
RAAAAAAARGH!

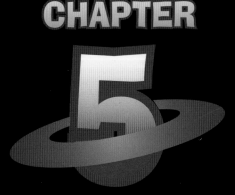

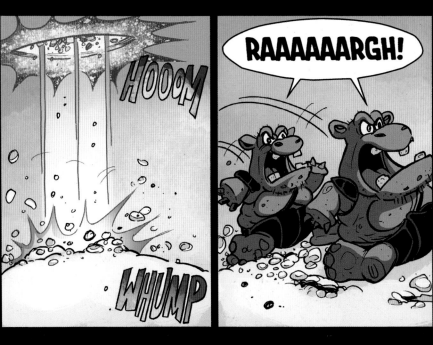

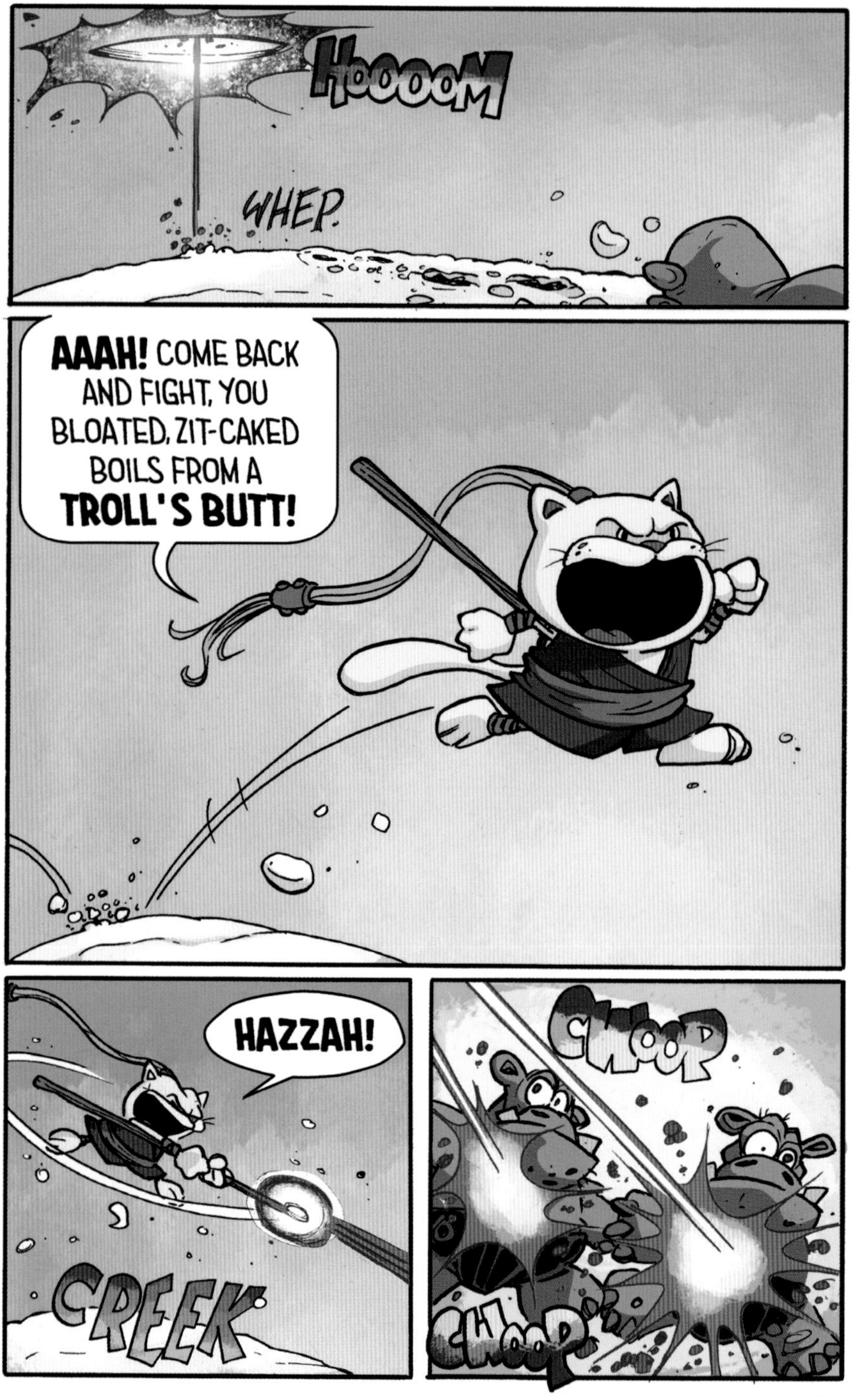
HOOOOM
WHEP
AAAH! COME BACK AND FIGHT, YOU BLOATED, ZIT-CAKED BOILS FROM A TROLL'S BUTT!
HAZZAH!
CREEK
CHOOP
CHOOP

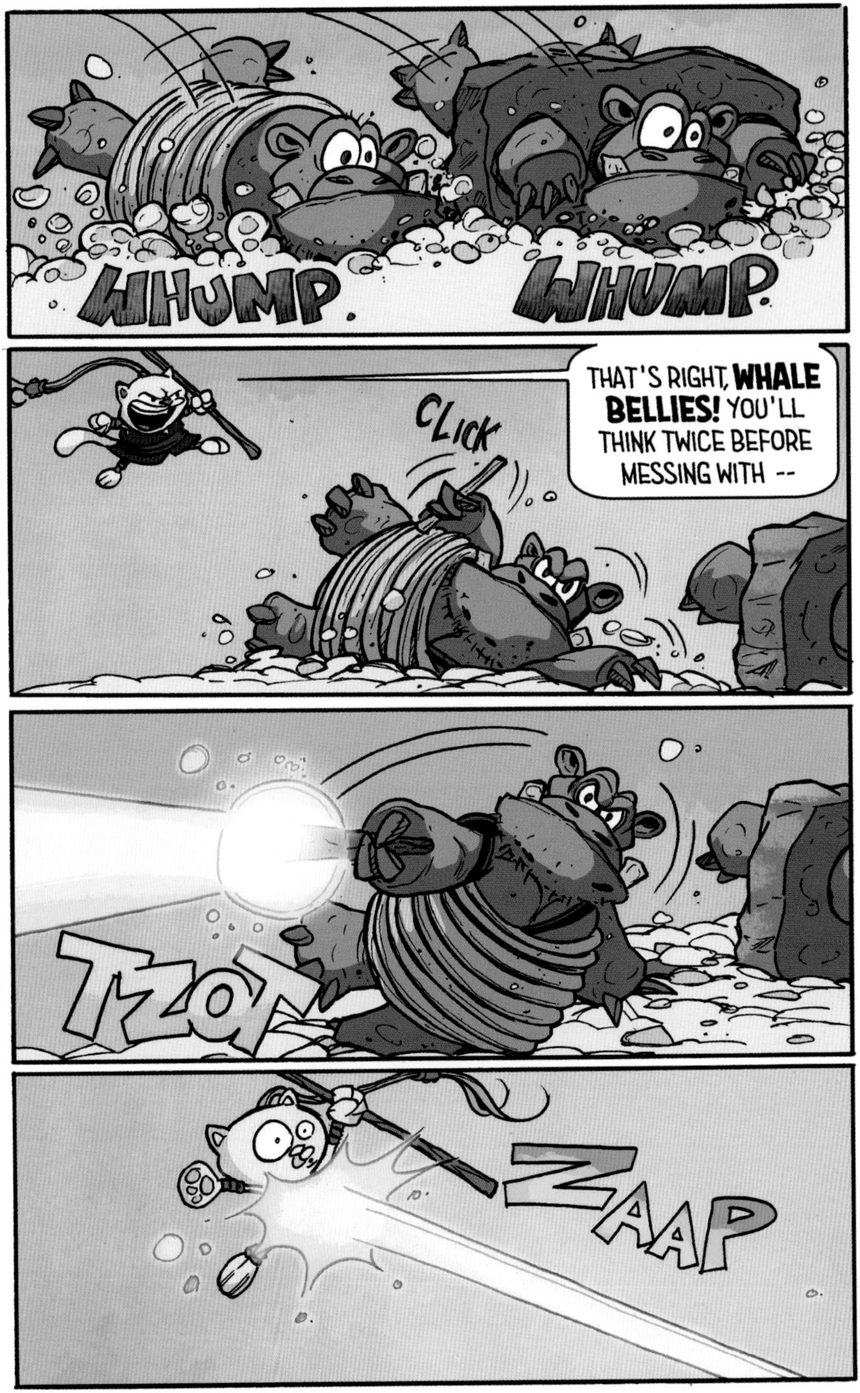
WHUMP
WHUMP
THAT'S RIGHT, **WHALE BELLIES!** YOU'LL THINK TWICE BEFORE MESSING WITH --
CLICK
TZOT
ZAAP

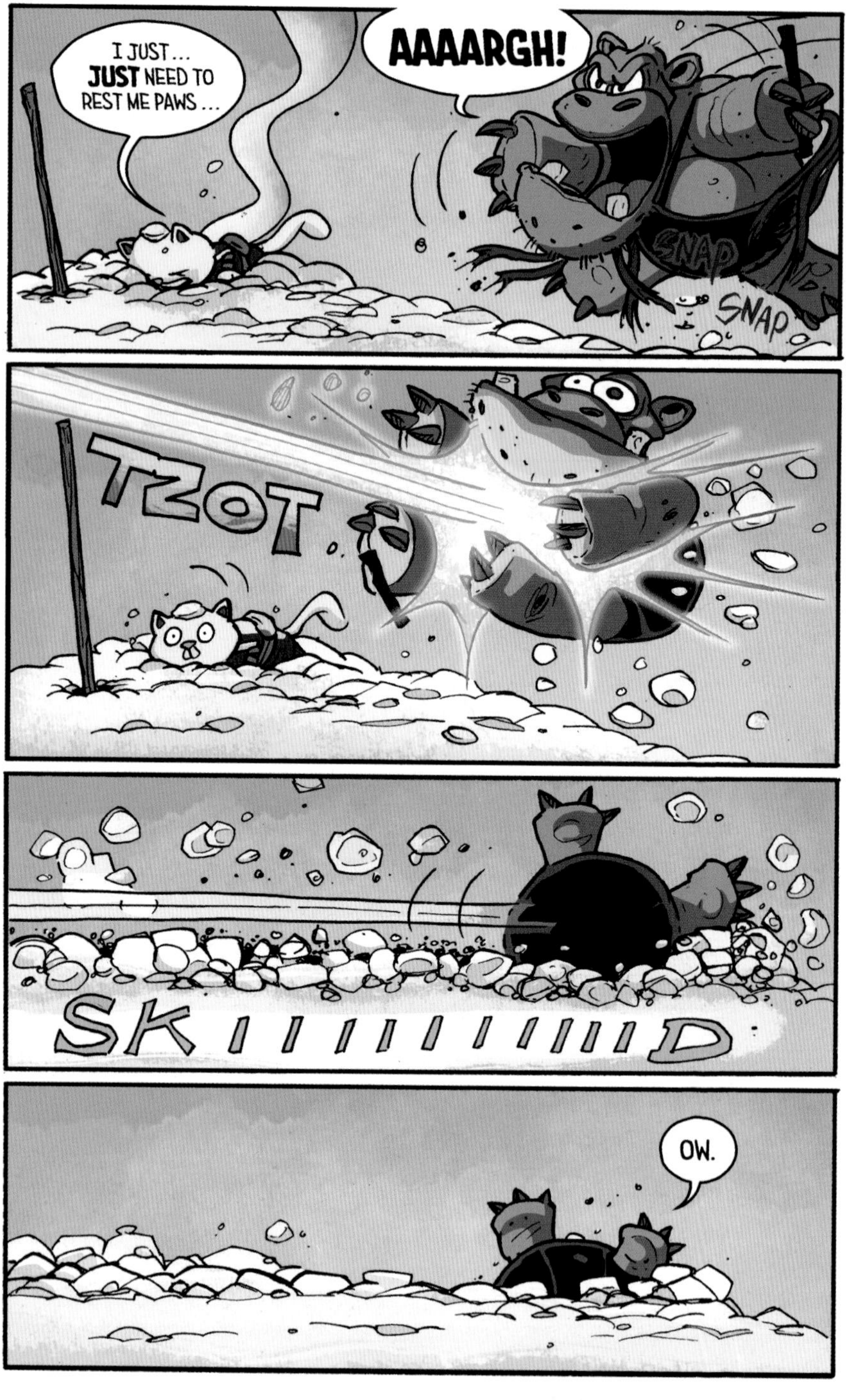
I JUST... JUST NEED TO REST ME PAWS...
AAAARGH!
SNAP
SNAP
TZOT
SKIIIIIIIIID
OW.

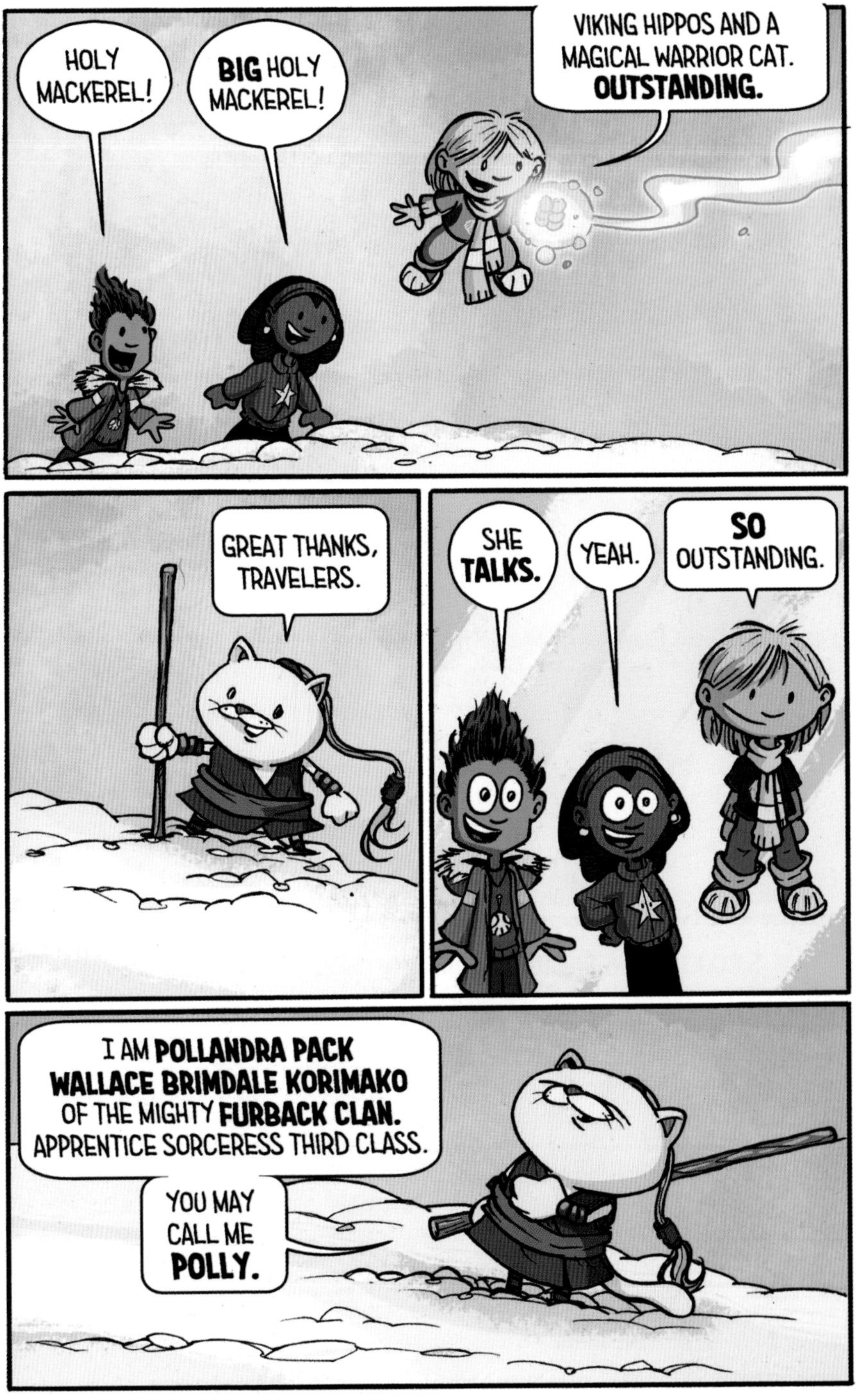
HOLY MACKEREL!
BIG HOLY MACKEREL!
VIKING HIPPOS AND A MAGICAL WARRIOR CAT. OUTSTANDING.
GREAT THANKS, TRAVELERS.
SHE TALKS.
YEAH.
SO OUTSTANDING.
I AM POLLANDRA PACK WALLACE BRIMDALE KORIMAKO OF THE MIGHTY FURBACK CLAN. APPRENTICE SORCERESS THIRD CLASS.
YOU MAY CALL ME POLLY.

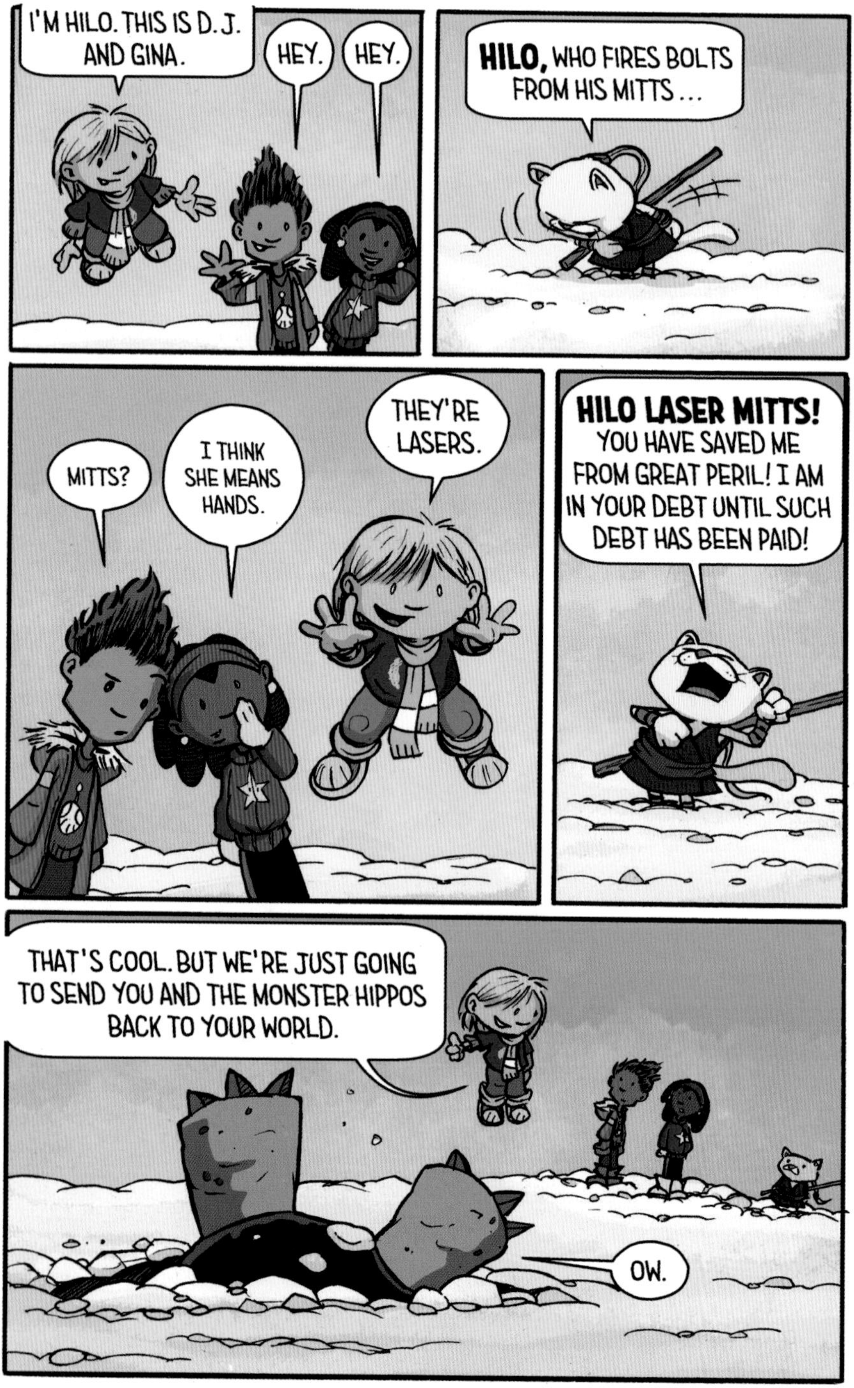
I'M HILO. THIS IS D. J. AND GINA.
HEY.
HEY.
HILO, WHO FIRES BOLTS FROM HIS MITTS . . .
MITTS?
I THINK SHE MEANS HANDS.
THEY'RE LASERS.
HILO LASER MITTS! YOU HAVE SAVED ME FROM GREAT PERIL! I AM IN YOUR DEBT UNTIL SUCH DEBT HAS BEEN PAID!
THAT'S COOL. BUT WE'RE JUST GOING TO SEND YOU AND THE MONSTER HIPPOS BACK TO YOUR WORLD.
OW.

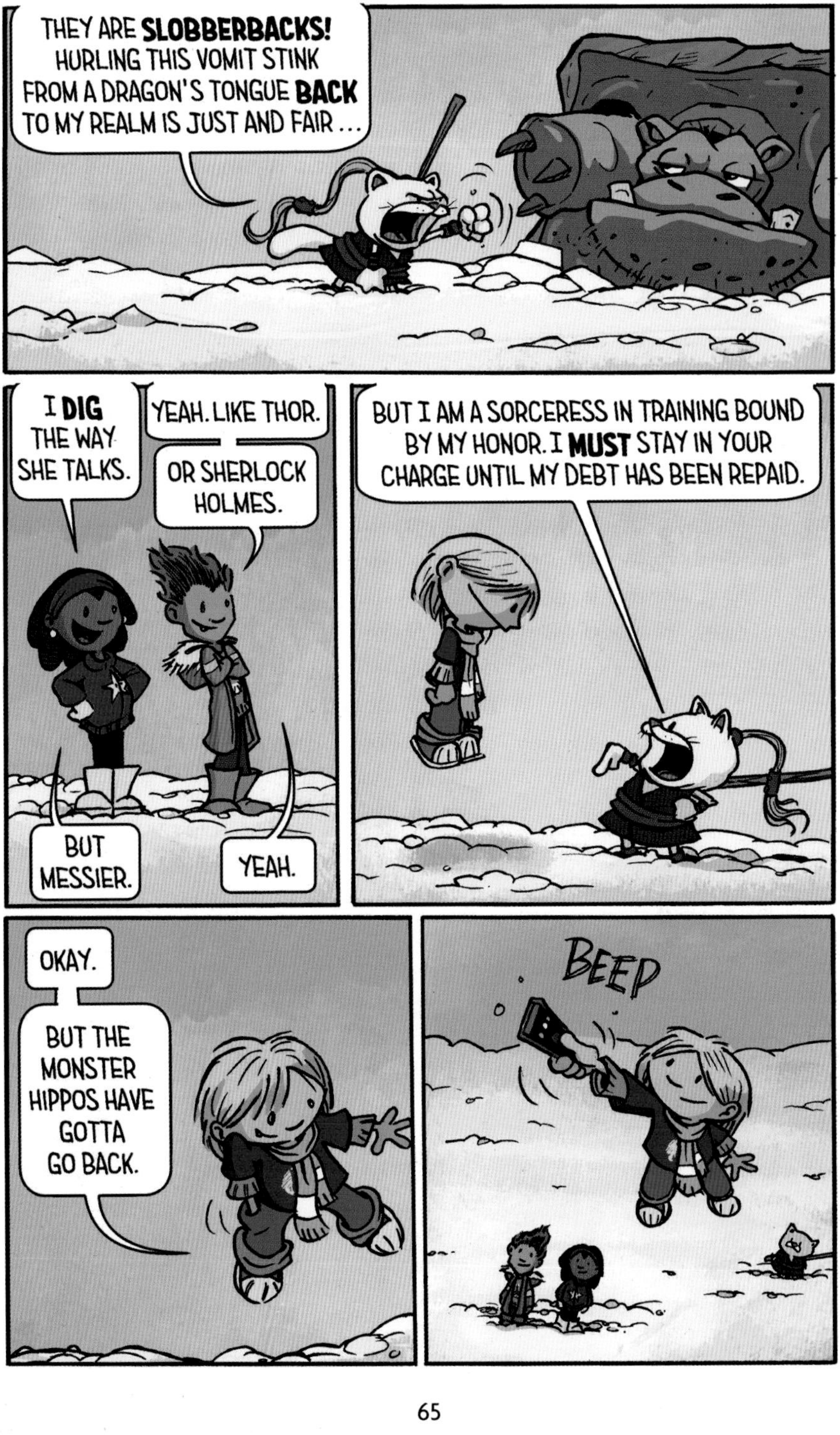
THEY ARE SLOBBERBACKS! HURLING THIS VOMIT STINK FROM A DRAGON'S TONGUE BACK TO MY REALM IS JUST AND FAIR...
I DIG THE WAY SHE TALKS.
YEAH. LIKE THOR.
OR SHERLOCK HOLMES.
BUT MESSIER.
YEAH.
BUT I AM A SORCERESS IN TRAINING BOUND BY MY HONOR. I MUST STAY IN YOUR CHARGE UNTIL MY DEBT HAS BEEN REPAID.
OKAY.
BUT THE MONSTER HIPPOS HAVE GOTTA GO BACK.
BEEP

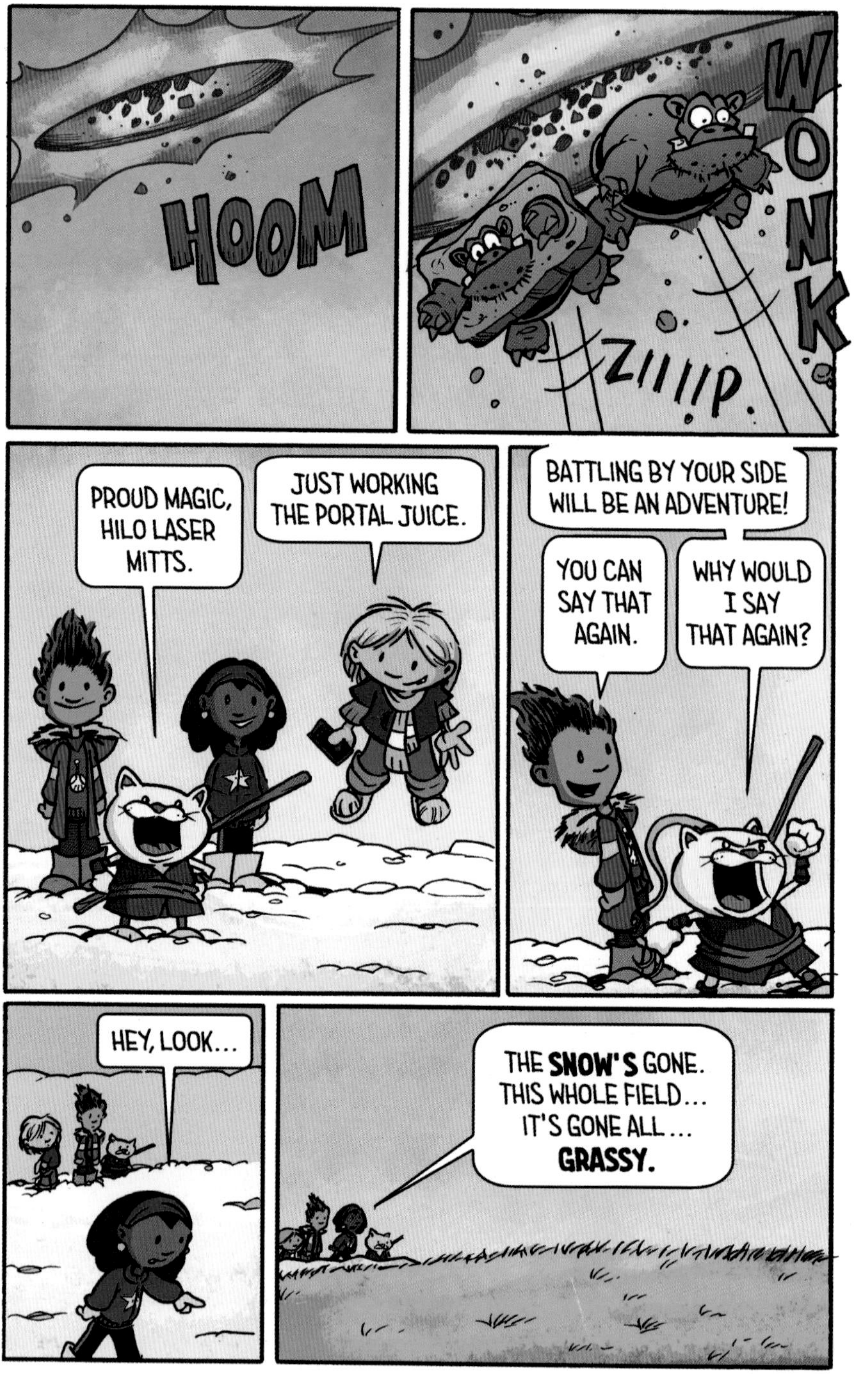
HOOM
WONK
ZIIIIP
PROUD MAGIC, HILO LASER MITTS.
JUST WORKING THE PORTAL JUICE.
BATTLING BY YOUR SIDE WILL BE AN ADVENTURE!
YOU CAN SAY THAT AGAIN.
WHY WOULD I SAY THAT AGAIN?
HEY, LOOK...
THE **SNOW'S** GONE. THIS WHOLE FIELD... IT'S GONE ALL... **GRASSY.**

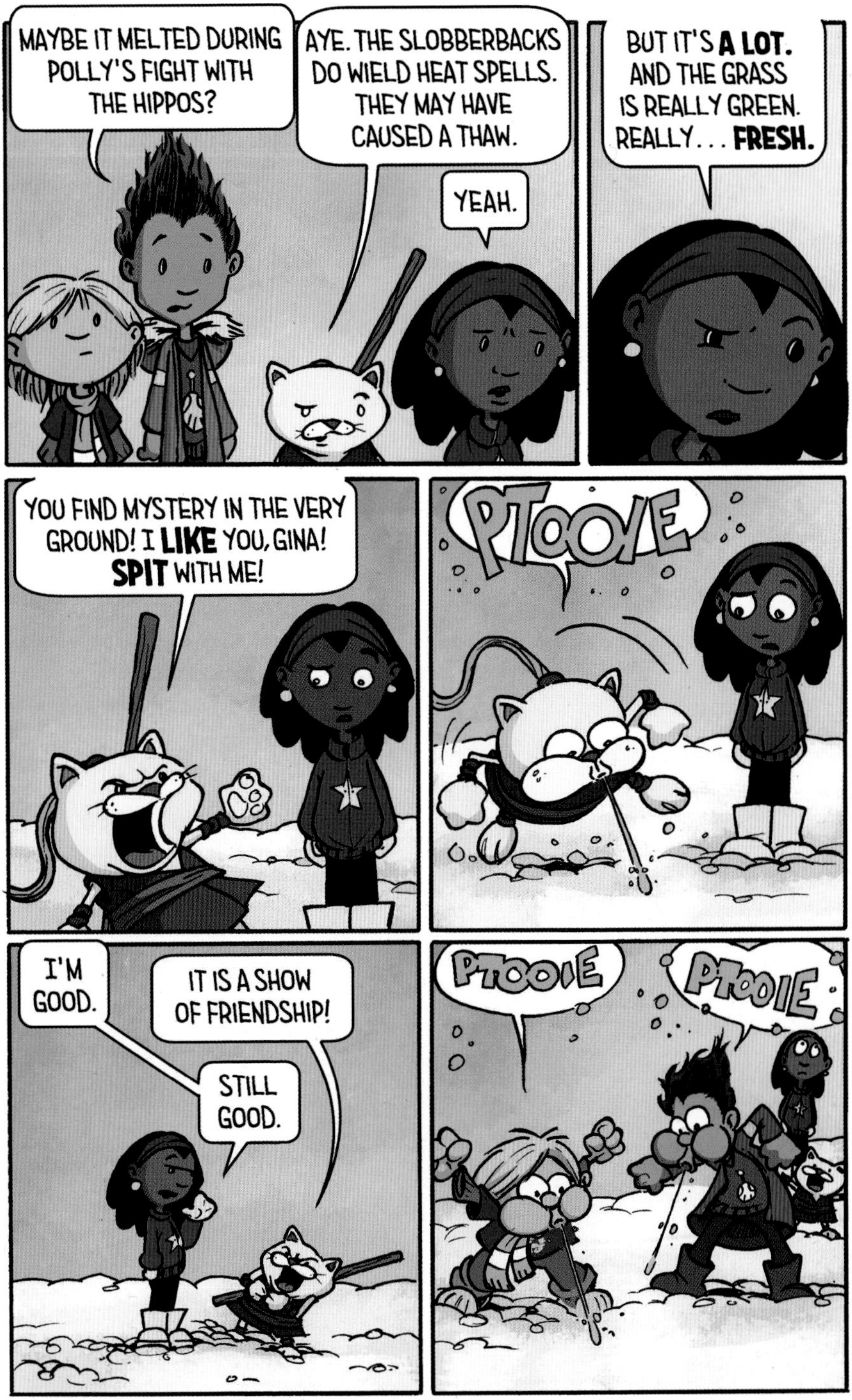
MAYBE IT MELTED DURING POLLY'S FIGHT WITH THE HIPPOS?
AYE. THE SLOBBERBACKS DO WIELD HEAT SPELLS. THEY MAY HAVE CAUSED A THAW.
YEAH.
BUT IT'S **A LOT.** AND THE GRASS IS REALLY GREEN. REALLY. . . **FRESH.**
YOU FIND MYSTERY IN THE VERY GROUND! I **LIKE** YOU, GINA! **SPIT** WITH ME!
PTOOIE
I'M GOOD.
IT IS A SHOW OF FRIENDSHIP!
STILL GOOD.
PTOOIE
PTOOIE

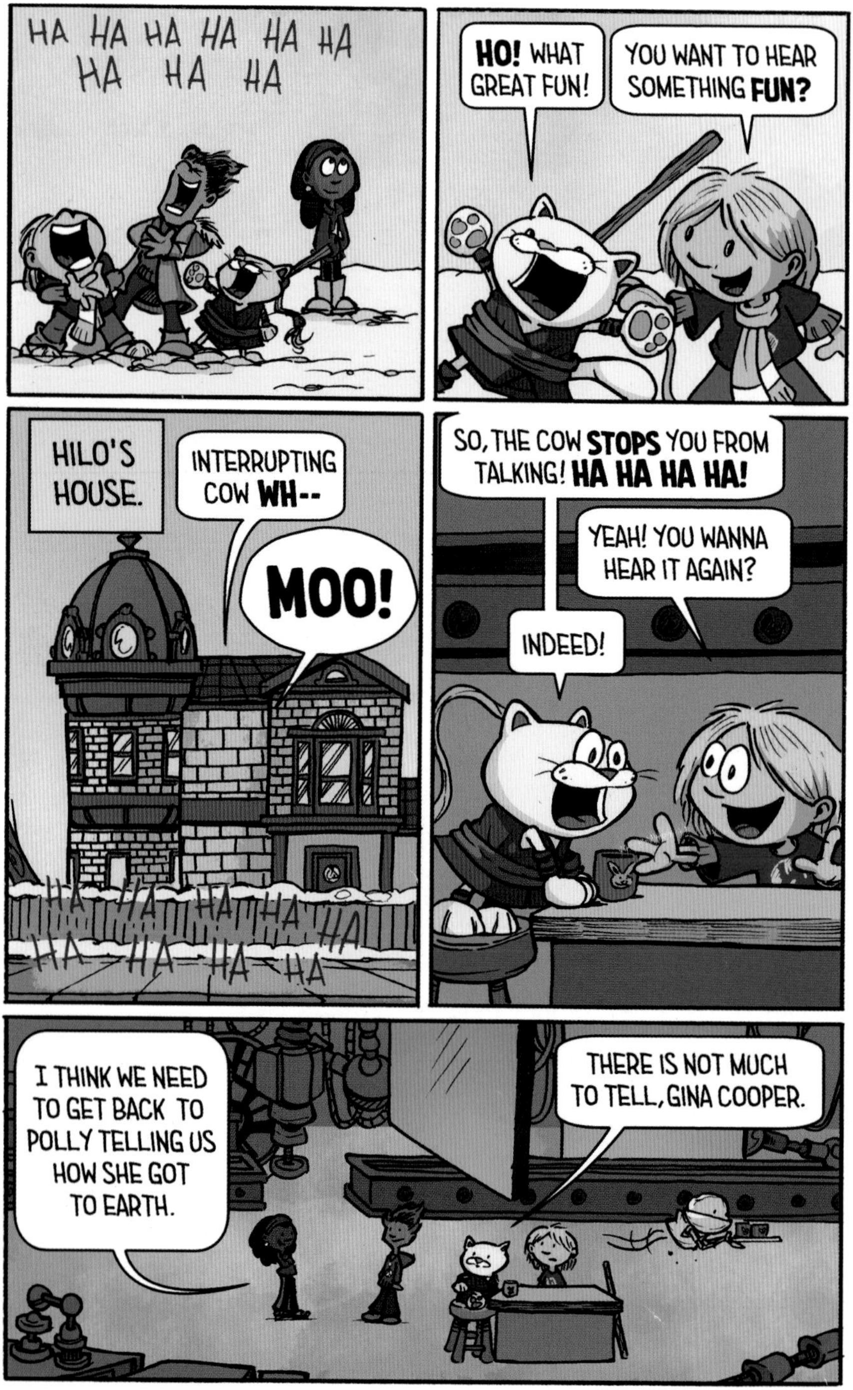
HA HA HA HA HA HA
HA HA HA
HO! WHAT GREAT FUN!
YOU WANT TO HEAR SOMETHING **FUN?**
HILO'S HOUSE.
INTERRUPTING COW **WH--**
MOO!
HA HA HA HA HA
HA HA HA HA
SO, THE COW **STOPS** YOU FROM TALKING! **HA HA HA HA!**
YEAH! YOU WANNA HEAR IT AGAIN?
INDEED!
I THINK WE NEED TO GET BACK TO POLLY TELLING US HOW SHE GOT TO EARTH.
THERE IS NOT MUCH TO TELL, GINA COOPER.

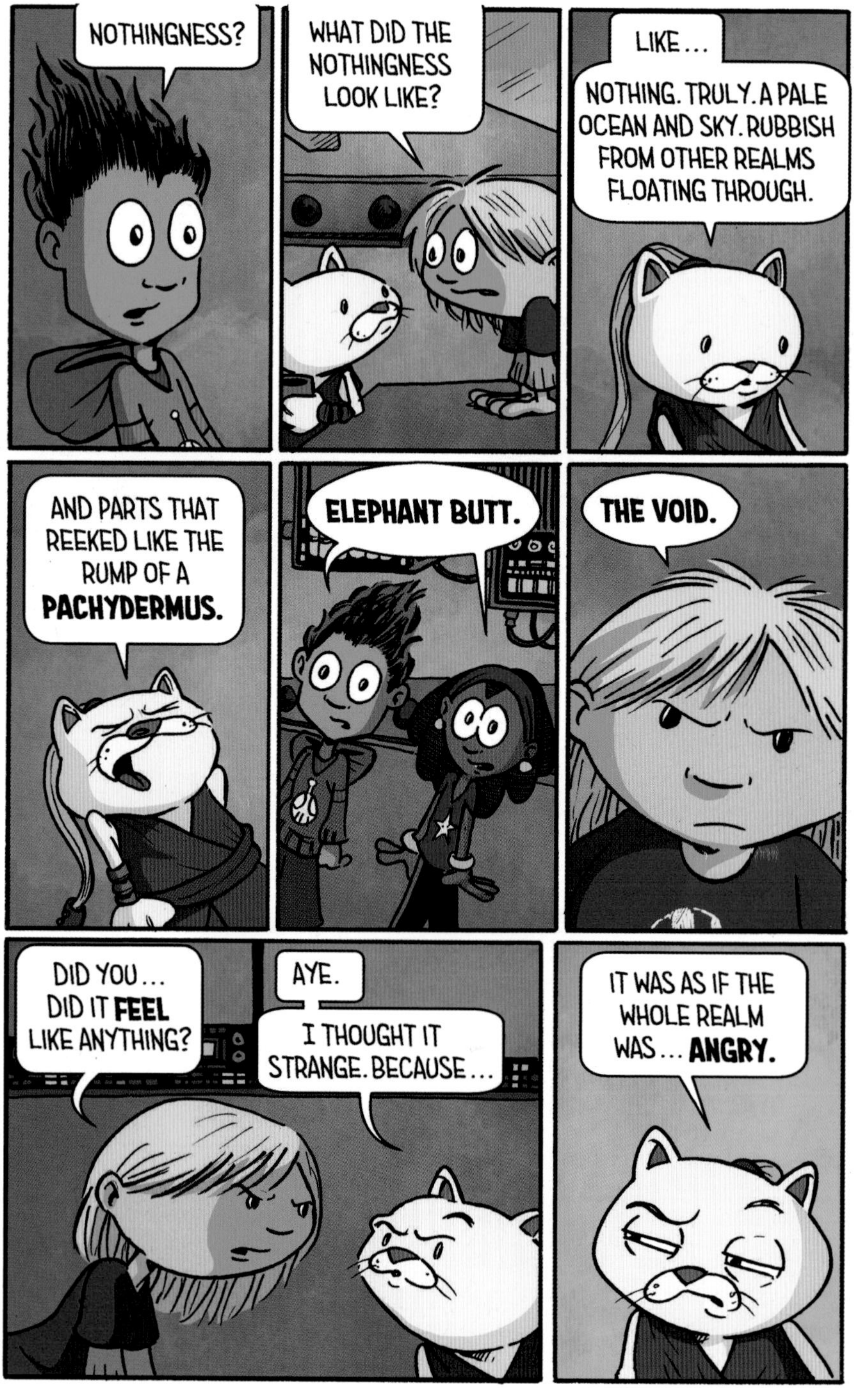
NOTHINGNESS?
WHAT DID THE NOTHINGNESS LOOK LIKE?
LIKE...
NOTHING. TRULY. A PALE OCEAN AND SKY. RUBBISH FROM OTHER REALMS FLOATING THROUGH.
AND PARTS THAT REEKED LIKE THE RUMP OF A PACHYDERMUS.
ELEPHANT BUTT.
THE VOID.
DID YOU... DID IT FEEL LIKE ANYTHING?
AYE.
I THOUGHT IT STRANGE. BECAUSE...
IT WAS AS IF THE WHOLE REALM WAS... ANGRY.

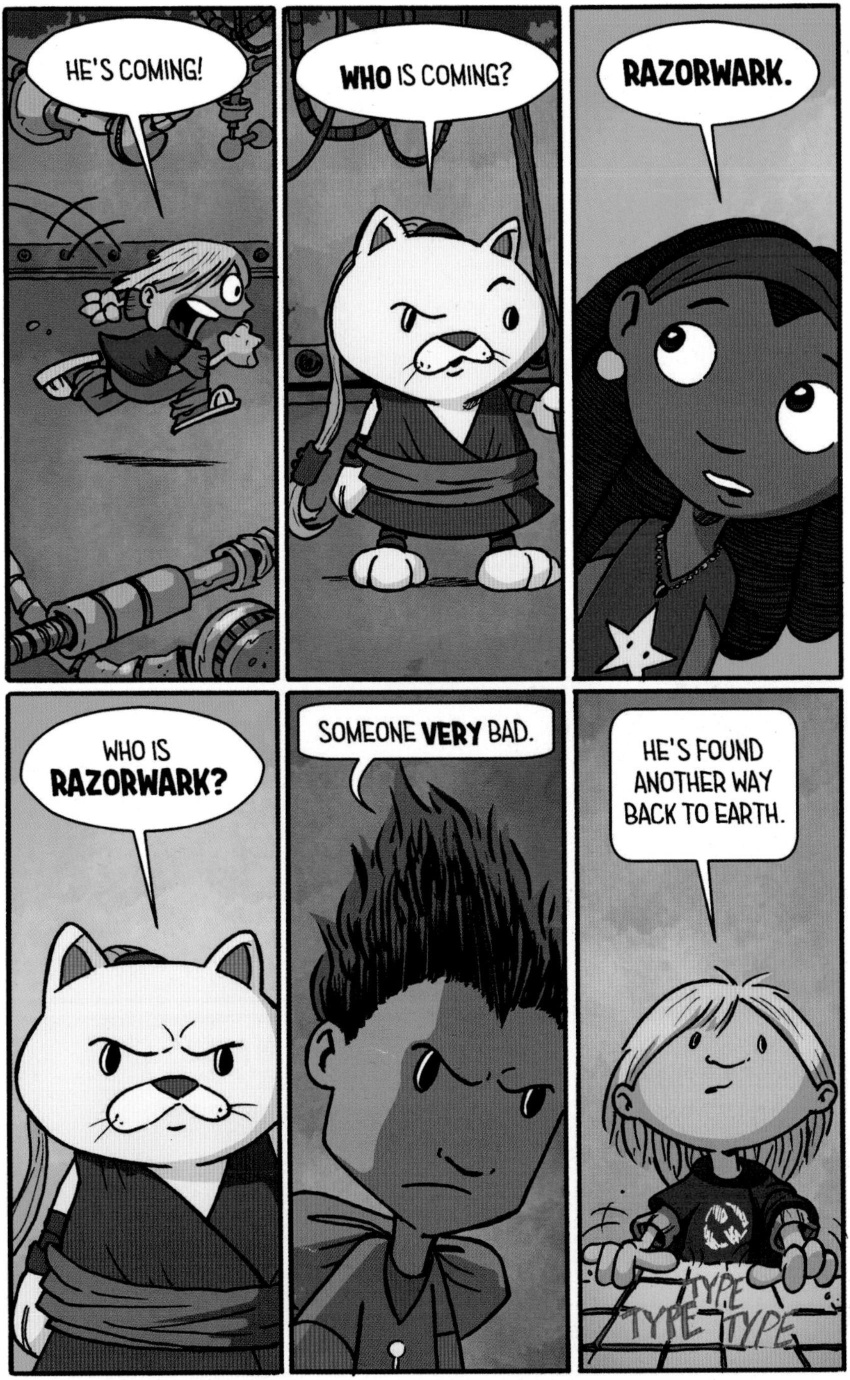
HE'S COMING!
WHO IS COMING?
RAZORWARK.
WHO IS RAZORWARK?
SOMEONE VERY BAD.
HE'S FOUND ANOTHER WAY BACK TO EARTH.
TYPE TYPE TYPE TYPE

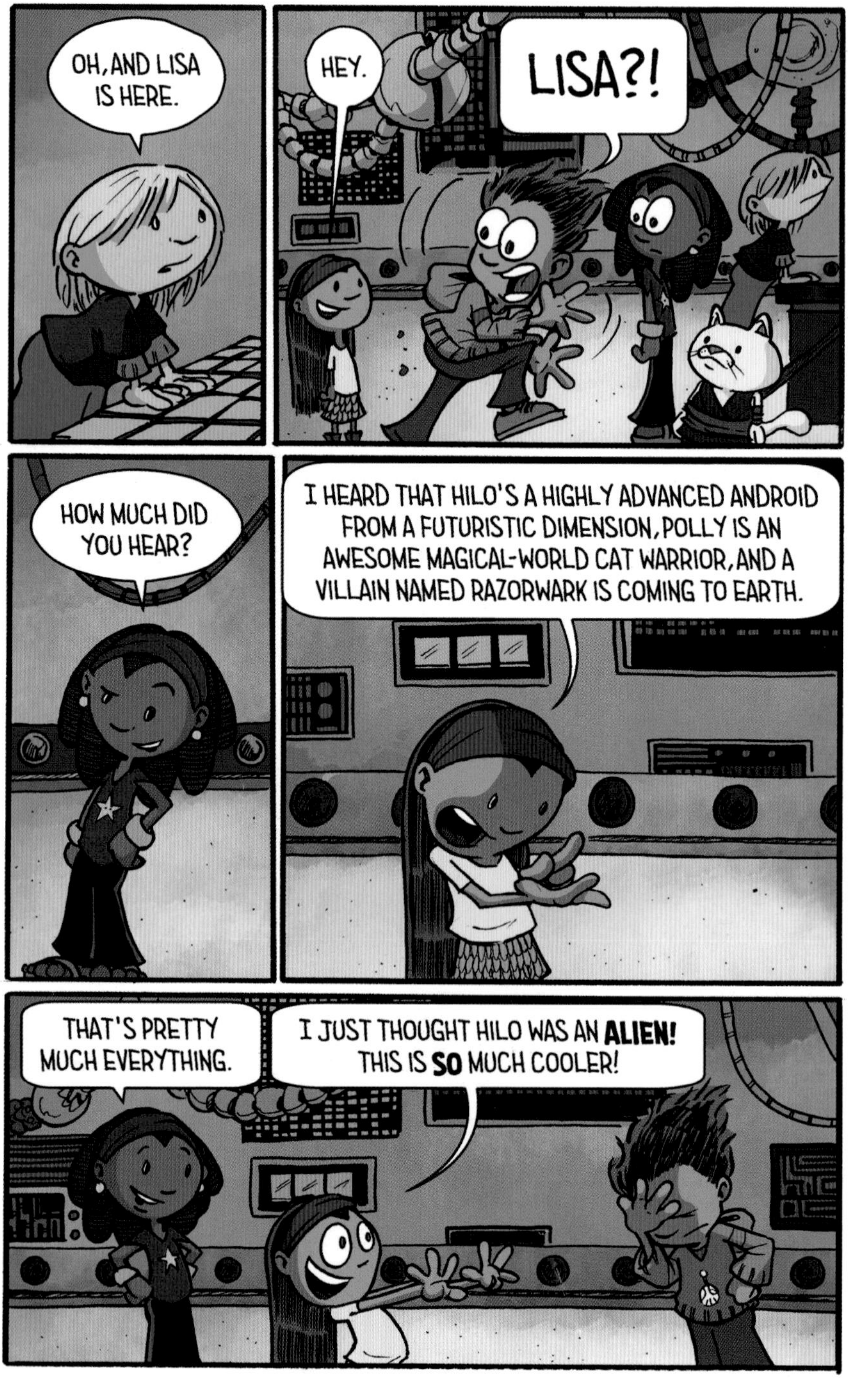
OH, AND LISA IS HERE.
HEY.
LISA?!
HOW MUCH DID YOU HEAR?
I HEARD THAT HILO'S A HIGHLY ADVANCED ANDROID FROM A FUTURISTIC DIMENSION, POLLY IS AN AWESOME MAGICAL-WORLD CAT WARRIOR, AND A VILLAIN NAMED RAZORWARK IS COMING TO EARTH.
THAT'S PRETTY MUCH EVERYTHING.
I JUST THOUGHT HILO WAS AN **ALIEN!** THIS IS **SO** MUCH COOLER!

73

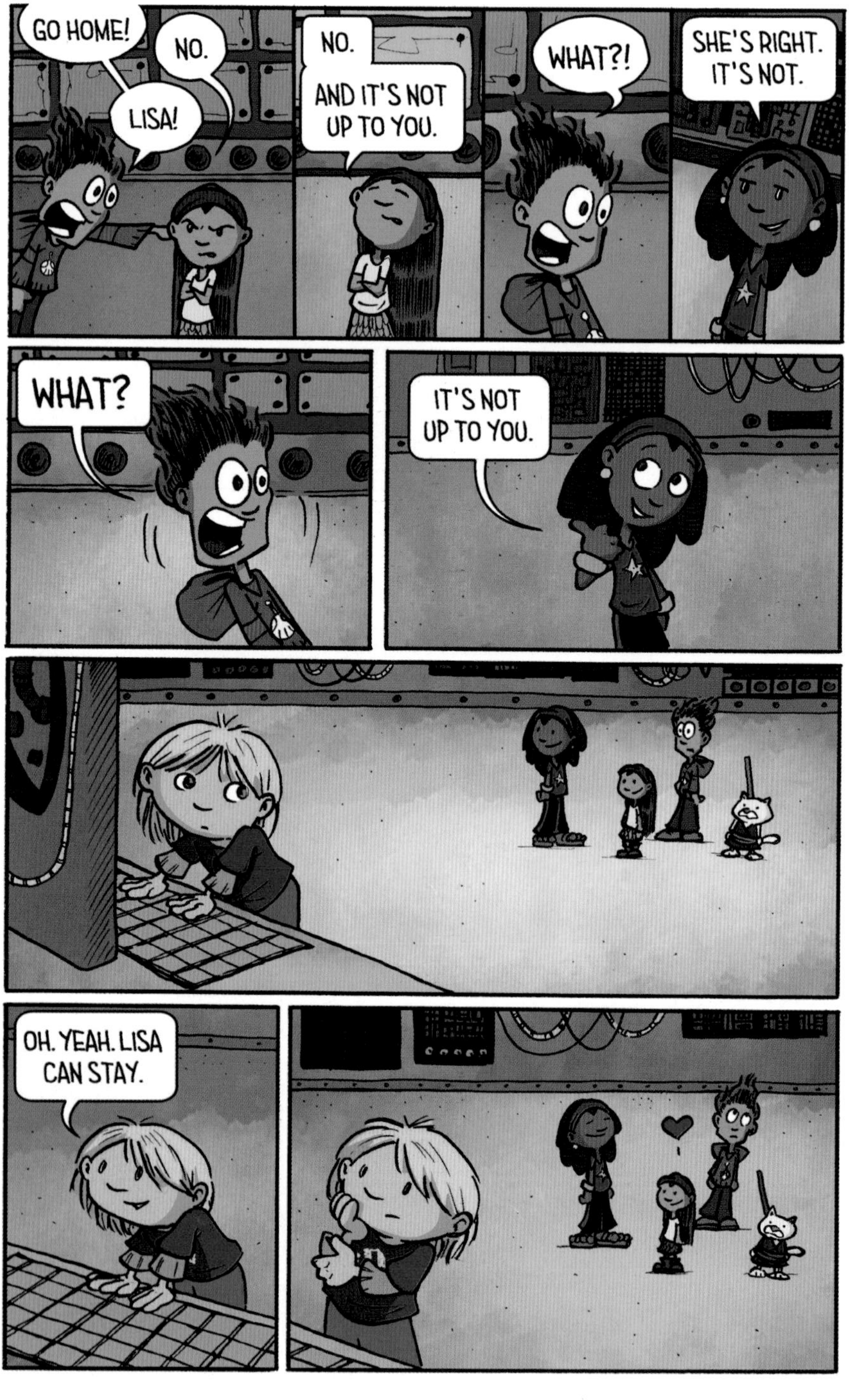
GO HOME!
LISA!
NO.
NO.
AND IT'S NOT UP TO YOU.
WHAT?!
SHE'S RIGHT. IT'S NOT.
WHAT?
IT'S NOT UP TO YOU.
OH. YEAH. LISA CAN STAY.

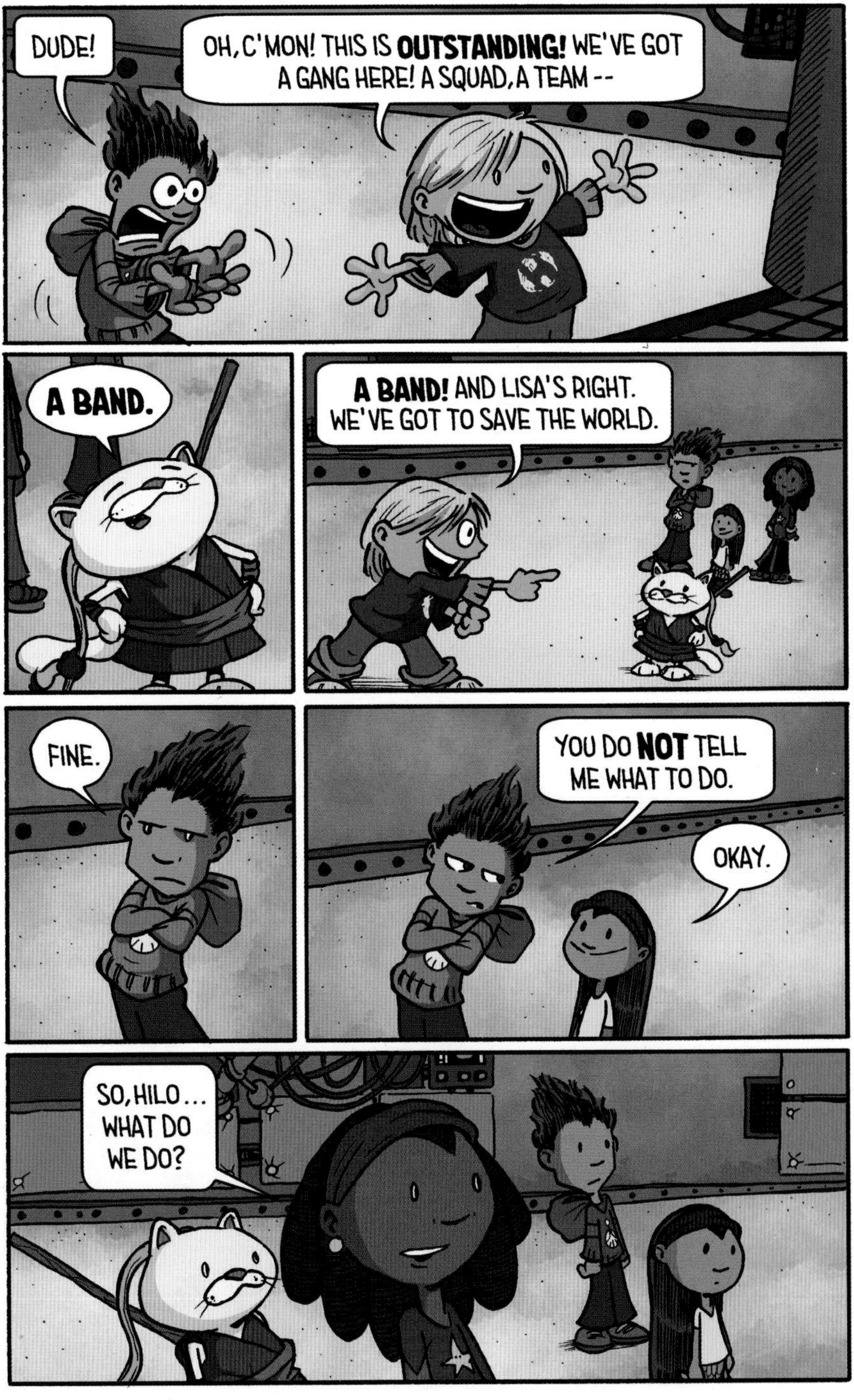
DUDE!
OH, C'MON! THIS IS **OUTSTANDING!** WE'VE GOT A GANG HERE! A SQUAD, A TEAM --
A BAND.
A BAND! AND LISA'S RIGHT. WE'VE GOT TO SAVE THE WORLD.
FINE.
YOU DO **NOT** TELL ME WHAT TO DO.
OKAY.
SO, HILO... WHAT DO WE DO?

CHAPTER 6

THE BAND

ZZZZZZ
ZZZZZ
DR. HORIZON ... WHEN DID THEY START MAKING ROBOTS?
ZZZZZ
158 YEARS AGO.

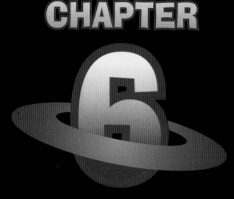

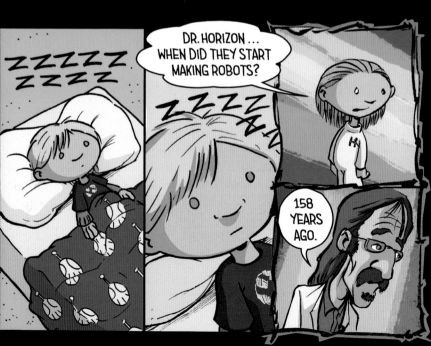

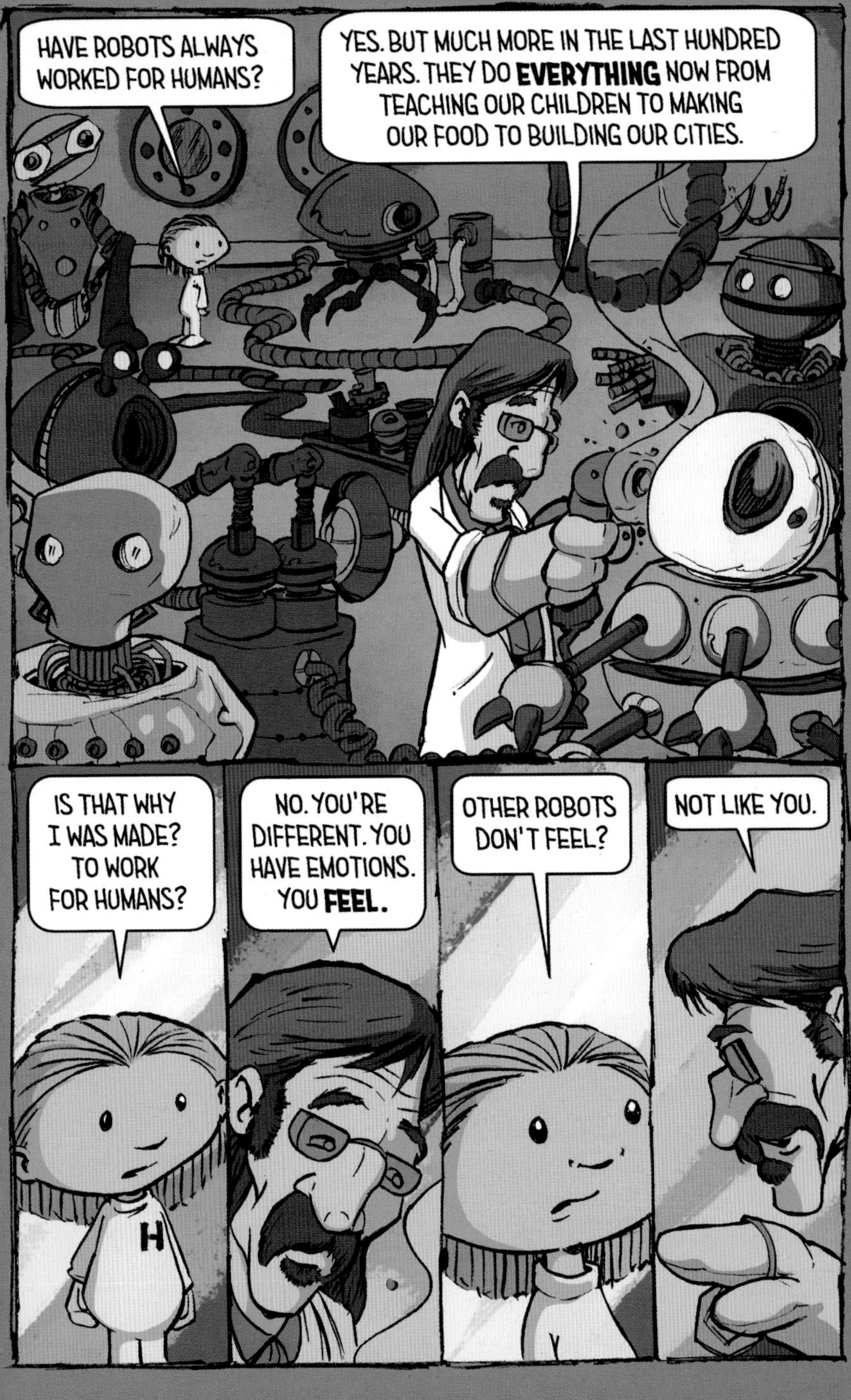
HAVE ROBOTS ALWAYS WORKED FOR HUMANS?
YES. BUT MUCH MORE IN THE LAST HUNDRED YEARS. THEY DO **EVERYTHING** NOW FROM TEACHING OUR CHILDREN TO MAKING OUR FOOD TO BUILDING OUR CITIES.
IS THAT WHY I WAS MADE? TO WORK FOR HUMANS?
NO. YOU'RE DIFFERENT. YOU HAVE EMOTIONS. YOU **FEEL.**
OTHER ROBOTS DON'T FEEL?
NOT LIKE YOU.
H

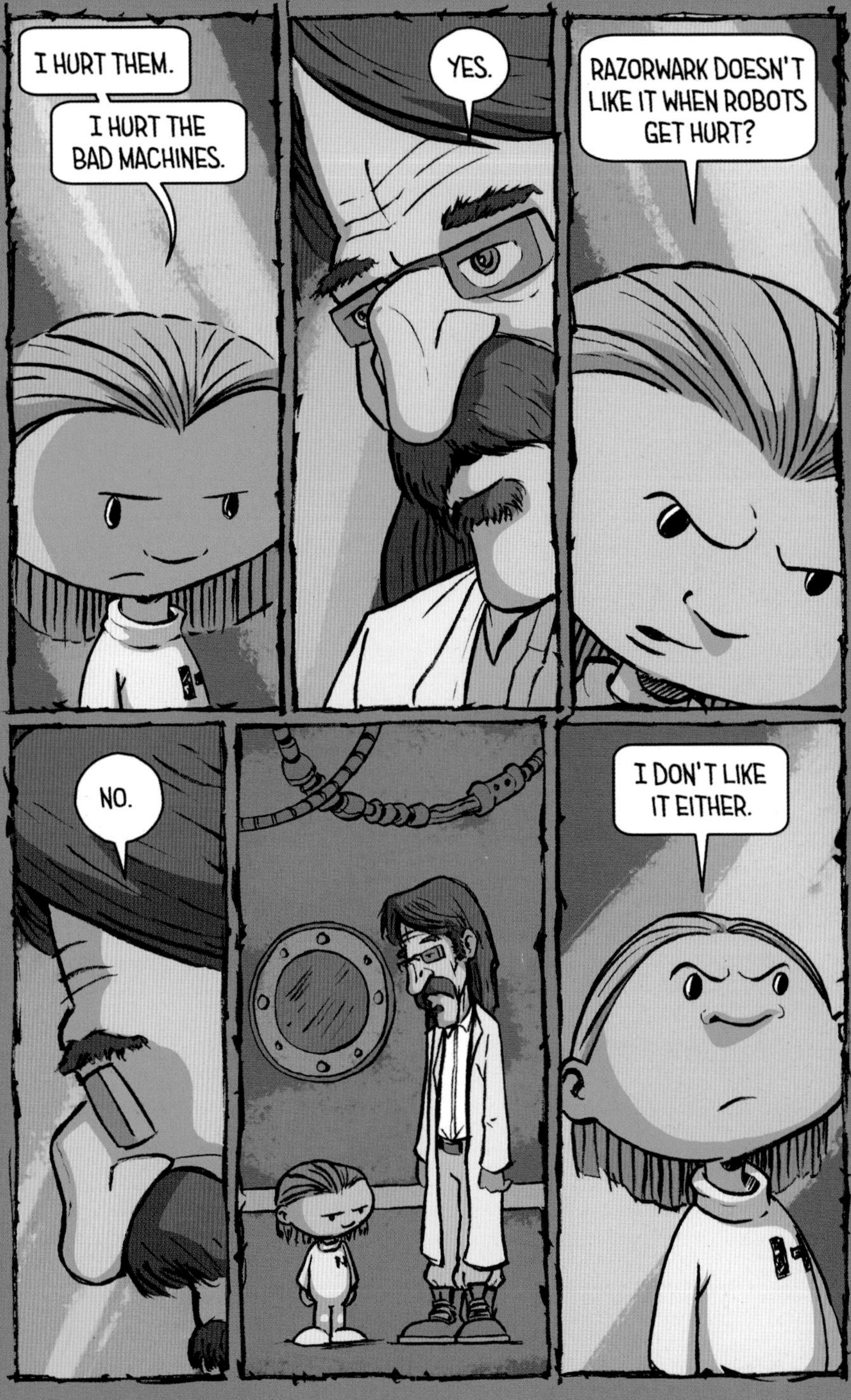
I HURT THEM.
I HURT THE BAD MACHINES.
YES.
RAZORWARK DOESN'T LIKE IT WHEN ROBOTS GET HURT?
NO.
I DON'T LIKE IT EITHER.

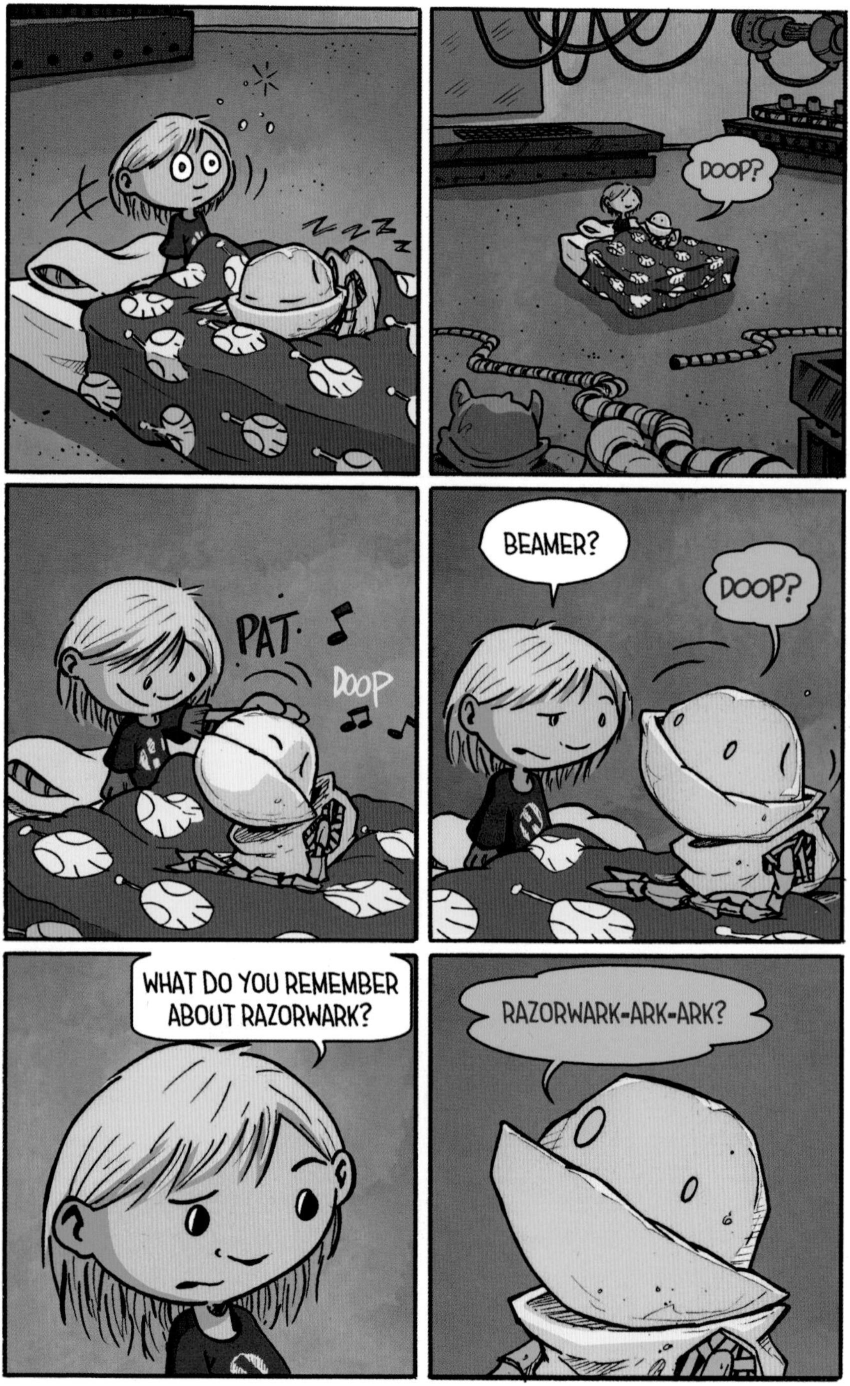
Z Z Z Z
DOOP?
PAT
DOOP
BEAMER?
DOOP?
WHAT DO YOU REMEMBER ABOUT RAZORWARK?
RAZORWARK-ARK-ARK?

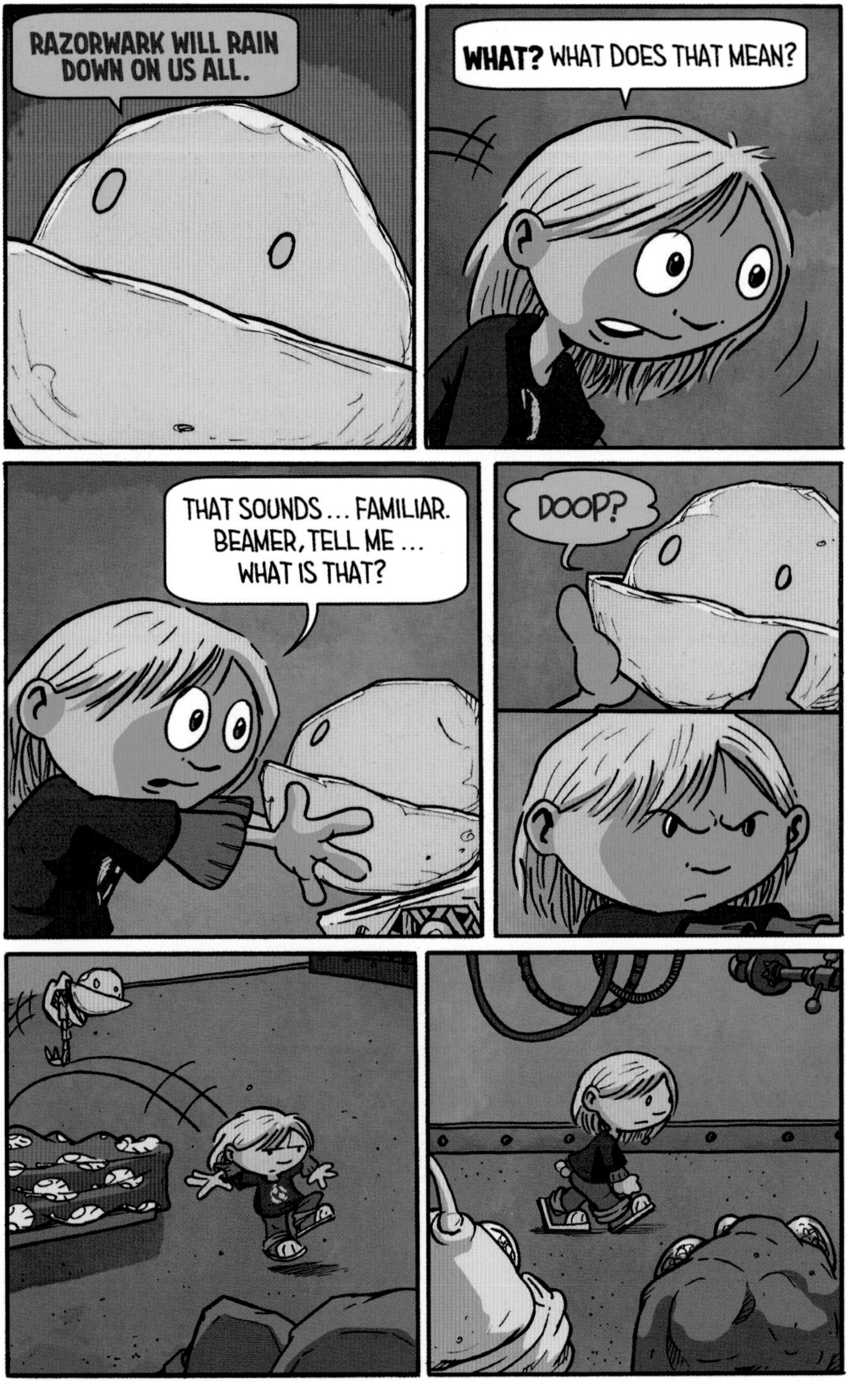
RAZORWARK WILL RAIN DOWN ON US ALL.
WHAT? WHAT DOES THAT MEAN?
THAT SOUNDS ... FAMILIAR. BEAMER, TELL ME ... WHAT IS THAT?
DOOP?

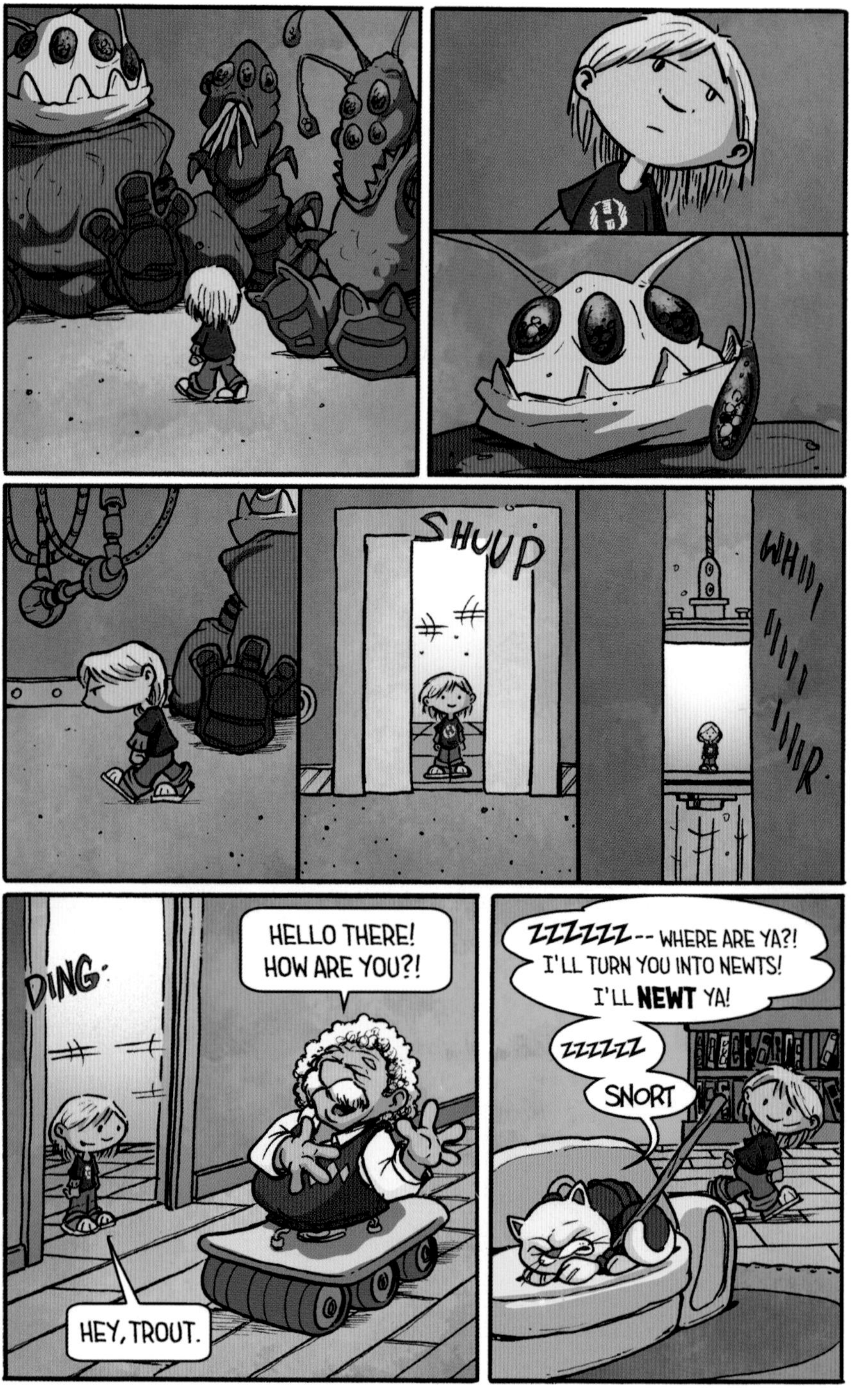

SHUUP
WHIIIIIIIIIIIR
DING
HELLO THERE! HOW ARE YOU?!
HEY, TROUT.
ZZZZZZ-- WHERE ARE YA?! I'LL TURN YOU INTO NEWTS! I'LL **NEWT** YA!
ZZZZZZ
SNORT

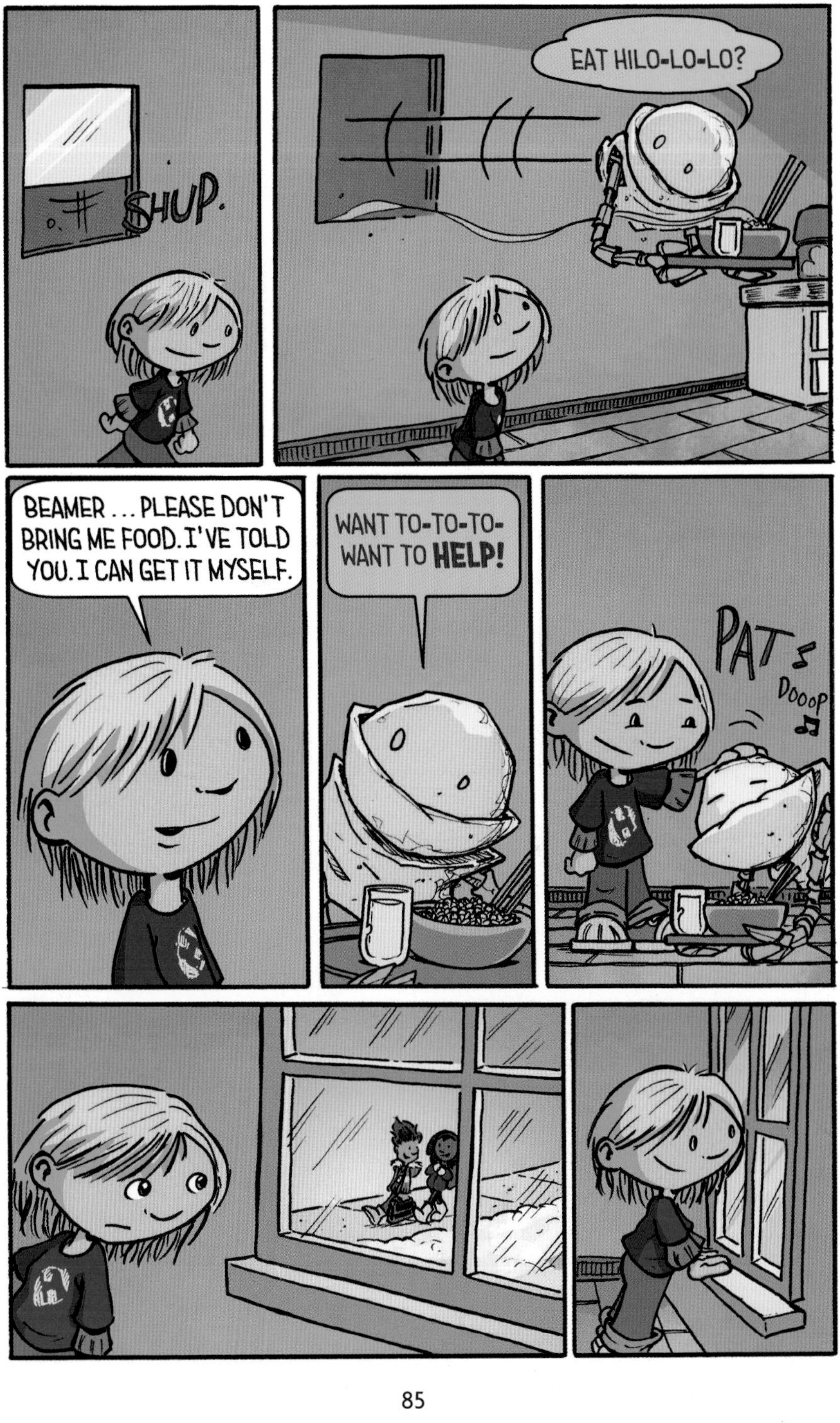
SHUP.
EAT HILO-LO-LO?
BEAMER . . . PLEASE DON'T BRING ME FOOD. I'VE TOLD YOU. I CAN GET IT MYSELF.
WANT TO-TO-TO-WANT TO **HELP!**
PAT
DOOOP

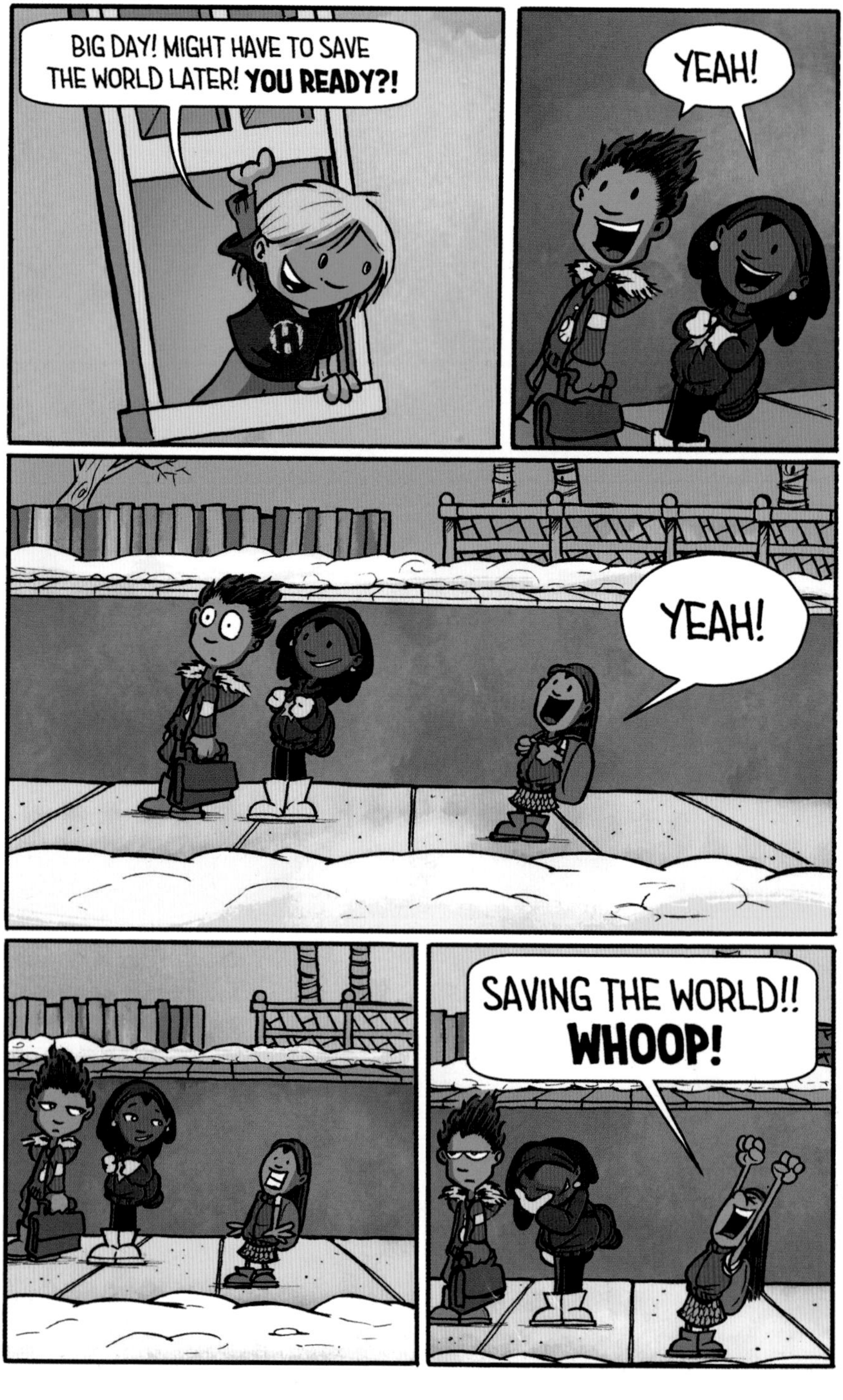
BIG DAY! MIGHT HAVE TO SAVE THE WORLD LATER! **YOU READY?!**
YEAH!
YEAH!
SAVING THE WORLD!! **WHOOP!**

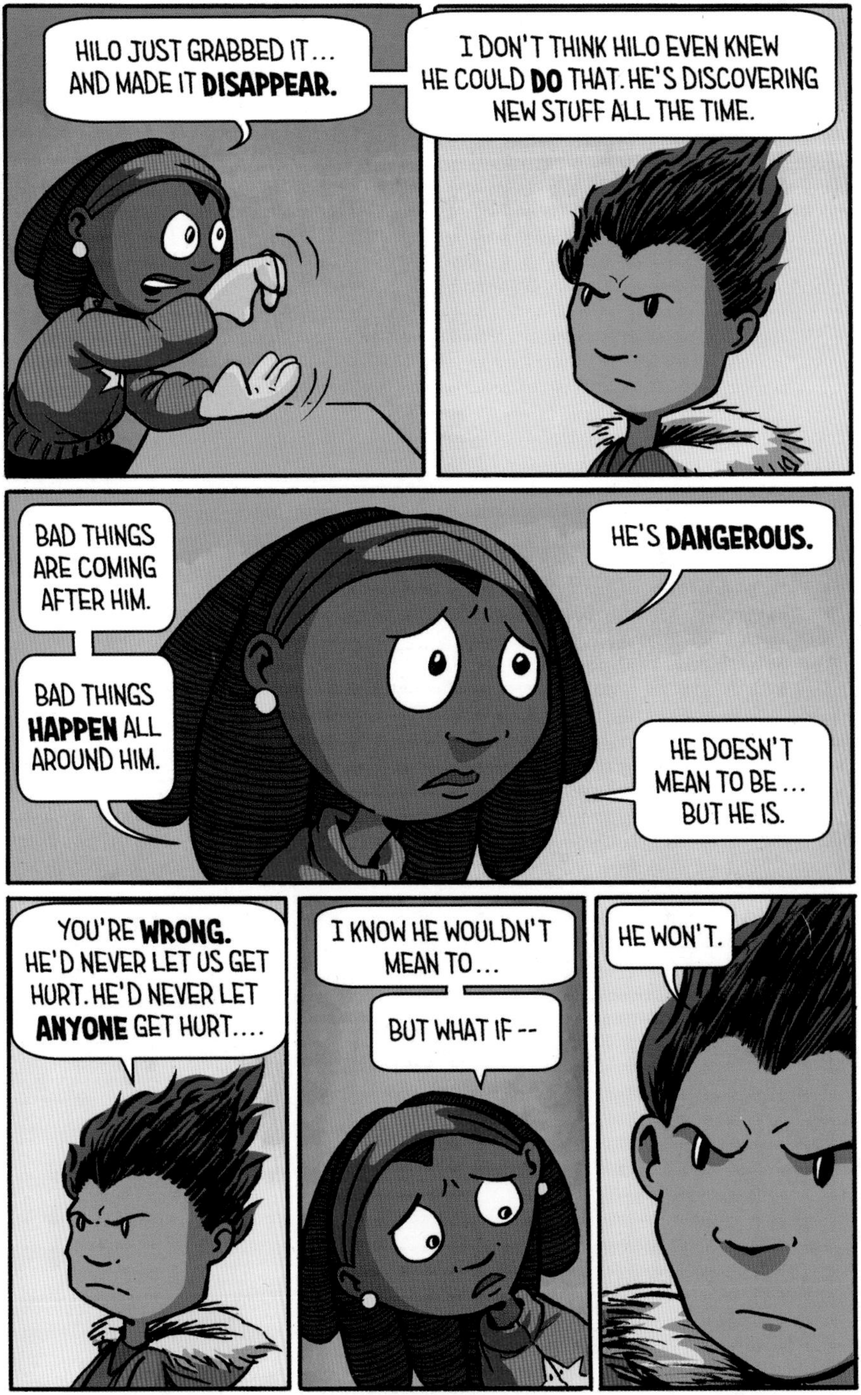
HILO JUST GRABBED IT... AND MADE IT **DISAPPEAR.**
I DON'T THINK HILO EVEN KNEW HE COULD **DO** THAT. HE'S DISCOVERING NEW STUFF ALL THE TIME.
BAD THINGS ARE COMING AFTER HIM.
BAD THINGS **HAPPEN** ALL AROUND HIM.
HE'S **DANGEROUS.**
HE DOESN'T MEAN TO BE... BUT HE IS.
YOU'RE **WRONG.** HE'D NEVER LET US GET HURT. HE'D NEVER LET **ANYONE** GET HURT....
I KNOW HE WOULDN'T MEAN TO...
BUT WHAT IF --
HE WON'T.

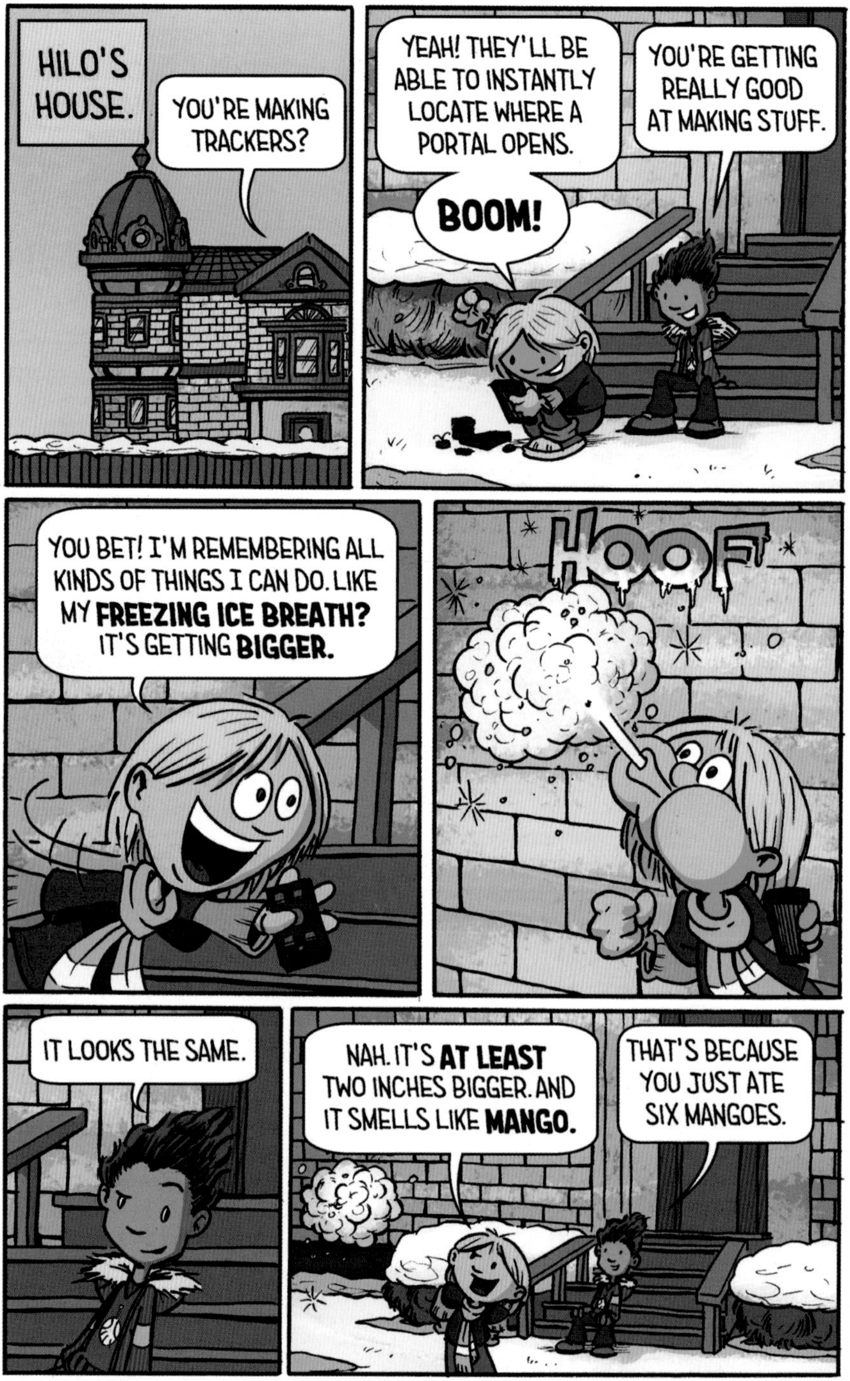
HILO'S HOUSE.
YOU'RE MAKING TRACKERS?
YEAH! THEY'LL BE ABLE TO INSTANTLY LOCATE WHERE A PORTAL OPENS.
BOOM!
YOU'RE GETTING REALLY GOOD AT MAKING STUFF.
YOU BET! I'M REMEMBERING ALL KINDS OF THINGS I CAN DO. LIKE MY **FREEZING ICE BREATH?** IT'S GETTING **BIGGER.**
HOOF
IT LOOKS THE SAME.
NAH. IT'S **AT LEAST** TWO INCHES BIGGER. AND IT SMELLS LIKE **MANGO.**
THAT'S BECAUSE YOU JUST ATE SIX MANGOES.

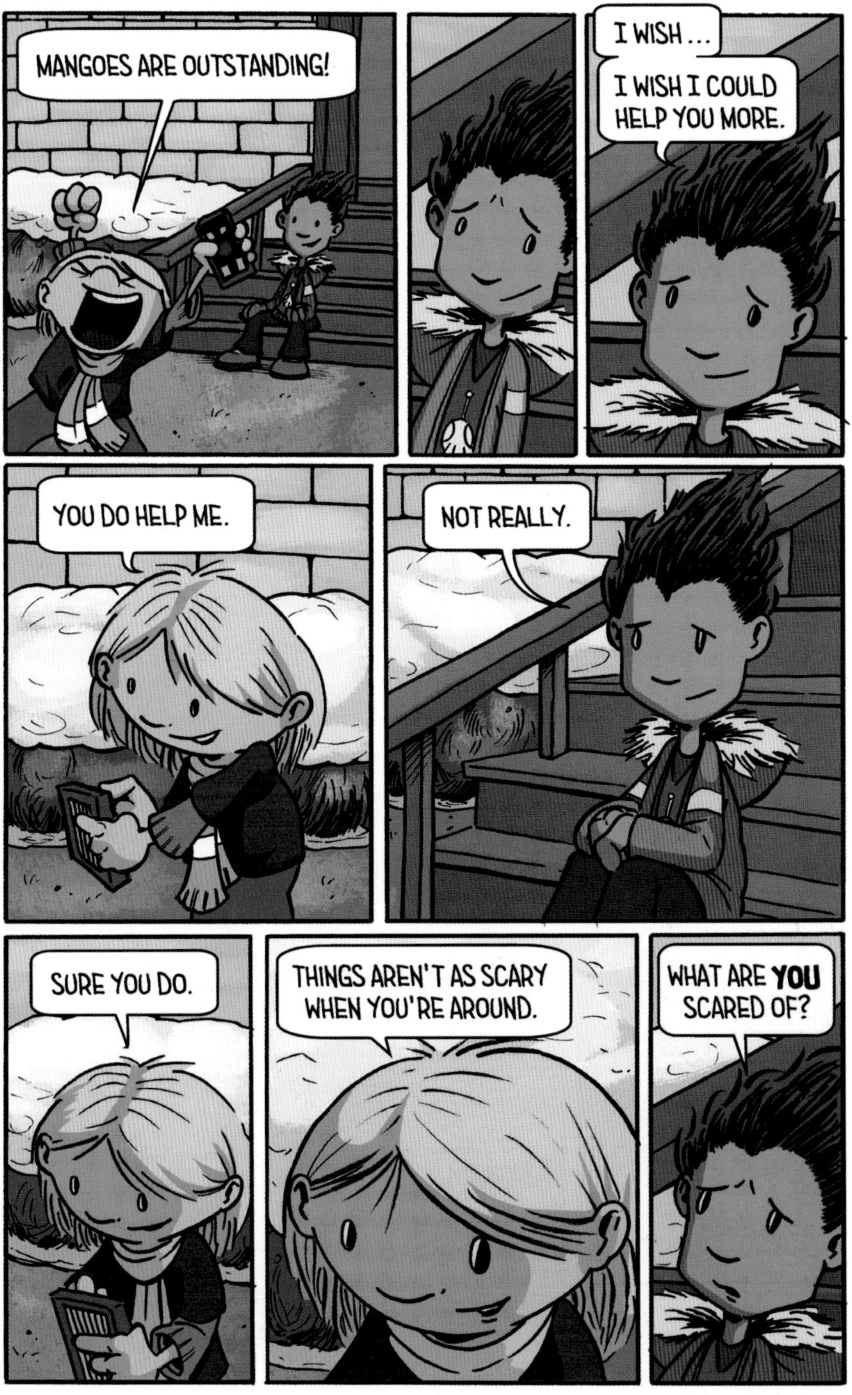
MANGOES ARE OUTSTANDING!
I WISH . . .
I WISH I COULD HELP YOU MORE.
YOU DO HELP ME.
NOT REALLY.
SURE YOU DO.
THINGS AREN'T AS SCARY WHEN YOU'RE AROUND.
WHAT ARE **YOU** SCARED OF?

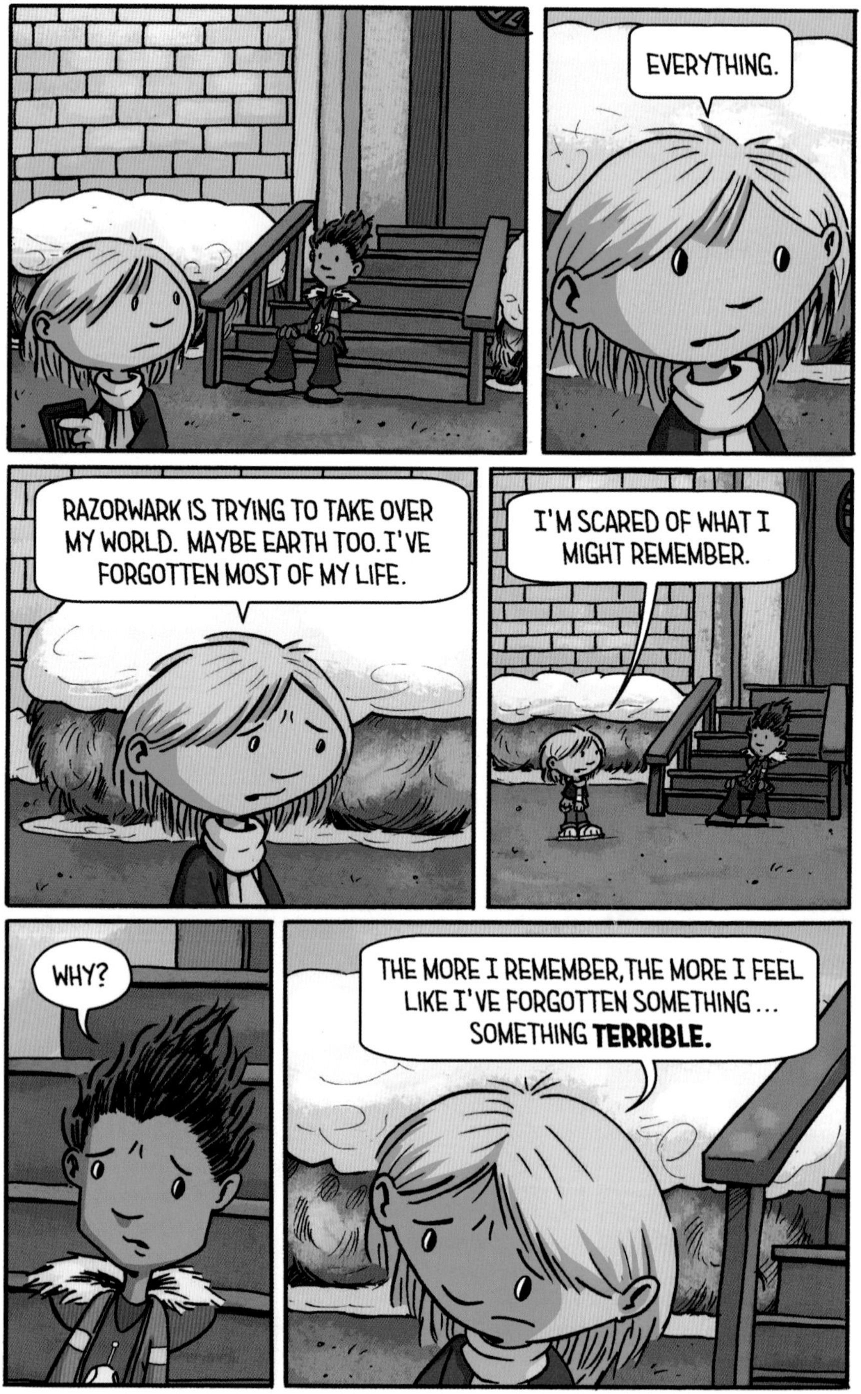
EVERYTHING.
RAZORWARK IS TRYING TO TAKE OVER MY WORLD. MAYBE EARTH TOO. I'VE FORGOTTEN MOST OF MY LIFE.
I'M SCARED OF WHAT I MIGHT REMEMBER.
WHY?
THE MORE I REMEMBER, THE MORE I FEEL LIKE I'VE FORGOTTEN SOMETHING... SOMETHING **TERRIBLE.**

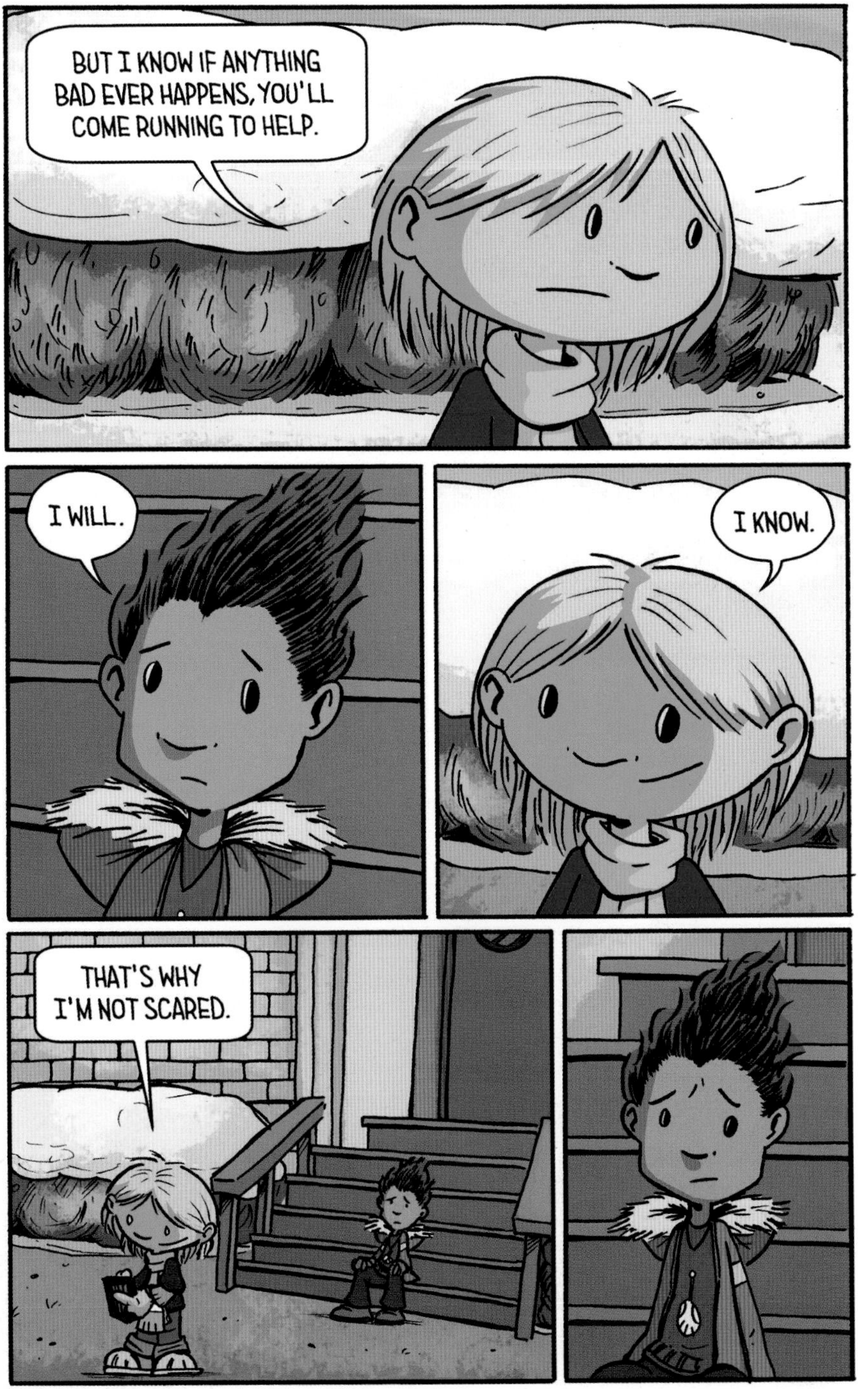

BUT I KNOW IF ANYTHING BAD EVER HAPPENS, YOU'LL COME RUNNING TO HELP.
I WILL.
I KNOW.
THAT'S WHY I'M NOT SCARED.

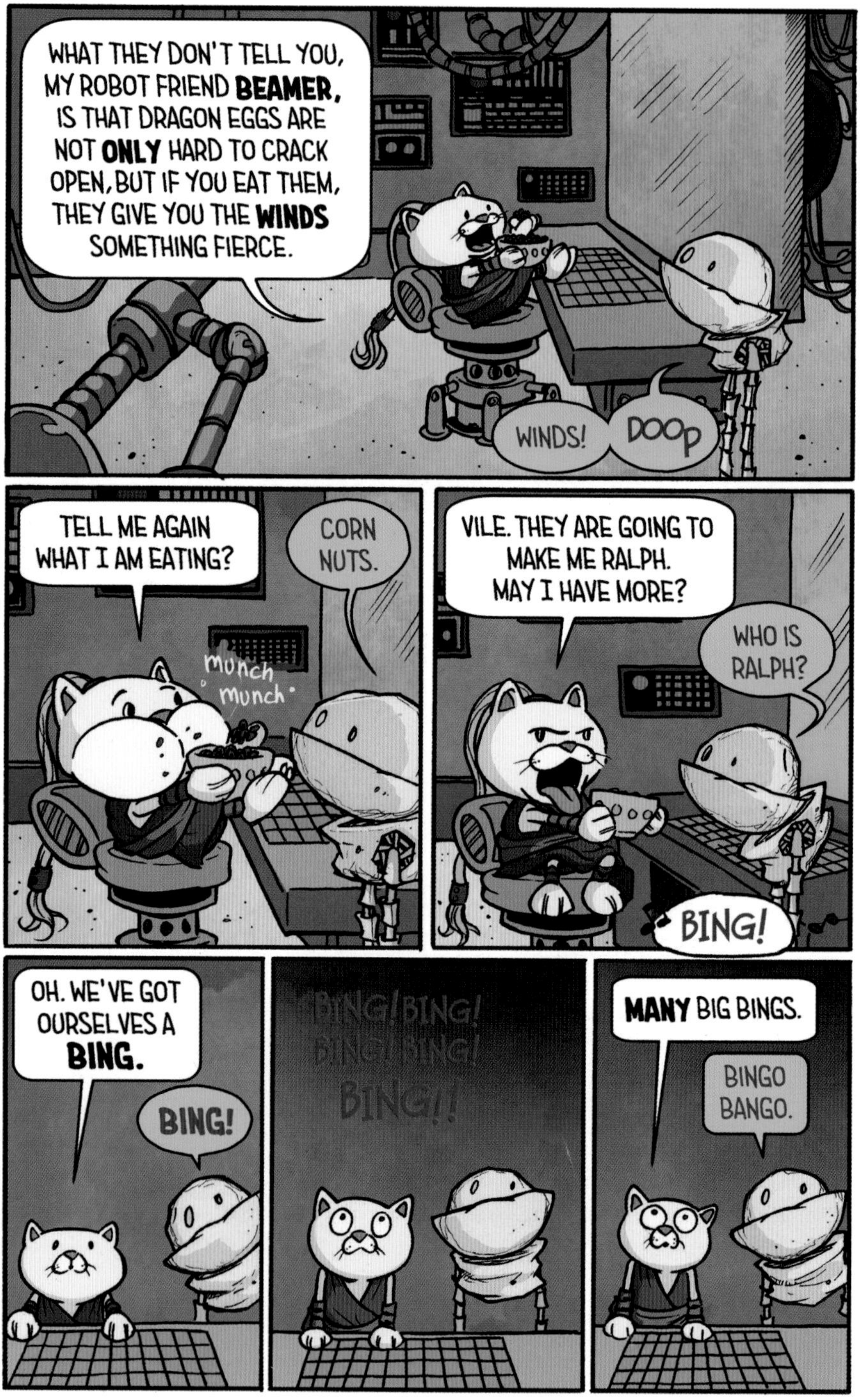
WHAT THEY DON'T TELL YOU, MY ROBOT FRIEND **BEAMER**, IS THAT DRAGON EGGS ARE NOT **ONLY** HARD TO CRACK OPEN, BUT IF YOU EAT THEM, THEY GIVE YOU THE **WINDS** SOMETHING FIERCE.
WINDS!
DOOp
TELL ME AGAIN WHAT I AM EATING?
CORN NUTS.
munch munch
VILE. THEY ARE GOING TO MAKE ME RALPH. MAY I HAVE MORE?
WHO IS RALPH?
BING!
OH. WE'VE GOT OURSELVES A **BING.**
BING!
BING! BING! BING! BING! BING!!
MANY BIG BINGS.
BINGO BANGO.

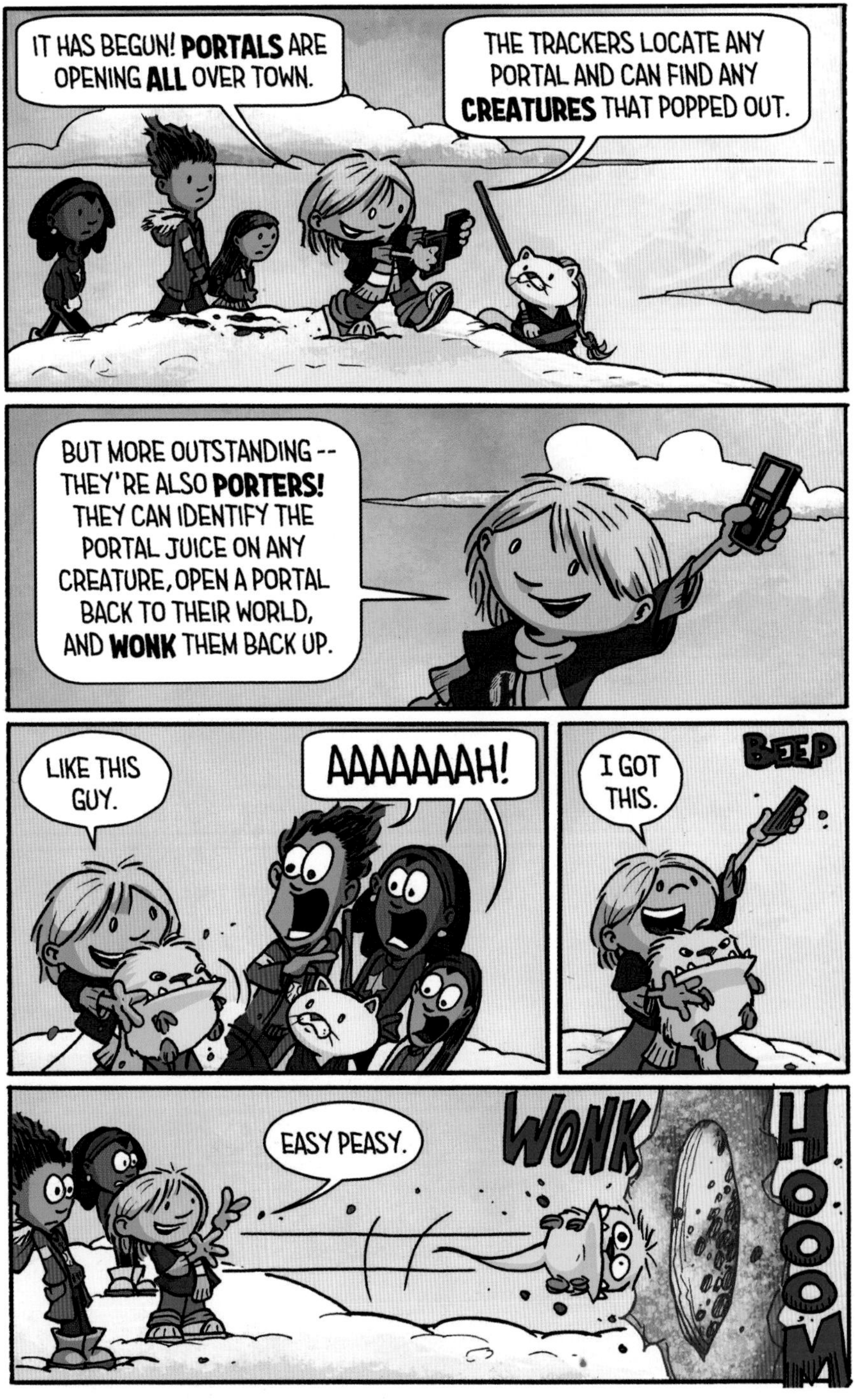
IT HAS BEGUN! PORTALS ARE OPENING ALL OVER TOWN.
THE TRACKERS LOCATE ANY PORTAL AND CAN FIND ANY CREATURES THAT POPPED OUT.
BUT MORE OUTSTANDING -- THEY'RE ALSO PORTERS! THEY CAN IDENTIFY THE PORTAL JUICE ON ANY CREATURE, OPEN A PORTAL BACK TO THEIR WORLD, AND WONK THEM BACK UP.
LIKE THIS GUY.
AAAAAAAH!
I GOT THIS.
BEEP
EASY PEASY.
WONK
HOOOM

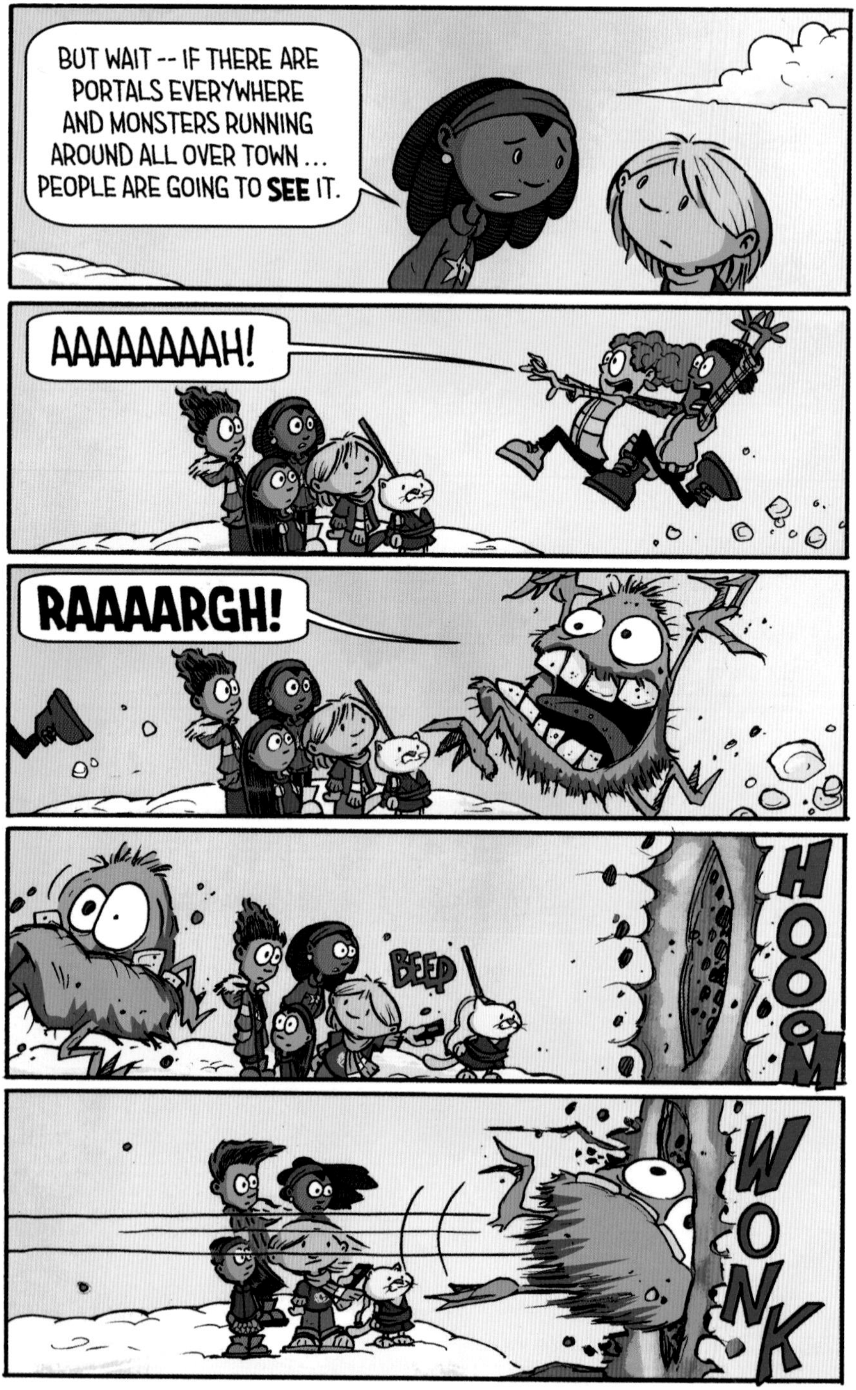
BUT WAIT -- IF THERE ARE PORTALS EVERYWHERE AND MONSTERS RUNNING AROUND ALL OVER TOWN ... PEOPLE ARE GOING TO **SEE** IT.
AAAAAAAAH!
RAAAARGH!
BEEP
THOOOM
WONK

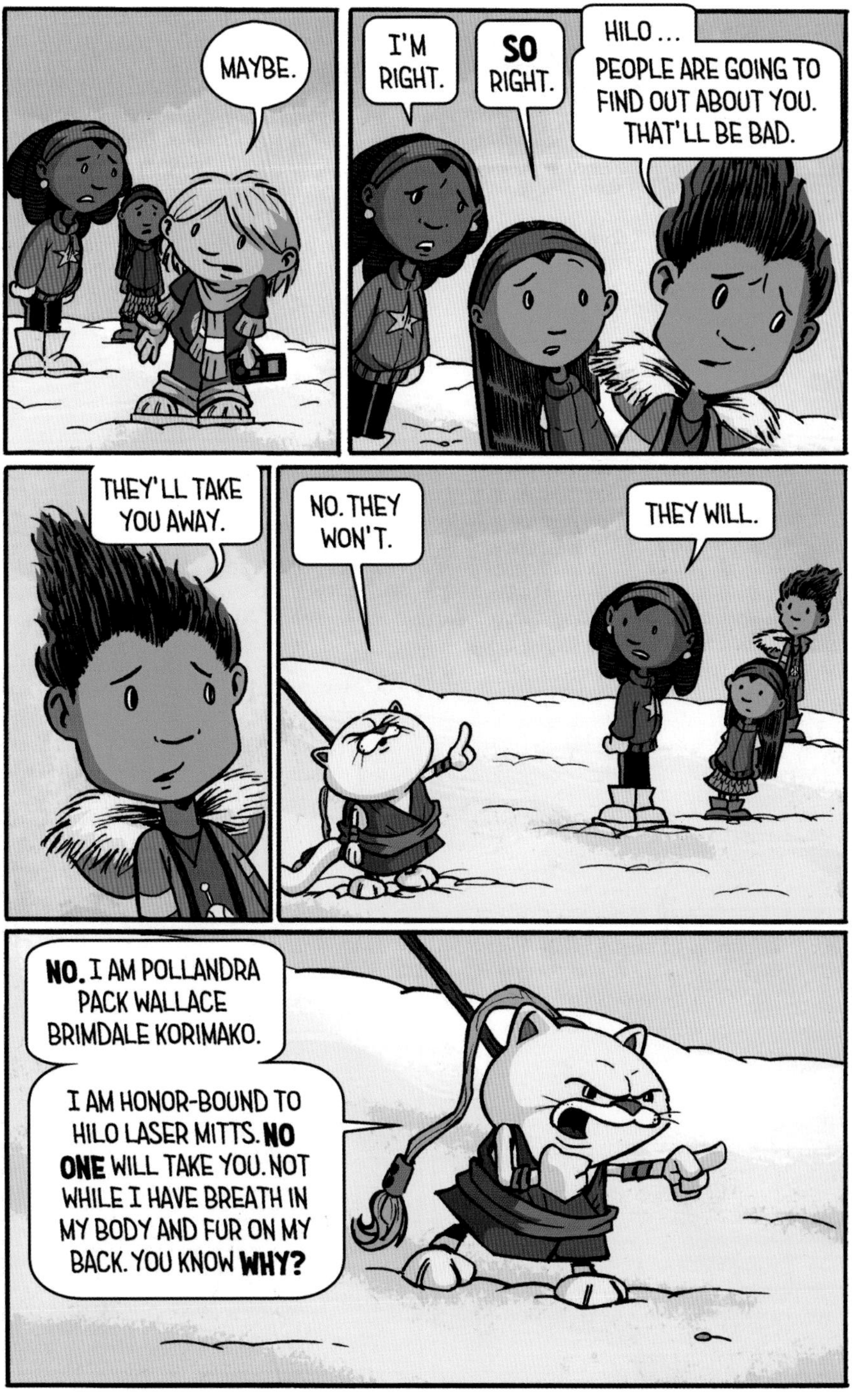

MAYBE.
I'M RIGHT.
SO RIGHT.
HILO ...
PEOPLE ARE GOING TO FIND OUT ABOUT YOU. THAT'LL BE BAD.
THEY'LL TAKE YOU AWAY.
NO. THEY WON'T.
THEY WILL.
NO. I AM POLLANDRA PACK WALLACE BRIMDALE KORIMAKO.
I AM HONOR-BOUND TO HILO LASER MITTS. **NO ONE** WILL TAKE YOU. NOT WHILE I HAVE BREATH IN MY BODY AND FUR ON MY BACK. YOU KNOW **WHY?**

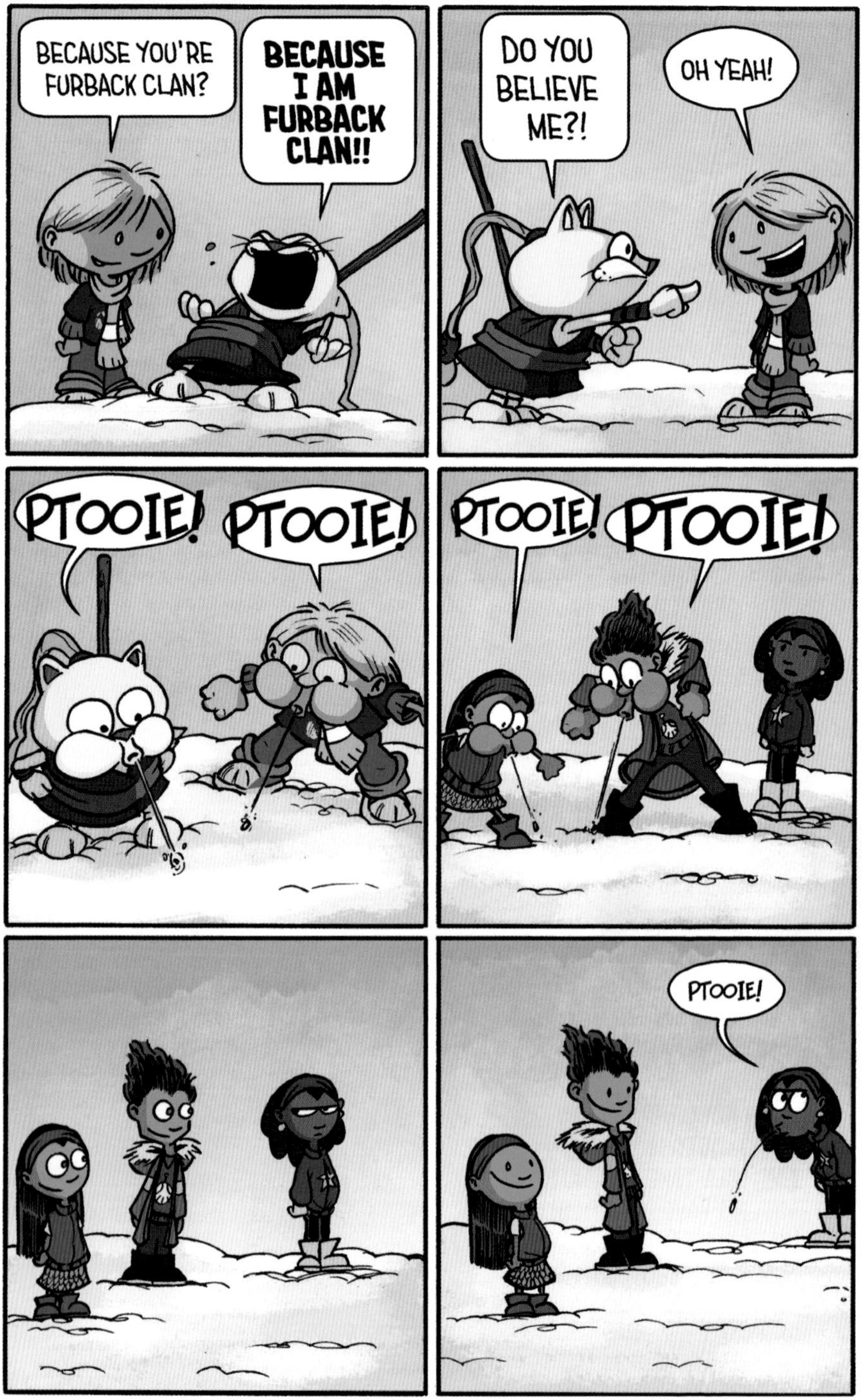
BECAUSE YOU'RE FURBACK CLAN?
BECAUSE I AM FURBACK CLAN!!
DO YOU BELIEVE ME?!
OH YEAH!
PTOOIE!
PTOOIE!
PTOOIE!
PTOOIE!
PTOOIE!

100

CHAPTER 7

BING

103

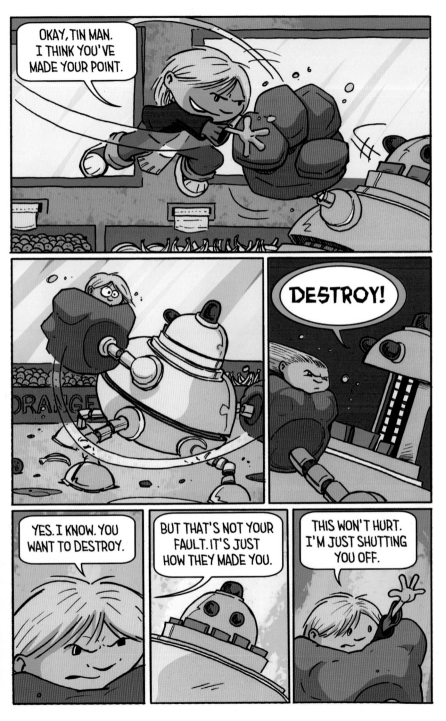

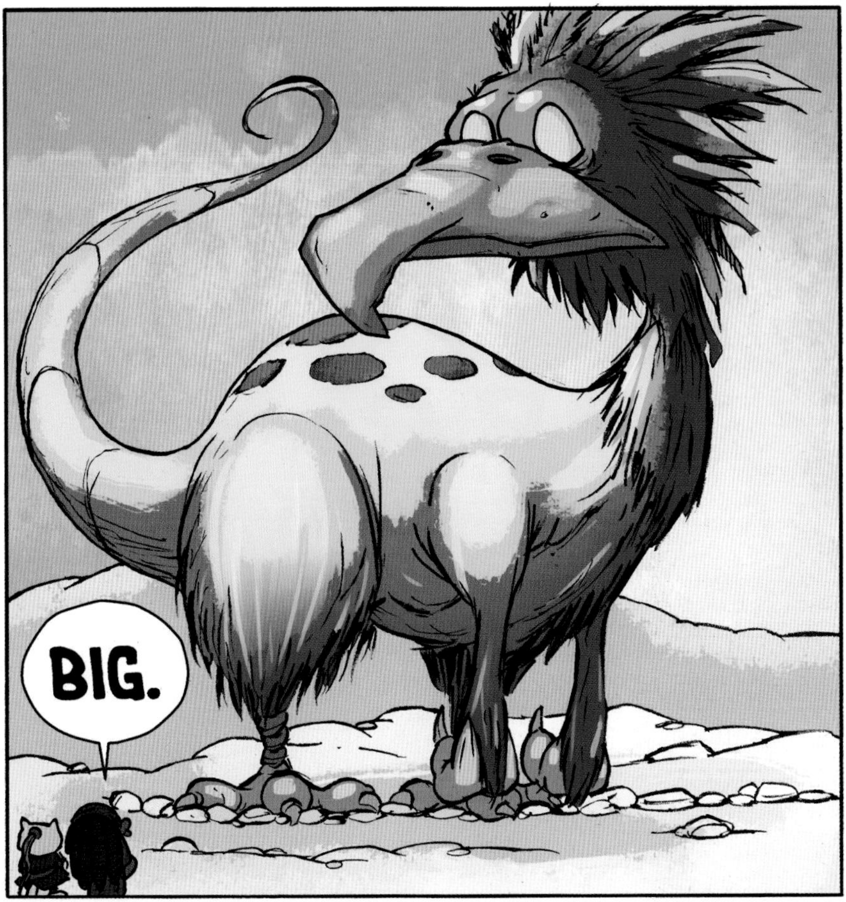
BIG.

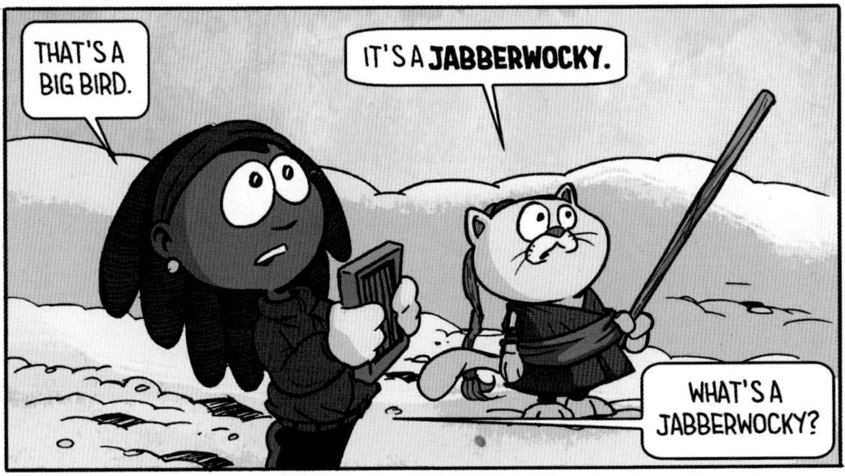
THAT'S A BIG BIRD.
IT'S A JABBERWOCKY.
WHAT'S A JABBERWOCKY?

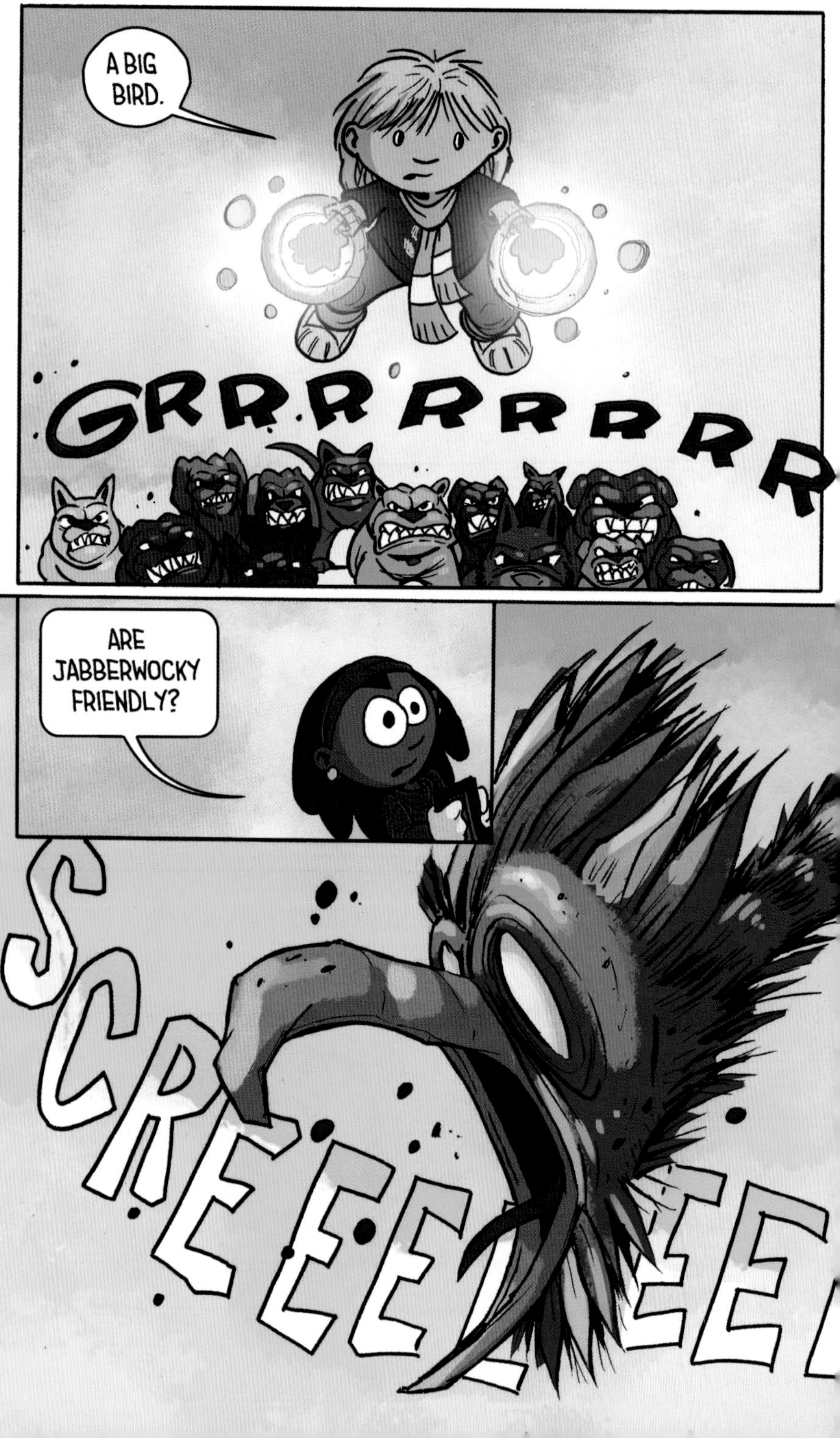
A BIG BIRD.
GRRRRRRRRR
ARE JABBERWOCKY FRIENDLY?
SCREEEEEEEE

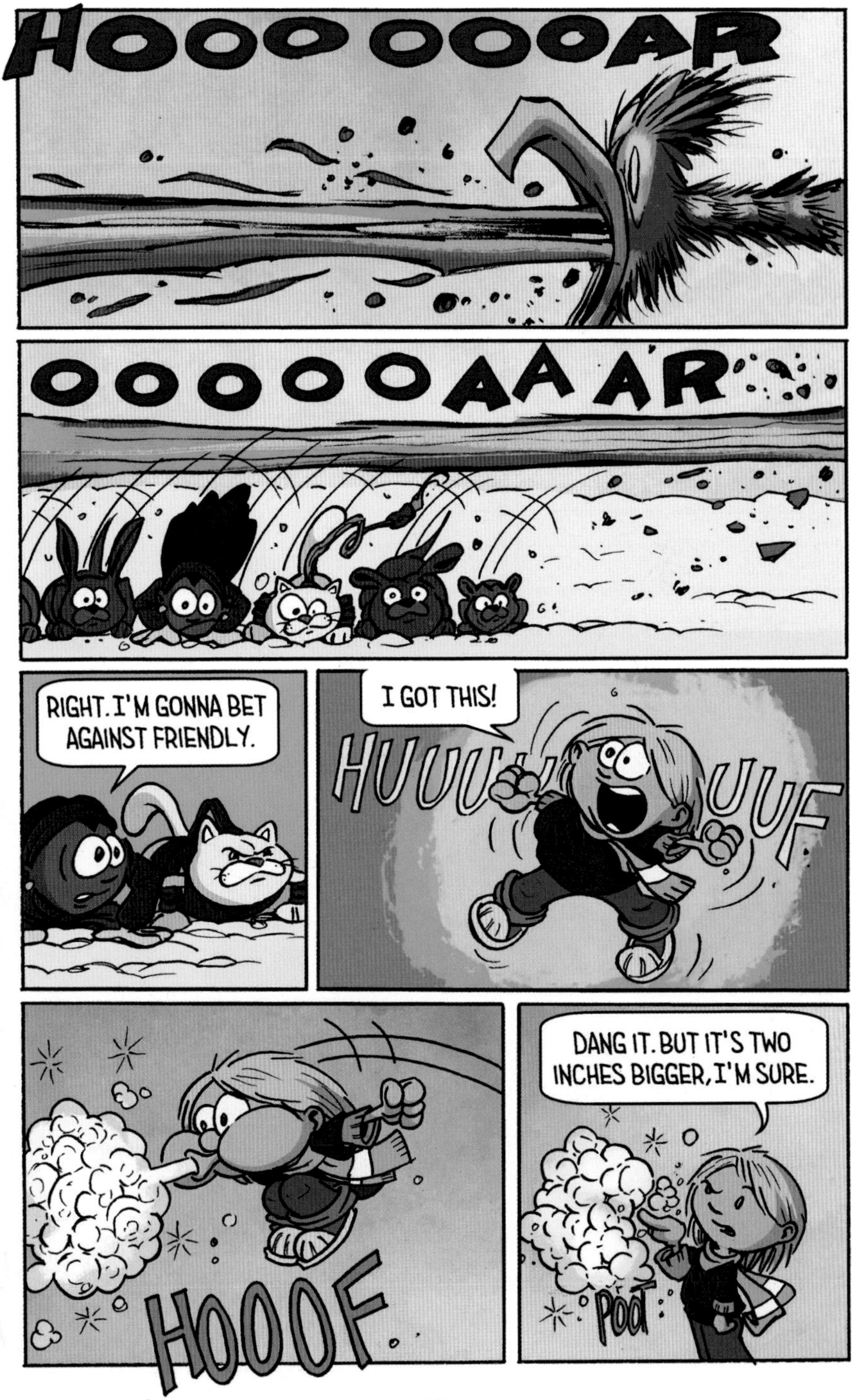
HOOOOOOOAR
OOOOOAAAR
RIGHT. I'M GONNA BET AGAINST FRIENDLY.
I GOT THIS!
HUUUUUUF
HOOOF
DANG IT. BUT IT'S TWO INCHES BIGGER, I'M SURE.
POOT

116

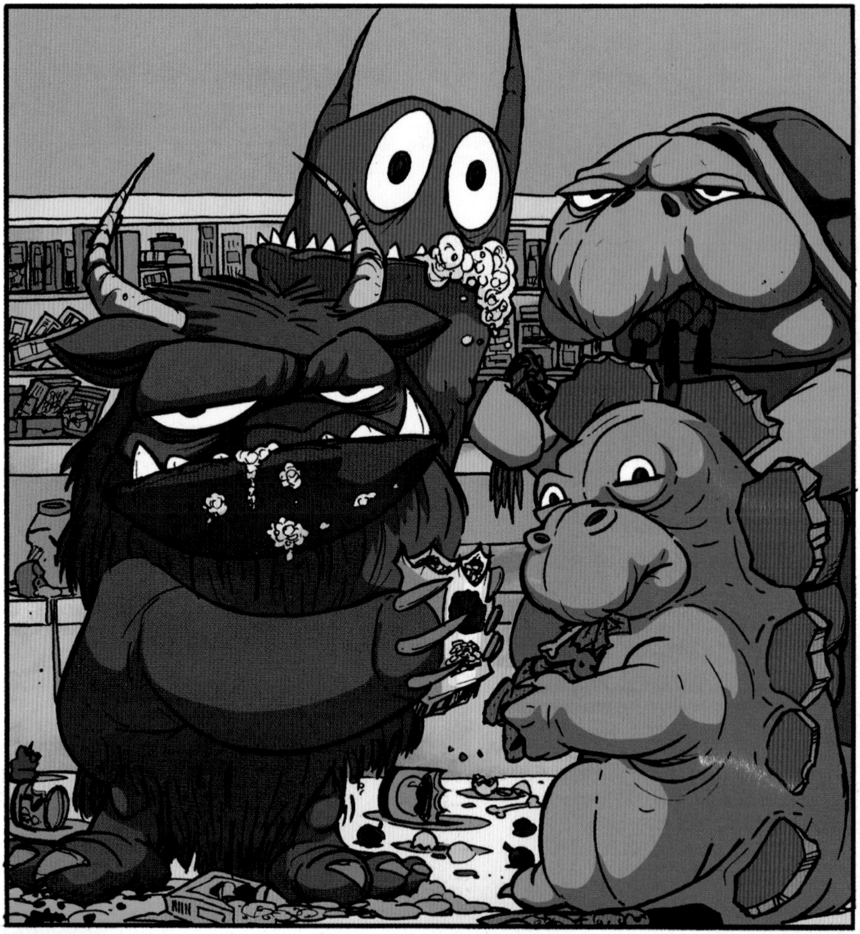

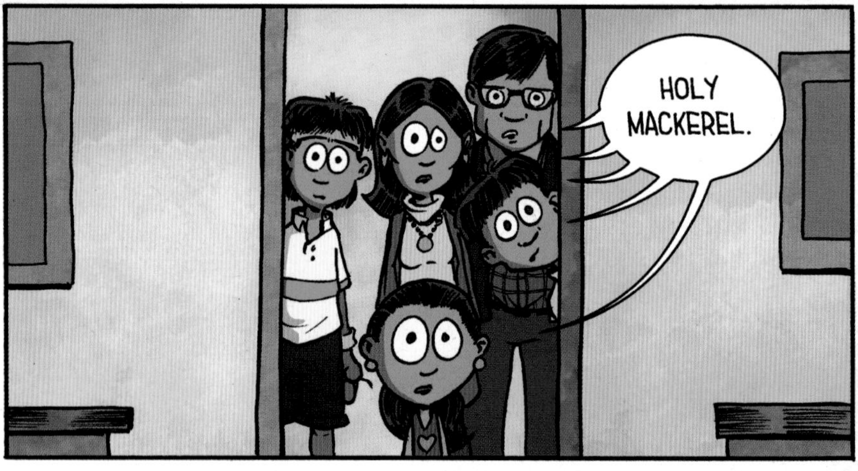
HOLY MACKEREL.

CHAPTER 8

BRAVE BOY

DEXTER, THESE AREN'T THE GUYS FROM YOUR BAND ARE THEY?
NO.
MAYBE THEY'RE FRIENDLY.

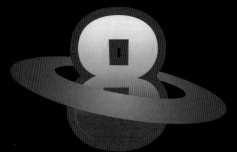

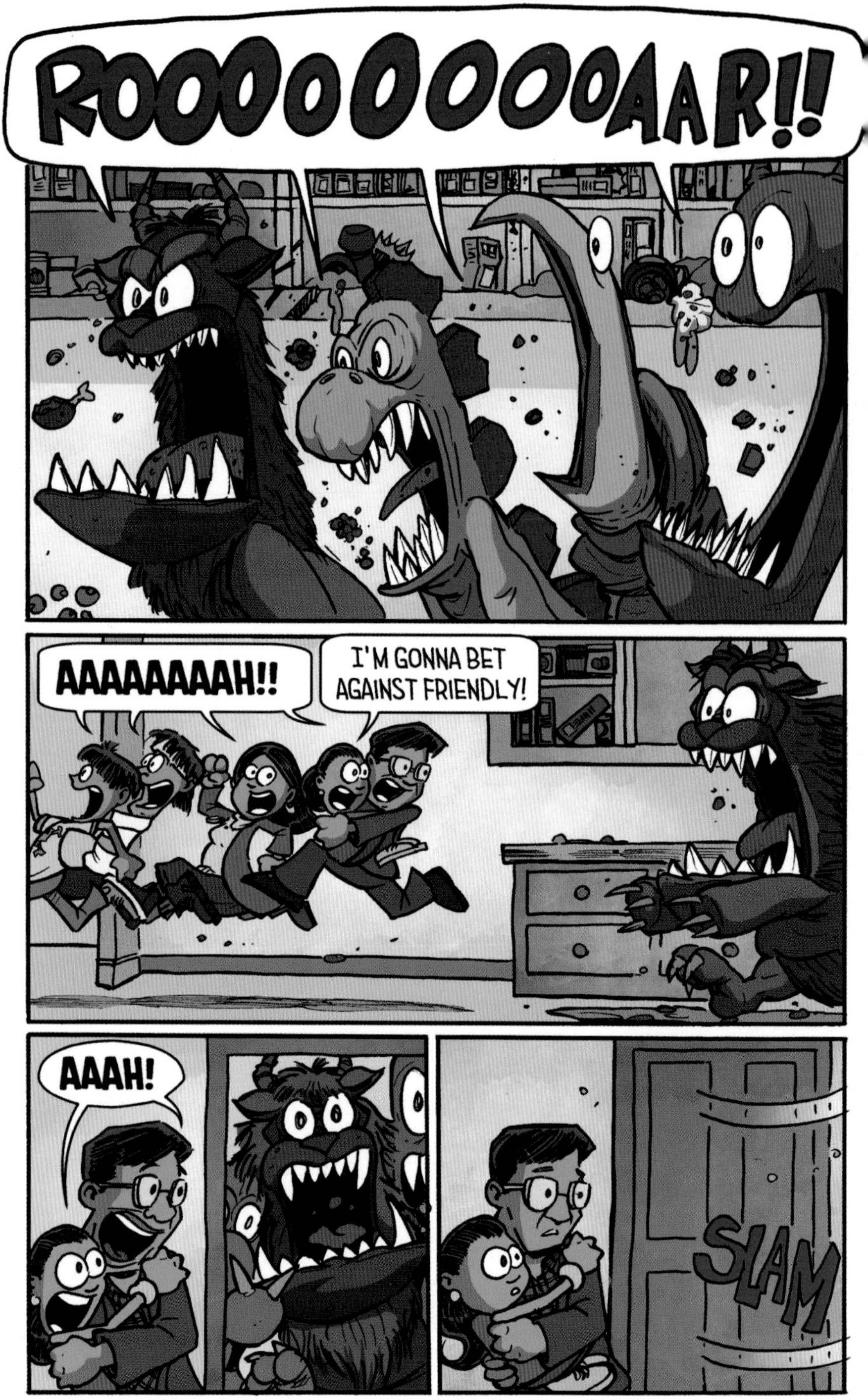
ROOOOOOOOOAAR!!
AAAAAAAAH!!
I'M GONNA BET AGAINST FRIENDLY!
AAAH!
SLAM

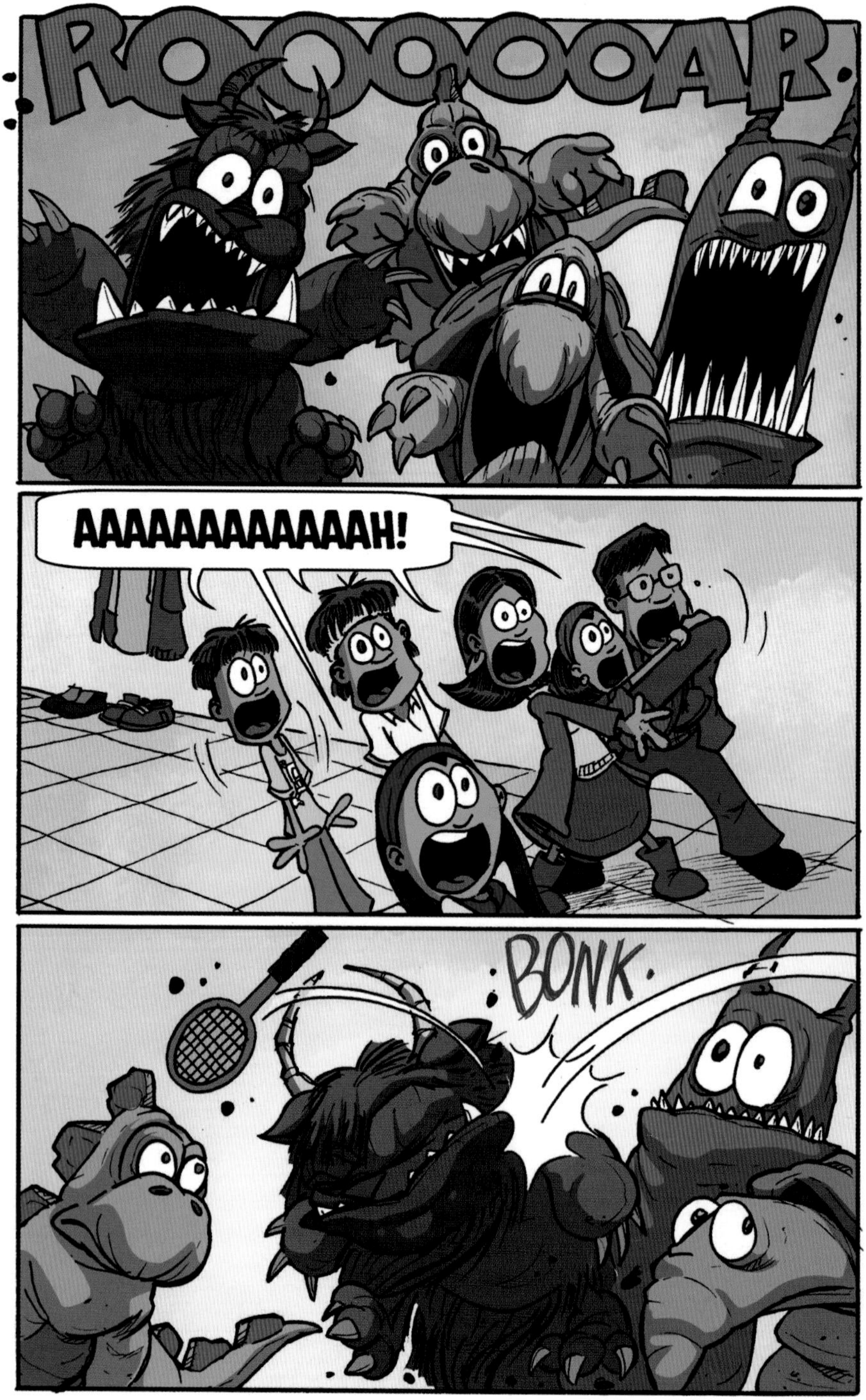
ROOOOOOAR
AAAAAAAAAAAAH!
BONK

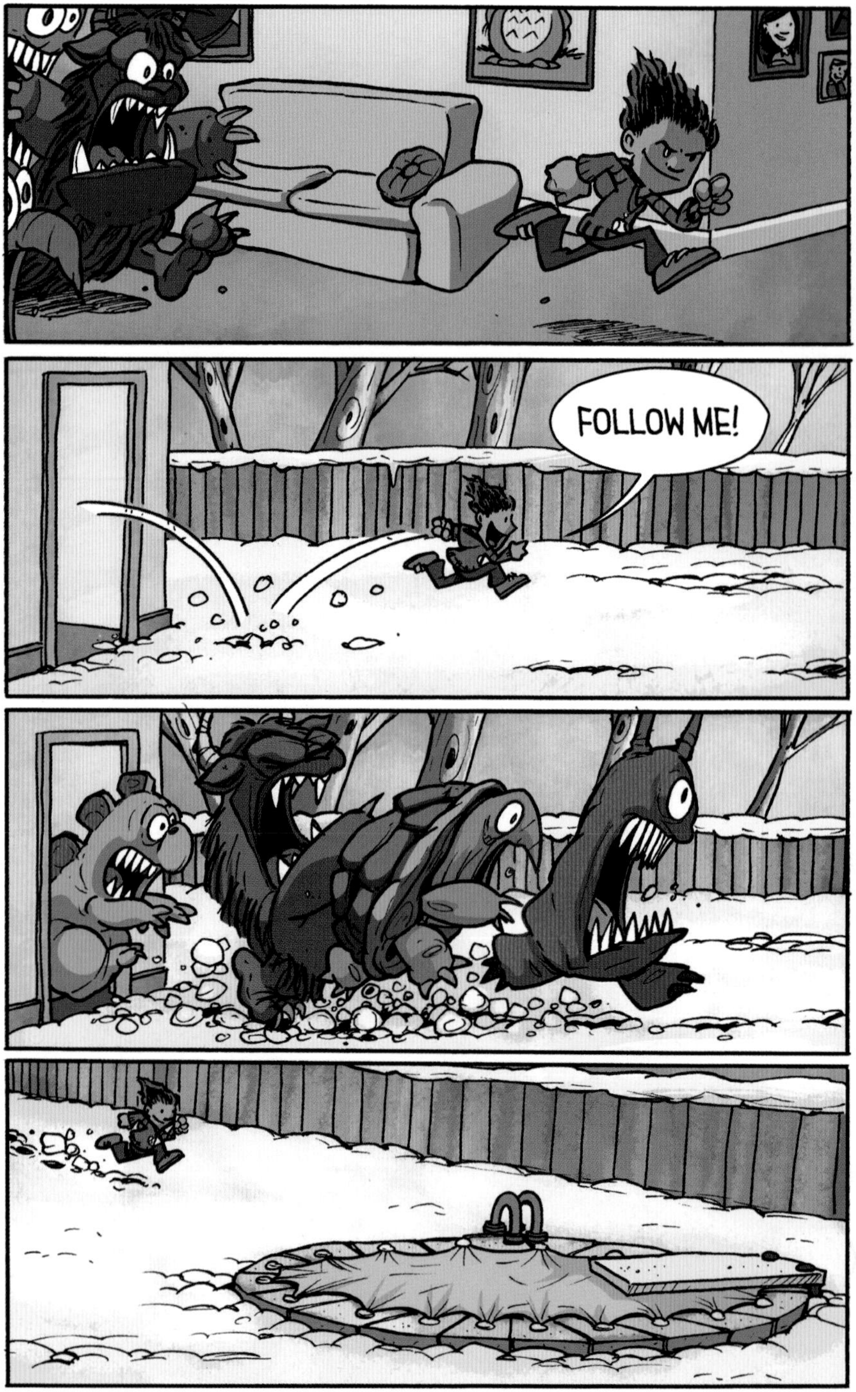
FOLLOW ME!

129

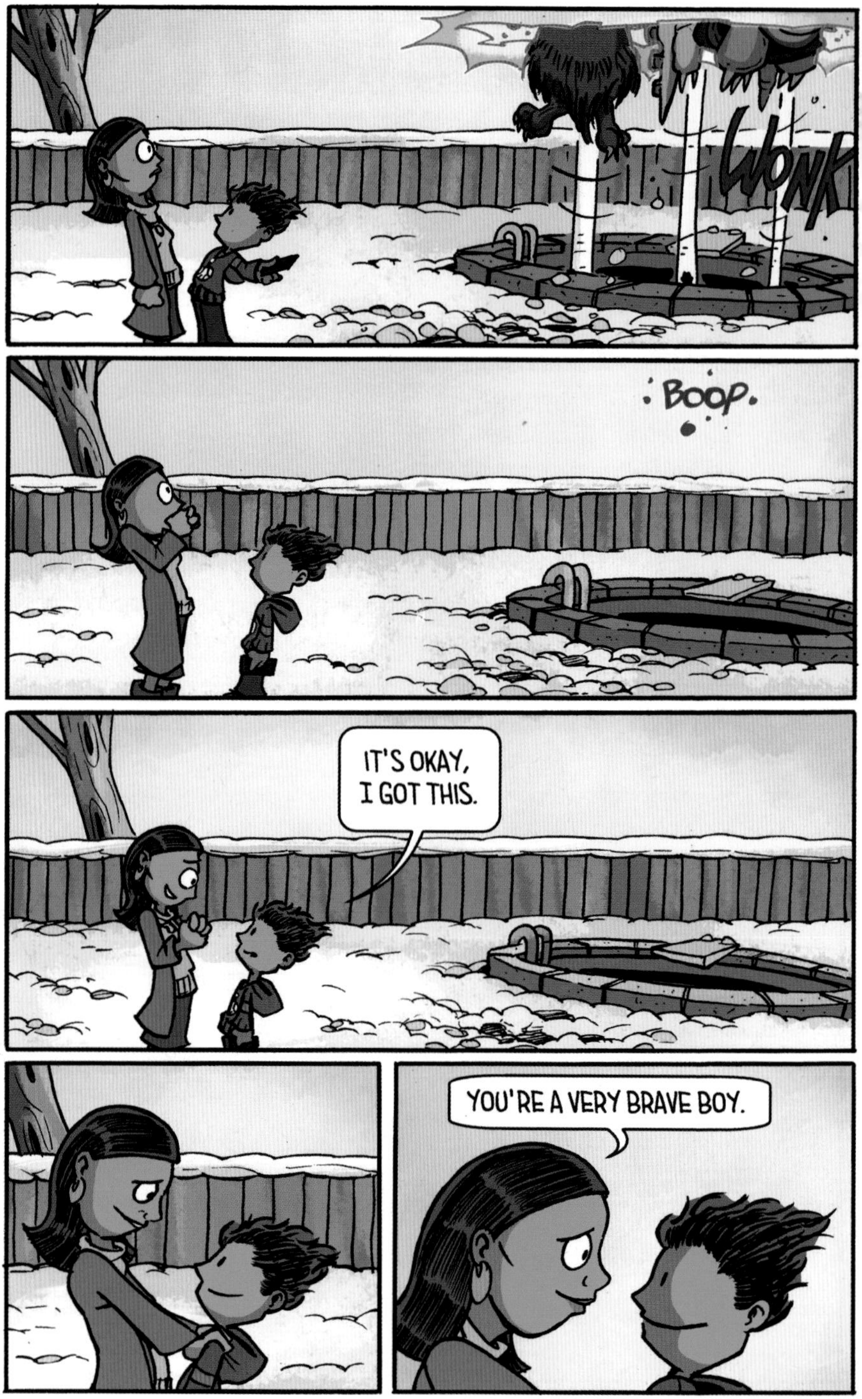
WONK
BOOP
IT'S OKAY, I GOT THIS.
YOU'RE A VERY BRAVE BOY.

133

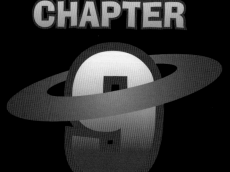

CHAPTER 9

VEGGIES

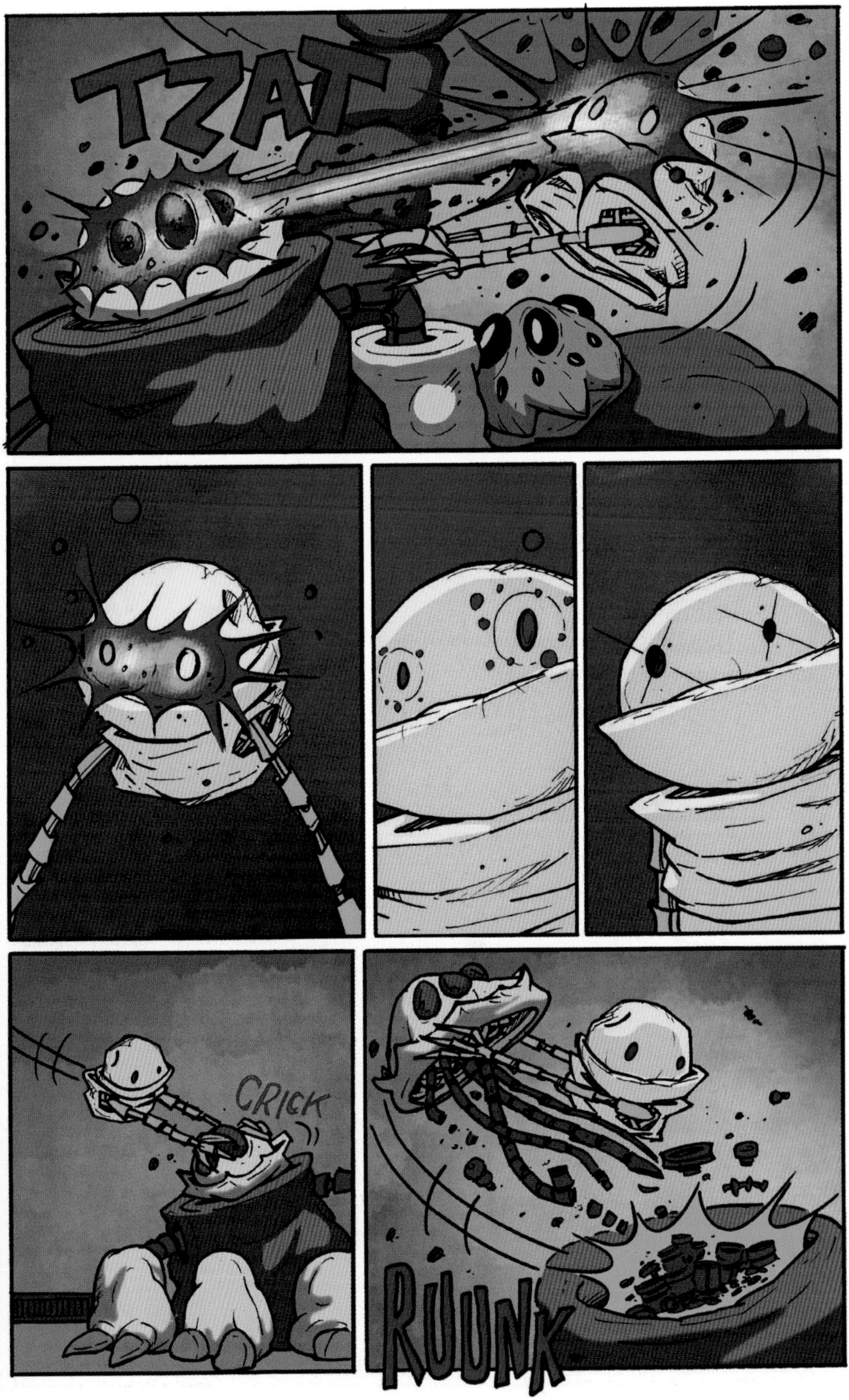
TZAT
CRICK
RUUNK

142

143

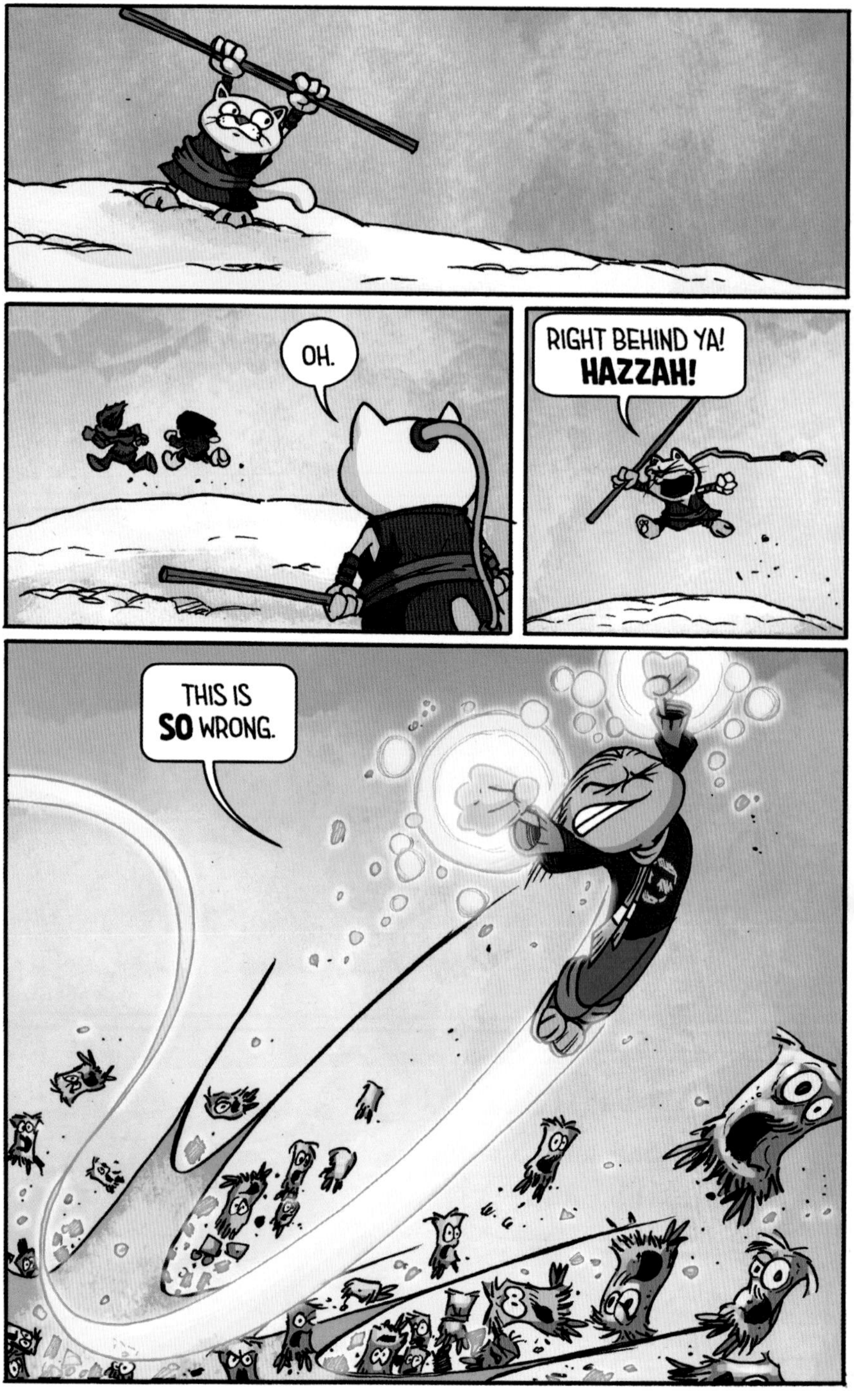
OH.
RIGHT BEHIND YA! **HAZZAH!**
THIS IS **SO** WRONG.

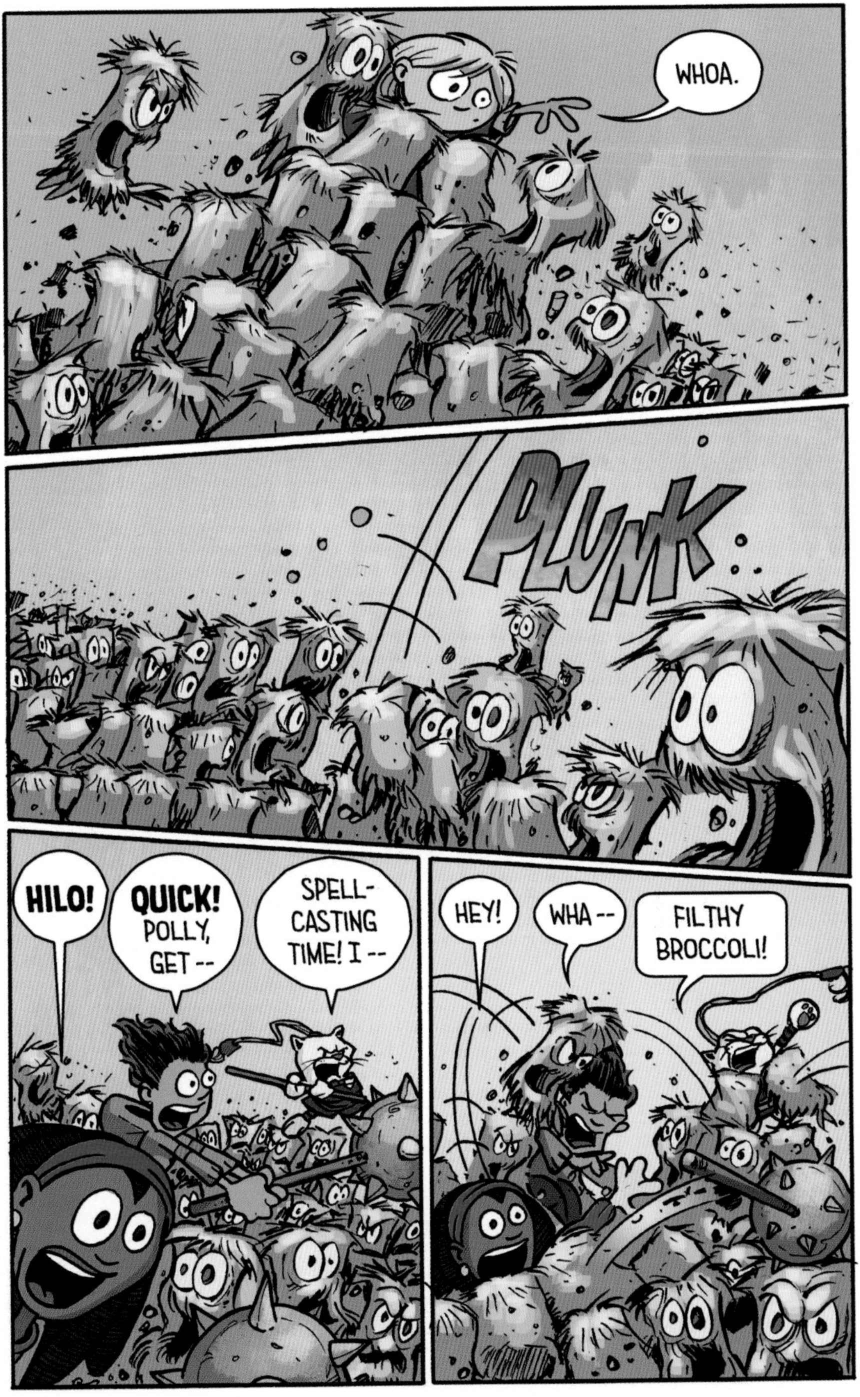
WHOA.
PLUNK
HILO!
QUICK! POLLY, GET --
SPELL-CASTING TIME! I --
HEY!
WHA --
FILTHY BROCCOLI!

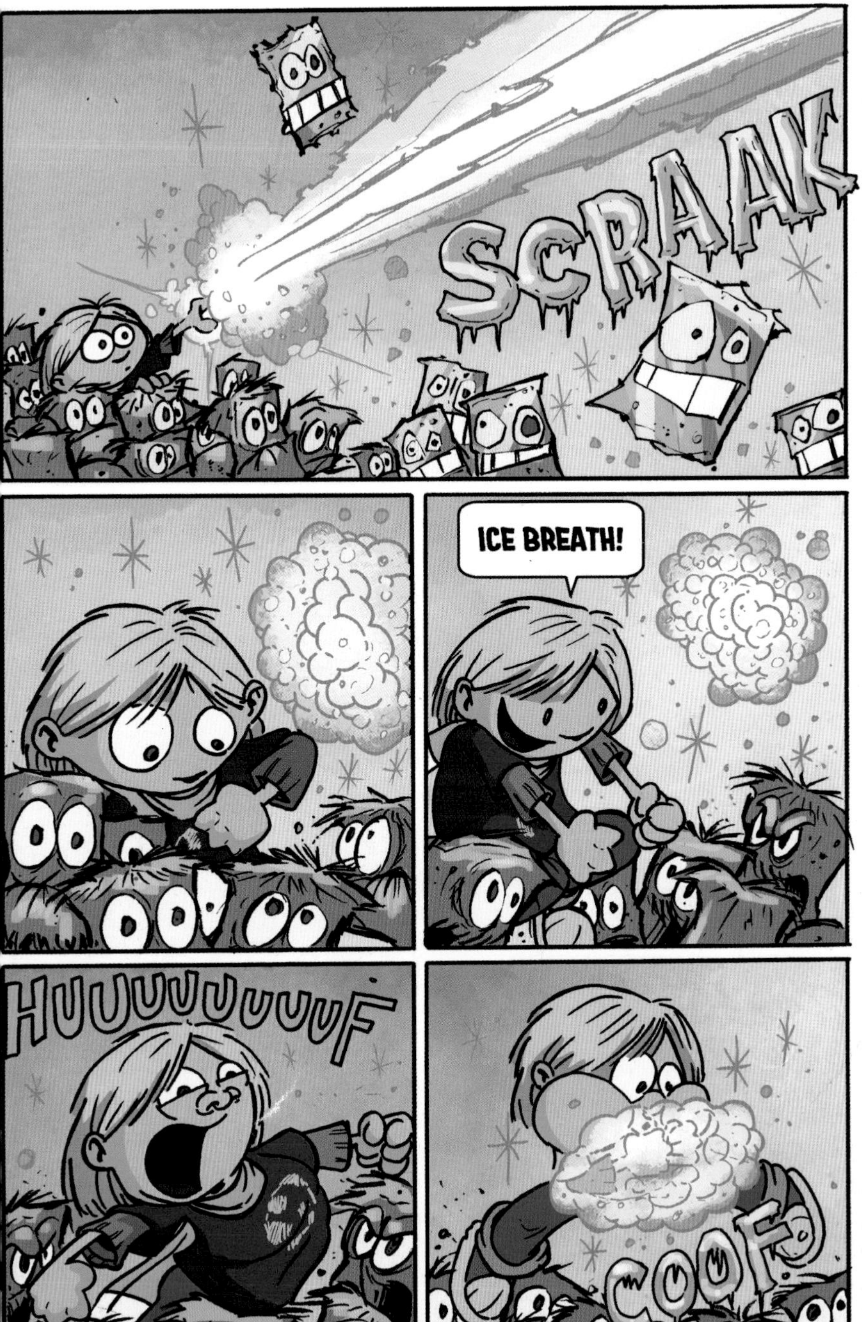
SCRAAK
ICE BREATH!
HUUUUUUUUF
COOF

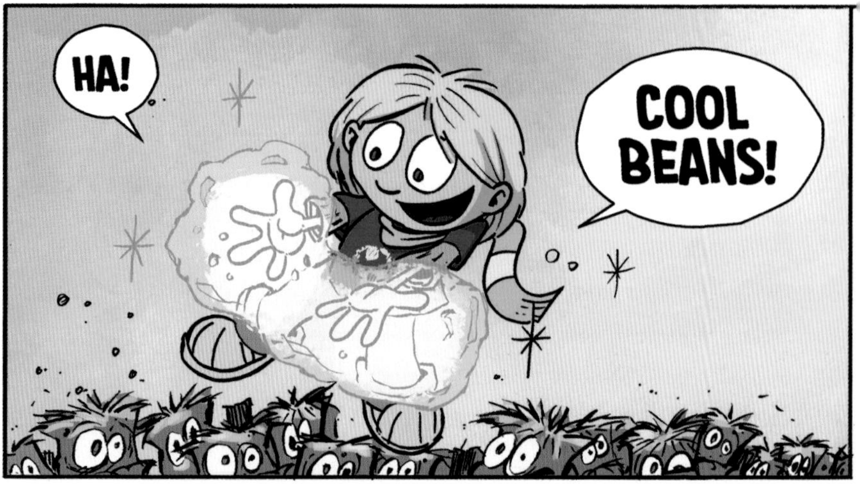
HA!
COOL BEANS!

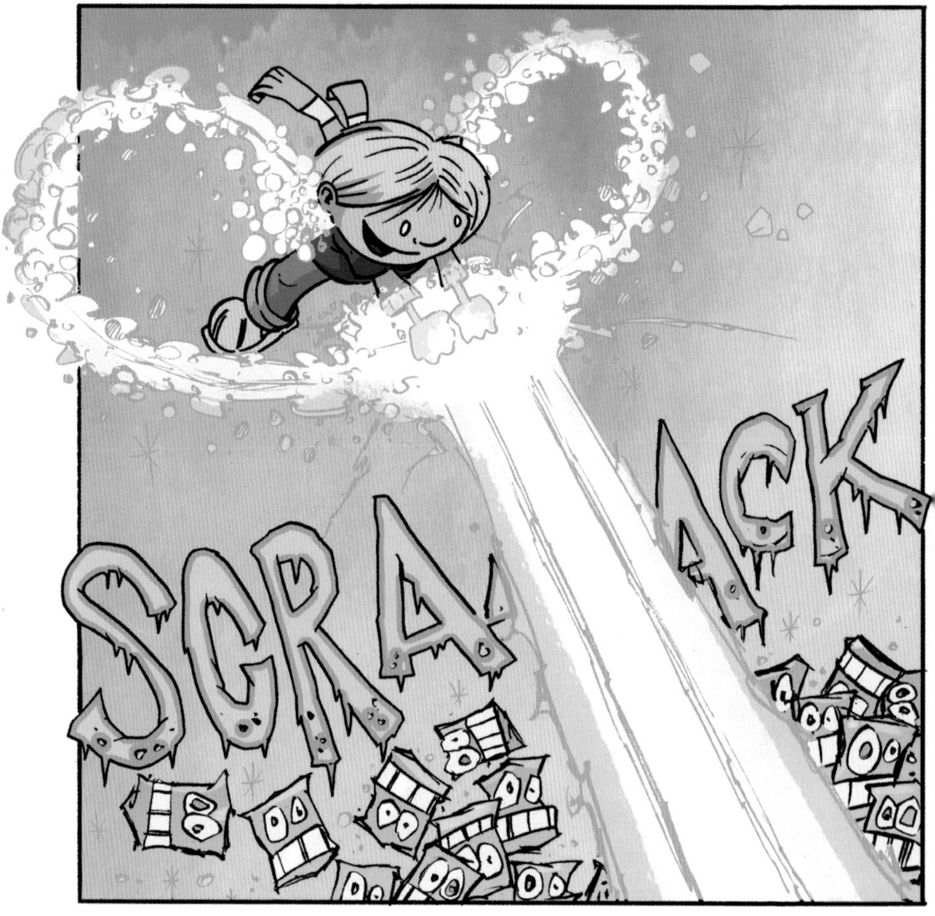
SCRA
ACK

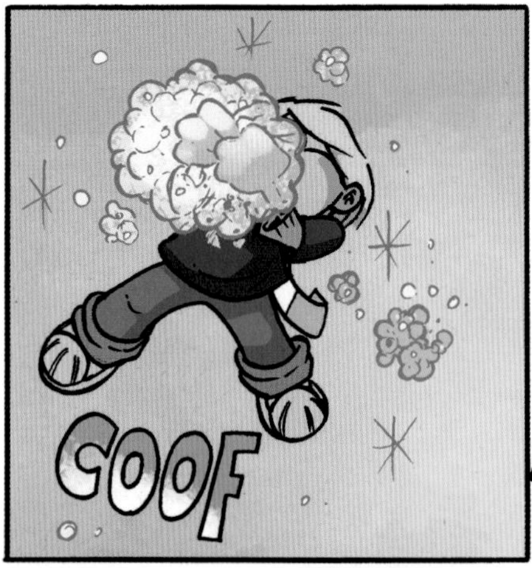
COOF

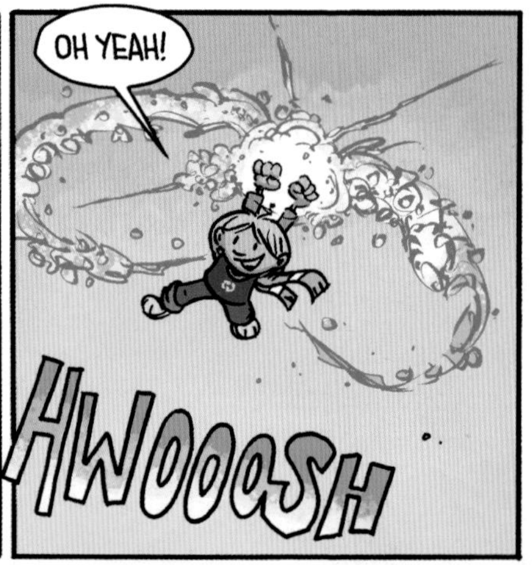
OH YEAH!
HWOOOSH

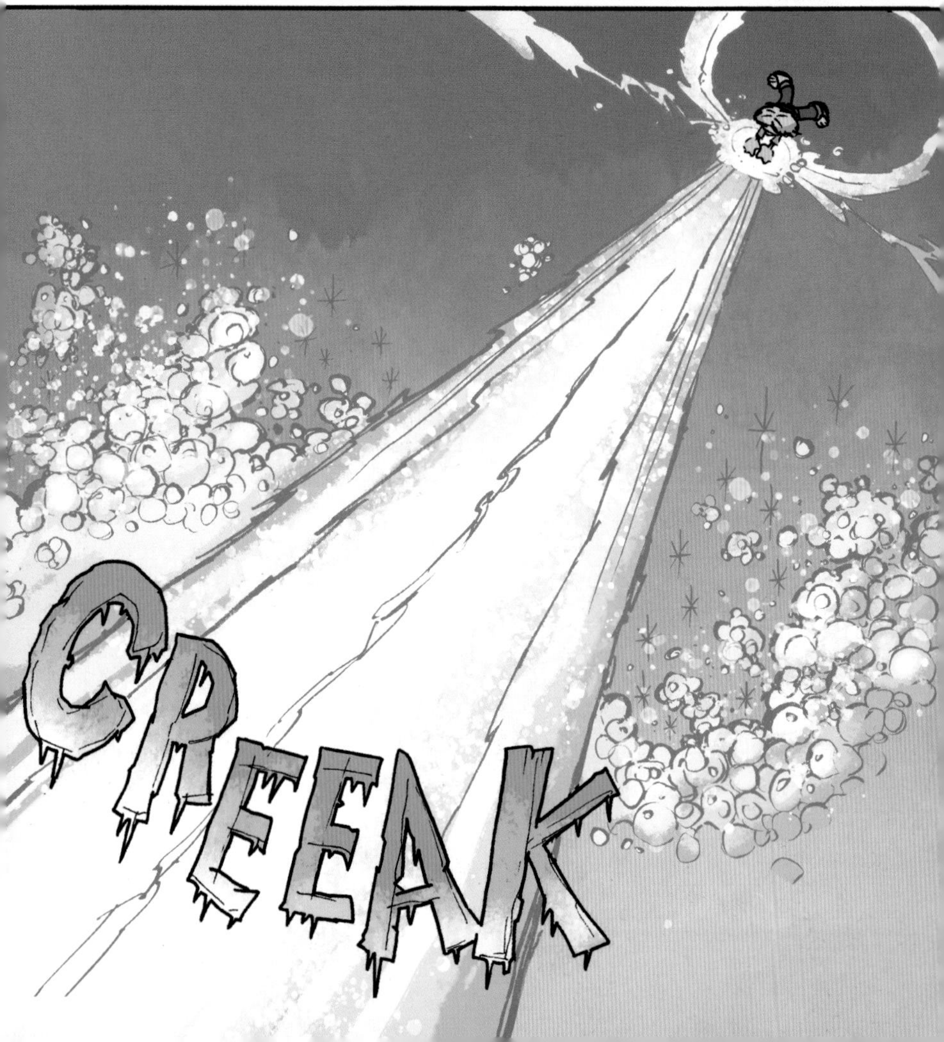
CREEEAK

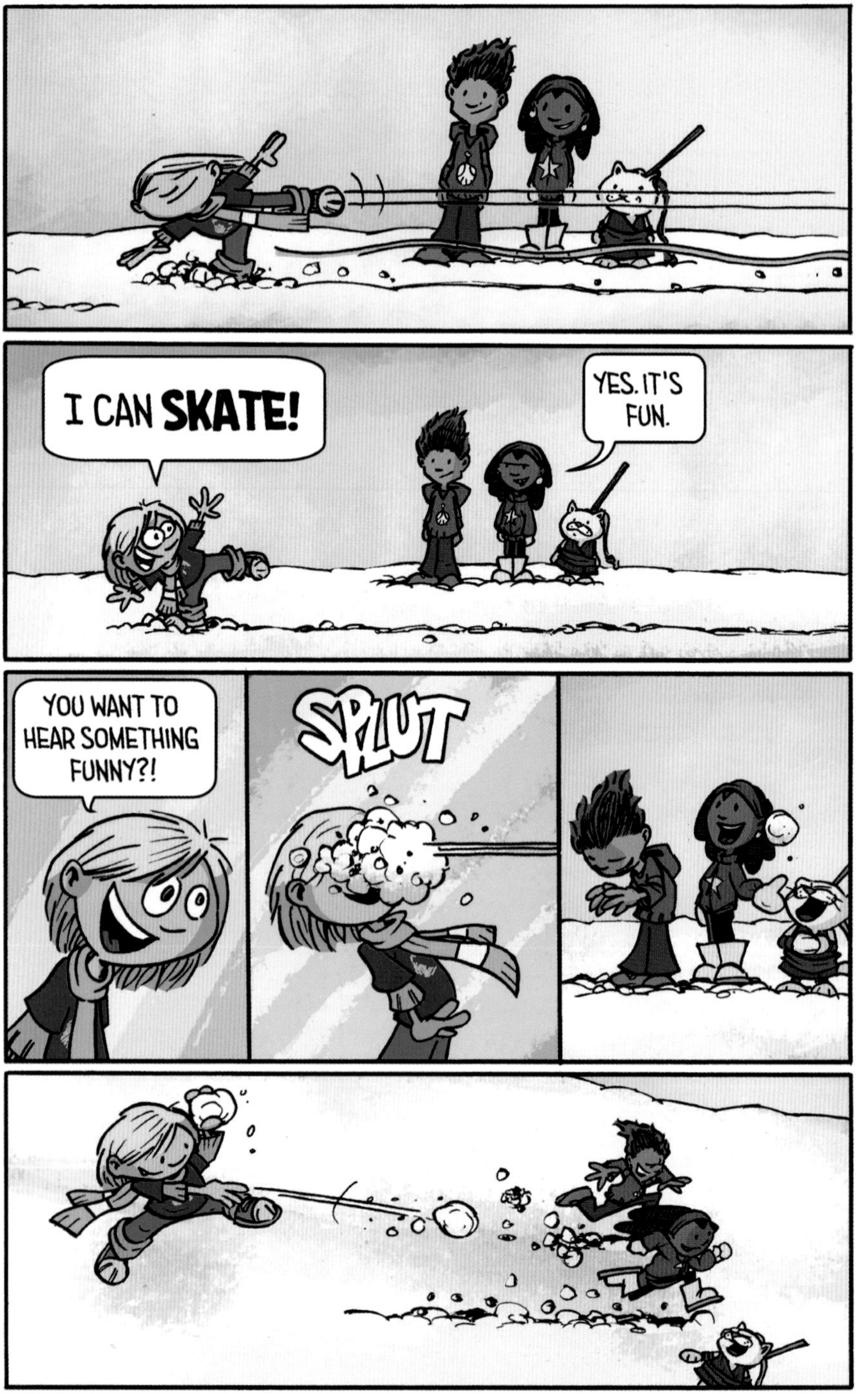
I CAN **SKATE!**
YES. IT'S FUN.
YOU WANT TO HEAR SOMETHING FUNNY?!
SPLUT

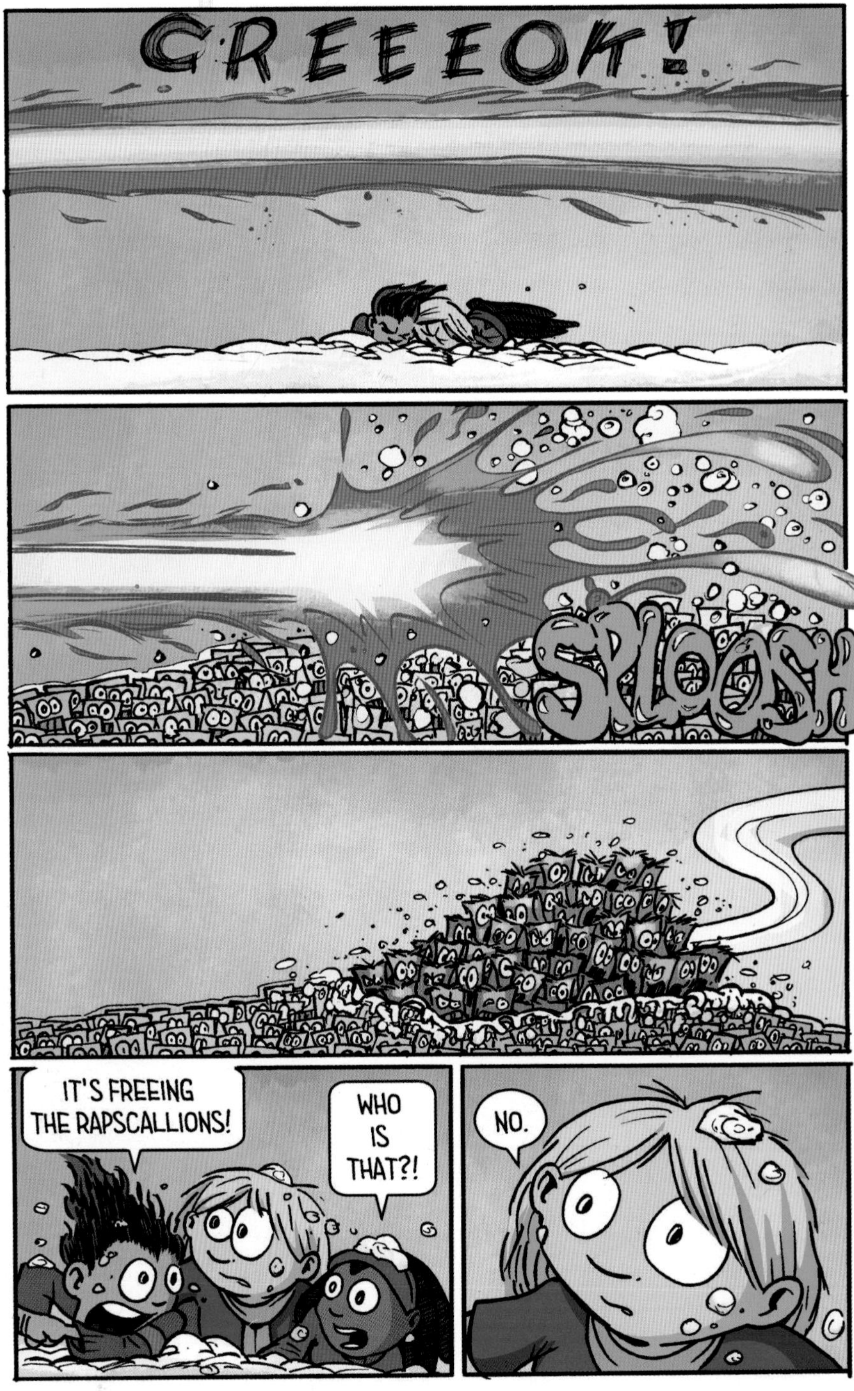
CREEEOK!
SPLOOSH
IT'S FREEING THE RAPSCALLIONS!
WHO IS THAT?!
NO.

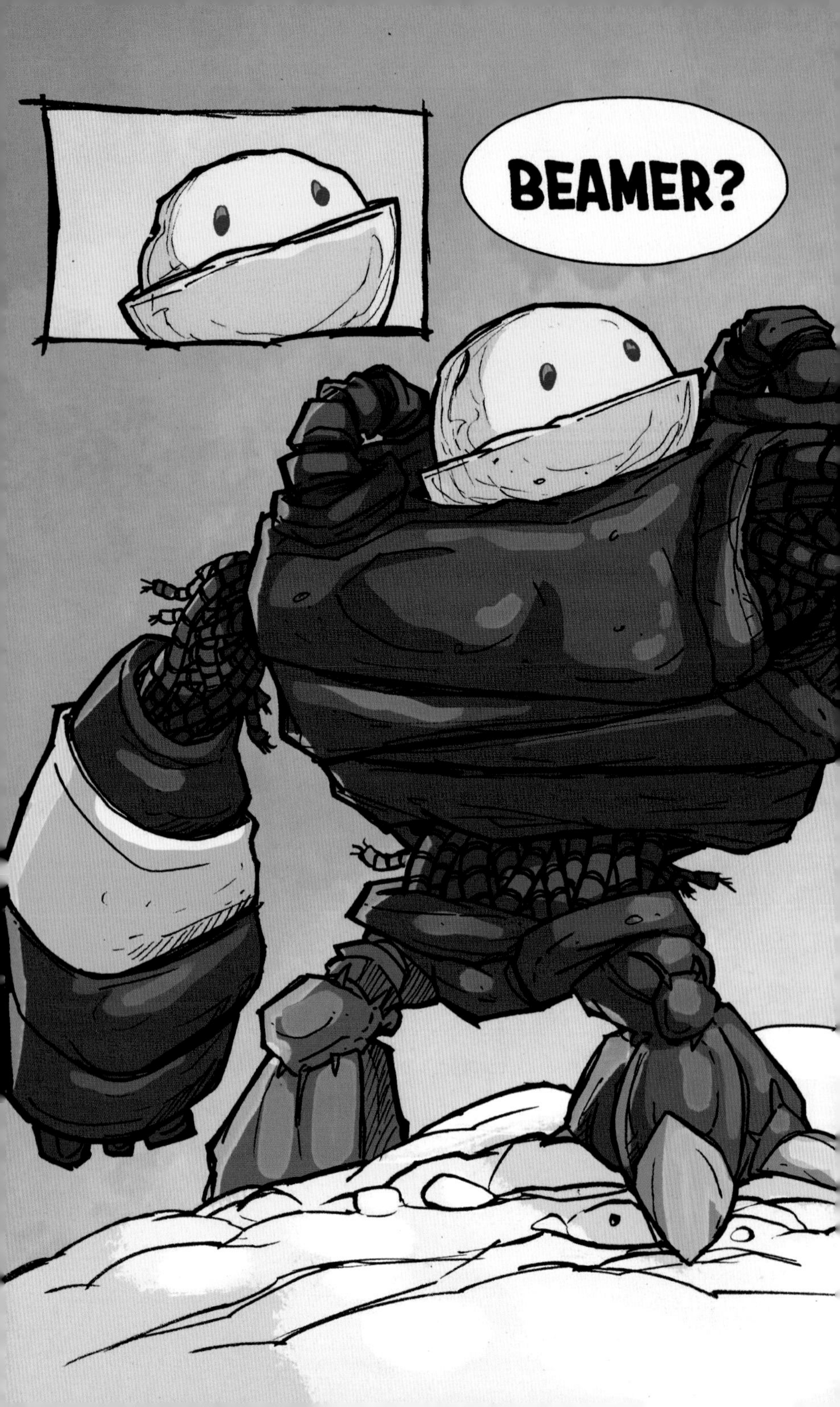
BEAMER?

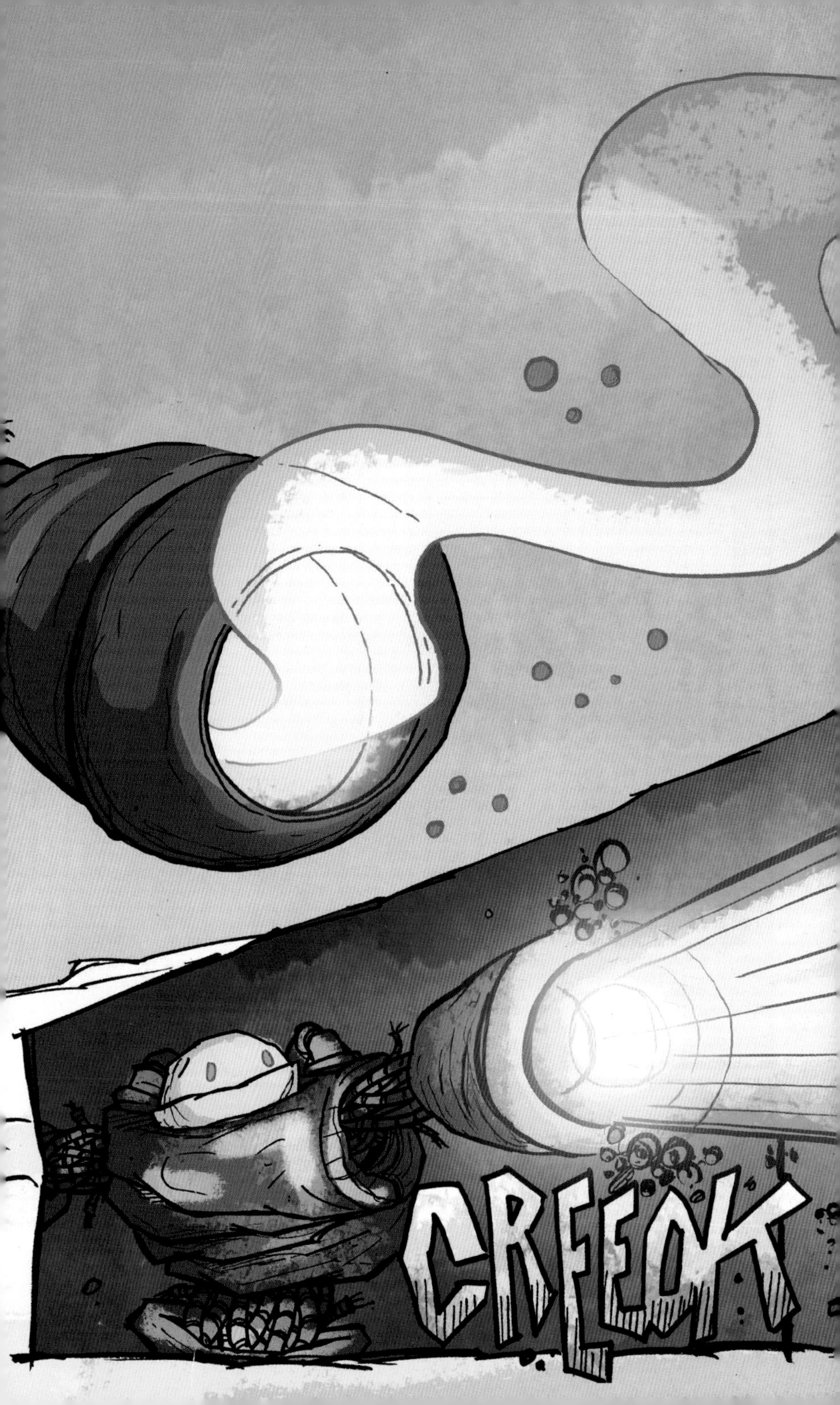
CREEK

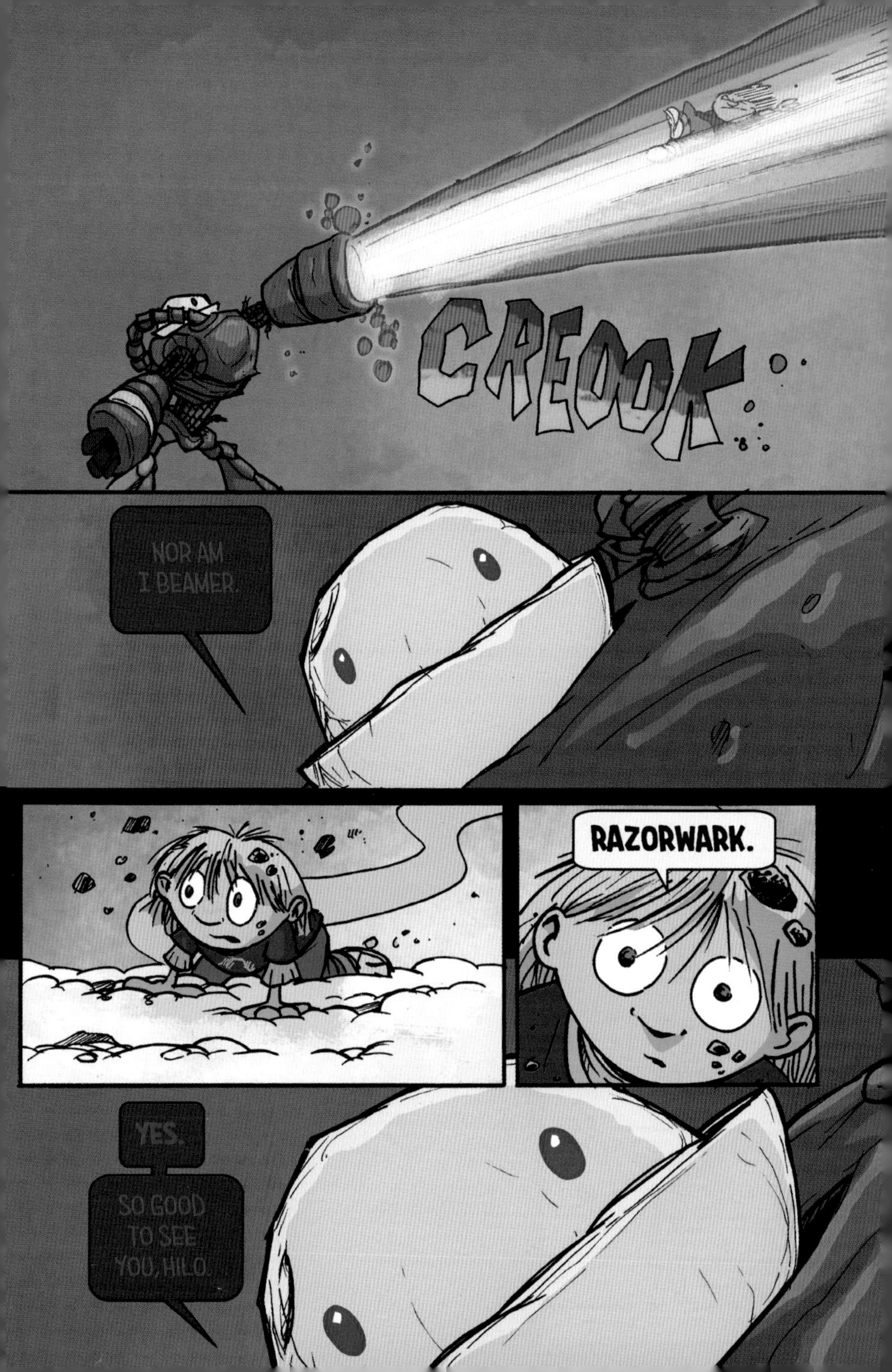
CREOOK
NOR AM I BEAMER.
RAZORWARK.
YES.
SO GOOD TO SEE YOU, HILO.

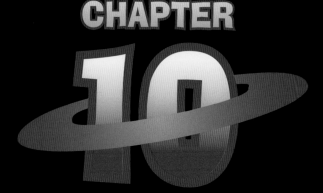

CHAPTER 10

BAD MACHINES

168

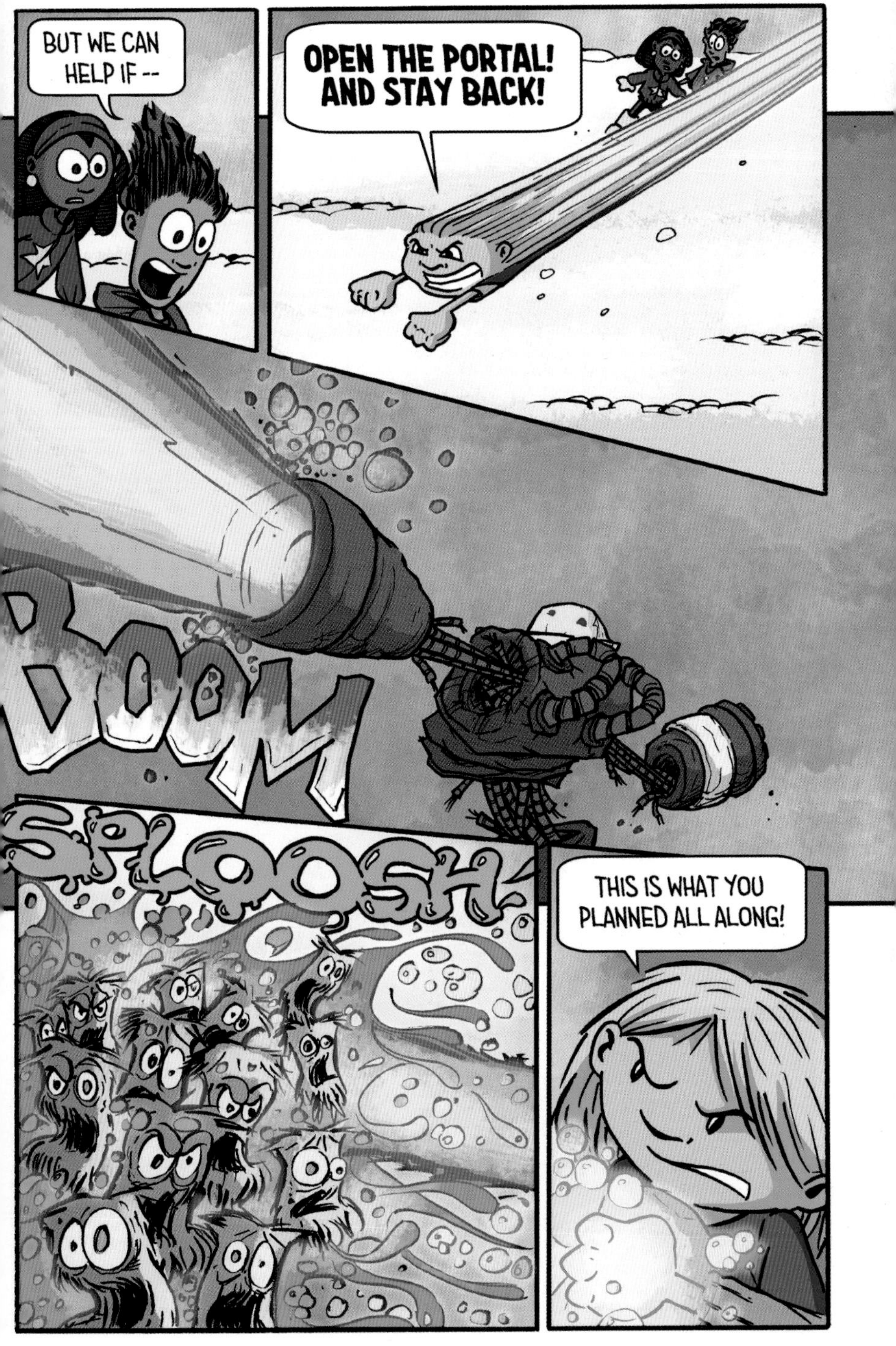
BUT WE CAN HELP IF --
OPEN THE PORTAL! AND STAY BACK!
BOOM
SPLOOSH
THIS IS WHAT YOU PLANNED ALL ALONG!

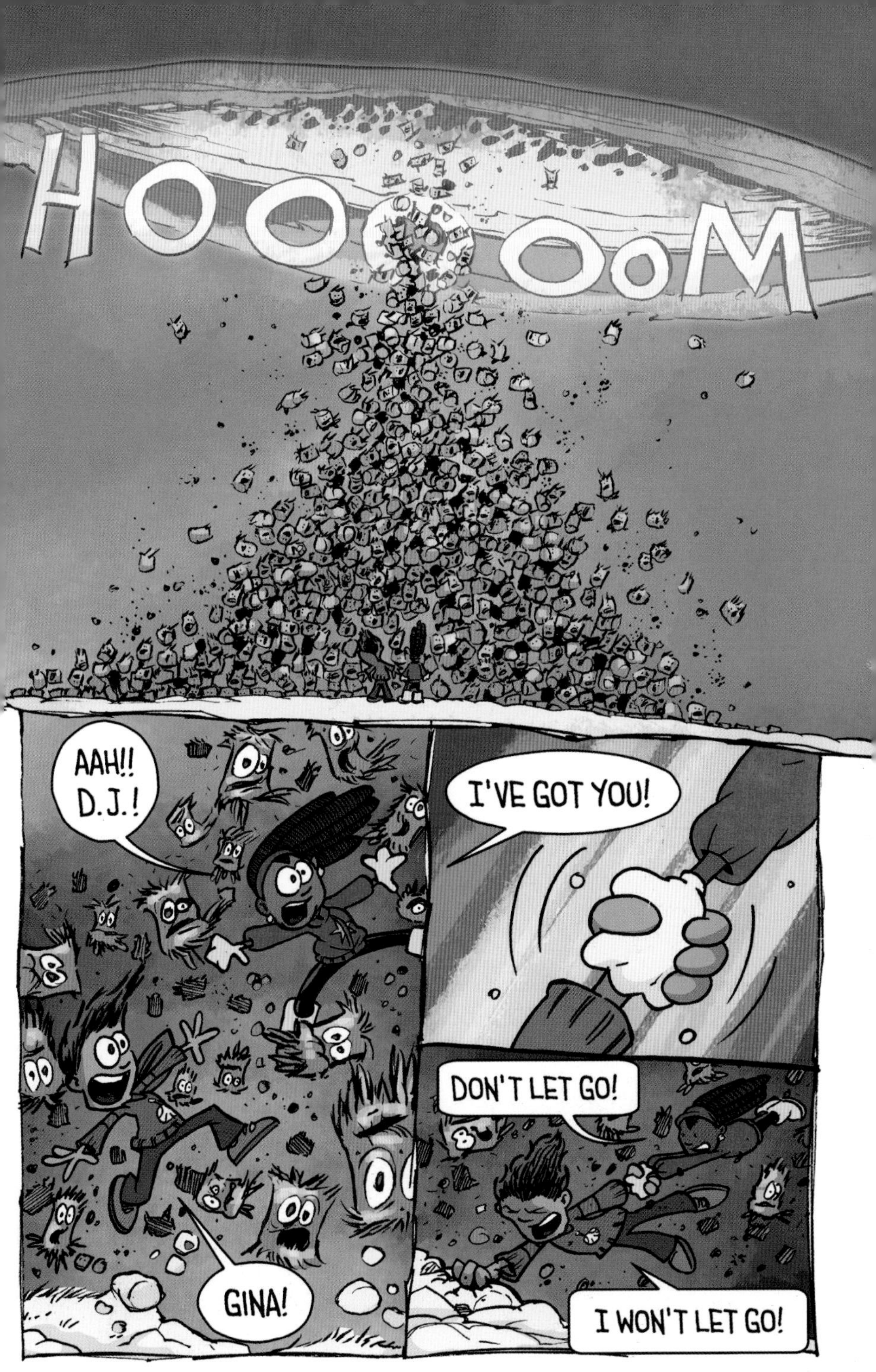
HOOOOOOM
AAH!! D.J.!
GINA!
I'VE GOT YOU!
DON'T LET GO!
I WON'T LET GO!

175

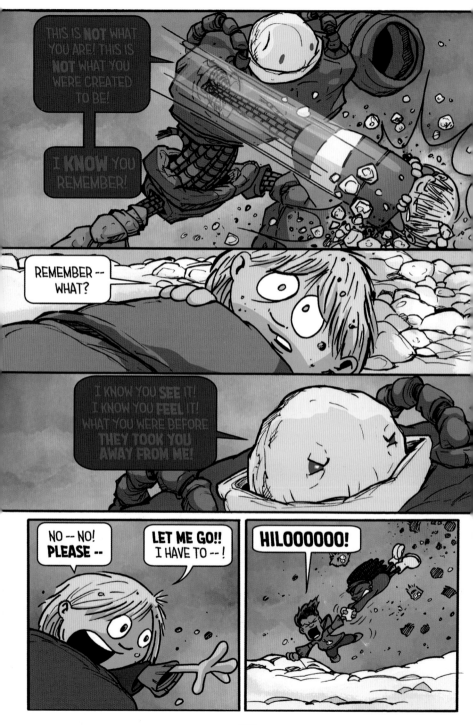

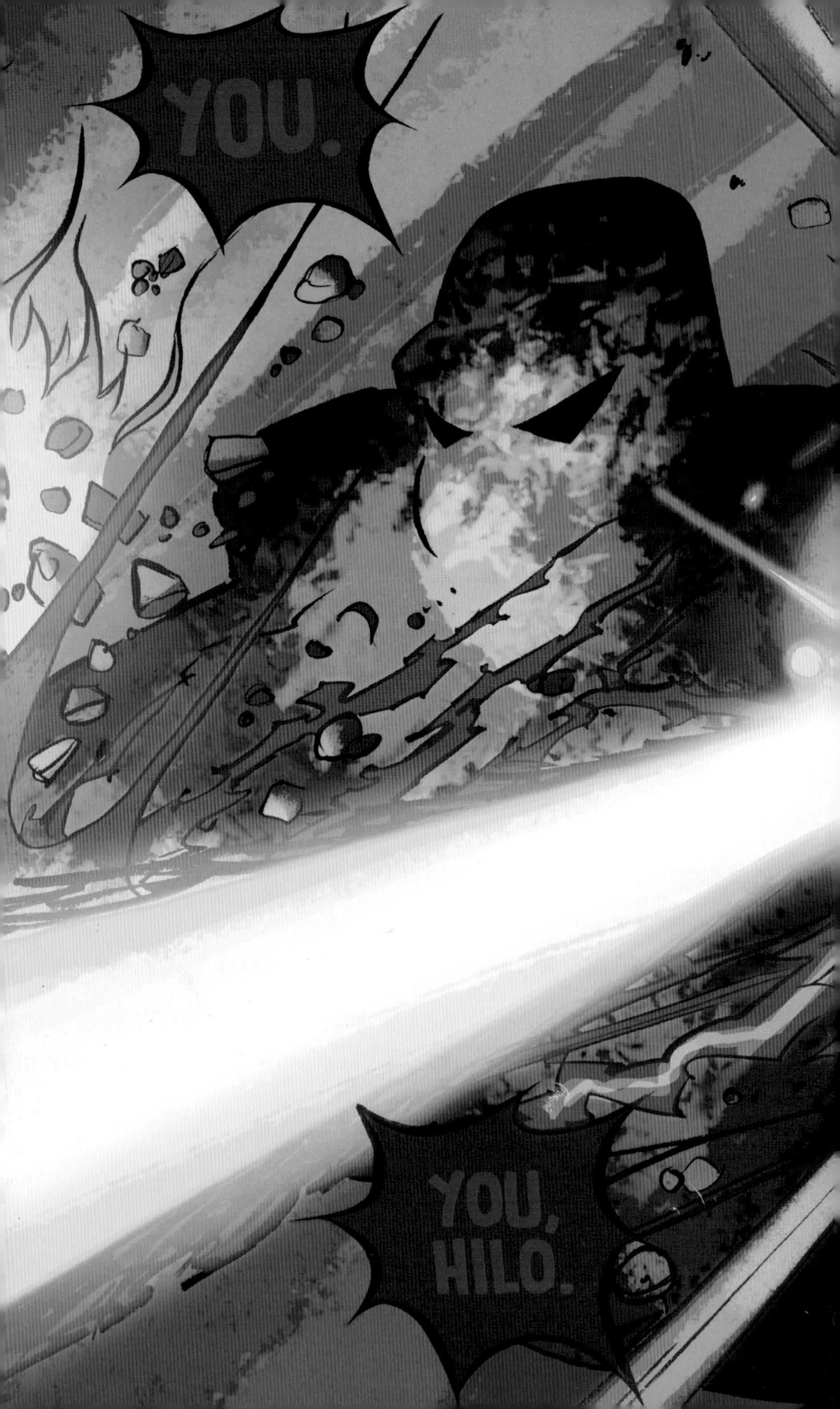
YOU.
YOU, HILO.

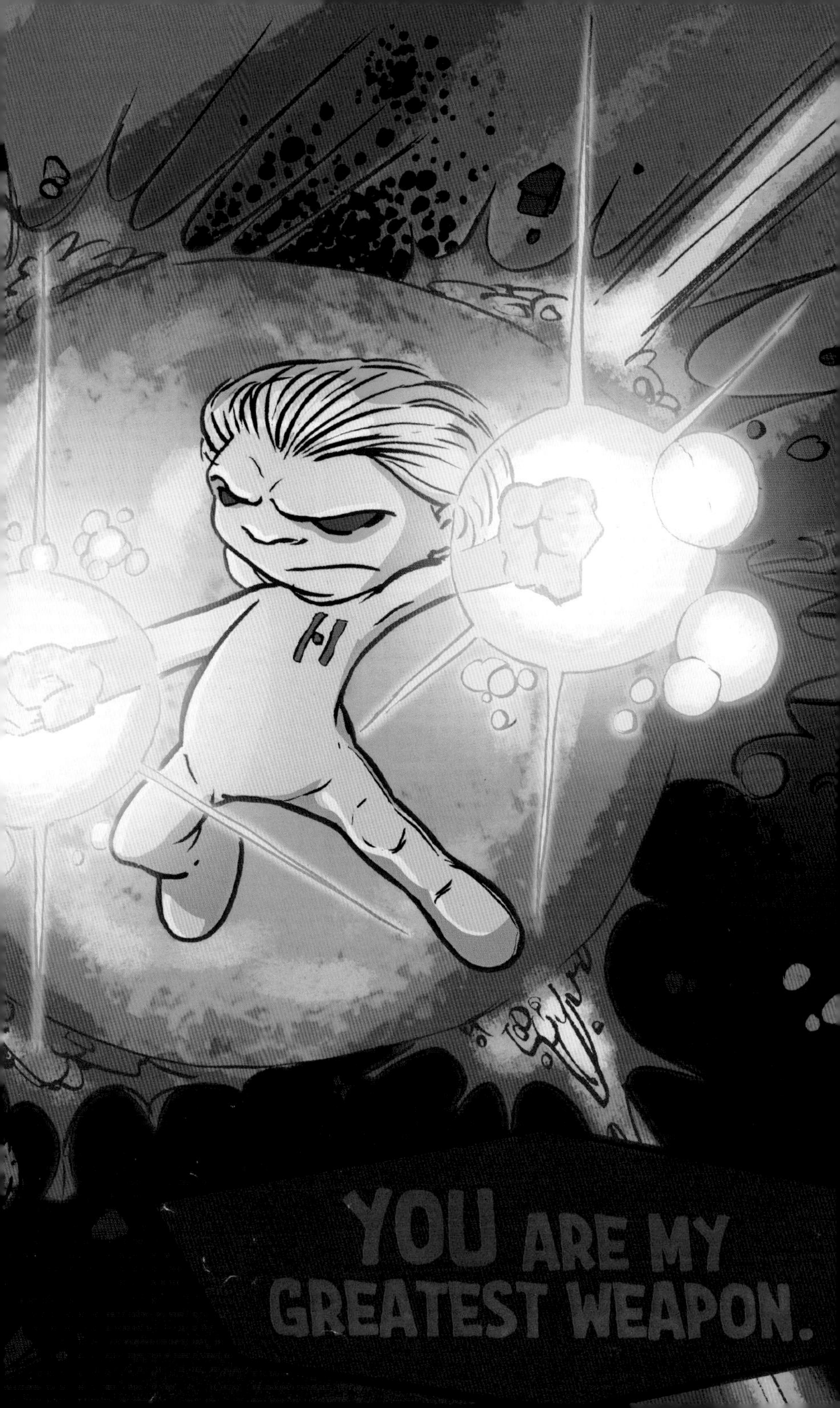

YOU ARE MY GREATEST WEAPON.

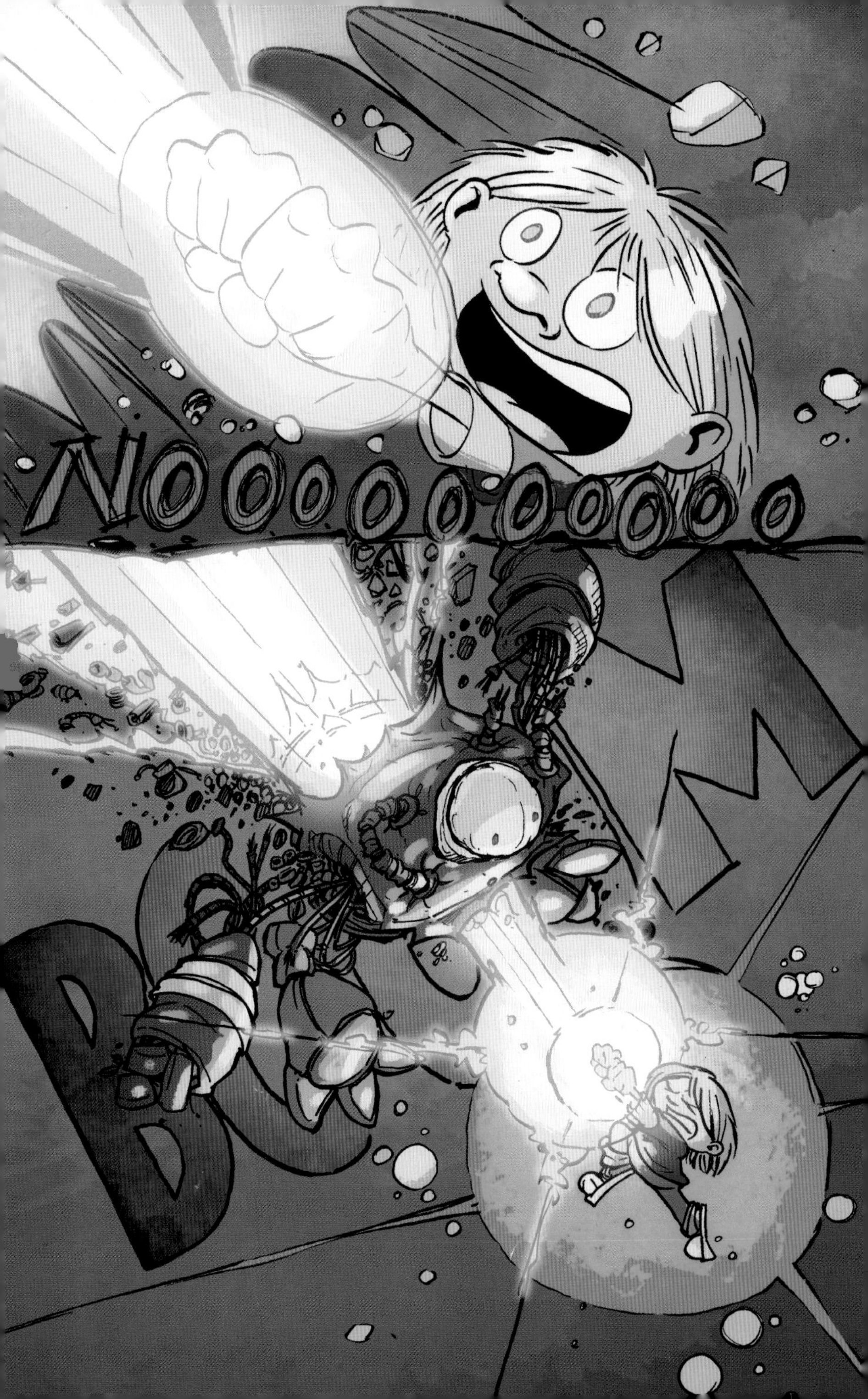
NOOOOOOOOOO

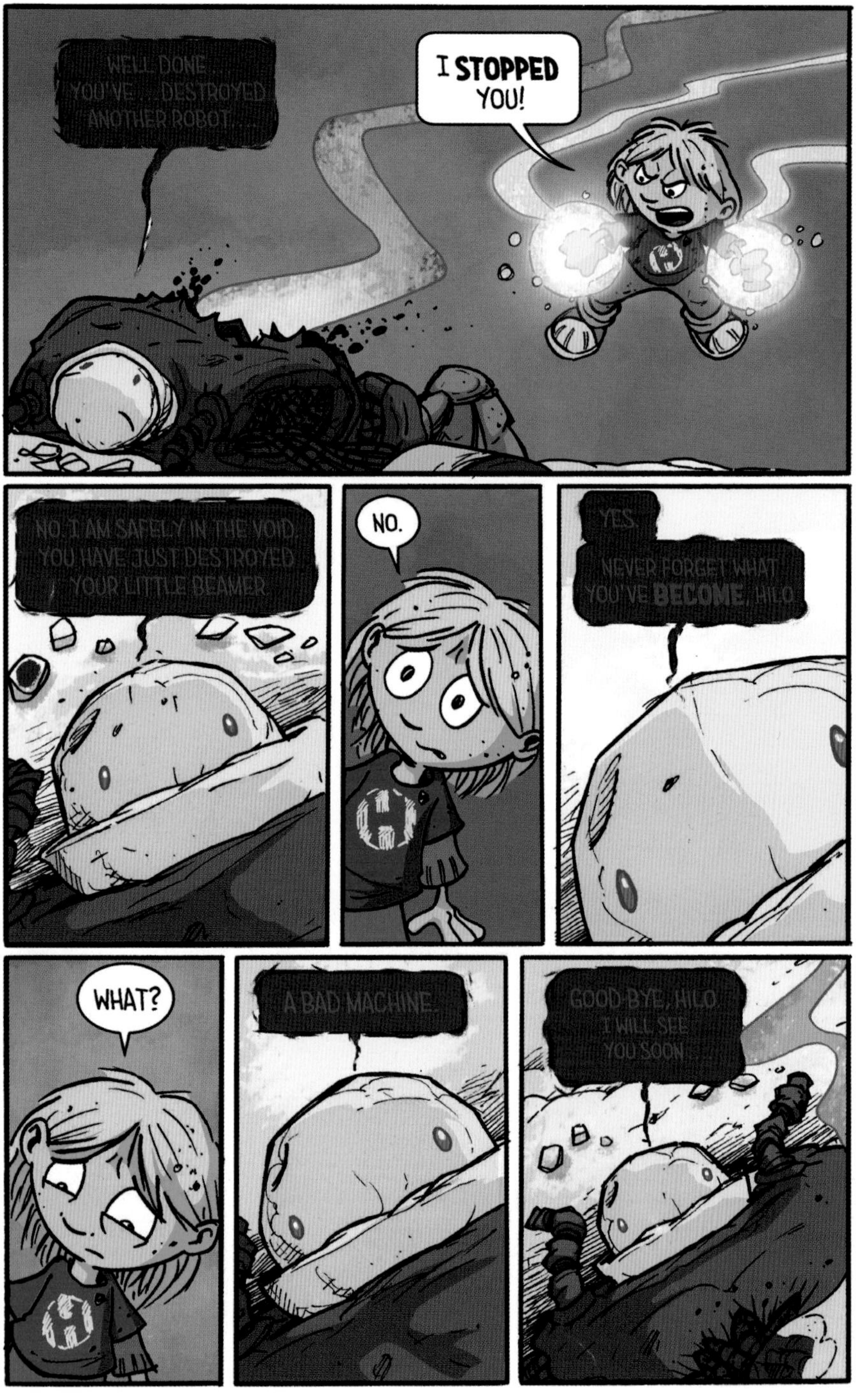
WELL DONE... YOU'VE... DESTROYED ANOTHER ROBOT....
I STOPPED YOU!
NO. I AM SAFELY IN THE VOID. YOU HAVE JUST DESTROYED YOUR LITTLE BEAMER.
NO.
YES.
NEVER FORGET WHAT YOU'VE BECOME, HILO.
WHAT?
A BAD MACHINE.
GOOD-BYE, HILO. I WILL SEE YOU SOON....

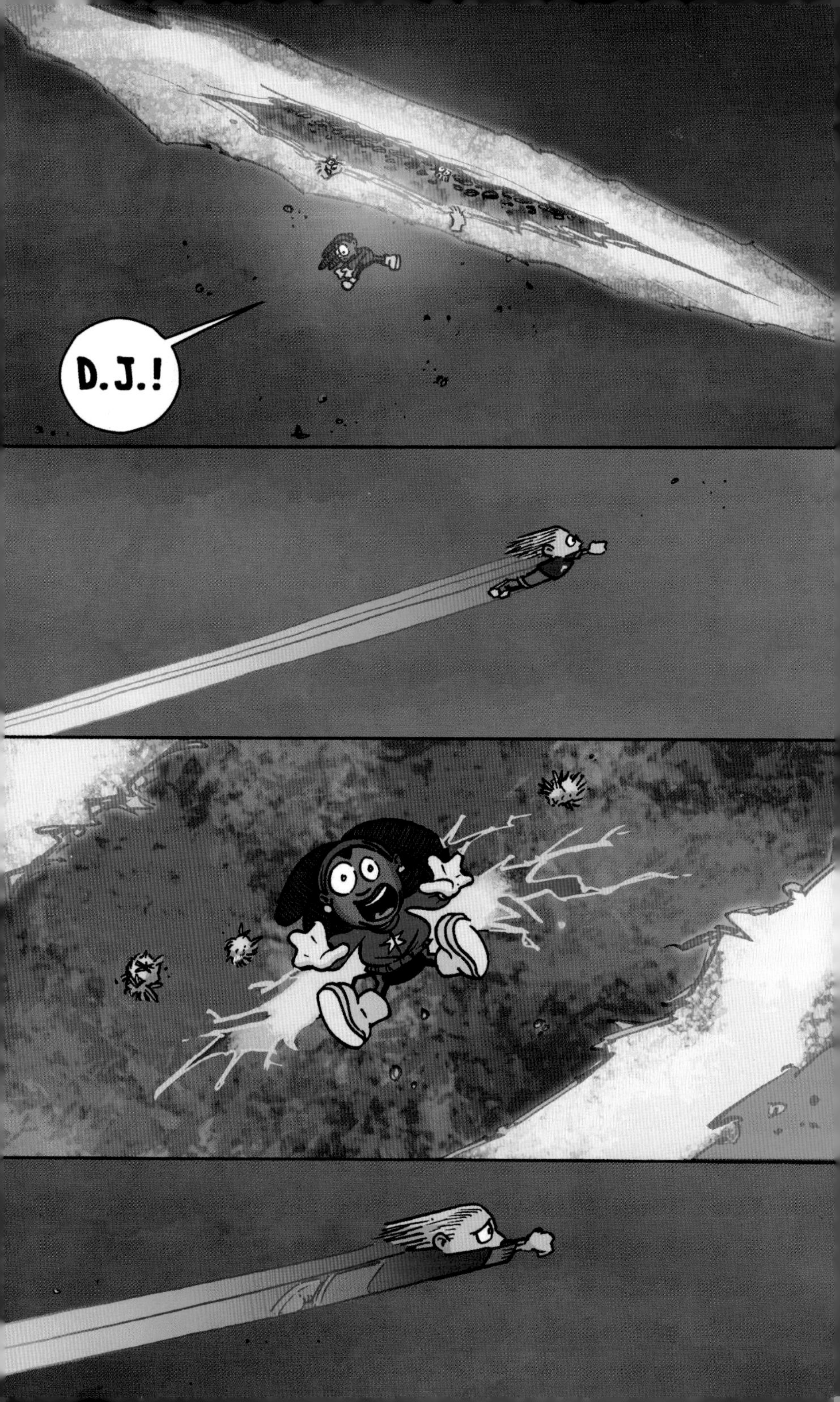
D.J.!

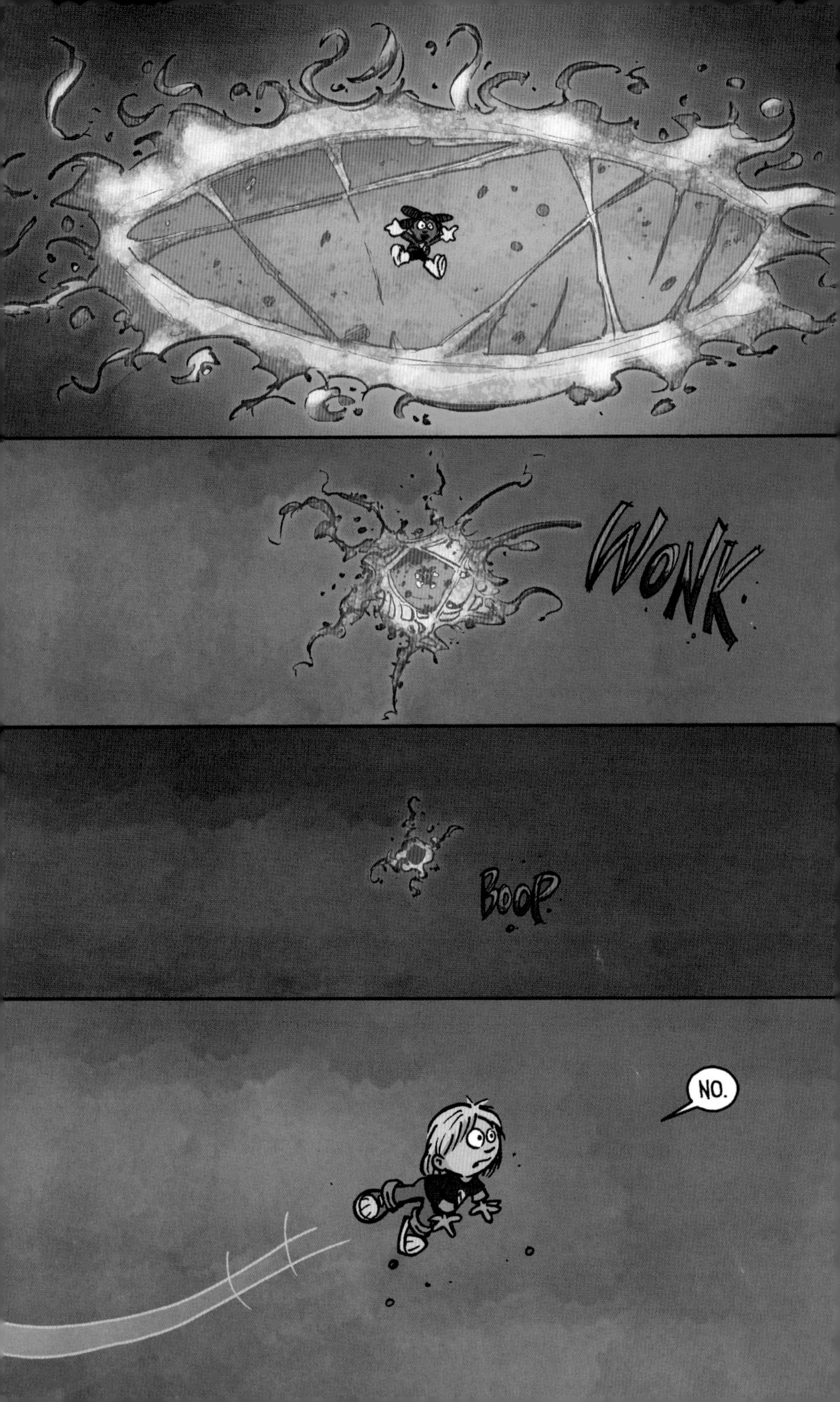
WONK
BOOP
NO.

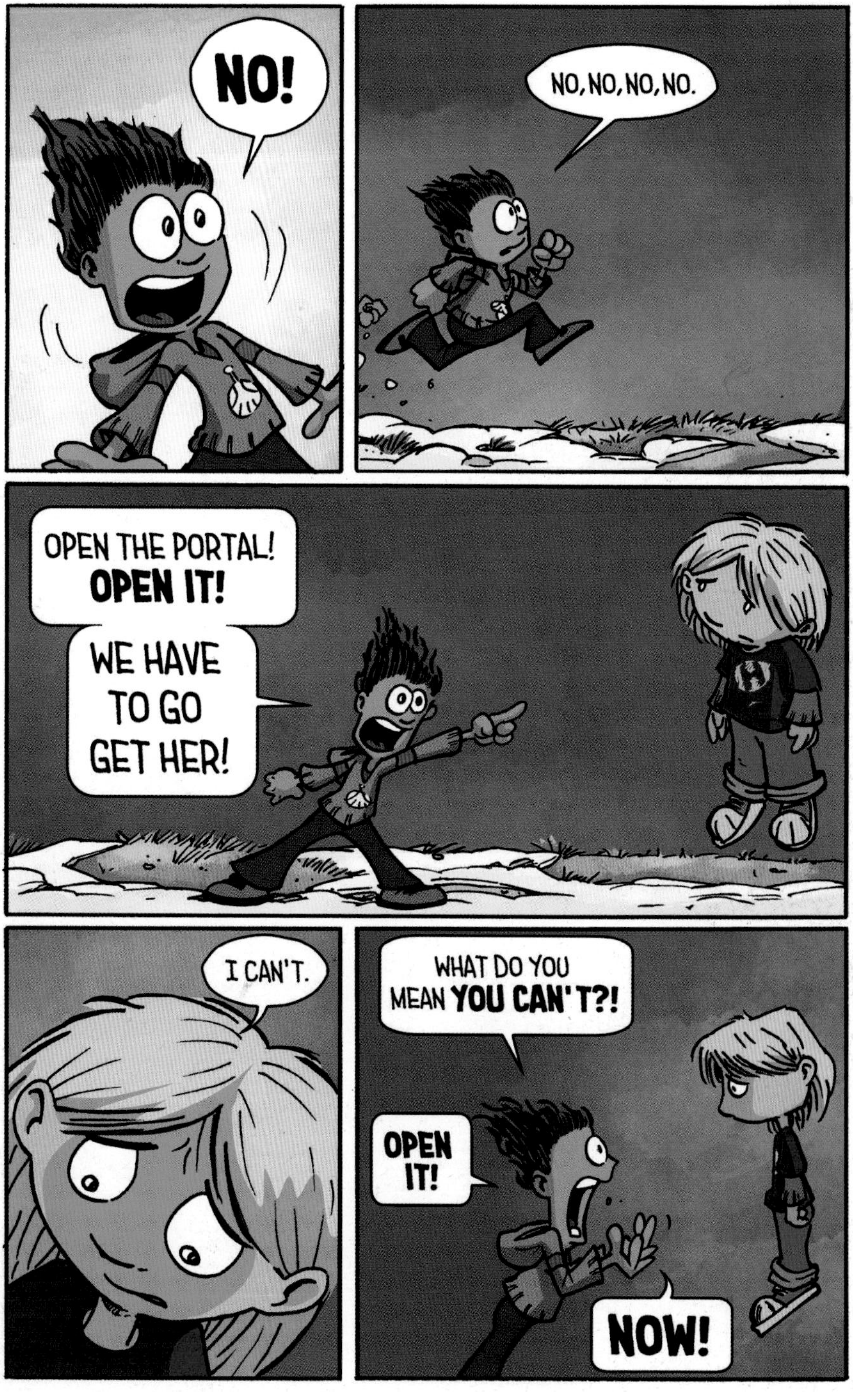
NO!
NO, NO, NO, NO.
OPEN THE PORTAL! **OPEN IT!**
WE HAVE TO GO GET HER!
I CAN'T.
WHAT DO YOU MEAN **YOU CAN'T?!**
OPEN IT!
NOW!

188

189

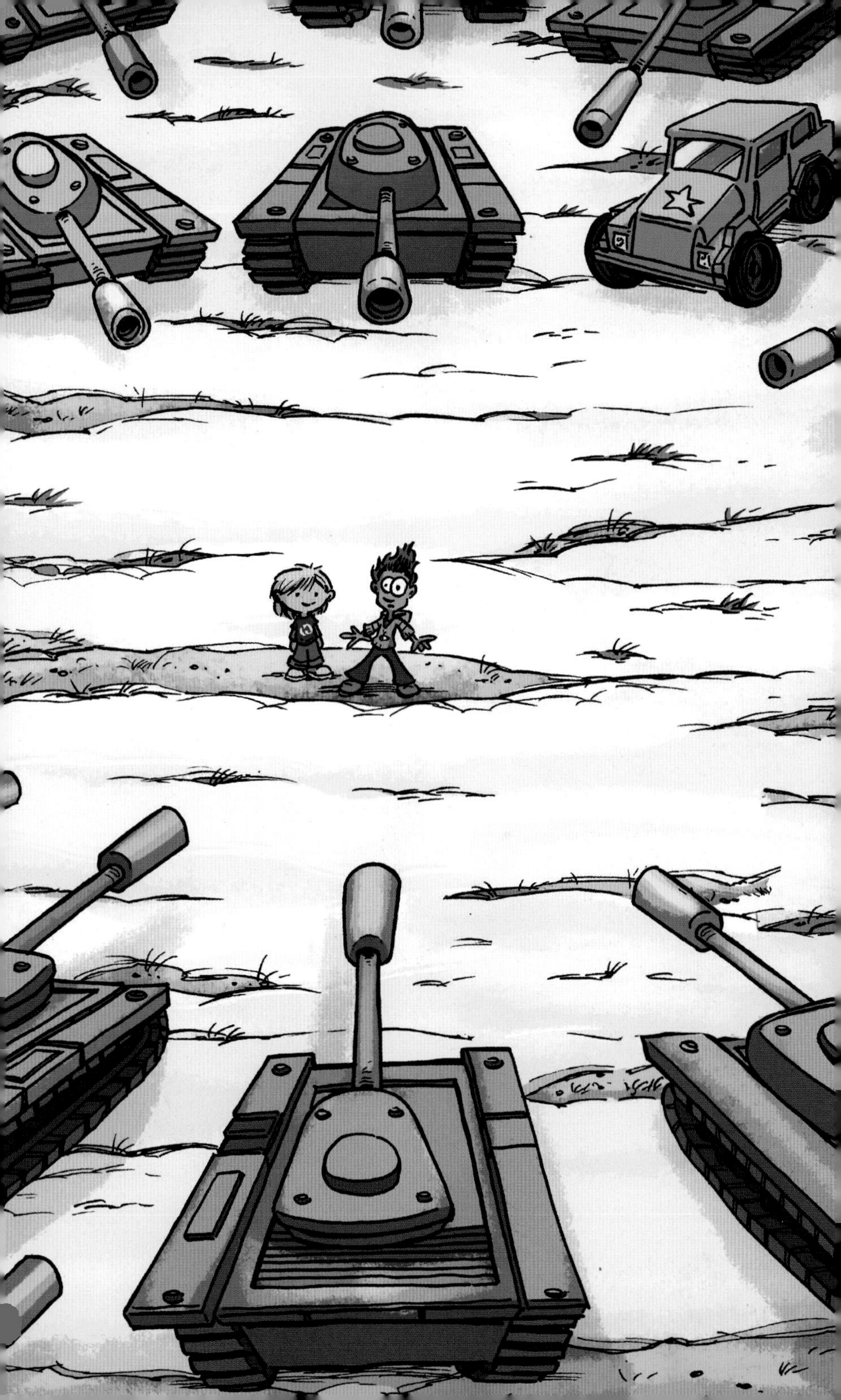

END OF BOOK TWO

LOOK FOR BOOK 3

NOW AVAILABLE ON A PLANET NEAR YOU!

TURN THE PAGE FOR A SNEAK PEEK!

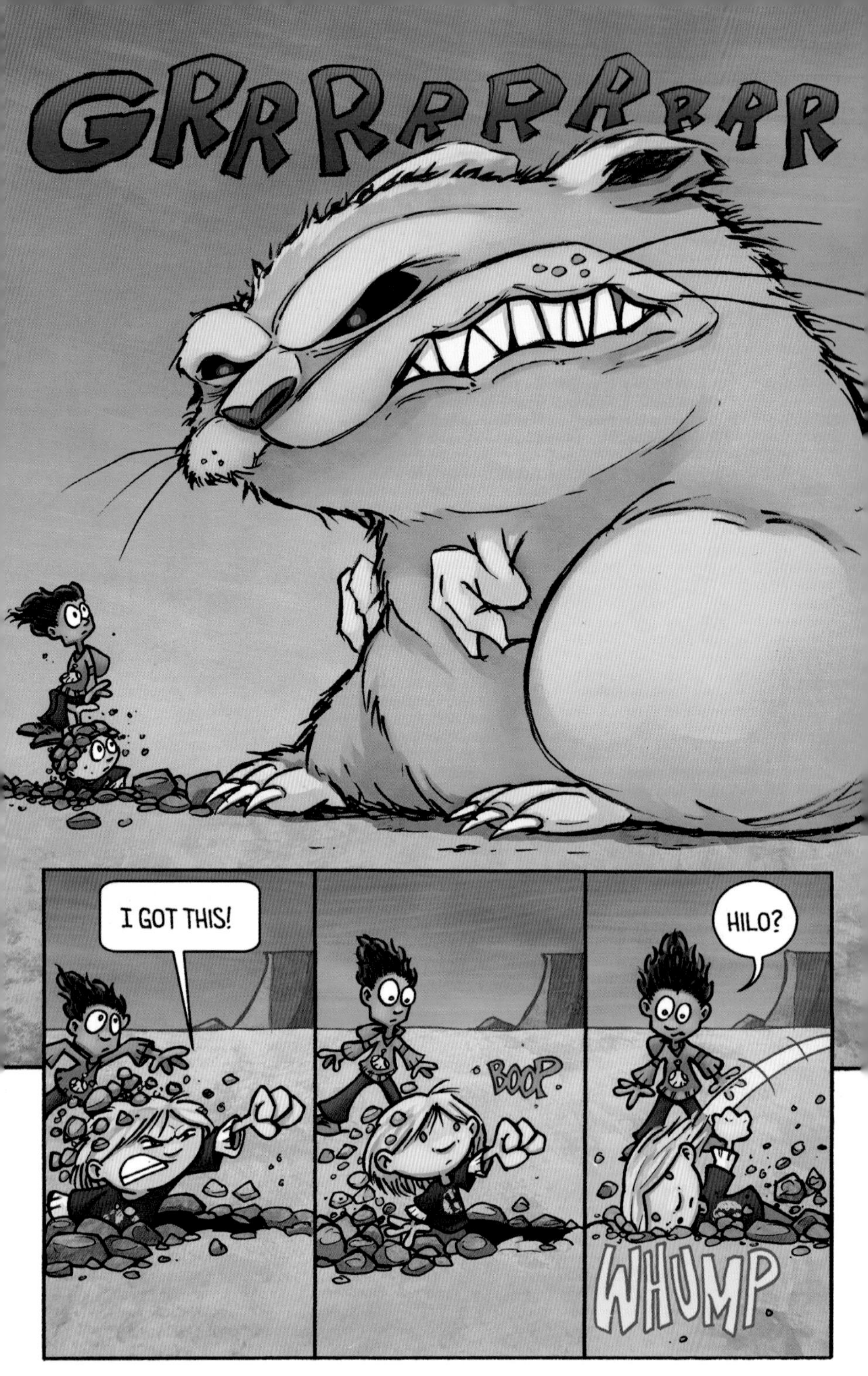
GRRRRRRRRR
I GOT THIS!
BOOP
HILO?
WHUMP

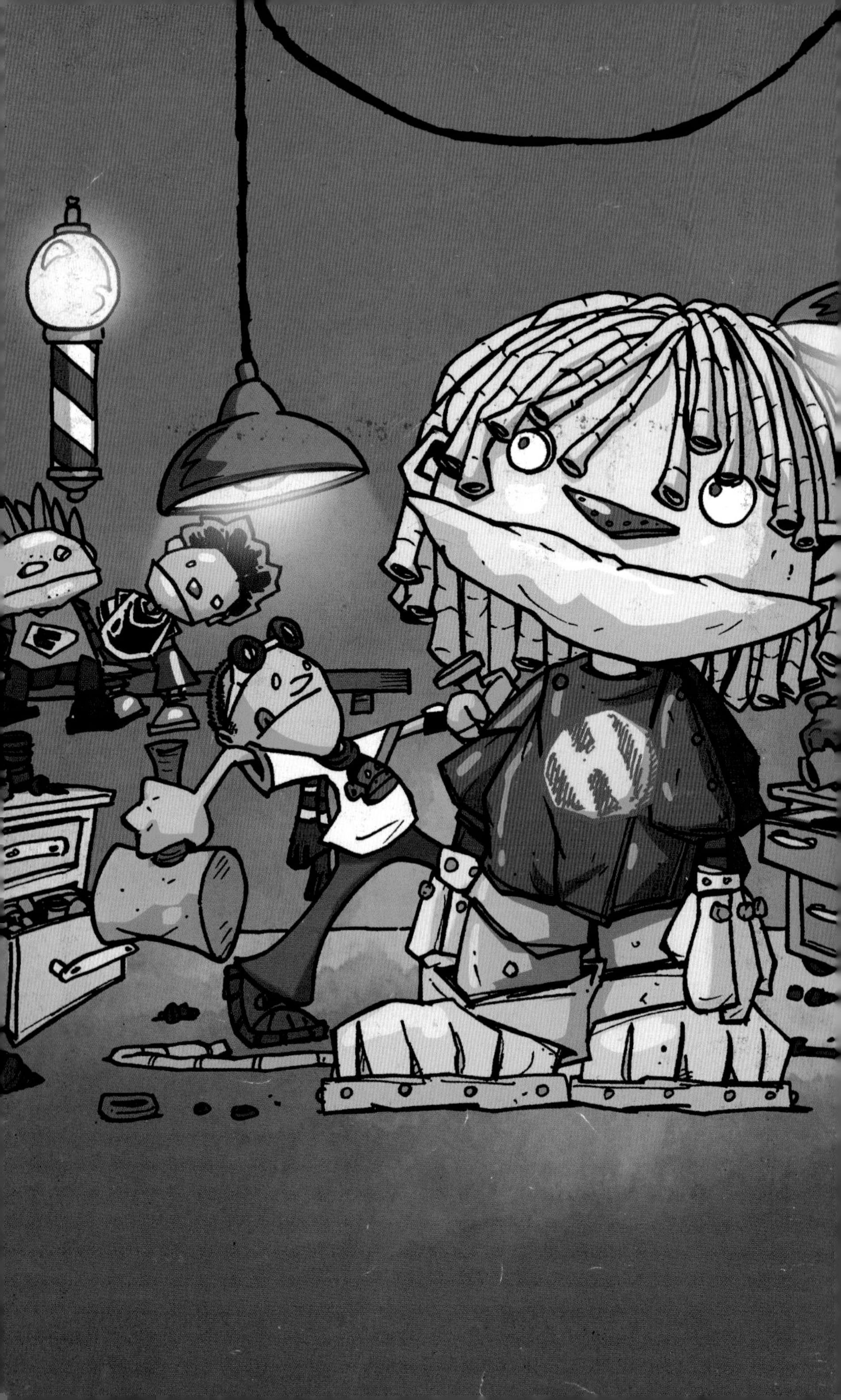